W9-BNR-686

PRAISE FOR
I CAN SEE YOU

"Compelling . . . if you like creepy, gripping mysteries, romantic leading men, and brainy leading ladies, you will enjoy I CAN SEE YOU."
—Examiner.com

"A terrific whodunit . . . a great poignant work . . . Karen Rose is gaining a well-deserved reputation for great romantic suspense thrillers; her latest winner, I CAN SEE YOU, is a super Minneapolis police procedural that also showcases the double-edged sword of online communities."
—*Midwest Book Review*

"Complex, chilling, and intense romantic suspense . . . Rose's greatest strength has always been her astute gift at getting into the heart and soul of her characters. Eve and Noah rank among her best . . . Rose is equally meticulous about getting into the head of her antagonists."
—BookLoons.com

"A hair-raising climax. For romantic suspense fans who don't mind some edge, or thriller fans."
—*Booklist*

more . . .

"I loved it! Read it! Races into overdrive . . . with many fascinating twists and turns, and I couldn't put it down . . . A great read, and a complex love story between two people who should be bitter but have decided to take the risk to trust, as the scars that bind Eve and Noah also heal them."

—TheReviewBroads.com

"Will chill you to the bone . . . With deeply drawn characters and a twisted plot, I CAN SEE YOU will snare you in its clutches, leaving you breathless and eager for more. The suspense sizzles. It builds and builds until you think you might come apart at the seams before the climax crashes down around you. I had no fingernails left after I finished this gripping read. Karen Rose is probably the best romantic suspense author in existence, and she proves it once again with the unpredictable and unsettling I CAN SEE YOU."

—NightsAndWeekends.com

PRAISE FOR KAREN ROSE'S
PREVIOUS NOVELS
KILL FOR ME

"Rose juggles a large cast, a huge body count, and a complex plot with terrifying ease."

—*Publishers Weekly*

"4½ Stars! TOP PICK! Gritty and thrilling . . . A page-turner from the get-go."
—*RT Book Reviews*

"Stupendous . . . an exhilarating thriller . . . filled with action from the onset and never slows down."
—*Midwest Book Review*

SCREAM FOR ME

"Intense, complex, and unforgettable."
—JAMES PATTERSON

"Cold chills, hot thrills, and characters that come alive."
—**Allison Brennan, author of** *Killing Fear*

"Blistering, high-octane suspense that never lets up."
—**Karen Robards,** *New York Times* **bestselling author**

"Strong and sexy . . . truly frightening."
—*BookPage*

"Memorable . . . page-turning."
—*Minneapolis Star-Tribune*

"Mesmerizing. Fabulous suspense. Masterful writing."
—**Betina Krahn,** *New York Times*
bestselling author of *The Marriage Test*

"4½ Stars! Terrifying . . . Rose is a force to be reckoned with!"
—*RT Book Reviews*

more . . .

"A first-rate, top-tier thriller . . . loudly announces that there could well be a new thriller sheriff in town."
— **Lorenzo Carcaterra**, *New York Times*
bestselling author of *Sleepers*

COUNT TO TEN

"Takes off like a house afire . . . There's action and chills galore in this nonstop thriller."
— **Tess Gerritsen**, *New York Times*
bestselling author

"Rose cranks up the heat in more ways than one . . . Emotional subplots, engaging characters, and a string of red herrings will keep readers hooked."
— *Publishers Weekly*

YOU CAN'T HIDE

"This novel is, in a word, riveting."
— *RT Book Reviews*

"An immensely enjoyable read . . . that will have the reader glued to the pages from beginning to end."
— *Romance Reviews Today*

"[Karen Rose] is the queen of murder and suspense . . . just terrific!"
— **RomanceReviewsMag.com**

NOTHING TO FEAR

"A pulse-pounding tale that has it all: suspense, action, and a very hunky private investigator."
—*Cosmopolitan*

"4½ Stars! Top pick! . . . Filled with heart-stopping suspense and graphic terror . . . In the pantheon of horrific killers, [this one] surely ranks near the top."
—*RT Book Reviews*

"Readers can always count on Rose to deliver an action-packed book, and this one is no exception."
—*Southern Pines Pilot* (NC)

"A tense, chilling suspense."
—*Midwest Book Review*

"Sets pulses pounding and pages turning."
—*BookPage*

"Riveting . . . A caring women's advocate heroine, a determined, gritty hero, and a diabolical villain drive the plot of Rose's riveting story."
—*Library Journal*

I'M WATCHING YOU

"TOP PICK! Terrifying and gritty."
—*RT Book Reviews*

"The suspense unfolds right up to the last page."
—*Southern Pines Pilot* (NC)

more . . .

"Action-packed . . . a thrilling police procedural romance."

—*Midwest Book Review*

"It's perfect . . . Love the characters, loved the side stories. It doesn't get any better than this!"

—*Romantic Review*

HAVE YOU SEEN HER?

"Heart-racing thrills . . . showcases her growing talent . . . readers will . . . rush to the novel's thrilling conclusion."

—*Publishers Weekly*

"Terrifying and gripping."

—*RT Book Reviews*

DON'T TELL

"As gripping as a cold hand on the back of one's neck . . . and tempered by lovable characters and a moving romance."

—*Publishers Weekly*

"A definite page-turner that never lets up until the last page."

—*RomRevToday.com*

KAREN ROSE

❧

I CAN SEE YOU

GRAND CENTRAL
PUBLISHING

NEW YORK   BOSTON

If you purchase this book without a cover you should be aware that this book may have been stolen property and reported as "unsold and destroyed" to the publisher. In such case neither the author nor the publisher has received any payment for this "stripped book."

This book is a work of fiction. Names, characters, places, and incidents are the product of the author's imagination or are used fictitiously. Any resemblance to actual events, locales, or persons, living or dead, is coincidental.

Copyright © 2009 by Karen Rose Hafer
Excerpt from *Silent Scream* copyright © 2009 by Karen Rose Hafer
All rights reserved. Except as permitted under the U.S. Copyright Act of 1976, no part of this publication may be reproduced, distributed, or transmitted in any form or by any means, or stored in a database or retrieval system, without the prior written permission of the publisher.

Cover design by Diane Luger
Cover photograph by Herman Estevez

Grand Central Publishing
Hachette Book Group
237 Park Avenue
New York, NY 10017
Visit our website at www.HachetteBookGroup.com

Grand Central Publishing is a division of Hachette Book Group, Inc. The Grand Central Publishing name and logo is a trademark of Hachette Book Group, Inc.

Printed in the United States of America

Originally published in hardcover by Hachette Book Group
First mass market edition: May 2010

10 9 8 7 6 5 4 3 2 1

ATTENTION CORPORATIONS AND ORGANIZATIONS:
Most HACHETTE BOOK GROUP books are available at quantity discounts with bulk purchase for educational, business, or sales promotional use. For information, please call or write:

Special Markets Department, Hachette Book Group
237 Park Avenue, New York, NY 10017
Telephone: 1-800-222-6747 Fax: 1-800-477-5925

To Lieutenant Danny Agan, Atlanta PD, retired, and to the real-life Hat Squad. Thank you all for your careers of service and your dedication to finding justice for the victims of crime. Special thanks to Danny for your friendship and help in bringing my books to life.

To Sonie Lasker, my *sempai* and my friend. Your discipline and dedication inspire me. Your workouts make me stronger, your friendship nurtures me, and your insight into my characters enriches my work.

And as always, to Martin. You are my reason.

Acknowledgments

Danny Agan, for the Hat Squad. And as always, thank you for answering all my many questions on police procedure, even though I keep promising, "Just one more!"

Marc Conterato, for always answering all my medical questions in a way I can always understand.

Sonie Lasker, for introducing me to the notion of the virtual world. I truly thought you were making it up!

Pamela Bolton-Holifield, for the facts on embalming. Someday, we'll have our gurney race.

Lynn Gutierrez, Colleen Tripp, and Janet Ware, for all the bartending information and wonderful anecdotes.

TinMan, for the hacking jargon from "exploits" to "white hats."

Terri Bolyard and Kay Conterato, who always listen.

Karen Kosztolnyik, Robin Rue, and Vicki Mellor, for simply everything.

Martin Hafer, for his help in psychological research protocol. And for bringing my dinner when I was on a roll.

As always, all mistakes are my own.

Dear Readers,

I introduce a new group of law enforcement officers in I CAN SEE YOU—the homicide detectives of Minneapolis and their "Hat Squad."

In reality, the Hat Squad is a group of homicide detectives in Atlanta, Georgia. I was intrigued by the concept and the tradition started by Lieutenant Danny Agan, Atlanta PD, retired. The homicide detectives of Atlanta are presented with a classic felt fedora soon after solving their first homicide—a gift from the other more experienced detectives. They wear their hats on the job, the fabric and styles changing with the seasons. In the words of Danny Agan, "You dress the part, you dress like a detective, you get better results. It commands respect: Who's showing up to take charge of this mess?"

When I started this book, I wanted to pay tribute to the Hat Squad. The Minneapolis Hat Squad is a product of my imagination, but based on real detectives who strive to get justice for victims every day.

Hope you enjoy meeting this new group!

All my best,
Karen Rose

I CAN
SEE YOU

Prologue

Minneapolis, Saturday, February 13, 9:10 p.m.

She was shy. Nervous. Mousy. Midforties and dowdy, even though she'd obviously dressed for the occasion in an ugly brown suit. She shouldn't have bothered.

Martha Brisbane was just as he'd expected. He'd been watching her from across the crowded coffee shop for close to an hour now. Every time the door opened, she'd straighten, her eyes growing bright if a man entered. But the man would always sit elsewhere, ignoring her, and each time, her eyes grew a little less bright. Still she waited, watching the door. After an hour, the anticipation in her eyes had become desperation. He wondered how much longer her bottom-of-the-barrel self-esteem would keep her waiting. Hoping.

He'd found bursting their bubbles simply added to his fun.

Finally she glanced at her watch with a sigh and began to gather her purse and coat. One hour, six minutes, and forty-two seconds. Not bad. Not bad at all.

The barista behind the counter aimed her a sympathetic look from behind his horn-rimmed glasses. "It's snowing outside. Maybe he got tied up."

Martha shook her head, defeat in the gesture. "I'm sure that's it."

The barista flashed an earnest smile. "You be careful driving home."

"I will."

It was his cue to exit, stage left. He slipped out of the side door in time to see Martha Brisbane huddled against the wind as she made her way to her beat-up old Ford Escort, mincing her steps in the two-inch heels that looked as if they pinched her fat feet. She managed to get to her car before the waterworks began, but once started, Martha didn't stop crying, not when she pulled out of her parking place, not when she got on the highway. It was a wonder she didn't run off the road and kill herself.

Drive carefully, Martha. I need you to arrive home in one piece.

By the time she parked in front of her apartment, her tears had ceased and she was sniffling, her face red and puffy and chapped from the wind. She stumbled up the stairs to her apartment building, grappling with the heavy bags of cat food and litter she'd purchased at the pet store before arriving at the coffee shop.

There was a security camera in the building's lobby, but it was broken. He'd made sure of that days ago. He swept up the stairs and opened the door for her.

"Your hands are full. Can I help you?"

She shook her head, but managed a teary smile. "No, I'm fine. But thank you."

He smiled back. "The pleasure is mine." Which would soon be very true.

Wearily she trudged up three flights of stairs to her apartment, teetering on the two-inch heels as she balanced the heavy bags. She wasn't paying attention. She didn't know he stood behind her, waiting for her to put the key in her lock.

She set the bags down, fumbled for her key. *For God's sake, woman. I don't have all night. Hurry up.* Finally she opened her door, picked up the bags, and pushed the door open with her shoulder.

Now. He leapt forward, clamping his hand over her mouth and twisting her around into the apartment with a fluid motion. She struggled, swinging her heavy bags as he closed her door and leaned back against it, dragging her against him. A pistol against her temple had her struggles magically ceasing.

"Hold still, Martha," he murmured, "and I just might let you live." As if that was going to happen. *Not.* "Now put down the bags."

Her bags dropped to the floor.

"Better," he murmured. She was shaking in terror, just the way he liked it.

Her words, muffled against his hand, sounded like a terrified "Please, please." That's what his victims always said. He liked a polite victim.

He looked around with a sneer. Her apartment was a disgusting mess, books and magazines stacked everywhere. The surface of her desk was obscured by the cups of coagulated coffee, Post-it notes, and newspapers that she'd packed around her state-of-the-art computer.

Her clothes were pure nineties, but her computer was brand new. It figured. Nothing but the best for her forays into fantasyland.

He pressed the gun to her temple harder and felt her flinch against him. "I'm going to move my hand. If you scream, I will kill you."

Sometimes they screamed. Always he killed them.

He slid his hand from her mouth to her throat. "Don't

hurt me," she whimpered. "Please. I'll give you my valu-
ables. Take what you want."

"Oh, I will," he said quietly. "Desiree."

She stiffened. "How did you know that?"

"Because I know everything about you, Martha. What
you really do for a living. What you love. And what you
fear the very most." Still pressing the gun to her temple,
he reached into his coat pocket for the syringe. "I see all.
I know all. Up to and including the moment you will die.
Which would be tonight."

Chapter One

Homicide detective Noah Webster stared up into the wide, lifeless eyes of Martha Brisbane with a sigh that hung in the freezing air, just as she did. Within him was deep sadness, cold rage, and an awful dread that had his heart plodding hard in his chest.

It should have been an unremarkable crime scene. Martha Brisbane had hung herself in the conventional way. She'd looped a rope over a hook in her bedroom ceiling and tied a very traditional noose. She'd climbed up on an upholstered stool, which she'd then kicked aside. The only thing remotely untraditional was the bedroom window she'd left open and the thermostats she'd turned off. The Minnesota winter had served to preserve her body well. Establishing time of death would be a bitch.

Like many hangers, she was dressed for the occasion, makeup applied with a heavy hand. Her red dress plunged daringly, the skirt frozen around her dangling legs. She'd worn her sexiest five-inch red stilettos, which now lay on the carpet at her feet. One red shoe had fallen on its side while the other stood upright, the heel stuck into the carpet.

It should have been an unremarkable crime scene.

But it wasn't. And as he stared up into the victim's

empty eyes, a chill that had nothing to do with the near-zero temps in Martha Brisbane's bedroom went sliding down his spine. They were supposed to believe she'd hung herself. They were supposed to chalk it up to one more depressed, middle-aged single woman. They were supposed to close the case and walk away, without a second thought.

At least that's what the one who'd hung her here had intended. And why not? That's exactly what had happened before.

"The neighbor found her," the first responding officer said. "CSU is on the way. So are the ME techs. Do you need anything else?"

Anything else to close it quickly, was the implication. Noah forced his eyes from the body to look at the officer. "The window, Officer Pratt. Was it open when you got here?"

Pratt frowned slightly. "Yes. Nobody touched anything."

"The neighbor who called it in," Noah pressed. "She didn't open the window?"

"She didn't enter the apartment. She tried knocking on the door but the victim didn't answer, so she went around back, planning to bang on the window. She thought the victim would be asleep since she works nights. Instead, she saw this. Why?"

Because I've seen this scene before, he thought, déjà vu squeezing his chest so hard he could barely breathe. The body, the stool, the open window. Her dress and shoes, one standing up, one lying on its side. *And her eyes*.

Noah hadn't been able to forget the last victim's eyes, lids glued open, cruelly forced to remain wide and empty. This was going to be very bad. Very bad indeed.

"See if you can find the building manager," he said. "I'll wait for CSU and the ME."

Officer Pratt gave him a sharp look. "And Detective GQ?"

Noah winced. That Jack Phelps wasn't here yet was not, unfortunately, unusual. His partner had been distracted recently. Which was the polite way of saying he'd dropped the ball more than a few times.

"Detective Phelps is on his way," he said, with more confidence than he felt.

Pratt grunted as he left in search of the manager and Noah felt a twinge of sympathy for Jack. Officers who'd never met Jack disrespected him. *Thanks to that magazine.* A recent article on the homicide squad had portrayed them as supermen. But Jack had borne the brunt, his face adorning the damn cover.

But Jack's rep as a party-loving lightweight started long before the magazine hit the stands three weeks before and it was a shame. Focused, Jack Phelps was a good cop. Noah knew his partner had a quick mind, seeing connections others passed over.

Noah looked up into Martha Brisbane's empty eyes. They were going to need all the quick minds they could get.

His cell buzzed. *Jack.* But it was his cousin Brock, from whose dinner table Noah had been called. Brock and his wife, Trina, were cops, they'd taken it in stride. In a family of cops, it was a rare Sunday dinner when one of them wasn't called away.

"I'm tied up," Noah answered, bypassing greeting.

"So is your partner," Brock responded. Brock had been headed to Sal's Bar to watch the game. Which meant that Jack was at Sal's, too. *Damn him.*

"I've called him *twice*," Noah gritted. Both calls had gone to Jack's voicemail.

"He's having drinks with his newest blonde. You want me to talk to him?"

Noah looked up at Martha Brisbane's lifeless eyes and his anger bubbled tightly. It wasn't the first time Jack had blown off his duty, but by God, it would be his last. "No. I'm going to get the first responder back in here and come down there myself."

Sunday, February 21, 6:55 p.m.

"Come on, Eve, it's just a little magazine quiz."

Eve Wilson glanced across the bar at her friend with an exasperated shake of her head before returning her eyes to the beer tap. "I get enough quizzes at school."

"But this one is fun," Callie insisted, "unlike that psycho research project that has you tied up in knots. Don't worry. You always get the best grade in class. Just one question."

If only it was the grade. A few months ago, getting A's was at the top of Eve's mind. A few months ago the participants in her thesis research had been nameless, faceless numbers on a page. The mug filled, she replaced it with the next. The bar was busy tonight. She'd hoped to numb her mind with work, but the worry was always there.

Because a few months ago Eve never would have entertained the possibility of breaking university rules, of compromising her own ethics. But she'd done both of those things. Because now the test subjects were more than numbers on a page. Desiree and Gwenivere and the others were real people, in serious trouble.

Desiree had been missing for more than a week. *I should do something. But what?* She wasn't supposed to know that Desiree existed, much less that she was Martha Brisbane in real life. Test subjects were assured their privacy.

But Eve did know, because she'd broken the rules. *And I'll have to pay for that.*

Across the bar, Callie cleared her throat dramatically, taking Eve's silence for assent. "Question one. Have you ever gone on a romantic dinner to—"

"I'm busy," Eve interrupted. For the next few hours there was nothing she could do about Martha and her other test subjects, but Callie's quiz was not welcome respite. *Do you believe in love at first sight, my ass. I hate those quizzes.* Which, of course, was the reason Callie insisted on reading them. "Look, Cal, I took your shift so you could party."

Callie shrugged the shoulders her cocktail dress left bare. "Nice try. I had somebody to cover for me. You should be studying, but you're here, procrastinating."

It was fair. Grasping three mug handles in each fist, Eve clenched her teeth against the pain that speared through her right hand. But until last year that hand couldn't hold a coffee cup, so a little pain seemed a small price to pay for mobility. And independence.

She lifted the mugs into the waiting hands of one of her most regular regulars, quirking the responsive side of her mouth in the three-cornered smile that, after years of practice, appeared normal. "Normal" was right up there with mobility and independence.

"You've been buying all night, Jeff," she said, surreptitiously flexing her fingers, "and haven't had a drop yourself." Which was so not normal. "You lose a bet?"

Officer Jeff Betz was a big guy with a sweet grin. "Don't tell my wife. She'll kill me."

Eve nodded sagely. "Bartenders never tell. It's part of the oath."

He met her eyes, gratitude in his. "I know," he said, then turned to Callie. "Hot date?"

"You betcha." Callie nodded, comfortable with the scrutiny she'd received since gliding into Sal's on ridiculously high heels. Her tiny dress would earn her significantly better tips were she to wear it next time she tended bar. Not that she needed any help.

Clerking for the county prosecutor was Callie's primary means of putting herself through law school, but she'd recently started picking up extra cash working at Sal's on weekends, her tip jar consistently filled to the brim. That dress combined with Callie's substantial cleavage would send her cup running over, so to speak.

Hopefully Callie's dress wouldn't give their boss any ideas, Eve thought darkly. *Because there's no way in hell I'm wearing anything like that, tips or no.*

So to speak. Eve squashed the envy. Never pompous, Callie was a beautiful woman comfortable in her own skin, something that Eve had not been in a long time.

Eve made her voice light. "Her date's taking her to Chez León."

Jeff whistled. "Spendy." Then he frowned. "Do we know this guy?"

The "we" was understood—it included every cop that hung at Sal's. Eighty percent of Sal's customers were police, which made the bar one of the safest places in town. An ex-cop, Sal was one of their own, and by extension so was everyone on Sal's payroll. It was like having a hundred big brothers. Which was pretty nice, Eve thought.

"I don't think so," Callie demurred. Her date was a defense attorney, which earned him poor opinion among their cops. Callie agreed, which was precisely why she'd accepted the date. Callie's constant challenge of her own worldview was something Eve had always admired. "But he's late, so I'm trying to get Eve to take this little quiz."

"Is that that *MSP* rag with Jack Phelps on the cover?" Jeff asked, his lip curled.

MSP was the women's magazine that juggled Minneapolis–St. Paul gossip, culture, and local concerns. Their recent exposé on the homicide squad had made instant, if temporary, celebrities of Sal's regulars. It was a decent piece, although it did make their cops into white knights, a fact that had embarrassed the hell out of the detectives.

Jeff gave Eve a pitying look. "My wife made me take that damn quiz."

Eve's lips twitched. "Did you pass?"

"Of course. A man can't stay happily married without knowing how to BS his way through one of those things." With a parting wink, he carried the beer back to his waiting friends, all off-duty cops who made Sal's their home away from home.

Callie rolled her eyes when Jeff was gone. "If he spent half the time he's here with his wife, he wouldn't have had to BS his way through this 'damn quiz,'" she muttered.

"Don't judge," Eve murmured, dumping two shots of gin over ice. "Jeff's wife works second shift at the hospital. When he's on days, he hangs here, then takes her home."

Callie frowned. "What about their kids? Who's watching them?"

"No kids." But not from lack of trying, Jeff had confided one night when the bar was empty and he'd had a little too much to drink. The stress had nearly torn his marriage apart. Eve understood his pain far more than Jeff had realized. Far more than she'd ever let anyone see. Even Callie. "I guess his house is kind of quiet."

Callie sighed. "What else should I know so I don't put my foot in my mouth again?"

Eve tried to think of something she could share without breaking a confidence. She wouldn't tell Callie about the cop at Jeff's table who was worried his wife was leaving him, or the policewoman at the end of the bar, just diagnosed with breast cancer.

So many secrets, Eve thought. Listening, keeping their secrets, was a way she could help them while she worked on her master's in counseling. If she ever made it through her damn thesis she'd be a therapist, trading one listening career for another.

But I'll miss this place. She'd miss Sal and his wife, Josie, who'd given her a chance to work, to support herself in the new life she'd started in Minneapolis. She'd miss Jeff and all the regulars, who'd become more like friends than customers.

Some she'd miss more than others, she admitted. The one she'd miss most never came in on Sundays, but that didn't stop her eyes from straying to the door every time the bell jingled. Watching Noah Webster come through the door still caught her breath, every time. Tall, dark. Powerful. *Look, but don't touch.* Not anymore. Probably not ever again.

She looked up to find Callie watching her carefully. Eve pointed to a couple who'd confided nothing, but whose behavior screamed volumes. "They're having an affair."

Callie glanced over her shoulder. "How do you know?"

"Hunch. They never socialize, are always checking their cells, but never answer. She twists her wedding ring and when the guy comes to the bar for their wine, he's twitchy. So they're either having an affair or planning a bank heist." Callie chuckled and Eve's lips quirked. "I suspect the former. They think nobody notices them."

Callie shook her head. "Why do people always think they're invisible?"

"They don't see anyone but each other. They assume nobody sees them either."

Callie pointed to a young man who sat at a table alone, his expression grim. "Him?"

"Tony Falcone." Tony had shared his experience in the open, so Eve felt no guilt in repeating it. "He caught his first suicide victim last week. Shook him up."

"From the looks of him, he still is," Callie said softly. "Poor kid."

"He couldn't forget the woman's eyes. She'd glued them open, then hung herself."

Callie flinched. "God. How do any of these cops sleep at night?"

"They learn to deal." She met Callie's eyes. "Just like you did."

"Like *we* did," Callie said quietly. "You a lot more so than me."

Yes, I dealt. But how well? Surgery could fix hands and minimize scars, but in the end one still had to *be*. It was easier here, surrounded by others who saw the darkness in the world. But when the noise was gone and the memories echoed in her mind . . .

Uneasy, Eve mixed another drink. "We all do what we have to do. Some have addictions, some have hobbies. Some come here." She shrugged. "Hell, I come here."

"To forget about life for a while," Callie murmured, then shook off her mood. "I'll take those out for you. It's the least I can do since I've left you with the whole bar tonight."

Eve arched her right brow, one of the few facial features that still obeyed her command. "It's going to Detective Phelps and his bimbo *du jour.*" Who were necking at a table next to the TV wall where everyone would see them. Eve didn't have to wonder if the choice was deliberate. Jack Phelps liked everyone to know when he'd scored.

Phelps should take a lesson from his way-too-serious partner. Eve stifled her sigh. Or perhaps Noah Webster should borrow just a smidge of Jack's cheek. Jack hit on her every time he came to the bar, but in the year he'd been coming to Sal's, Webster had never said more than "please" and "thank you" when she served his tonic water.

He came in on Mondays with Phelps, who'd order a gin and tonic for them both. Phelps always got the gin, Webster always the tonic. Then Phelps would flirt with the women and Webster would nurse his water, green eyes alert, but unreadable.

For a while she'd thought he'd come to watch her, but after weeks had gone by she'd given up on any such notion. Not that she'd reciprocate any move he made, so the question was moot. Although her mind still stubbornly wandered, imagining what she'd say if Noah ever uttered the lines that fell so meaninglessly from Jack's lips.

Of course, fantasy and reality were very different things. This fact Eve knew well.

"We have to be fair here, Eve," Callie said dryly. "Katie's more than a bimbo *du jour.* She's been with Phelps for three whole weeks. That could be a record for him."

Katie had come in with the other groupies after the *MSP* article had hit the stands and Jack had reeled her in like a walleye. Or maybe it was the other way around. Either way, Katie would be gone soon and Jack would move to his next conquest. "So she's more the flavor of the month. You gonna take these drinks or not?"

"Not on your life. Katie doesn't like me much. You're on your own, pal."

"I thought so. I have to talk to Phelps anyway. That magazine you found is Sal's copy. He wants Phelps to sign the cover so he can add it to the Hat wall."

Sal had covered one wall of his bar with TVs, but the others were covered in photos, most taken by Sal, all of cops. One wall he'd dedicated to his favorites—the homicide detectives known as the Hat Squad for the classic fedoras they wore. The wall had, in fact, inspired the *MSP* article. One day one of their staff writers had wandered in to Sal's and been instantly charmed. To the public, the hats were an unofficial uniform, but to the detectives who proudly wore them, the hats were a badge of honor. Every member of the squad owned at least one fedora.

When a newly promoted detective solved his first case, he was presented with a fedora by his or her peers. It was tradition. Eve liked that. As years passed and more murders were solved, the detectives supplemented their own hat collections according to their personal style and the season—felt in the winter, sometimes straw in the summer.

Eve had never seen Noah Webster wear anything but black felt. It suited him.

"I was wondering why Sal moved the picture frames around," Callie said, pointing to the large, new bare spot on the wall. "But not even Phelps's head is that big."

Eve chuckled. "Sal's done a collage. He got all the detectives whose pictures were in the article to sign the page from the magazine. Phelps's cover is supposed to be at the center." She sobered. "But Phelps won't sign it, even though Sal all but begged him."

Callie's brows shot up in surprise. "Why? Jack's not going for humble now, is he?"

Eve studied Jack, who was discreetly checking his cell phone for the third time in a half hour. He returned the unanswered phone to his pocket, and his lips to Katie's pouting mouth. "Who knows why men like Jack Phelps do the things they do?"

A bitter frown creased Callie's brow. "Because they can. Poor Sal."

"I promised him I'd ask Phelps one more time."

Callie closed the magazine and Jack's face stared up from the cover. He was a dead ringer for Paul Newman, down to his baby blues. And, Eve thought, he knew it. "You're going to pander to that ego?" Callie huffed. "You hate Jack as much as I do."

Eve smiled. "But I love Sal. He's given me so much and this means a lot to him. He found some old photos of himself wearing his hat before his accident." Before he'd been forced to give up the career that had been his life. "He wanted to do a Hat Squad photo exposé of his own. For Sal, I can pander to Phelps's ego for a few minutes."

Callie's frown eased. "You have a good soul, Eve."

Embarrassed, Eve put the drinks on a tray. "Watch the bar for me." But she hadn't taken a step when the door opened, jingling the bell and letting in a gust of frigid air. Her eyes shot to the door before she reminded herself that it was Sunday.

She started to turn back to the bar, then stopped. Because Sunday or no, there he was. Noah Webster. Filling the doorway like a photo in a frame.

Suddenly, as always, all the oxygen was sucked from the room. He paused in the doorway and Eve couldn't tear her eyes away. Dressed in black from his fedora to his shiny shoes, he looked, as always, as if he'd stepped straight from an old *film noir*. There was something edgy, almost thuggish in the way he carried himself, a coiled danger Eve didn't want to find attractive. As if she'd ever had a choice.

He was linebacker big, his shoulders nearly touching the sides of the door, so tall the top of his hat brushed the doorframe most men cleared with ease. Heavy stubble darkened his jaw and her fingers itched to touch. *Look, but don't touch.* The mantra was ingrained.

He closed the door and Eve dragged in a ragged breath. Normally she was prepared before he came through the door, defenses ready. Today he'd taken her by surprise.

"I'd say that's a yes," Callie said softly.

"Yes, what?" Eve asked, her gaze hungrily following Noah, who was striding across the bar toward Jack's table. He was angry. She could feel it from where she stood.

Apparently Jack did, too. Eve watched the briefest shiver of alarm pass through Jack's eyes, followed by sly calculation, then wide-eyed surprise. He frowned at his cell phone and Eve remembered seeing him check it, three times. *SOB*. His partner needed him and here he'd sat, showing off his sexual prowess with his bimbo *du jour*.

"Yes to number six," Callie murmured. "Do you believe in love at first sight?"

Eve jerked her eyes to Callie and saw she'd flipped the magazine open to that damn quiz again. "Will you cut it out? The answer is no. N-O."

"Lust then. Can't say that I blame you. He's a lot more potent in person, all burly and broody." She turned to the article and the picture of Webster. "Doesn't do him justice."

Eve refused to look. It didn't matter. She'd seen that picture hundreds of times. At home. In private. That Callie had seen her reaction to Noah's entrance *in public* was bad enough. But who else had seen? And worse, pitied her adolescent fascination with a man who'd never said more than please or thank you?

Her face heated, making it worse. She knew the scar on her cheek, almost invisible under her makeup, was now blazing white against her scarlet face. Out of habit, she turned her face away, reaching for his bottle of tonic water. Then she put it back. From the look of their conversation, Webster had come to fetch Jack. He wouldn't be staying.

She busied her hands, pouring coffee into two Styrofoam cups, adding spoonfuls of sugar. "Can you just put that damn magazine away?"

"Eve, I only could see it because I'm your best friend. Nobody else noticed a thing."

Eve's laugh was bitter. "You're just saying that to make me feel better."

Callie smiled wryly. "Did it work?"

"No." Eve lifted her eyes, saw Jack Phelps putting on his coat. "But on the upside, Phelps is leaving. I won't have to ask him to sign that damn cover for Sal."

"Unfortunately, he'll be back."

As will his partner. *Next time I'll be ready. And next time I won't even look.* Eve snapped lids on the coffee cups. "Do me a favor. Take these to them. It's cold tonight."

*   *   *

"Thank you." Noah took the cup of coffee from Sal's new weekend bartender. The men had been talking about her. Curvy and blonde, she was quite a package.

But she wasn't the woman he'd been coming to see for months. The one he thought about long before walking into Sal's every week, and long after leaving. That would be the tall, willowy brunette quietly standing behind the bar, dark eyes wide. *Watching me.*

Watching everyone. Eve Wilson reminded him of a doe, head always up. Always aware. He wondered what had happened to make her that way. There was a fragility, a vulnerability her eyes didn't always mask. Whatever had happened, it had been bad.

Which hadn't taken a detective to figure out. Up until six months ago, she'd borne a visible mark of past violence, a scar on her cheek. Rumor had it that a surgeon had worked magic with his knife, because now it was barely visible. Rumor also had it that the black leather choker she wore around her neck covered another scar, much worse.

Noah had lost count of the number of times he'd been a mouse click away from finding out what had put that wary guard behind the façade of calm. But he hadn't. He wanted to believe he respected her privacy, but knew he didn't want to know. Because once he knew, it would change . . . everything. The knowledge rattled him.

Conversely, very little seemed to rattle Eve, even the clumsy advances of drunken customers. More than once in the last year Noah had been tempted to come to her aid, but she always managed—either on her own or with the help of one of the other cops.

The men took care of her. They liked her. They lusted after Callie, but liked Eve, which left Noah grimly reassured. He would've had a much harder time sitting with his damned tonic water week after week had it been the other way around, because long before he walked in every week and long after he left, he wanted her. But he had only to look at the mugs of beer and glasses of liquor surrounding him to know he couldn't have everything that he wanted. Some things, like Eve, were best left untouched.

However difficult she was to rattle, Eve had been startled tonight. Her dark doe eyes had widened. Flared to life. And for that undefended split second, his heart stumbled, the hunger in her eyes stroking the ego he'd tried so hard to ignore. But he'd come to get Jack. And it didn't matter anyway. That Eve was interested didn't negate any of the reasons he'd vowed to keep his distance. If anything, it underscored them.

He pulled his eyes back to Callie, who still stood in front of him, studying him. "Eve thought you might want something to keep you warm when you went back out," she said, shivering in a skimpy black dress that left little to the imagination.

"Tell her I appreciate it. You should get away from the door. You'll catch cold."

Callie's smile was self-deprecating. "The things we women do for fashion."

Looking over his shoulder, Noah watched Callie take the other cup she held to Jack. She spared his partner no conversation, simply leaving the cup on the table. Jack wouldn't have heard her anyway. He was soothing Katie, who was pouting because he had to leave. Noah bit back what he really wanted to say, about both Katie's pout and Jack's idiotic song and dance about no cell phone reception in the bar.

Noah pulled out his own phone. Just as he'd thought,

strong reception. He wasn't sure if Jack believed his own excuses, thought Noah was stupid enough to believe them, or just didn't care if anyone believed him or not. Regardless, Noah was going to have to report him soon. Jack had missed too much work.

The thought of turning in his own partner made him sick. When Jack focused, he was a damn good cop. If he could just keep his fly zipped, there would be no issue.

"Noah. Over here." His cousin Brock was waving from his table along the far wall. "You found him, I see," Brock said quietly when Noah approached.

Noah nodded. "I need his eyes on the scene." He thought about Martha Brisbane, still hanging from her ceiling, eyes wide open. "This is going to be a bad one."

"Call if you need me." Brock glanced to the bar where Eve was shaking a martini, her gaze constantly roving the bar. "On *any* subject," he added, accusingly.

"I will," Noah said and Brock shook his head in disgust.

"That's what you always say. You gotta fish or cut bait, man. This has gone on long enough. You're playing with fire, every damn time you walk into this bar."

It was true. "I know." Still he shrugged. "When I close this case."

Brock's jaw hardened. "That's what you always say."

That was true, too. Noah always promised that this time would be the last he'd walk into Sal's, but he always came back. He'd spent ten years battling one addiction, only to find another. Eve Wilson was his weakness, dangerous in more ways than one.

"I know," Noah repeated, reaching for the four packets of sugar he took in his coffee.

Brock pushed the sugar container away. "I'd taste it first if I were you."

Noah did and drew a quiet breath. Eve had added it already. He'd ordered coffee maybe twice in the last year, and had added his own sugar each time. She'd not only watched, she'd remembered. The look on Brock's face said he knew it, too.

"She's a good bartender," Noah said. "I bet she remembers what you always order."

Brock rolled his eyes. "You're a goddamn fool, Noah."

Noah sighed. "Yeah, I know that, too. Tell Trina thanks for dinner. I have to go."

Jack had just left, Katie clinging to his arm. He'd said he'd go home and change, then join Noah at the scene where they'd focus their full attention on finding out who'd killed Martha Brisbane. They'd do their jobs. For Noah, the job was all. When he'd hit rock bottom, the job was what led him out. He'd do well to remember that.

But Noah felt Eve's steady gaze as he made his way toward the door and he stopped. He wouldn't be coming back. Wouldn't see her again. He hadn't come within fifteen feet of the bar in six months, Jack eager to get their orders once Eve's scar disappeared, shallow jerk that he was. *And you? What are you?* He'd sat there, and watched.

I'm a fool. Deliberately, he turned to the bar. Her eyes were quiet as he approached, but he could see the pulse hammering in the hollow of her throat beneath the choker she wore, and knew he hadn't been wrong about that flash of hunger he'd seen before. He lifted the cup, a million things he wanted to say stampeding through his mind. In the end, he said the only thing that he could say. The only thing that made any sense.

"Thank you."

She nodded once, swallowed hard. "It's just a cup of coffee, Detective."

But it was more. It was kindness, one more in a string of many he'd witnessed over the months, most when she thought no one was watching. But he'd seen.

Turn around and go. But he didn't say anything, nor did he go, his eyes dropping to her hands. Her left cradled the right. A jagged scar wrapped around her thumb and disappeared up the sleeve of a black sweater that matched her short hair and dipped just low enough to be considered modest, yet still make a man look twice. And wish.

Calmly she splayed her hands flat on the bar as if to say, "Nothing to see here, please move along." But for a brief moment her eyes flickered, and he glimpsed a yearning so profound it stole his breath. As quickly as it had come, it was controlled, gone, and she was back to guardedly serene. "Stay safe, Detective," she said quietly.

He touched the brim of his hat. "Take care." *And good-bye.*

Noah gulped a mouthful of the scalding coffee as he walked to his car, the sweet liquid sour on his tongue. *Fish or cut bait.* It would be the second one. As long as he'd clung to the belief that he was only hurting himself, he could go to the bar, just to see her. But tonight she'd nibbled, just a light tug on the line, but a tug nonetheless.

He'd reel in his line before he hooked her. *And hurt her.* Whatever she'd been through, it had been bad. *I won't make it worse by dragging her down with me.*

*   *   *

Sunday, February 21, 7:15 p.m.

Lindsay Barkley woke screaming. *Dogs.* Snarling, baring their teeth, chasing. *Run.* But she couldn't run. She was tied and couldn't run. They were on her, teeth ripping . . .

She screamed and the jagged teeth disappeared, the snarling abruptly silenced.

A dream. She was panting, gasping for breath. *Just a bad dream.* A nightmare, she thought, as her mind cleared. She tried to move and the terror returned in a dizzying rush. *This is no nightmare.* The bed to which she'd been tied was real, as was the dark room. Ropes bit into her wrists and ankles. The air was dry. Her mouth was like chalk and the pillow beneath her head smelled of sweat and vomit. Her eyes burned like fire.

She tried to blink, but her eyes merely stared straight ahead into the darkness. Her eyes were glued open. She was naked. And so cold. *No. This can't be happening.*

"Help." What in her mind had been a shrill scream escaped from her throat in a hoarse whisper. *Dry.* Her throat was too dry to scream. *He's going to kill me.*

No. I'll get away. Think. Think. The last thing she remembered was being pushed to the backseat floor of his black SUV and the jab of a needle on her neck.

He'd looked so . . . respectable. Clean. Trustworthy. When she'd quoted her price he'd smiled politely. So she'd gotten into his SUV. She didn't like getting into cars with her johns, but it was cold outside, so she had. *I'm so cold. Somebody help me.*

He said he had a hotel, that he'd take her someplace warm. Nice. He'd lied. He'd pulled over, dragged her from the front seat to the back, holding a gun to her head. Then he'd jabbed a needle into her neck. And he'd laughed, told her when she woke, she'd be torn apart by wild beasts, limb from limb. And that she'd die tonight.

He'd been right about the dogs. *I don't want to die. I'm sorry,* she prayed, hoping God would still hear. *You can't let me die. Who will take care of Liza?*

Upstairs a door opened, closed, and she heard the click of a deadbolt. *He's coming.* He flicked on the light and she could see. And her thundering heart simply stopped.

Shoes. The walls were lined with shelves that held more shoes than she'd ever seen outside a store. They were grouped by the pair, heels out. Dozens of shoes.

At the end of the top row was a pair of stretched-out pumps with a tiny heel next to the five-inch leopard skin stilettos she'd pulled from her own closet, just hours before.

My shoes. God, please help me. I swear I'll never turn a trick again. I'll flip burgers, I'll do anything. Don't let me die here.

Desperate, Lindsay yanked at the ropes as he came down the stairs, but they were too strong. She drew another breath to scream, but again it came out hoarsely pathetic.

His expression went from expectant to furious the instant he came into view. "You're awake. When did you wake up? Goddammit," he snarled. "I was only gone five minutes."

"Please," she begged. "Don't kill me. I won't tell. I promise I won't tell."

Pain speared through her when the back of his hand hit her mouth. She tasted blood.

"I didn't say you could speak," he snarled. "You're nothing. Less than nothing."

Terror clawed. "Please." The pain was worse the second time, his ring hitting her lip.

"*Silence*." He was naked and erect and she tried to get calm. It was just sex. Maybe this was a bondage fantasy.

She dropped her dry, burning eyes suggestively to his groin. "I'll make it good for you. I'll give you what you need."

She cried out when his palm struck her cheek.

"Like I'd put anything of mine in anything of yours," he said with contempt. He climbed on the bed, straddling her. "You *give* me nothing. I *take* what I need."

His hands closed around her throat, tightening his grip. *Can't breathe. God, please.* Lights danced before her eyes and she flailed, trying to draw just one breath. *Just one.*

His laugh was faraway, tinny. Like she was in a tunnel. The last thing she heard was his groan as he climaxed, his seed hot on her frozen skin. And then . . . darkness.

Breathing hard, he stared into her face, now slack in death. Withdrawing his hands from her throat, he clenched them into fists. It should have been *better*. He'd needed it to be *better. Dammit*. She'd woken earlier than he'd calculated and he'd missed her postsedation hallucinations. During the hallucinations was always the optimal moment.

Whatever he whispered as they were going under, they experienced as they awoke. The abject terror in their eyes when they were waking . . . He'd learned long ago that their fear was far better than any drug, sending his orgasm into the stratosphere.

That had been denied him today. His breathing began to slow, his racing thoughts to settle. Which was the primary objective. The orgasm was just . . . incidental.

Nice, but completely unnecessary. He climbed off her, staying away from the blood sullenly oozing from her lip. He was always careful with the trash he collected. Hookers and addicts, crawling with disease. *Disgusting.*

It was late. He'd shower her stink off of his skin, get dressed, and do what needed to be done. He hoped somebody had found Martha Brisbane. He'd been waiting for days, the need to move forward to the next victim growing every hour. He couldn't move to the next victim until the police found the last one. That was his own rule.

Rules kept order and order controlled chaos. The higher the chaos, the greater the chances of discovery and that wouldn't do at all. So he'd follow his own rules.

He looked at the body on the narrow bed. She'd served her purpose. A diversion, a means to keep his mind clear while he waited for someone to discover Martha. Once he got his mind prepared for a kill, he had to move. If he didn't, his mind raced too fast.

Options, scenarios, outcomes. It was distracting, and he couldn't afford to be distracted. In his line of work, he had to be sharp, every day. *Now, more than ever.*

He grabbed the steel handle in the concrete floor. The slab moved silently on well-oiled bearings, revealing the pit where he'd disposed of dozens of bodies over the years. Hookers. Addicts. Trash nobody would miss. *The world is a better place without them here.* Dozens of victims and the police had never had even a whiff of suspicion.

He sniffed in disdain. "Modern-day heroes," he muttered, quoting the shallow, pathetically written article all the detectives claimed embarrassed them, but he knew better. They'd secretly preened, thrilled to be so elevated in the public's regard.

They were simply thugs with big guns and very small

brains. Easily manipulated. He should know. He'd been manipulating them for years. They just didn't know it.

That was about to change. He'd bring them down, humiliate them. Show everyone what they really were. The premise of his plan was quite simple. He'd do what he'd been doing for years—killing women right under their noses. He looked into the pit. *But not like this*. Not quietly. Not discreetly. *And not the dregs of society no one would miss.*

He considered the six women he'd chosen. Single women who lived alone, but who had family and friends who'd grieve their loss in sound bites covered by a sympathetic press who'd quickly lose patience with their precious Hat Squad.

Which was the point of it all. The six he'd chosen would capture the public's attention, command their ire in a way no skanky, lice-infested prostitutes ever could.

Of course the irony of his choices wasn't lost. His six had never walked a street or shot up, but they were hookers and addicts just the same. They simply plied their trade and fed their addictions in less traditional venues. *They were women, after all.*

He'd had to change his MO in other ways. No bringing them here where he had disposal down to a science. Instead he'd posed them in their homes, leaving clues of his choosing. He didn't touch them, couldn't risk putting his hands around their necks. He'd correctly anticipated the loss of the tactile would detract from the experience.

And he'd had to hold back. He couldn't release himself on them. Any killer that left DNA behind was a fool. The strain of killing without the physical release had been a bit more difficult than he'd expected, but this hooker had taken off the edge.

It would be worth it. Headlines would scream SERIAL KILLER UNCHALLENGED and COPS CLUELESS. *So true.* A serial killer, the people would quail, in their own midst. *Oh my.* If they only knew he'd killed in their midst for years. *Oh my.*

How many victims would it take before they wised up? Martha was the third of his six. But they hadn't found Martha yet and he was growing impatient. Fortunately he was disciplined enough to stick with his plan, falling back on the tried and true for relief.

He dragged the hooker's body to the pit and rolled her in. He threw her clothes in after, except for her shoes. Those he would keep, as he'd done dozens of times before.

He donned the coveralls he'd taken from the man he'd hired to dig the pit, twenty years before. Who, bullet in his head, had become its first inhabitant. He shoveled lime from the steel drum into the pit, covering the body.

Quicklime hastened decomposition of flesh without the fuss and muss and foul odor, but one had to be careful. It was powerful stuff, highly reactive with moisture. He kept his basement dry with dehumidifiers, with a side benefit the preservation of his shoes.

The pumps he'd taken from the feet of his first victim nearly thirty years ago were in as good condition as the shoes he'd taken from victims over the last three weeks.

He finished the hooker's burial by adding dirt to cover the lime, pulled the handle on the slab to cover the pit. Just as he'd done dozens of times before.

But although this killing had fulfilled its purpose, it was a shadow next to the triumph he'd feel when the police realized they had a bona fide serial killer on their hands.

Chapter Two

Sorry again. I gotta get a new phone," Jack said, crossing Martha's bedroom.

Noah had been waiting, stewing for half an hour. Jack had said he'd change clothes, but his eyes held a satisfaction any man would recognize. He'd had sex with Katie. While a victim hung from her damn ceiling. That was it. *I'm going to have to report him.*

"Whatever, Jack," he said coldly, but if Jack detected his fury, it didn't show.

"So, introduce me to the lady with the Bette Davis eyes and get this party swinging."

The ME techs were impatiently waiting to cut the body down, but Noah had wanted Jack to see the scene. *I shouldn't have bothered. I might have a new partner soon.*

"Martha Brisbane," Noah said tightly. "Forty-two, single. Found by her neighbor."

"It's cold in here. Did the neighbor open the window or did Ms. Brisbane?"

"The neighbor said the window was open."

"Well, it could be worse. It could be August. Shit. Are her eyes glued open?"

"Yes," Noah bit out. "They are." *Just like the other one.*

"That's one you don't see every day." Then Jack shrugged.

"At least this should be quick. I might even get back to Katie in time for dessert. *If* you know what I mean."

Noah bit his tongue, saved from a response by ME tech Isaac Londo. "So now that Detective GQ's *finally* here, can we *finally* cut her down?"

"No," Noah said sharply.

"I got twenty on tonight's game," Londo grumbled. "I want to get out of here."

CSU's Micki Ridgewell looked up from putting her camera away. "What's the big deal, Web? The vic strung herself from the ceiling, kicked the stool away, and died."

Jack frowned, as if finally realizing something was up. "What's wrong here?"

You want a damn list? "This scene," Noah said. "I've seen this scene before."

"Well, of course you have," Micki said reasonably. "After fifteen years, you've seen almost every crime scene before. So have I."

"No. I've seen *this* scene before, down to the placement of the victim's shoes."

"I haven't," Jack said, dead serious now. "When did you see it and why didn't I?"

"Friday morning, a week ago. You were home ... sick."

Jack tensed at Noah's hesitation, flags of angry color staining his cheeks. "I was."

Noah let it slide. This was not the place for confrontation. "It was Gus Dixon's scene. I'd borrowed his mini recorder because mine broke and I needed to interview a witness." For a case he'd closed without Jack, because Jack had been *sick*. "On my way back from the interview, Dix called. He needed his recorder at a scene, so I took it to him."

"And it was this scene?" Jack asked, eyes narrowing. "A hanging?"

"Exactly. The stool was overturned, same distance and angle from the body. The vic wore this dress and the same style shoes. One shoe lying on its side, the other standing straight up. The type of hook, the noose, the open window, everything is the same."

Micki frowned. "Déjà vu all over again."

"But this victim was hung," Londo said. "Petechiae in the eyes, the ligatures on her throat . . . All the injuries are consistent with a short-drop hanging."

"Dix's was the same," Noah said. "But her eyes are glued open just like Dix's victim."

Jack winced. "I was just kidding about the Bette Davis eyes." Studying the scene again, Jack pointed to the stool. "You done with it, Mick?" He picked it up and, placing it directly under the body, stepped back, and Noah's suspicion was confirmed.

The stool sat two full inches lower than the tips of Martha Brisbane's toes.

"Holy fuck," Londo muttered. "Was that the same on the other hanger, too?"

"I don't know. When I got there some other ME techs had already cut her down."

"This vic couldn't have stuck her neck in the noose and still been able to kick the stool away," Micki said quietly. "Somebody helped her."

Noah looked up into Martha's wide eyes. "Somebody killed her."

"And went to a lot of trouble to make it look like a suicide," Jack said. "Any note?"

"We haven't found one," Noah said.

Micki took more close-ups of the red stilettos. "No

scuffs." She held a shoe next to the victim's foot. "And too small. Why go to all this trouble and leave the wrong shoes?"

"I wonder how many others he's staged," Jack said.

"And how many we missed." Noah nodded at Londo. "You can take her down now."

"Let's check this apartment," Jack said, "then go talk to the neighbor who found her."

"Sarah Dwyer. Martha promised to water Dwyer's plants while she was away."

"How long ago was that?" Jack asked.

"Two weeks," Noah said. "Officer Pratt said Dwyer got back today, pissed because her plants were dead. She came to yell at Martha, but nobody answered the door so she climbed the fire escape to bang on the bedroom window, and saw her hanging."

Micki's brows went up. "She went to all the trouble to climb the fire escape?"

Jack's lips twitched. "Three guesses as to the plants she was so attached to."

"I thought the same thing," Noah admitted. "But I bet she got rid of any pot she was growing on her windowsill before she called 911. Let's finish up here. I've already searched the bedroom and bath. You take the kitchen, I'll take the living room."

Noah was searching Martha Brisbane's empty desk drawers when Jack came in from the kitchen, a can of cat food in his hand. "The vic had a cat," he said.

"There weren't any cats here," Noah said and Jack frowned.

"A multiple murderer and a missing cat. Not good. You finding anything?"

"Nothing, and nobody's desk is this clean. Let's see the neighbor, get a next of kin."

"You talk to the neighbor," Jack said. "I'll go door to door and find anyone who may have seen her more recently than two weeks ago."

Sunday, February 21, 8:20 p.m.

Dell stretched out his hand. "Gimme the zoom."

Harvey shook his head. "You should have brought your own tools."

Dell shifted in the passenger seat. "They've been in there a long time."

"Means it's a big case," Harvey said. "Bigger the case, harder they fall."

"Sonsofbitches," Dell muttered. "That article made them look like damn Messiahs."

Harvey heard the hate in his son's voice. He felt the same. "Which is why we'll show the world the truth. Which is why you won't be taking that gun out of your pocket."

Dell's jaw tightened. "How did you know?"

"I didn't, not till now. But it seemed like the kind of damn fool thing you would have done. You shoot, and they become martyrs on top of being heroes. And you go to prison." He shot Dell a glare. "I lost one son. I don't want to lose another. We'll be patient. We'll watch and take pictures and prove exactly what kind of men they are."

"They deserve to die," Dell said.

"Of course they do. But once we show the world what they really are, they'll go to prison." Harvey's brows lifted. "Do you know what happens to cops in prison?"

Dell's smile was a mere baring of teeth. "They'll wish they were dead."

Sunday, February 21, 8:25 p.m.

Noah placed his mini recorder on Sarah Dwyer's coffee table. "So I don't have to take notes," he said when she eyed the recorder. "How well did you know Martha?"

"I'd see her occasionally in the laundry room. We weren't friends."

"But you gave her a key to your apartment, so you must have trusted her."

"She was a lady in my building," Dwyer said impatiently. "Sometimes we talked."

Noah watched her wring her hands. "You seem agitated, ma'am."

Her eyes narrowed. "I just flew in from Hong Kong and haven't slept in twenty-four hours." She pointed to a small hothouse on her dining room table. "I get home, find my prize orchids dead, and my neighbor deader. And you have the nerve to ac*cuse* me?"

"No one's accusing you." Jetlag and shock could account for her nerves, and fury over dead orchids could have sent her up a fire escape. "What did Martha do?"

"She was a computer consultant. I'm pretty sure she worked out of her apartment."

Noah thought about the empty desk. No papers, no CDs. Only the computer. Odd that a consultant who'd worked out of her home would have no evidence of work.

"In any of your conversations, did she seem depressed or afraid?"

"No. Usually we talked about how much we hated Mrs.

Kobrecki. She's the building manager. Kobrecki and Martha did not get along."

He'd paged Mrs. Kobrecki several times, with no returned call. "Why not?"

"Kobrecki said Martha was a pig. Martha took exception. That's all I know. If you want more, you'll need to talk to Mrs. Kobrecki." She grimaced. "Or her grandson."

"Why don't you like her grandson?" Noah asked.

"He's a creep. Once I caught him taking my lingerie out of the dryer and sniffing it. I made sure never to do laundry at night again. He only seems to come around at night."

"What's his name?"

"Taylor Kobrecki. Why?"

"Just gathering the facts, ma'am. Do you know Martha's next of kin?"

"Her mom. She's in a nursing home, in St. Paul."

Noah stood, giving her his card. "Thanks. If you remember anything, please call me."

"What is this?" she asked suspiciously. "*Did* Martha kill herself?"

Noah smiled vaguely. "We're just following procedure, Miss Dwyer."

"Uh-huh," she said. "I'll have my gun loaded and next to my bed tonight."

"Anything?" Jack asked, meeting him as he left Dwyer's apartment.

"Maybe. You?"

"Bupkiss. You get a next of kin?"

"Nursing home, St. Paul. You get any calls back from the building manager?"

"Nope. I couldn't find any tenants who seemed to care for her."

"She has a grandson." Noah's brows went up. "Panty fetish."

"Interesting. I wonder if Mr. Panty Fetish has a record."

"I'll run the grandson, you find the mom. Call and I'll meet you at the nursing home."

"What about Gus Dixon's case reports?"

"Records said they'd have everything pulled when we got back to the station."

Jack checked his watch with a sigh. "No dessert for me tonight."

Noah gritted his teeth. "You get too much dessert, *partner*."

Jack snorted. "This from the man who hasn't had dessert in how long?"

Noah shook his head. Everyone saw that Jack was a train wreck. Everyone but Jack. "Just find Brisbane's mother. I'll meet you there."

"I'll call Abbott," Jack said, "and give him a heads up."

Abbott was their boss. "I already did, while you were having your 'quickie dessert.'" Jack's eyes flashed, his lie called out. "And no, I didn't tell him you weren't there."

Jack let out a careful breath. "I owe you one."

Noah met Jack's eyes, held them. "Don't make me sorry, Jack. Please."

Jack looked away. "I'll call you when I find Brisbane's mother."

Sunday, February 21, 8:45 p.m.

The crowd was cheering at the largest of Sal's flat-screen TVs. It was college hoops and home team star Tom Hunter had the ball. Not much more needed to be said.

Eve watched her oldest friend fly across the screen, dropping the ball through the hoop like it was nothing. A cheer shook the room and Eve rocked back on her heels.

"Yes," she whispered, then jumped when a stream of cold beer ran up her sleeve. She jerked the overflowing pitcher out from under the tap and shook her sleeve with a grimace. *Careless.* She'd have to let it dry, as there was no time to change.

Tonight's other bartender hadn't shown. The line at the bar had been unending, but so far, no one was complaining. As long as the home team kept winning, that shouldn't change. As long as the team kept passing to Tom Hunter, winning was assured.

"Your friend's got a real gift," Sal said behind her, quiet approval in his voice.

Eve jumped. For a man with a bad leg, Sal moved with surprising stealth. Then again, the bar was so noisy that she couldn't hear herself think. Tonight, that was good.

"I know," she said. She'd known Tom was gifted the first time she'd seen him play on a crumbling blacktop in a poor Chicago neighborhood. She'd been fourteen, Tom ten, both older than their years. She'd been a runaway, and in a different way, so had he.

They'd become friends, raised under the sheltering wings of three amazing Chicago women who had become Eve's family. But her bond with Tom went far deeper.

Tom was one of the few who truly understood Eve's nightmares, because the same monster haunted his. Both of them bore scars inflicted by Tom's biological father, Rob Winters. But now they were both past all that. Reinvented.

Tom was the reason she was here, in Minneapolis. When he'd been awarded a basketball scholarship to one of the country's top schools, he'd challenged her to come with him, to take her life back. To come out of the dark and start anew.

And she had. Now Tom was on his way to becoming a basketball legend, like his adopted father, Max Hunter. *And I'm finally out of the darkness and into the light.* "Tom makes it look easy," she said. "Size fourteen feet should not be able to move like that."

"I'm not talking about his game," Sal said. "I'm talking about his talk to Josie's kids."

Eve glanced up at him, puzzled. Sal's wife, Josie, was a high school guidance counselor in one of Minneapolis's tougher neighborhoods. "When was this?"

"Last week. He said he planned to go to all the high schools, to tell kids to stay in school. Promised Josie's kids he'd be back to play a game with their team, for the ones that stuck it out. The kids are still talking about him," he said and Eve smiled, touched.

"It's like Tom to do something like that without bragging. He comes from good stock."

Sal lightly knocked his shoulder against hers. "You come from the same place."

"Not exactly." Tom's mother, Caroline, was one of the amazing women who'd raised her. Eve had no idea where her own mother was, doubted she was still alive. "But I've been lucky enough to be taken in by good folks everywhere I go."

She finished filling a second pitcher, lifting both into the customer's hands. She'd stopped gritting her teeth against the pain. It was a constant throb now, but she thought she'd been hiding it pretty well. Until Sal nudged her aside.

"Ice your hand," he said, then shot down her protest with a warning look. "Do it."

"Yes, sir," she said meekly and filled a bag with ice, wincing as she placed it on her hand. "Why are you here?" she asked. "Rich was supposed to be on with me tonight."

"He called in sick." Sal's hands made quick work of the waiting orders. "Why are you here? Callie was on tonight."

"She had a date." Who'd finally shown up with a dozen roses and a story of a client who'd gotten himself arrested in an afternoon hockey brawl.

Sal frowned. "You worked every day last week."

"I need the money. The leak in my roof is worse," she said, but he shook his head.

"No, you need to go out on your own dates. You're too pretty to hide in this bar."

Being called "pretty" still startled her. Being accused of hiding, however, could not be borne. "I don't hide," she said more sharply than she'd intended. "Not anymore."

She knew Sal studied her face even though she kept her eyes averted. For years people had stared at her face when they thought she didn't see, but she'd always been aware of the horrified stares and the whispers. At least people didn't do *that* anymore and for that reason alone her plastic surgeon should be a nominee for sainthood.

"I'm sorry," Sal said. "It's just that you work so hard here, then you go home and study, then go to school. And any moment you have free you spend in that Fantasy Island computer game of yours, what with its aviators and orgies. It's not natural."

That "Fantasy Island" computer game was really called Shadowland, an online virtual playground. There was no Mr. Roarke in a crisp white suit, but like the old TV show, it was a place where adults could pretend to be anyone they wanted to be, interacting with millions of players all over the world while pursuing virtual fantasies.

Eve discovered Shadowland's lure after the assault that had taken her life, literally and figuratively. The virtual world had been more than a game. It was a vital link to the outside world from which Eve, scarred and ashamed, had hidden for too many years.

Thankfully those dark years were gone. Like Tom Hunter, she'd reinvented herself. Shadowland was no longer an escape, but a tool for her graduate research.

At least it had started out that way. But the tool of her research had become a glitzy, gaping black hole, sucking her subjects into its virtual world of fantasy faster than she could grab them. The research that started out with such therapeutic potential had somehow become a trap, luring and endangering the very people she'd sought to help.

"It's not 'aviators,'" she said to Sal, irritated. "It's 'avatars.' The characters are *avatars*. And where are you getting this orgy stuff?"

Sal's eyes twinkled and she knew he'd poked at her on purpose. "I imagine that would be a lot of men's fantasy. But not mine," he added quickly. "Josie wouldn't like it."

"I'm sure," Eve said dryly. Then she shrugged. "Besides, I'm not wasting my time playing computer games. Shadowland's for my thesis, and you know it."

Sal's eyes stopped twinkling. "Exactly my point. Even when you play a game, you're working. When was the last time you went on a date?"

Five years, eleven months, and seven days ago. That the amount of time should come back to her so quickly, after all this time, was . . . terrifying.

"I thought so," Sal said quietly when she said nothing.

"You've been under so much stress lately. This project of yours is putting dark circles under your eyes. I want you to take some time off. Take a vacation. Go to Florida and get some sun."

Eve tossed the ice bag into the sink and started mixing a martini, the usual drink of the next customer in line. "Vacations take money, Sal. I don't have any."

"I'll loan you some," he said simply. "Tell me what you need."

Abruptly she put the shaker down, her heart in her throat. "Damn, I hate it when you're nice. Why can't you be a mean boss?" Swallowing back what would have been embarrassing tears, she patted his beefy shoulder. "Keep your money. I'm fine."

He shook his head. "You're not fine. You're worried. I see it in your eyes."

She finished the martini and started with the next order. "I wish everyone would stop looking into my eyes," she muttered, Callie's observation about Noah Webster still fresh. She looked for a subject change and found it in the magazine Callie had left behind. "Jack Phelps was in here tonight, but he left before I could ask him to sign the *MSP* cover."

"I heard it was more like he got called out," Sal remarked mildly. "By Webster."

She turned and stared at his profile. "How did you know that?"

His sideways glance was almost amused. "I know what goes on in my own bar, Eve. I'm surprised it's taken Webster this long. There was a pool, you know—how long Web would put up with Phelps before he requested a transfer or cleaned Jack's clock."

The mental image of such an altercation left Eve disturbingly aroused. "Who won?"

"Nobody. Webster's outlasted all of our predictions. Man's either a saint or a fool." He slanted another glance her way, this one annoyed. "Maybe both."

Eve thought of the parting words Noah had uttered with grim resignation, more a good-bye than a thank-you. "Doesn't matter. I don't think he's coming back."

Which was for the best. She didn't have time for anything more than work, school, and her Fantasy Island computer game. *Not true.* It wasn't the time she didn't have. It was the heart. And various other internal organs that made a huge difference.

Sal sighed. "I'm sorry, honey."

She made herself smile. "Don't be." She poured the martini and reached for an olive, relieved to find the canister empty. She needed a minute to herself. For just a moment or two, she needed to hide. "We're out of olives. Hold the fort. I'll get them."

Sunday, February 21, 9:10 p.m.

Finally. The Hat Squad finally knew they had a homicide. It had taken them long enough. Three homicides, carefully staged. At least they'd seen it with Martha Brisbane.

He hadn't realized how impatient he'd grow, waiting for them to engage. But as frustrating as the wait had been, the Hat Squad's ineptitude better furthered his goal—to see them humiliated, degraded, their stature in the community obliterated.

To see stripped away that infuriating self-importance they wore along with their badges and guns. And their hats. He wanted each of those hat-wearing, knuckle-scraping Neanderthals to see themselves for what they really were. Worthless failures.

Which was precisely why he'd staged these murders as suicides.

He'd known they'd miss the first victim, perhaps even the second. That they'd be so eager to close a suicide that they'd miss the clues he'd left behind. He didn't know what had finally tipped them off, whether it was that they'd finally seen the clues or because they'd finally connected Martha to the other two. Regardless, they would soon know that there had been others, that through their carelessness they had *missed* two homicides.

Now they were on victim three of his six, halfway through the game already.

Because they had God complexes, they would blame themselves. They would know that if they'd been smarter, quicker, *competent*, they would have seen victim number one hadn't killed herself. That they might have prevented the deaths of the others.

They'd begin to second-guess themselves, and each other. And as the body count climbed, all that they believed they were, the mirage of strength they'd built of their own hubris would disappear. Because their strength had never been.

He would move on, stronger through their weakness. And he alone would know the truth, because they'd never find the one who'd brought demise to their public façade.

But enough of that for now. They'd finally discovered Martha Brisbane, aka victim number three of his six, aka Desiree. The game had officially begun.

On to victim four. He opened his laptop and logged in to his new hunting ground. There was a great deal to be said about the supposed anonymity of Shadowland's virtual "world." His victims were there to play, their guard down. In the virtual world they could say and do things they'd never dream of doing in the real world. He could earn their trust more easily because they believed he didn't know who they really were.

But he knew. It was why he'd chosen these particular six out of the millions online.

He knew their names, addresses, occupations, marital status, and—of great personal value—their phobias, their worst fears. He'd tailored each experience to the victim, so although he hadn't put his hands around their throats or allowed himself release, he'd been able to stoke the first three to more intense terror than he'd ever achieved with his hookers.

In the past, the fears had been only in his victims' minds, a by-product of the ketamine he'd used to sedate them. Not so with these six. They played in the virtual world, but he'd make certain they died terrified in the real one.

His first of six had been so terrified of small spaces. After minutes in a box, Amy had been hysterical. Pulling that twine around her neck as her heart had thundered, her body unable to flee . . . It had taken real discipline to keep from losing control.

He'd managed to conjure the memory of her terror later, when he was back at home, alone. But his climax was only a pale shadow of what it would have been had he taken it as his first of six gasped her last. *But one had to make sacrifices for the greater goal.*

Samantha, his second of six, had been afraid of being buried alive. He'd had a bad moment when he thought she'd passed out, lying under feet of dirt, a snorkel her only access to air. He wanted her conscious when he killed her, completely aware. To his relief she'd struggled like an animal when he'd unearthed her. It had been magnificent.

Martha . . . not so much. She hadn't been that afraid of water. So he'd made her pay in other ways. One had only to look at her apartment to know she was obsessive about the *stuff* she'd accumulated. Excepting her computer, nothing was of value, but its loss induced nothing less than sheer panic. So he'd forced her to throw it all away.

And she'd loved her cat. Those threats had resulted in extreme disturbance.

When he put Martha back in the water, he finally achieved terror. By the end, she'd begged him to kill her. He rolled his eyes. By the end, he'd been happy to oblige.

Christy Lewis would be number four of six. He had high hopes for Christy. *Oh, yesssss.* He chuckled aloud. Christy's phobia was especially intense.

"Gwenivere, are you online tonight?" Of course she was. She always was. Christy wasn't Gwenivere any more than Martha had been Desiree. But Shadowland's motto said it all. *Sometimes you want to go where no one knows your name.* "Except me."

Gwenivere was at Ninth Circle, the virtual club she visited every night. Here she was a former Miss Universe, a pianist as well as an avid dancer and witty conversationalist.

Shadowland was truly a fantasyland. *Gwenivere*, he typed. *I've missed you.*

Christy's avatar smiled at him. Her avatar had one of Pandora's nicer faces. He also had invested in a quality face and body-builder physique for his own avatar. Pandora's Façades Face Emporium had good stock and wasn't nearly as expensive as some of the other avatar designers.

After all, one had to look one's best when hunting shallow, narcissistic fantasy addicts. But one also had to save a little cash for expenses. Like his Ninth Circle bar tab or his account at the Casino Royale's most elite poker table.

Long time no see, Christy typed back. *Where have you been?*

Waiting for someone to find Martha Brisbane, he thought.

His avatar took the bar stool Christy had saved, his long legs easily allowing his feet to touch the floor. He'd chosen Pandora's tallest, most muscular model because that's what would most easily attract his prey. As the hunter, he had to choose the best bait, even when it sickened him.

Off on business, he typed. *You know, bought an island, built a resort, made a million. Can I buy you a drink?*

Christy's avatar smiled again. *Oh, maybe just one.*

He'd chat with her awhile, get her talking. It never took more than a few minutes for Christy to abandon her Gwenivere persona and become herself. Once he'd "slipped," telling her he lived near Minneapolis. She'd been surprised, revealing that she did, too.

Of course she did. That's one of the reasons he'd picked her.

She'd suggested they meet several times, but he'd always put her off. He'd still been waiting for Martha to be found. Tonight he'd suggest they meet, just for coffee.

Just to talk. They always fell for it. Every single time. So why change what worked?

* * *

Sunday, February 21, 9:55 p.m.

"Normally we don't allow visitors this late," the nurse said.

"We're sorry. It took longer to find Mrs. Brisbane than we expected," Jack said.

"If Mrs. Brisbane is asleep, you'll have to come back tomorrow. Department policy."

"We understand," Noah said. Martha Brisbane had chosen a nice place for her mother, he thought. Must've run Martha a pretty chunk of change.

Noah thought of his own mother who wintered in Arizona because of her health. Between his dead father's police pension and a sizable percentage of his own salary, he'd settled her pretty comfortably. It was a financial sacrifice, but she was his mom and he wouldn't have it any other way. He imagined Martha had felt the same.

"Will getting this news about her daughter's death affect her heart?" Noah asked.

"It might, if she had one," the nurse said, then sighed. "I'm sorry. That was uncalled for." She opened the door, revealing a woman who nearly disappeared against the white sheets. "Mrs. Brisbane, these men are detectives. They're here to talk to you."

The old woman's eyes narrowed. "What about?" she demanded sharply.

Noah had lost the toss. "I'm Detective Webster and this is my partner, Detective Phelps," he said, keeping his voice as gentle as possible. "We're here about your daughter, Martha. She's dead, ma'am. We're very sorry for your loss."

Mrs. Brisbane's mouth pinched as if she'd eaten something sour. "How?"

They'd agreed to keep Martha's death a suicide until the ME filed his report. That said, they were questioning witnesses assuming Dr. Gilles would confirm a homicide.

"It appears she killed herself," Noah said.

"Then she got what she deserved. The wages of sin is death, Detective. It's as simple as that." And with that Mrs. Brisbane closed her eyes, dismissing them.

"Whoa," Jack mouthed silently, then cleared his throat. "Ma'am, we have a few more questions, if you don't mind."

"I do mind," Mrs. Brisbane snapped, not opening her eyes. "Make them leave. Now."

"You have to leave." In the hallway the nurse shrugged. "That was pretty mild."

"'She got what she deserved,' was mild?" Jack asked, incredulous. "Hell."

"Mrs. Brisbane didn't approve of Martha," she said, "and I have no idea why."

"Was this disapproval something new?" Noah asked.

"No. It's been that way since she got here, about six months ago."

"When was the last time Martha came in to visit her mother?" Jack asked.

"At least a month ago. Martha would leave looking like a whipped pup. I tried to help but Mrs. Brisbane complained. I got a warning not to ask again. I wish I knew more."

"'The wages of sin is death,'" Jack mused when they were back in the parking lot.

"The Bible, book of Romans," Noah said. "My uncle was a minister."

Jack frowned. "Your uncle's a retired cop."

"That's Brock's father, on my father's side. My minister uncle was my mother's older brother." He'd been dead five years now and Noah missed his guidance. Missed him.

"What*ever*. Brisbane's mother knew something. We have to try her again tomorrow. Assuming whoever did this did it once before, it stands to reason they'll do it again."

"So let's see what Martha and Dix's vic had in common before he has a chance."

Sunday, February 21, 10:55 p.m.

"Lindsay?" Liza Barkley locked the front door. No one answered. She so hoped Lin would come tonight. It was only a high school play, but she'd worked hard on her role.

But Liza knew her sister was working her ass off to pay the rent. And the gas and the groceries, all the while insisting Liza spend her time studying. *Keep your grades up. Get a scholarship.* They had no savings left for college, every dime gone to doctors who hadn't been able to save their mother anyway. After a year, it still hurt. *I still miss her.*

Now Lindsay had cleaned office building toilets all night, every night so they could survive. *One day it'll be my turn to pay the bills.*

She shivered. It was so cold in their apartment she could see her breath. But heat cost money, so she pulled on two more sweaters and snuggled under a pile of blankets, setting the alarm for five-thirty. She still had a little homework to finish and Lindsay would just be getting home by then, tired and hungry. *I can do trig and fry eggs at the same time*, she thought sleepily and drifted off.

Chapter Three

Eve curled up in her favorite chair, grateful Sal had let her off early. She'd come home, logged into Shadowland, and sent her avatar straight to Ninth Circle, the bar and social center. It was, as usual, dark, smoky, and teeming with avatars.

Desiree, be there. Be in your normal spot, doing whatever it is you do. Or did. It had been a week since Martha Brisbane's avatar had been seen in Ninth Circle. Maybe Martha was on a real-world vacation, but Eve didn't think so.

If Martha didn't show up soon . . . *I'll have to do something.* But what?

Eve could see herself now, filing a missing person report on an imaginary person who dwelt in a Fantasy Island computer game. The cops would think she was nuts.

For now, she could only keep a virtual eye on Martha and the others, and she wasn't supposed to be doing even that. She wasn't supposed to know the names of her subjects. Double-blind tests were not to be broken. But she had, and wasn't sorry.

Just worried. And wincing from the cacophony blasting from Ninth Circle's stage where a computer-animated band "performed." Ninth Circle's "band" was probably one middle-aged man with a synthesizer, but he wasn't hurting anyone. Some objected to his cover of AC/DC, but those snobby rock purists could turn down the volume.

Eve muted the sound. She was one of those purists. *When did I become . . . old?*

Five years, eleven months, and seven days ago. That she'd remembered it twice in one night made her angry. But she'd put it behind her. Mostly. Sometimes.

No, you haven't, Evie, whispered the voice in the back of her mind, annoyingly logical. Smug bitch. And she wasn't Evie anymore. She'd left Evie behind in Chicago.

"I'm Eve now," she said aloud, just to hear the sound of her own voice. It was too quiet in her apartment tonight. With the Ninth Circle band muted, the only sound was the constant dripping of water into the pots she'd placed below the leaks in her roof.

I've gotta get that fixed before I lose my mind. But her scum-sucking landlord ignored her repeated requests for roof repair. Myron Daulton had inherited the house from his mother, but none of her responsibility for her tenants, all of whom had finally had enough and left. Eve was the last holdout.

If Myron forced her out, he'd be able to sell. Developers were buying these old houses, refurbing them, then flipping them for big bucks. Myron didn't deserve a dime. He'd never visited his mother. Never called on her birthday. Sometimes made her cry.

Eve had loved old Mrs. Daulton dearly and she'd be damned before she let Myron make even one penny off his mother. Eve had fixed the plumbing, dealt with the mice problem, and even replaced the garbage disposal. But a roof was a much bigger deal.

I'm not going to move. So she'd have to figure out how

to fix the roof herself, too. She turned the volume of the band back up to drown out the constant dripping. *Get to work, Eve. Find Desiree and Gwenivere so you can concentrate on your day job.*

Sal's filled her evenings, but her day job was not failing grad school. She had a ten-page Abnormal Psych paper due in ten hours. *I shouldn't be in Shadowland, spying on my test subjects.* But she felt a responsibility to Desiree, Gwenivere, and all the others.

Many of them were older than she. Chronologically, anyway. All had signed releases before participating in her study, but Eve felt compelled to keep them safe. She figured she came by the compulsion honestly. It wasn't possible to grow up with a bevy of meddling social workers without *some* of their nurturing overprotectiveness rubbing off.

Eve guided her own avatar through the virtual dancers, searching for the ones she'd come to find. Her heart sank when, once again, she saw Desiree's corner table. *Empty.*

She moved to the next "red-zone" case—slinky, sexy Gwenivere, aka Christy Lewis, real-world secretary by day, dancer extraordinaire by night. Hours and hours every night and lately, during the day as well. Christy had been escaping into the game from her computer at work. Christy had confessed it last week, on one of her frequent visits to Pandora's shop. If her boss found out, Christy Lewis would be fired.

Eve did not want that on her head. She was worried enough about Martha Brisbane. Martha's Desiree had been a regular both at Ninth Circle and at Pandora's Façades Face Emporium, Eve's virtual avatar shop. Desiree had come every week to check Eve's inventory of "Ready-to-Walk" avatars as well as her assorted mix-and-match body parts. Martha had upgraded her avatar's face six times in the last three months.

Up until a week ago, Martha Brisbane had been a resident of Shadowland an average of eighteen hours a day. *Eighteen.* Considering the woman had to sleep sometime, that didn't leave much time for anything else. Martha was an ultra-user, one of the many who comprised the negative control group of Eve's study.

They'd had so many applicants they'd had to turn gamers away. Too many people lived their lives in Shadowland. *Like I did*, Eve thought. She desperately wanted to bring those people back to the real world. Into the sunlight. *Like I did.*

Hey, honey, can I buy you a drink?

Eve stopped scanning the crowd and frowned at the message at the bottom of her screen. She maneuvered her camera, staring into a nice face. Quality merchandise, if she did say so herself, and she did. She had, after all, designed it herself.

But the gamer wouldn't know that. Tonight she wasn't Pandora, the avatar designer who only hung out at Façades. Tonight she was her new character, Greer, the private investigator. Tonight Greer was searching for Christy Lewis and had no time to play.

Sorry, but I'm not interested, she typed back.

Then why are you here? he asked logically. This was, after all, the place to hook up.

Really not interested. Good night, she typed. She turned away and resumed scanning the crowd, hoping rudeness was a language he better understood.

Ah, there she was, Gwenivere, aka Christy Lewis. Christy was five-two, and while her real-world face was pleasant, she wasn't gorgeous. Not true for Gwenivere, a six-foot blonde with a very expensive face. One of Eve's, or Pandora's, finest designs.

Gwenivere was dancing with a very handsome avatar, one of Claudio's designs. Claudio was the best. Which was fine. Eve had started Pandora's Façades to observe her subjects without them knowing she did so.

Without *anyone* knowing she did so. Especially Dr. Donner, her graduate advisor.

She winced. If Donner found out . . . That didn't even bear consideration because if it ever happened, all her research would be nullified. She would probably be kicked out of the grad program. Expelled from Marshall University. And that could not happen. She'd worked too hard to come into the sunlight, to establish a real life for herself.

But at what cost? She'd believed in this research when she first started.

Now . . . Now she wasn't so sure. But that wasn't something she could resolve tonight. Christy was okay, flirting as usual. Eve had five more red-zone cases, three here in the Ninth Circle bar. Two others hung out in the Casino Royale, dancing and playing poker. She'd check up on them, then get busy on her Abnormal paper, the topic of which was the pathology of serial killers.

Eve flinched when she realized she was tracing the scar that she could now barely see, but still couldn't feel. She didn't need to research. She had all the background any professor could ever want. It was always in her mind, that voice that still taunted. It was, after five years, eleven months, and seven days, still written on her face.

* * *

Sunday, February 21, 11:55 p.m.

Noah locked his front door, worn. He and Jack had spent an hour going over the missed homicide, trying to glean any detail that would connect her to Martha Brisbane but so far, nothing. The two were connected in the most obvious way, of course. They'd been killed in the same exact way. But why? And who? And why those two women?

Then he and Jack read months of suicide reports, praying there would be no similar scenes. They'd found none, but after reading all of those accounts of suicide, Noah's relief was mixed with sadness and a feeling of hopelessness he was finding difficult to shake. *There but for the grace of God*, he'd thought more than once.

He sat wearily on his bed. Jack had no understanding, no compassion for those who'd taken their own lives. *But I do. I understand all too well.*

One night, ten years ago, he'd been so close . . . He'd been sitting right here on the edge of his bed, his revolver in one hand, their picture in the other.

His eyes strayed to their picture on his nightstand, the frame worn smooth by years of rubbing. The boy was only two and looked just like the woman who held him. A woman who, twelve long years later, could still make him wish for just one more day. *If only.*

It hadn't been twelve years the night he'd decided to end it. It had only been two years since the night his car spun out of control, taking his world with it. Two years that he'd sunk deep into the darkness and crawled deeper into a bottle.

He'd been drunk that night he'd held his gun in his hand. Almost drunk enough to pull the trigger and end the pain that never seemed to fade. But he hadn't been quite drunk enough. It had been Brock that he'd called, Brock who'd come, Brock who'd dragged his ass to AA. Brock who'd saved his godforsaken life.

Ten years, Noah thought. *Sober for ten years.* But there were times, unguarded moments when the pain still speared deep. Tonight was one of those times.

It was no longer grief as much as loneliness. The house was so quiet. Too quiet. Brock had Trina and the kids. *What do I have? Or who?*

He picked up the novel he kept next to his bed for nights he couldn't sleep, pulled out the glossy postcard he'd shoved between the pages. It was Sal's holiday card. Sal and Josie stood in the middle, surrounded by all their employees. Sal's arm was solidly around Eve's shoulders, as if holding her in place for the picture. Her lips curved in her little sideways smile, but her dark eyes were serious. Too serious.

Eve had drawn him the moment he'd laid eyes on her, and he'd convinced himself to approach her a million times. But in the end it was his own voice he heard. *Hi, I'm Noah, and I'm an alcoholic.* It was a hell of a burden to ask any woman to share.

Anyone with eyes could see that Eve bore her own burdens. There was no way he'd add his to her shoulders. His heart heavy, he put Sal's holiday card in his drawer.

Tonight, after reading all those suicide accounts, he'd wanted a drink so goddamn bad . . . If he'd had any booze in the house, he'd be halfway to drunk this very moment. If the craving got any worse, he'd be calling Brock for a midnight workout. A few rounds in the boxing ring usually got him through the worst of it.

Somehow Eve didn't strike him as much of a boxer. He thought of her slender hands and the pain in her eyes every time she lifted a heavy pitcher to the bar. A million times he'd nearly jumped out of his chair at Sal's and done the lifting for her, but he hadn't. Because along with her pain was a determination, and then satisfaction that she'd done it. Determination and satisfaction, he understood.

Brock had told him that when Sal first hired her, one of her hands had been useless, but that she'd just worked faster with the good hand, somehow managing to keep up. She was a woman who'd been through a hell of her own. And persevered.

She deserved a hell of a lot more than . . . *me.* Brock was right. He played with fire every time he walked into that bar. He couldn't go back to Sal's. Not ever again. Which meant he wouldn't see Eve, ever again. Which in the end, was for the best.

He would do his job. Two women, murdered. He would find out by whom, and why.

And then? And then he'd take one day at time, as he'd been doing for ten years.

Monday, February 22, 2:20 a.m.

Christy Lewis puckered her lips in a kiss, checking her lipstick and the rest of her reflection. The lipstick was new, just like the outfit she'd been saving for a night like this.

Her eyes were bright with anticipation. She'd never done anything like this before. Anything so naughtily tawdry. She'd met him in Shadowland, mingling in Ninth Circle. He'd said his name was John. She was pretty sure it wasn't, just as she was pretty sure he wasn't divorced. She wouldn't be at all surprised if he was married with two point five kids and a dog. But she wouldn't ask. She didn't want to know.

He was in sales and traveled. She'd left the open invitation that if he was ever in the Twin Cities . . . Tonight he was. For just one night. The words "one-night stand" tickled her imagination. She'd never done one, not even in college when all of her friends did. She might not even do one tonight. It would depend on him, how he looked.

She didn't expect him to look like his avatar. *Who does? If we looked like our avatars, we'd have real lives.*

But, if he was cute and clean, then why not? It had been a while since she'd had her watch wound. And men did it all the time. Her miserable ex-husband had. All the time. *So now it's my turn.*

And if "John" had a wife, two point five kids, and a dog? Christy's shoulders sagged. She knew if he did, she couldn't go through with it. She'd been the "injured party."

But just maybe, he didn't. She dropped her lipstick in her purse. Maybe he was telling the truth. And if not? She'd get out, drink a cup of coffee with someone who was flesh and bone. And then she'd come home alone, like she always did.

Finally. He'd thought she'd never leave. He watched Christy Lewis drive away, then pulled into her driveway. She lived out in the country, her nearest neighbor a quarter mile away. The location was logistically inconvenient to get to, but once they returned together later, there would be no need to tape her mouth closed as he'd done to the others. She could scream as long and loud as she wanted and no one would hear her.

And she would scream. Or maybe she'd be so terrified

she'd go completely silent. One never knew how people would react when confronted with their worst fear. Either way, he had very high hopes for an intense experience.

He looked into his backseat with a smile. Christy Lewis's worst fear was safely contained in a metal box with holes poked in the top. One couldn't be too careful. He himself wasn't terrified, but he wasn't foolish either. He'd put the box in the house where it and its occupant could grow warm. The occupant of the box didn't like the cold, hibernating this time of year. By the time he returned with Christy, the occupant of the box should be quite warm and quite . . . mobile.

He grabbed the box by its handle, gratified at the soft stirring that came from within. *Excellent.* Christy's worst fear was waking. It would be hungry. Of course he'd planned for that. He grabbed a small cage from the floor, ignoring the high-pitched chatter.

He shivered deliciously, anticipating. This would be one to remember for a long time.

Monday, February 22, 2:40 a.m.

Brock dragged his forearm across his brow, clumsily wiping the sweat. "You good?"

Noah leaned against the ropes, panting. He was very nearly hollowed out. They'd set up the boxing ring in Brock's basement years ago, along with free weights, punching bags, everything they needed for their own gym. Everything Noah needed to battle his way out of the bottle, away from the prying eyes of other cops at the department gym.

Noah had thrown more punches here than he wanted

to count. It was a way to get through the gnawing need for a drink before it became a craving. Sometimes he used a punching bag, but when it got really bad, he needed something that punched back.

Brock had absorbed more of Noah's punches than either of them wanted to count.

Noah exhaled slowly, considering. The gnawing need was still there. It was always there. But the worst of the craving had passed. "I think so."

"Thank God," Brock muttered. Spitting out his mouth guard, he straightened his back with a quiet groan and waggled his jaw. "You got me with that last one."

Normally he and Brock were evenly matched, but tonight the craving had been especially vicious, its claws razor sharp. The dream woke him, left him shuddering in his bed like a frightened child. Then the craving had barreled out of the darkness like a freight train. It had been a long time since he'd come so close to giving in.

"I'm sorry." Noah pulled at his gloves with his teeth, wincing when he got a good look at his cousin's face. "I got your eye, too. God, Brock, I'm sorry. Dammit."

"S'okay." Brock tried to rip at his own gloves with his teeth, but stopped, grimacing from the pain in his jaw. "I've had worse. Not in a while, but I have had worse."

"Shoulda' kept your hands up." Brock's wife, Trina, rose from the basement stairs where she'd been sitting, hidden from their view. She reached over the ropes to pull off her husband's gloves. "One of these days, you're gonna really get creamed."

Brock frowned down at her. "Don't I get any sympathy?" he grumbled.

She lifted her chin to meet his eyes, unmoved. "I made you an ice pack."

Noah almost smiled. Trina was one of his all-time favorite people. They'd gone through the academy together and he'd introduced her to Brock, toasted them at their wedding. He was godfather to two of their sons. A decorated cop, Trina was as close as any sister could ever have been. She knew all his faults and loved him anyway.

Trina turned, assessing Noah with eyes that missed very little. "Not that I mind watching two ripped guys without shirts duking it out in my basement, but what gives?"

Noah rubbed a towel over his face. "Bad dream," he said shortly.

"Hm," she said. She pulled a cold bottle of water from each of the deep pockets of her robe, tossing one to Noah. The other she pressed to Brock's eye, which was already turning purple. "Ice pack for your jaw is upstairs. I put on a pot of coffee. Come."

They followed her up to the kitchen table where Trina filled their cups and pressed an ice pack to Brock's jaw. "Must have been one hell of a bad dream," she said quietly.

"Yeah." Noah dragged his palms down his face. "I caught a hanger tonight, but it was staged." He knew he could tell these two anything and it would never leave the room. They were more than family, they were cops. "And it was the second one."

"Not good," Trina murmured. "You're thinking serial?"

"Maybe. Jack and I went back to the station, combing the suicide reports to see if there were any more. Luckily there weren't."

Trina sipped at her coffee. "So what did you dream?"

Noah drew a breath. It was still so real. So disturbing. "That I was the hanger."

"Upsetting," she said matter-of-factly. "But you've had suicide dreams before and you've never messed up Brock's face this bad."

"It's not that bad," Brock mumbled and she patted his hand.

"Not from where I'm sitting, baby," she said. She turned back to Noah. "So?"

"The victims had their eyes glued open. Grisly." He shrugged. "In the dream I saw these dark eyes staring up at me." Dark brown doe eyes, filled with pain.

"The victim's?" she asked.

Noah shook his head, not wanting to say. "No. Just somebody I know."

Brock's eyes grew sharp. "Eve, then."

Noah looked down at the cup in his hands. "Yeah."

Trina sighed heavily. "So you did go to Sal's tonight. You had me confused there for a minute. You normally only come over to punch on Brock on Monday nights."

Noah barely fought the urge to fidget in his seat. "Well, I won't be going back."

"Glad to hear it," Trina said cautiously. "What about Eve?"

"Not meant to be," Noah said, ignoring the disappointment. "I'm moving on."

"Really, now?" she asked, her tone deceptively mild. "Then I have a friend you'd like. She's Joey's kindergarten teacher. Really pretty and she likes those dark philosophers you like to read. Y'know, the ones that make you want to drown your head in a bucket."

Brock looked away, but failed to hide his smirk.

Trina leaned forward, all charm and smiles. "I think

I'll invite her to dinner for you. You can bring a pie or something. How does tomorrow night look?"

Noah hated when Trina read him like a book. "Busy."

"Tuesday? Wednesday? Busy?" She made a scoffing noise. "You're a lousy liar."

He frowned darkly. "I won't go back to Sal's. You have my word."

"Good. But don't lie to me about Eve. You don't move on. You linger and wallow."

"I do not," he said, offended. "Brock?"

Brock shook his head. "I already got beat up once tonight."

Trina threw a sympathetic glance at Brock before turning serious eyes on Noah. "You don't have to go to a bar to see a bartender. She has a life outside of Sal's." She brightened, wryly. "I bet she even eats. I know. Why not invite Eve to dinner, instead?"

Noah clenched his teeth. "It isn't meant to be, Tree. Just leave it. Promise me."

Trina pushed away from the table, annoyed. "Fine. I promise. Satisfied?"

Not really. Part of him hadn't wanted her to give up so easily. But Noah stood, kissed her cheek, and said what he needed to. "Yes. Go back to bed. I'm going home."

"I'll walk you to the door," she said and Noah swallowed his sigh. This meant she had more to say. Dutifully Noah followed her to the door where she buttoned his coat as if he was one of her sons. She looked up, troubled. "You know I love you, right?"

"Yes," he said, without hesitation, and she smiled, but sadly.

"Tonight . . . you scared me, Noah. If you two hadn't

stopped when you did, I would have stopped you. You were so angry."

He closed his eyes, shame washing through him. "I know."

"You will always be welcome here, no matter what time of the day or night. But you can't go after Brock like that again. He won't say so because he's too proud, but you could seriously hurt him. You were rocked tonight by that dream. But there was more to it than that." She tugged on his coat. "Dammit, you look at me."

He opened his eyes and swallowed hard. There was no accusation in her eyes, just love, fierce and sharp. "You're not ready to move on, Noah. Eve's touched something in you that you don't want to walk away from, whether you want to admit it or not. And I think that's what was pushing you tonight, not a dream and not this case."

"I know," he murmured, miserably. "But I don't know what to do about it."

Trina hugged him hard. "Trust yourself. You're a good man, Noah Webster. You don't deserve to be alone forever." She gave him a shrewd look. "You're not the only one with bad dreams. Brock and I see bad shit every day, just like you do."

"So what do you do when you have dreams, Tree?"

"Sometimes I raid the fridge for anything chocolate. Sometimes I work out. And sometimes I just fuck Brock's brains out." He snorted a surprised laugh and she lifted a brow. "There's something to be said for therapeutic sex. Maybe you should get some."

Her words sent instant images of Eve, long and lithe, sliding her body down his. He thought of the yearning he'd seen in her eyes tonight, the need she'd tried so hard to hide. He shuddered, clenching his fists in his pockets. "I won't drag her down with me."

"Sometimes, Noah, it's just out of your hands."

"You promised," he warned, but wearily and without bite.

"Yeah, I did. But sometimes fate steps in and kicks your ass. You think you know what she needs. Hell," she scoffed, "you don't even know what you need."

"What I need is sleep." He kissed the tip of her nose. "Go, before you get sick."

Monday, February 22, 4:00 a.m.

Christy had been sitting in the booth by the window for over an hour. She'd had five cups of coffee, having finished the waffles she'd ordered when the waitress got testy.

He didn't dare go inside. Unlike the coffee shop where he'd watched Martha, in this diner he'd stick out like a sore thumb. The diner served all night, but most of their clients were truckers and the occasional hungry traveler. And Christy Lewis.

"Who is finally tired of waiting for John," he murmured as she dug into her purse. She paid her bill before disappearing for several minutes, which he assumed was a trip to the ladies' room. Reappearing with her face blotchy, which he assumed meant she'd indulged in a fit of tears, she walked to her car, her head down against the wind.

One hour, twenty minutes, and fifty-five seconds. So far Christy Lewis had waited longer than any of them. He might have enjoyed that fact, except that the car he was driving was too small, even for him. But the little car was part of the plan, just like the choice of this particular diner. More "clues" for the Hat Squad. It was going to drive them crazy. That Christy had consumed food while she'd waited seemed an unfair autopsy freebie, but he couldn't change that now.

With a defiant tilt of her chin, she pulled down her visor mirror and slashed on fresh lipstick before capping the tube and throwing it hard at her windshield. He hoped her anger would carry her home faster. He got a shiver of anticipation, just thinking about what lay ahead, and pulled out of the diner's parking lot behind her.

Monday, February 22, 4:35 a.m.

Christy slammed her car door, the noise echoing in the night. *I am so stupid.* How many times had she heard about lies online? *You should know. You tell them yourself.* That was different. That was Shadowland. This was real life and he'd lied.

Maybe he was there. Maybe he took one look at you and ran the other way.

"Goddammit." She stumbled up the sidewalk, tripping in the heels she's spent next month's grocery money on. *You're a stupid idiot, just like Jerry said.* She struggled with her keys, hands shaking as her ex-husband's voice rolled through her mind. *Clumsy, ugly. You'll never find anyone else willing to look at your face every morning.*

He's right. There's nobody out there for somebody like me. She'd been suckered tonight, waited like a fool for an online asshole that never showed, who'd probably never intended to show. "John," whoever he was, was probably laughing at her right now.

Just like Jerry had when she'd caught him with that slut. *In my bed.*

She shoved the front-door key into the lock, her eyes narrowing at a new thought.

"Jerry." It made sense. Her ex knew computers, but he wouldn't even have needed to hack in. She hadn't logged out of Shadowland in God only knew how long. She'd changed the locks, but that wouldn't have kept him out. He'd broken into the house. Her cheeks flamed. *Read my Ninth Circle conversations.* Why on earth had she saved them? So, like a loser, she could read them again and again, pretending to have a life.

"He set me up," she hissed. "Sonofafuckingbitch set me up."

She pushed the door open, furious. She'd get him, the lying, screwing SOB, if it was the last thing she— A hand clamped over her mouth and her heart froze. *Jerry.* Fury supplanted the fear. This was taking it too damn far. *I'll kill you for this.*

Then fury evaporated away as she was viciously yanked back, her head smacking against a hard shoulder. *Not Jerry,* she thought wildly. *It's not Jerry.*

"Hello, Gwenivere," he crooned into her ear and she thrashed against him. *Get away. Get away.* She felt the jab of a needle into her neck. "Welcome to Camelot."

She could hear him calmly counting back from ten as her body went numb. He let her go and she teetered for a split second before collapsing on the floor.

"Snakes," she heard him say, from a distance. She was floating now. *Get away. Must get away.* But she couldn't move. She heard him kneel beside her, felt his breath in her ear. "A pit of vipers slithering over your skin, Christy. No escape. No escape."

* * *

No. No. Everywhere, they're everywhere. It was a deep pit. Twisting snakes, all around. Hissing. Her heart pounded and cold sweat drenched her skin. *Don't move. Don't breathe. Oh God.* One slithered across her foot, and she clenched her eyes shut. Another dropped from above to her shoulder and she screamed. *Run. Get away.*

Help me. Christy Lewis heard the shrieking and was suddenly aware it came from her own throat. She opened her eyes, heart pounding, lungs gasping for air. *Just a dream.* She was in her own living room. *But not.* Her eyes darted side to side as she took it in. Her furniture was moved. Pushed against the wall. She lunged. *But not.*

I can't move. She struggled wildly, her mind fighting to clear the haze. *No snakes*, she told herself. *Just a dream. But I still can't move.* Her arms hugged her body, her ankles burned like fire, her head . . . God, her head hurt. *Stop. And think.*

She blinked hard, but her living room was still changed. Her arms . . . She was sitting up, bound shoulder to waist, warm. *Trapped.* Horror flooded her mind as the mist cleared away. Her ankles were tied to her chair with rope and there was hideous pressure on her temples, like a . . . "A vise?" she whispered in disbelief.

"Indeed, my dear. And a straitjacket," he said and it came back in a rush.

She'd gone to meet John. She'd waited for him, but he'd never come. *But he was here.* She jerked around to see, crying out at the shearing pain in her head.

"I suggest you not try to move," he said dryly, still behind her.

"Why?" she begged, agonized. Tears filled her eyes and she blinked them away.

"Maybe because your empty *head* is in a *vise*?" he said with contempt.

"No." She wanted to sound angry, but instead she whimpered in fear. "Why me?"

"Because I needed you," he said logically. "And because you're here. And because I can. Pick one, it doesn't matter which. Did you like the snakes, Christy?"

She shuddered. It was her very worst fear. How did he know? "Go to hell."

He chuckled, sending another shiver racing coldly down her spine. "Ladies firssssst," he whispered, hissing into her ear. Her insides rolled at the memory, at the total, immobilizing fear.

No. Stay focused. You have to get away. Pay attention. Remember important things to tell the police. When you get away. "They weren't real," she muttered.

"Those weren't," he agreed. "But *he* is." A gloved hand came into her peripheral vision, pointing. She could see a gold ring through his opaque latex glove.

Remember the ring. Tell the cops about it.

But he *is.* His words suddenly registered as did the metal box on the floor. The size of a tool box, it had holes in the top. Tied to the latch was twine that ran along the floor, ending somewhere behind her. Behind her he moved and his hand reappeared in her line of vision, holding one end of the twine. He yanked and was then that she heard it.

A rattle. Ominous. Quiet. Her breath began to hitch. "Not happening. Not real."

"Oh, he's real," he whispered, "and he's hungry and he won't like being disturbed. Shall we disturb him?"

"No," she whimpered. She clenched her eyes closed but he forced one of her eyes open, pinching her eyelid hard. He smeared something cold under her eyebrow and quickly pressed her eyelid against it. *Glue.* She struggled to blink, and could not.

"You'll watch," he said, angry now. "Because I say you will." He glued her other eye open, then brought something around her head. A cage. Inside was something white, and completely still. A mouse. "Not dead," he said. "Blood's still nice and warm. He's sedated with the same drug I gave you. I wonder if he'll be half as terrified as you."

He took the mouse from the cage and placed it against her foot. She could feel its fur tickling her skin. She tried to flinch away, but her ankles were tied too tightly. He yanked the twine again. Again she heard the rattle. She panted, trying to fill her lungs.

Breathe. Can't breathe. It's coming. Run. She struggled, tried to draw a breath to scream, but all she could manage was a terrified mew. *Trapped. I'm trapped.*

He yanked the string again and the front of the box lowered with a clatter.

It lifted its head and stared. *At me.* Frozen, she could only stare back.

"It's coming," he whispered, his breath hot in her ear. "For you."

Monday, February 22, 6:15 a.m.

Harvey Farmer was tired. He'd followed Noah Webster for hours, only to return home to an empty house. Dell was AWOL again. Unable to sleep, he was staring stonily at his front door when it opened. Dell closed it, surprise flickering in his eyes. "Where have you been?" Harvey asked, not kindly.

"Out."

Abruptly Harvey lurched to his feet. "Don't you talk to me like that, boy."

Dell took a step back. "I'm not a boy. I can go where I like."

Harvey's eyes narrowed as he smelled leftover perfume. He grabbed his son's arm, stunned when Dell grabbed it back. "Who is she?" Harvey growled.

Dell's smile was tight. "No one you'll ever meet. Now if you'll excuse me . . ."

Harvey watched his son's retreating back, his anger rising. "If you fuck up what we're doing because of some slut . . ."

Dell didn't stop. "I won't. Now, I've had a long night. I'm going to sleep."

Chapter Four

Captain Bruce Abbott stopped at their desks. "You two are here early. Progress on the Brisbane investigation? Did you get the report on Dix's victim? The first hanger?"

"Samantha Altman," Noah said, "was thirty-five, lived alone, recently divorced and recently unemployed. She was found by her parents, who said she wasn't depressed."

"Parents always say that," Abbott said. "It's a coping mechanism."

Jack rubbed his hands over his face, trying to wake up. "Dix is ripped up, Captain. He kept going over his scene, trying to figure out what he'd missed."

"Dix did what most of us would have done," Abbott said. "It quacked like a duck, so he called it a duck. Did he remember anything that wasn't in his report?"

"Only that the parents swore the clothes weren't hers," Jack said. "Dix gave them back the dress and shoes. We're hoping the Altmans haven't thrown them out."

"Any connections between the two women?"

"Not so far," Noah said. "Martha was a little older, self-employed. Samantha was downsized from a manufacturing job and found two days after she died, by her parents. Martha was dead at least a week, but no one reported her missing. We didn't find an address book, but whoever hung her probably took it. Her desk was too damn clean."

"The lab's going over her computer, checking emails, contacts," Jack added. "She was a computer consultant, so we should at least find a client list on her PC."

"Motive? Any suspects?"

"Martha's mother knows something," Noah said. "We'll pay her another visit today."

"And we still haven't heard from Mrs. Kobrecki, the building manager," Jack said.

"Grandmother of the panty pervert," Abbott said.

"He's got a jacket," Noah said. "Three complaints from former building residents, all improper advances. Nothing came of them. It was always he said, she said."

"Go get the 'she said' from the women who lodged the complaints. See if anything pops. And find out if the grandson would have any contact with the first victim." Abbott hesitated. "So for the million-dollar question. Do we think there are any other victims?"

"No," Noah said. "We've gone through the reports on all the suicides in the Twin Cities going back two years. No scenes resemble the two we're dealing with."

Abbott looked relieved. "That's something, at least. Have you heard from the ME?"

"Not yet," Jack said, "but we're expecting to any moment. Ian normally starts autopsies after the morgue's morning review. He knows this one's a high priority."

"Well, hurry it up. I don't want the press getting wind of this until we know what's what. We just got rid of all those damn reporters from the magazine."

"I saw reporters last night," Jack said. "They've been shadowing us for three weeks."

"They're shadowing everyone in the department." Abbott pushed away from Jack's desk. "Don't do anything exciting and maybe they'll go away."

The phone rang and Jack picked up. "Ian's got something," he said. "Let's go."

Monday, February 22, 7:30 a.m.

Liza Barkley frowned at her cell. Lindsay had never come home. She hadn't called and she wasn't picking up. If her sister was going to be late, she always called.

Liza bit at her lip, wondering what to do. She didn't know any of Lindsay's friends anymore and had never called the cleaning service where she worked.

But if she didn't leave the apartment now, she'd miss her bus. *Maybe Lin met a friend for breakfast.* Liza hoped so. Lindsay worked so hard, her social life had become more endangered than the blue whale, the subject of Liza's second-period science test. She slipped her cell into her pocket. *Call me, Lin. Let me know you're okay.*

Monday, February 22, 8:15 a.m.

He folded his newspaper. Martha's suicide was way back in the Metro section, but it was there. Soon Martha's murder would be headlines, maybe as early as tomorrow. That would depend on how skilled the ME was, he supposed. And then, he'd be front-page news, every day. Coverage would explode when they found Christy Lewis hanging from her bedroom ceiling. SERIAL KILLER STALKS WOMEN, the headline would read.

He'd have to keep clippings. He smiled. *Frame and hang them in my basement.*

That the dynamic duo had caught Brisbane's case would only help. They were media darlings, after all. The press would hang on their every word, put every missed clue under the microscope. Then the headlines would change. POLICE CLUELESS.

He wondered how long it would take someone to find Christy Lewis. She'd be missed faster than Martha. Although she was divorced and her parents were deceased, she had a job and daily contact with people in the real world. Unlike Martha, who had lived in Shadowland.

Christy should be discovered by tomorrow when she failed to show up for work a second day. He didn't have time to rest. He had to start preparing for his fifth of six.

Monday, February 22, 8:32 a.m.

"You work fast, Ian," Noah commented. "I didn't expect a ruling until later."

"I don't have anything official yet," Ian Gilles said. "Where's Jack?"

"Right here." Jack came through the door, perturbed. "I got delayed outside by a reporter. Wanted to know why we had two CSU vans at a suicide last night."

"What did you tell him?" Noah asked.

Jack shrugged. " 'No comment.' What else could I say? So, what do you have, Ian?"

Ian tilted Brisbane's head so that her throat was exposed. "I haven't started the autopsy yet, but I thought you should see this. Right in the middle of the ligature marks is a needle puncture. The rope was placed precisely so the puncture would be hidden."

"Injected with what?" Noah asked.

"Don't know yet. Urine tox didn't show anything. I'm expecting results from the blood test this afternoon. So far, no other obvious injuries, the X-rays show no broken bones, and I found no evidence of any sexual activity."

"Did you check the suicide Dixon processed last week?" Noah asked.

"Janice did that exam. She's at the national ME's convention, but I read her report."

"What do MEs do at a convention?" Jack asked. "Never mind, I don't want to know."

"Probably not," Ian said without a trace of humor. "Janice noted that establishing time of death was difficult as the deceased's window was open."

"Same as Martha," Jack said, nodding toward the body on the table.

"Right. Samantha's eyelids were glued open with super glue, same as this victim."

"Didn't that send up any alarms?" Jack asked, and Ian shrugged.

"We see people do weird things. All the other signs of suicidal hanging were there."

"What about the puncture wound?" Noah asked. "Does Samantha have one?"

"I think so. Janice took a photo of Samantha's ligature wounds. I blew it up. You lose resolution, but I'm pretty sure I saw a puncture wound. I'll need to re-examine the body to be sure. Unfortunately we released the body to the funeral home a week ago."

Jack grimaced. "Exhumation?"

Noah nodded, resigned. "How long to get an exam on Samantha Altman?"

"I'll start as soon as the body arrives. I had the blood samples from her autopsy pulled from storage this morning and they're already submitted for the same blood tests I ordered for Martha. That's all I can do until I get the body back."

Noah put on his hat. "We're going to interview the Altman family today. We'll grease the skids for the exhumation order. You'll call us when Martha's autopsy is finished?"

"Absolutely." Ian pushed the gurney into the examination room.

"Next stop Altman family?" Jack said.

"I'll drive." They'd gotten to Noah's car when his cell rang. "Webster."

"It's Abbott." Who sounded displeased. "Brisbane's suicide hit the papers and I just got a call from a reporter who said he would've called it a homicide on page one, but his editor wouldn't allow it without corroboration. Apparently he got corroboration because he's saying his next headline will be 'More Than a Suicide.' Which of you corroborated?"

"Neither. Jack was approached, but said 'no comment.' Who was this guy?"

"Name was Kurt Buckland. How close are you to having an official homicide ruling?"

"Ian's doing the autopsy this morning, but he found signs that Brisbane was drugged. We're going to interview the Altman family while Ian files for exhumation."

"Good. I'll give a statement as soon as Ian rules it a homicide. That'll take some of the wind out of the reporter's headline. Be back at four. Tell Micki to be here."

"Will do. What about a shrink? We need to start a profile."

"Carleton Pierce will be here at four. I've put Sutherland and Kane on standby."

Noah dropped his cell in his pocket. "Let's move. We have a deadline."

Monday, February 22, 9:35 a.m.

Eve carefully placed the receiver in the cradle on her desk in the graduate office. "Fuck you, asshole," she muttered.

A chuckle had her swiveling her chair. Callie sat behind her, laughing. "I knew you couldn't hold it in. What was that all about, then?"

"I got a new leak in my roof, right over my bed. I moved my bed, but then it dripped into a bucket for the rest of the night. I didn't sleep a wink."

"You have to find a new place." Callie brightened. "My building has a vacancy."

"Your building costs twice as much as I can afford."

"The concept is called a roommate." Callie drew the word out. "My roommate and I split the rent and utilities and everybody is happy. You should get a roommate, too."

"No." After years of living with others, she wanted privacy. "My rent's cheap."

"Your rent is a *gift*. You're just lucky that old woman liked you."

Eve smiled sadly. "Mrs. Daulton liked everybody."

"I know. And I know you miss her. How much longer till your lease runs out?"

"Six more months. And I'll be damned if Myron

Daulton gets his greedy little mitts on my house a second before that."

"Um, Eve, it's not your house. Legally, it's his."

"Greedy SOB, thinking he can run all his mother's tenants out. Wouldn't surprise me if he was up on the roof with an ice pick himself, making the damn leaks."

"Now you're sounding paranoid. So was the asshole on the phone the greedy SOB?"

"No, that was a roofer who does not fix roofs. He only talks to people buying new roofs. Who needs a brand-new roof, for God's sake?"

"Sounds like you do. You shouldn't be paying for repairs on somebody else's house anyway. It's not your responsibility. It might even be a lease violation."

"Well, it's moot, because I can't get anyone to do it. I'm thinking that roofing would be a good skill to master. Lately I've done plumbing, some minor wiring . . ."

Callie's eyes widened. "You're *not* planning to fix your roof. You don't like heights."

"I like Myron less. I even called an old friend this morning to ask how I should do it."

"What did he say?"

"I got his voicemail. He'll call me back when he's off shift."

"You know him from the bar?"

"No, from back home. He's a firefighter."

"You touch your scar when you talk about Chicago," Callie said quietly.

Eve yanked her hand from her cheek. "Which is why I don't talk about it."

"Don't you miss them?" Callie asked. "Your family?"

Dana, Caroline, and Mia. The thought of them and their growing families, so far away, made Eve's heart ache. Not a day went by that she didn't miss them. "Yes. But I couldn't stay." To stay was to remember. To hide in the dark.

"At least Tom is here," Callie said. "And me. But I ain't helping with your roof."

"Tom offered. He said he'd bring a half dozen friends when the season is over."

Callie's smile became wry. "Tom Hunter plus six college basketball players. On your roof. In the winter. You're a foolish girl. If you'd wait till summer they'd work shirtless."

"If I wait till summer, everything I own will be underwater and Myron Daulton will have won. I've got to go. I've got Abnormal in fifteen." Eve reached to shut down her laptop, then stopped. Abruptly. "Oh my God," she murmured staring at her email inbox.

"Eve, who is Martha Brisbane and why do you have her on Google Alert?"

Eve had put Martha on Google Alert a week ago, after she'd been missing from Shadowland for two days. Any mention of Martha on the Internet would be flagged.

And it had indeed. Her heart in her throat, Eve read the short article that had been published in today's *Mirror*. *Martha Brisbane, 42, was found dead in her apartment last night, the victim of an apparent suicide. She had hanged herself.* The article went on, giving statistics of Twin Cities suicides, but Eve could only see one line.

Suicide. I should have seen this coming. I should have stopped it.

But Martha had spent eighteen hours a day in Shadowland for months before joining their study. Who knew what had driven her to do so? Still . . . Martha was dead.

And Eve wasn't even supposed to know she'd existed.

"Eve?" Callie tapped her shoulder gently. "Who is she?"

"Just someone I know." *Someone I shouldn't have known. But I did.* Eve closed her laptop with a snap. "I have to get to class."

Callie hung back, studying her. "Will you go to the funeral?"

She slid her laptop into her computer bag. "If I can figure out where it is, yes."

"You want me to go with you?"

Eve drew a shaky breath. "Yes. Thanks."

"You bet. Don't go climbing on the roof by yourself."

Eve made herself smile. Her roof was now the least of her concerns. "I won't."

Monday, February 22, 9:40 a.m.

"Thank you for seeing us." Jack set his hat next to Noah's on the coffee table.

Mrs. Altman's hands were clutched tightly in her lap. "What is this about?"

"Your daughter, ma'am," Noah said. He'd lost the toss again. "We know Samantha's death was ruled a suicide, but you and your husband weren't convinced."

"It's a mortal sin. Samantha was a good Catholic. She never missed Mass."

"We believe your daughter didn't commit suicide. She may have been murdered."

Mrs. Altman closed her eyes. "Dear God."

Jack gave her a moment. "Do you have the clothing your daughter was wearing?"

"We put everything in a box," she murmured. "We haven't been able to look at it."

"What about the stool found in her bedroom?" Jack asked.

"I gave it to a thrift shop. I couldn't look at it."

Noah wanted to sigh. "Can you tell us which location you took it to?"

"Grand Avenue. Why?"

"It may be important," Noah said, then damned the toss he'd lost. He suspected Jack kept a two-faced coin in his pocket, because Noah lost the toss most of the time. "To rule your daughter's death a homicide, we need to examine your daughter's body."

Mrs. Altman's eyes filled with tears. "No. I won't allow it. It's a desecration."

"I won't say I understand how you feel," Noah said gently, "because there is no way that I can. But please know we'd never take this action if it wasn't absolutely necessary. If someone killed your daughter, he needs to be caught. Stopped. Punished."

She was rocking pitifully, tears streaming down her face. "You can't do this to her."

"Mrs. Altman," Noah said, his voice still gentle, "there's nothing stopping the person who killed your Samantha from killing someone else's daughter. I know you don't want that. You don't want another family to go through the pain you've endured."

"No," she whispered. "We don't." She looked away, closed her eyes. "All right."

"Thank you," Noah said. "If you tell us where you put her things, we'll be going."

She stood up, still crying. "In the spare bedroom closet."

"I'll get it," Jack said while Mrs. Altman covered her face with her hands and wept.

Exhumation was like waiting until a wound had almost healed, then ripping it open again in the vilest of ways. "Sit down, ma'am," Noah said, patting her back as she cried.

Jack returned and Mrs. Altman stood uncertainly as Noah and Jack put on their hats.

"Detective Phelps and I will update you on the investigation ourselves. And don't worry. We'll make sure they put the ground back the way it was."

Mrs. Altman shook her head. "She's not in the ground yet."

Noah's brows lifted. "Excuse me?"

"Our family has been buried in the same cemetery for generations. They don't have a backhoe so they can't dig yet. The ground's still frozen. We'd planned to bury her in the spring." Her chin lifted, her eyes now sharp as they met Noah's. "That will make it faster, won't it, Detective? That way you can find the monster that did this to my child."

"Yes, ma'am. This will speed things up considerably. Thank you."

Neither Jack nor Noah spoke until they reached the car. Jack cleared his throat, no humor in his eyes. "I'm glad you lost the toss. I never know what to say."

"She reminded me of my mom." Who worried about him constantly. She was a cop's widow. Noah supposed she was entitled to worry about her son.

"All the old ladies remind you of your mom."

"I always hoped somebody would be kind to her if something happened to me first."

Jack frowned. "Don't talk like that."

"We all gotta go sometime, Jack," Noah said, as he always did.

"I'm not anxious to go today," Jack replied, as he always did. "Let's find that stool."

"And then to Brisbane's apartment, see if Mrs. Kobrecki has returned."

"And with her, the panty fiend grandson, Taylor."

"Exactly."

Monday, February 22, 11:15 a.m.

Eve stood outside her advisor's office, her heart beating way too fast. For an hour she'd sat through her Abnormal seminar, unable to concentrate. *Martha's dead.*

You have to do something. But what? Martha's suicide might not have been related to her participation in Eve's study. *But I don't know that it wasn't.*

She had five more red-zones, whose game time had skyrocketed in recent weeks. None had been ultra-users before. They'd never played a role play game before. But when they'd been introduced to Shadowland, they'd been sucked in, just the same.

Lightly she rapped her knuckles on her grad advisor's office door. "Dr. Donner?"

Donner looked up. "Miss Wilson. I thought our meeting wasn't until Thursday."

"It's not. But something has come up."

"Then come in," he said, looking back at the journal he had been reading.

Eve had never liked him, not in the two years she'd been a grad student at Marshall. He'd asked to be her advisor, citing interest in her thesis concept. He thought it was publishable, critical in the "publish or perish" academic world. Everyone said he was overdue. He wouldn't be pleased with what she was about to say.

"Well." He tossed the journal onto a tall stack. "What did you need, Miss Wilson?"

"I'm having some concerns about a few of the test subjects, Dr. Donner." She opened her notebook where she'd written the subjects' ID numbers, as if she didn't know them by heart. None of whose real names she was supposed to know.

"Well?" he asked impatiently. "What about them?"

"They've posted increases in game time of more than three hundred percent. I'm concerned they're endangering quality of life and in some cases, their livelihood."

Donner fixed his gaze upon Eve's face and part of her wanted to back away. But of course she did not. She'd faced monsters far scarier than Donald Donner in her lifetime.

"Miss Wilson, how do you know how much time they've spent in game play?"

She was prepared for the question. "I can run a search to find out who's in Shadowland at any given time. I've programmed my computer to run these searches multiple times every day and these numbers represent an average." Which was no lie.

"Clever," he murmured. "But can you prove these subjects are engaged in active play versus, perhaps, just forgetting to log out?"

Yes. Because I'm in there, too. Talking, interacting with them. *Watching them.*

His eyes narrowed when she didn't answer. "Miss Wilson? Does your search differentiate active play time versus just forgetting to log out?"

"No, it doesn't," she murmured.

"Are they doing their self-esteem charts?"

"Yes, and the data is promising. Twenty percent indicate they are more confident in the real world after self-actualization exercises in the virtual world. But I'm concerned that the line between reality and imagination is blurring for some."

He frowned. "They've exhibited quantifiable depression or personality changes?"

"No. But they haven't been required to test for depression or personality changes in the last month. Most of these subjects aren't due for testing for another few weeks."

He relaxed. "Then in another few weeks we'll find out if they have a problem."

Not soon enough for Martha Brisbane. She's already dead. In a few weeks Christy Lewis might be unemployed. "We should be testing more frequently," she said firmly.

"So you've noted many times," he said, condescendingly. "And as I've attempted to explain to you each time, we need to use independent third-party testers to ensure our double-blind status. That costs money for the university and time for the subjects."

"There is surplus in the test budget. I've kept careful track of spending."

"You'd have subjects dropping like flies if they had to come in more frequently."

"But sir," she started and Donner lifted his hand.

"Miss Wilson," he said sharply, then smiled, but somehow a smile never worked on his face. "Eve. Your graduate research could help a lot of people. Role play in the real world has long been used to help our patients improve self-esteem. It's timely and relevant to explore using the virtual world of the Internet to do the same."

Timely, relevant, and publishable. She lifted her chin. "I never intended our subjects to participate to the point of ignoring their real lives. We're responsible for them."

His smile vanished. "Your subjects signed a release indemnifying us from liability. We are not responsible. Don't ever indicate that we are, spoken or written. I don't have time for this. I have a class to teach at noon, so if you'll excuse me."

Eve didn't move from her chair. "Dr. Donner, please. What if our subjects show evidence of depression, even . . . suicidal thoughts? What would we do then?"

"We'd ensure that subject was treated by an independent third-party therapist."

Eve looked down at her hands, clenched in her lap. *Too late for Martha.* "What if, hypothetically speaking, I knew one of our subjects was suicidal?"

"It's moot," he said coldly, warningly even. "You do not have that information."

She looked up. His eyes were narrowed, daring her to continue. "But if I did?"

"Then you'd be facing discipline from the committee. Perhaps worse."

Eve wanted to close her eyes, wanted to retreat back into the dark. But this was real. Martha was really dead. They might have seen it had they tested more frequently. *I should have insisted.* A year ago she'd been happy to have her research approved and funded. Rocking the boat hadn't seemed worthwhile. The situation had changed.

She took the copy she'd printed of Martha's death article from her notebook. "This was subject 92." Keeping her hand perfectly steady, she handed it to him over his desk.

He stared at the page, then grabbed it. His face darkened and Eve's throat closed. This was it. He'd throw her out of the program. Cancel her research.

"I think that if we'd tested her more often, we might have been able to get her help," she said. "Her death is on my head, Dr. Donner. I don't want any more suicides."

Deliberately he dropped the sheet onto his shredder and hit the switch. Instantly the page was gone and with it any minute respect she'd held for Donald Donner.

"I never saw that," he said. "*You* never saw it. Are we clear, Miss Wilson?"

Eve's knees were shaking, but she'd be damned before she'd let him see it. "Crystal."

For a long time she sat at her desk, staring at nothing, trying to figure out what to do.

What would Dana do? Dana Dupinsky Buchanan, one of the women who'd all but raised her in Hanover House, a Chicago shelter. Dana, who'd risked her freedom and her life helping battered women find hope and safety. *Helping runaways like me.*

Dana would do whatever was necessary to keep those people safe. *So should I.*

Maybe no more bad things would happen. But if they did . . . *I'll do what I need to do.* She knew where every one of her subjects resided in Shadowland. Now she'd seek them out in the real world, right here in Minneapolis. Starting with Christy Lewis.

If Donner found out, she'd be finished. *But I'd rather forfeit it all and be able to look in the mirror.* She'd do what she needed to do, but smartly. *If I'm lucky, nobody will ever know.* Her subjects would be safe and Donner would get his precious published study.

Then she'd get a new advisor. But first, Christy. She'd watched Christy's Gwenivere for weeks in the virtual world. It was time to set Christy straight in the real one.

Monday, February 22, 2:10 p.m.

Noah had expected Mrs. Kobrecki to look meaner. So when a sweet little old lady answered his knock, he had to swiftly control his surprise. "Mrs. Kobrecki?"

"You must be the detectives." She opened the door wide. "Please, sit down."

"Thank you," Jack said with an engaging smile. "You're a hard woman to reach."

"My cellular phone battery was dead. I was away for the weekend and returned just this morning. I called you all as soon as I saw the crime scene tape. Poor Martha."

"How long had you known Ms. Brisbane, ma'am?" Noah asked.

"Eight years. We had our differences, but I never dreamed she'd do this."

"What kind of differences?" Noah probed with a sympathetic smile.

"Her apartment," Mrs. Kobrecki said archly, as if it were obvious. "Not to speak ill of the dead, but that woman lived in total filth."

Noah thought of Martha's spotless apartment. "When did you last see her?"

"Week ago, Saturday. She was going out, which was odd. She didn't go out often."

"Did she say where she was going?" Jack asked.

"No." Mrs. Kobrecki's lips thinned.

"Did you have an argument, Mrs. Kobrecki?" Noah asked.

"Yes. I told her that if she didn't clean her place, I'd evict her. She just ignored me. That woman made me so mad." Then she sighed. "But I never would have wanted this."

"Of course not," Noah said soothingly. "Did you see when Martha returned home?"

"No. I would have been too angry to talk to her anyway." Her eyes narrowed. "Why?"

"It's routine, ma'am. We're trying to establish a time of death. For family."

"Her mother probably won't care what time Martha died."

Noah feigned surprised concern. "Martha didn't get along with her mother?"

"No, and I don't know why. I once went up to yell at Martha about the mess. I heard her through the door, on the phone, yelling at her mother. She came to the door crying."

"Did you hear what they were saying to each other?" Jack asked.

"Not really. I did hear Martha tell her mother she was doing it for her. I assumed she meant that was why she worked all the time and never visited her."

"Was it normal for a week to pass without seeing her?" Noah asked.

"Sometimes I'd go a month without seeing her. I hadn't planned to see her that night. I just ran into her at the door. I'd already decided to evict her before that last argument but my lawyer had told me to give her one more warning, and if she didn't listen, then get photos of the mess. Her going out gave me the opportunity to do that."

"Did you get the pictures?" Jack asked.

"Yes, after Martha left that evening. I don't normally intrude on my tenants' privacy, but I knew I needed to get her out or my whole place would be infested with roaches."

Noah felt a spurt of triumph. "Can we get a copy of those pictures? For our files."

Mrs. Kobrecki got them from her desk. "Oh, and I suppose you should take her mail, too. The postman gave me that on Friday as I was leaving for my weekend trip. Martha's mailbox was full. He couldn't stuff any more in there, so I cleaned it out."

"You didn't think it unusual that she didn't go to her mailbox?" Noah asked.

"She'd go weeks without checking her mail, like she was in her own little world."

"Did she pay her rent on time?" Noah asked.

"She'd never missed a payment until a year ago. She said she'd gotten wrapped up in a project and lost track of time. After that she did automatic payment from the bank."

Jack began sorting the mail, Noah the pictures. *Wow.* The kitchen sink was filled with dishes, the garbage can overflowing with paper plates. Her desk was covered with trash, coffee cups, and stacks of paper. In the living room were stacks of newspapers, so many the wall was totally obscured. Someone had done a very thorough cleanup.

Jack cleared his throat. "Mrs. Kobrecki, we'd like to have a last look around the apartment before we close this case. Can you unlock it for us?"

"Of course. I'll get my keys. They're in the back."

CSU had sealed the scene. Jack didn't need Kobrecki's keys. "What did you find?"

"Something that looks like a paycheck," Jack murmured, "plus a bank statement. Why don't you chat with Mrs. Kobrecki and I'll go to the car and check this out."

The two stood when Mrs. Kobrecki came back into the room. "Let's go," she said.

"I have to start wrapping up," Jack said. "Thank you so much, Mrs. Kobrecki."

Noah followed Mrs. Kobrecki upstairs. "I apologize. My partner and I forgot that CSU sealed the scene with our lock. We'll put your lock back when the case is closed."

"I didn't realize a suicide was a case," Mrs. Kobrecki said, suddenly suspicious.

"It's procedure, ma'am. Who lives in the apartment next to Miss Brisbane?"

"Nobody. The Smiths lived there, but they got transferred about three months ago."

The hair rose on the back of Noah's neck. "You mean this apartment was empty?"

"Yes. I won't rent either of them for months after this."

"Could you open it for me? The empty unit?"

Mrs. Kobrecki stiffened. "I don't have the key to that unit on this key ring."

Oh, really. "I thought you had a master."

"I do, but it only works on the doorknob and the last tenants installed a deadbolt. Could you hurry, please? I'd like to get this over with."

"Of course." Noah opened the door, waited for her reaction. She didn't disappoint.

Her gasp echoed off the walls. "Oh my God. Was she robbed?"

"We took her computer into our lab. But the rest of the place looks different?"

"Like day and night. I heard that people will call family and friends and give things away before they kill themselves. Do they clean, too?"

"Apparently Miss Brisbane did. Was her apartment always messy?"

"Not like at the end. She was always a little cluttered and always had dishes in the sink but the disgusting messes started . . . about a year ago."

Noah wondered what had happened a year ago that had so changed her life. "Ma'am, who does maintenance and repair for you?"

"My grandson," she said, still stunned and off-guard, as he had hoped she would be.

"I'd like to have his statement for the report, if that's all right."

Her eyes grew sharply suspicious once again. "Why? You have the pictures, why do you need to talk to Taylor?"

Smart old bird. "Just following procedure." Her defenses were up. That was telling.

"Taylor is out of town. He won't be home for weeks."

"Can I get a phone number?"

Her lips pursed. "It's stored in my cell phone, which as I mentioned, is dead. I don't remember it by heart. I'll have to call you with it."

Ooh, very smart old bird. "Please do that, Mrs. Kobrecki. Thank you for your time."

"Can I have my pictures back?"

"I'll need them for my report. I'll make copies and ensure you get these back."

Her cheeks darkened. "Thank you. If there's nothing else?"

"No ma'am. You've been very helpful."

She looked as if she wanted to curse. Instead she left silently fuming. Noah locked the door and attached the crime scene tape. They needed to find Taylor Kobrecki.

Chapter Five

Monday, February 22, 2:45 p.m.

Eve stood on Martha Brisbane's apartment building manager's welcome mat, her fist an inch from the woman's door. She'd stopped herself from knocking twice already.

Eve's attempt to talk with Christy Lewis had fallen flat. Christy hadn't come into the office and hadn't called in sick. That meant Christy had either overslept after spending all night online, or was still online. Frustrated and needing to *do something*, Eve had driven to Martha's, hoping to learn where the woman's funeral would be held.

But what if the building manager asks how I know Martha? You'll say you know her from work. That's not a lie. Drawing a breath, Eve lifted her hand to knock just as a little old lady came stomping down the stairs to the manager's basement apartment.

"I don't want any," she said. She slammed the door so hard the walls shook.

"I think I'll wait for the obituary," Eve murmured. She started up the stairs, then heard footsteps coming down. The hairs on the back of her neck lifted, and she'd learned long ago to trust her senses. Slowing, she waited until whoever was coming was gone.

It was a man, all in black. All the way up to the fedora on his head.

Oh. It was more quiet exhalation than a word, but he'd heard. He paused at the door, then turned, and her stomach rolled, just as it did every time she saw him.

Mr. Tonic Water himself. He came to the head of the stairs, eyes shadowed by the brim of his hat. *"Eve?"* He sounded as surprised as she was.

"Detective." It was the only word that would move from her brain to her lips. *Why was he here?* Why did her heart have to hammer like a piston every time she saw him?

"Why are you here?" he asked, which was a damn good question.

She walked past him to the door. "I was wondering when Martha's funeral would be."

"That I don't know," he said. "How did you know Miss Brisbane?"

She stared up at him unflinchingly, her mouth dry as dust. "From work."

His dark brows lifted slightly. "From Sal's? I never saw her there."

You only come in once a week. "Not from Sal's. I'll check the paper for her obituary."

"Eve, wait. I need to know more. You knew her from work, but not from Sal's?"

"I just wanted to pay my respects. Excuse me." She could feel his eyes on her as she escaped, staring from beneath the brim of his fedora.

Fedora. Why was the Hat Squad here? Abruptly she turned. "I read Martha committed suicide."

"That's what the paper said, yes," he said, his stare too penetrating for her comfort.

"But you're homicide."

"We investigate suicides."

"But that's not why you're here. If Martha killed

herself you would have closed it last night." When he'd come by to fetch Jack, he was so angry she'd felt it across the bar. She came closer, until she could see under the brim of his hat. "Did Martha kill herself?"

His jaw tightened, almost imperceptibly. "Why?"

Because if she didn't, I'm not guilty or responsible. Someone else was. *Oh my God. Martha was murdered.* By whom? And why? *She was in Shadowland eighteen fucking hours a day.* How could any real person have known her to murder her?

She drew a breath of frigid air. "It matters to me, okay? Martha mattered."

His eyes shifted and suddenly they were no longer unreadable. She saw a flash of pain, of grief, of anger. And suddenly she knew Martha mattered to him as well.

In that moment Eve wanted, needed to tell him everything. Which terrified her.

"She didn't kill herself," he said. "Where did you know her from? I need to know. Please."

I didn't do it. I didn't kill her. Relief sent a shudder down her spine. "Work. I knew her from her work. I have to go." And when she turned, he didn't try to stop her.

"Was that Eve from Sal's?" Jack asked when Noah got back to the car.

"Yeah. She said she knew Martha 'from work.'"

"Really? I never saw Martha at Sal's."

"No, Eve said it was from Martha's work."

Jack blinked, clearly taken aback. "*Really?* Well, well, well. Still waters, they say."

"What the hell are you babbling about?" Noah asked irritably.

Jack held out a paycheck. "Payable to Martha Brisbane from Siren Song, Inc."

"Siren Song. Never heard of them," Noah muttered.

"Me either, so I had Faye run them through the system."

"And?" Faye was their office administrator. "What did she say?"

"Siren Song is a phone sex business."

Noah's jaw dropped. *"What?"*

"Yep. I called the number on their business registration, but only got a voicemail. Here's the address. Let's go pay them a visit."

"Wait." Noah's mind was still spinning. *"Eve* is a *phone sex provider?"*

Jack looked amused. "Um, so was Martha. Our victim? Remember her?"

Noah opened his mouth. Closed it again. "Goddammit," he said.

He started the car and Jack shrugged. "I checked Martha's bank statement while you were in there. She spent almost every penny on that nursing home for her mother, which is expensive. She needed the money, Web. Maybe Eve does, too. It's not illegal."

I'm just disappointed. He'd thought more of Eve. For a moment, seeing her there, outside of a bar . . . For a moment he'd thought it was fate kicking him in the ass, like Trina said. But now . . . *A phone sex provider?* "Bartenders make good money."

"She's a grad student," Jack said. "College is expensive."

Noah's scowl deepened. "How did you know she's a grad student?"

"You think I've been going up to the bar to get your

water because I'm nice? I've been trying to get Eve to go out with me for six months, ever since . . . Well, you know."

Yeah, Noah thought bitterly. He knew. Before six months ago Jack wouldn't have given Eve the time of day. Her scar had put him off. The man was a prince.

Jack made a rude noise. "Don't you look at me like that, Web. *You* sure weren't making a move, before or after she got her face fixed."

Sometimes, I swear to God . . . Noah gripped the wheel to keep his hand from balling into an annoyed fist, but couldn't stop himself from asking, "What did she say?"

"She evades me every single time. She's a smooth one."

Noah thought about the way she'd bolted away minutes ago. Not so smooth. He'd known she was hiding something. A damn big something. His mind was still reeling.

"But I bet she's good at it," Jack added as Noah pulled out of the parking lot.

"What?"

"Eve. Phone sex. She's got that smoky voice. I bet she makes good money."

Noah knew Jack was riding him, but still the anger rose higher. "Shut. Up. Jack."

Jack chuckled. "God, you're easy. Ask her out. She'll say no and you can move on."

"No." Noah bit the word off, then regretted it. He was letting Jack bait him. Again.

"Whatever." Jack was quiet a moment. "One of Martha's clients may have killed her."

Noah made himself concentrate. "Possibly. Did Faye have Martha's LUDs yet?"

"Yeah, and there was a toll-free number she called at least ten times a day."

"Her connection into Siren Song's switchboard."

"I'm thinking that," Jack said. "When we get Samantha's LUDs, we'll see if Sammy called the same number. Maybe Siren's the connection between the two."

"Hell. If this perv is hitting on phone sex operators, and Eve is working for them . . ."

"Let's make sure all the other Sirens are still alive and heavy breathing."

"Not funny, Jack."

Jack's sigh was almost sincere. "Wasn't really meant to be. Sometimes they just come out on their own. Hey, my dad's a stand-up comic. It's genetic."

"Your dad's a retired podiatrist."

"He does stand-up part time at the comedy club. Said after looking at feet for forty years, it only seemed right. He's pretty good. Henny Youngman, watch out."

Noah laughed wearily. Just when he was ready to strangle Jack, his partner acted human and . . . almost likable. "Jack."

Jack's lips curved. "But you laughed. Look at the bright side. Maybe one of us can convince Eve to leave Siren and go into private practice. *If* you know what I mean."

Unbelievably, Noah felt his cheeks heat. "Are you a perpetual teenager?"

Jack considered it without rancor. "Yep. You wanna grab lunch, hit Siren Song, then head back to the nursing home to chat with Martha's Mommy Dearest?"

"Sounds like a plan."

* * *

Monday, February 22, 3:02 p.m

Liza Barkley flipped open her phone the moment she walked out of the school. She'd been checking surreptitiously all day, but Lindsay hadn't called back.

Worried sick, she called Information and was connected to Shotz Cleaning Service.

"Hi, my name is Liza Barkley and I'm trying to reach my sister Lindsay. She didn't come home last night, after working the night shift. Have you heard from her?"

There was a long silence on the other end and Liza's stomach turned inside out. Poised in front of her school bus, she froze. "Is my sister all right?"

"Um . . . we had to let Lindsay go last June. Business was bad."

Stunned, Lindsay stared at the ground. *June?* "She goes to work every night. She told me that business was bad, that she had to take the night shift to keep her job."

"I'm sorry, but we don't have a night shift. Good luck."

For a moment Liza stood, too numb to move. *Lindsay lied.* What had she been doing all these months? It didn't matter now. Lindsay was missing.

"Liza?" The bus driver leaned forward. "You need to get on. It's time to leave."

Do something. "I'm not going home. Which city bus goes to the police station?"

Monday, February 22, 3:35 p.m.

Eve sank into the stuffed chair in her living room. Someone had murdered Martha, who'd spent eighteen hours a day online. Was it random or connected to Shadowland?

"That's crazy," she said out loud. "Nobody knew who Desiree was in the real world."

You did. That stopped her cold. *And Christy Lewis didn't show up for work today.*

Oh my God. What if something had happened to Christy, too?

Eve logged in to Shadowland, chose her Greer avatar and went to Ninth Circle. But Greer searched, finding no Gwenivere. Eve navigated to Gwenivere's virtual house, and . . . the breath rushed out of her lungs. *A black wreath hung on the door.* The death of an avatar. Heart pounding, Eve had Greer open the door.

And everything real around her faded away. Eve stared at the screen until she heard a whimper and realized it had come from her own throat.

Gwenivere was hanging, a noose around her neck, her face made up like a garish clown. Her red shoes had fallen off. One lay on its side and the other sat straight up.

"Oh my God," Eve whispered. Her pulse now pounding out of control, she set the laptop aside and paced. Martha was found hanging. Now Christy's Gwenivere was hanging. It could be a coincidence. *But you know damn well it's not. Call 911.*

And tell them what? That a virtual-world character got whacked? *They'll laugh at me.*

So don't tell them about Shadowland. Just tell them to check on her.

And they'll ask why. So I'll say, she missed work today. They'll still laugh at me.

"I can't call 911," she said. "But I have to tell somebody." Somebody she could trust.

If this were Chicago, she'd call Detective Mia Mitchell

who, along with Dana and Caroline, had raised her. But this wasn't Chicago and Mia wasn't here.

She calmed until all she could hear was the dripping of the water into the pots in her living room and then she knew what to do. *Olivia Sutherland.* Olivia was Mia's sister and Hat Squad, too. Olivia was a kind person—she'd helped Eve get the job at Sal's. If Christy was in trouble, Olivia could tell Noah Webster and keep Eve out of the whole loop. If Christy was fine, Olivia would keep it to herself.

"Now you're finally thinking," Eve muttered. She dialed the precinct, asked for Olivia. And got voicemail. "Olivia, it's Eve Wilson. Could you call me please? It's urgent."

She hung up and stared at the hanging avatar on her laptop screen. "Now what?"

You have to check on Christy. Hands shaking, Eve searched the online phonebook. Martha had been listed, but there were twelve Christine Lewises in the Twin Cities.

The addresses of all the study subjects were in a file on the university's server under Dr. Donner's account. The one time she'd broken in, she'd done so from Donner's admin assistant's PC. Jeremy Lyons had typed the names in when the study began.

Jeremy Lyons was also careless and left his workstation unprotected when he took one of his many bathroom breaks during the day. It had taken Eve only minutes to find the file and write down the names of the subjects she'd thought at risk. There hadn't been time to write home addresses and she hadn't wanted to know them anyway.

That had been too close to real-world stalking. Now she wished she'd copied them.

"You could just call Noah Webster," she said aloud. And tell him what? *How about the truth?* She'd wanted to tell him when she stood in front of Martha's apartment. There was something in his eyes that she . . . trusted. Trust was a precious commodity.

So's my place in grad school. Eve needed access to the server in a way that couldn't be traced back to her. She knew someone who could do it. Dana's husband, Ethan, was a network security expert. When she lived in Chicago, Eve had worked for Ethan part-time and had learned a hell of a lot about networks. She needed to phone home.

If this doesn't work, I'll call Webster and come clean. Fingers crossed, Eve dialed and nearly cried when Dana's familiar voice answered. "Evie, how are you?"

"I'm fine." Dana was pregnant again, due in a month. There was no way Eve would tell her anything was wrong. "Can I talk to Ethan? My hard drive froze again."

"You *will* tell me what's wrong, sooner or later," Dana said. "Hold on, I'll get Ethan."

A minute later he picked up. "Eve. How the hell are you, kid?"

"I've had better days. Ethan, I need access to my university's server, but don't want anyone to know I've been there."

"Why?" The single word carried all of Ethan's unvoiced concerns.

That was a damn good question. "I told you about my thesis study."

"Building self-esteem in the virtual world. Your subjects get to play all day in Shadowland. I wish I were on your study."

"No, you really don't. I'm concerned about one of the

subjects. I need to get her home address. Can you trust me and not ask me any more?"

"I can do that. You'll tell me if you get into trouble? I can be there in a few hours."

Eve's heart squeezed. "Thank you." She gave him Jeremy Lyons's logon and password. "He wrote it on a sticky hidden under his blotter."

"He's an idiot," Ethan muttered. "Writing his password down like that."

"But so many do." One of her jobs for Ethan had been to hack into his clients' networks, to show them their vulnerabilities. It had been all too easy.

"Keeps me employed," he said. A minute passed, then two more while Eve watched Christy's avatar swing from a virtual noose. "I'm in. What do you want to know?"

"Home address for Lewis, Christy L., for now. Can you email me a copy of the file?"

"Done and done. Christy Lewis lives at 5492 Red Barn Lane in Woodfield."

It would take a little while to get there. "Thanks."

"Eve, wait. How much trouble are you in?"

"I broke the double-blind code on this test. If anyone finds out, I'll get expelled."

"Ooh." In her mind's eye she could see him wince. "That's bad, kid."

"I know, but it was the right thing to do."

"You're Dana's," he said quietly. "I'd expect no less. Call me if you need me. I can keep it from her for a little while. She and the baby are strong, so don't worry."

Eve hung up, staring at the hanging Gwenivere. "Easy for you to say."

Monday, February 22, 4:05 p.m.

"It's officially a homicide," Ian Gilles said when he joined the team that had gathered in Abbott's small office. "Martha was strangled. Among other things."

"What other things?" Noah asked, then put up his hand. "Wait, before you tell us, you know everybody, right? Micki Ridgewell and Carleton Pierce?"

"Of course I know Micki." Ian smiled at her, a rare look for his face. "And Dr. Pierce and I worked on a homicide last year. Good to see you."

"And you." Carleton had photographs of the two victims in front of him and he pointed to Samantha. "Have you re-examined her yet?"

"Not yet," Ian said. "I'll have her body tomorrow. For now, I can only tell you about Martha Brisbane. Her bloodwork was positive for ketamine."

"The puncture wound on her neck," Jack said. "Ket's a sedative."

"Exactly. It's sometimes used in field surgery because it sedates and immobilizes. This is interesting." Ian pulled a photo from the stack. "These are her lungs."

Micki frowned at the photo. "They're blue. Why did you stain them?"

"I didn't. She came that way."

"I've heard of holding your breath till you turn blue," Jack said, "but I never actually thought it worked. What is it?"

"Copper sulfate. I found traces in her tracheal wall and stomach. Copper sulfate is found in drain cleaners that clear tree roots. You flush it down your toilet."

Micki winced. "It eats through tree roots?"

"And skin. I found traces on her face, under the makeup."

"He held her face in the toilet?" Noah asked and Ian nodded.

"She was held under long and frequently enough that she'd inhaled and swallowed the liquid. If he hadn't strangled her, the copper sulfate might have eventually killed her. Also, she'd been cleaning right before her death. I found pieces of sponge beneath her nails. Her hands had also been in contact with some very strong bleach."

"Her landlady said the apartment was filthy," Noah said, "but it had been cleaned. The sonofabitch made Martha clean before he killed her?"

"Now, that's a new one." Jack looked at Ian. "No signs of sexual assault?"

Ian shook his head. "This woman had not been sexually active in some time."

"Well, not in the conventional way," Noah muttered. "You done, Ian?"

"Almost. I found a callus above her left ear. I've seen it before in victims who worked in phone sales. It was where the headset rested on their skin."

"Martha spent quite a lot of time on the phone," Jack said deliberately. "That we can't find her headset means he took the tool of her trade, painted her face up, made her clean up her apartment . . . It does all fit."

"Martha worked for Siren Song," Noah said. "It's a phone sex company."

Micki blinked. "She was a phone sex operator?"

"No wonder her mother was mad at her," Abbott said.

Noah sighed. "Perhaps Martha didn't consider it prostitution, but her mother did. We're thinking Martha may have been killed because of Siren."

"By a client or somebody who didn't approve," Jack added. "We don't know how Samantha Altman factors in, yet, although she had been laid off recently. Maybe she was working for Siren until she got something better."

"We want Siren Song's employee list. It could connect Samantha and tell us who's at risk for the next attack." *Like Eve*, Noah thought.

"I'll call the DA," Abbott said. "Get the subpoenas started. Mick, what do you have?"

"All the prints matched the victim except for one set we found on pipes, light fixtures, etc. I'm betting they belong to the maintenance man."

"Taylor Kobrecki," Noah said. "He does all her maintenance. He's still AWOL."

"Also, we've searched her computer," Micki said. "Looks like the drive was wiped."

"Can you work your magic and save the day?" Jack asked.

"Sugar's working on it," she said. "If anything's there, he'll find it. That stool that you two recovered from the thrift store this morning is a match to Martha's. I haven't traced the origin yet, and there are no usable prints. On the other hand, both victims' dresses and shoes came from The Fashion Club, an online shopping network. Unfortunately they sold hundreds of each this year, none to Martha or Samantha. If we get a suspect we may be able to use the list to confirm, but I don't see it being a beacon."

"If this killer bought those dresses, he had to have known his victims' sizes," Carleton said thoughtfully. "That's quite a bit of planning."

"I agree," Micki said. "Lots of planning and no mistakes. No fibers or hair, except the cat hair in Martha's carpet. She had food and a box of litter, but no litterbox."

"And nobody's seen the cat," Jack said.

"That's not good," Carleton said quietly. "Serial killers often begin by killing animals."

"Wonderful." Abbott shook his head. "What about the noose?"

"Ordinary rope," Micki said. "Could have been purchased at any hardware store. Same with the hook in the ceiling. Martha had really high ceilings in that apartment. I don't think she could have put the hook in herself. She would have needed a ladder."

"Or a handyman," Noah said. "Taylor Kobrecki, again."

"So the panty perv moves to the top of our list of suspects," Abbott said.

"Mrs. Kobrecki says Taylor's out of town," Noah said. "I'm thinking that as soon as I left, she called him, so we put in for her LUDs, cell and home phones."

"He could be hiding in an empty apartment unit next to Martha's place," Jack said.

"We called for a warrant," Noah said. "We didn't have cause. Now we might."

"I'll push it with the DA," Abbott said. "Carleton, any thoughts on profile?"

"White male, twenties or thirties. High IQ. He plans and he's dramatic. He's obsessive about detail." He sorted through all the photos until he found the ones of Samantha and Martha hanging in their identical poses. "There is something about the eyes that's important to him. He made sure they'd stay open."

"Which was very creepy," Micki said under her breath.

"Agreed," Carleton said. "Whoever did this thinks he got away with it with Samantha. So he did it again with

Martha. It's interesting that he used ketamine, and that he injected it in the neck. That indicates a level of . . . confidence. Except for Ian, how many of you would be comfortable shoving a syringe in a woman's neck?"

"You think he's had medical training?" Noah asked and Carleton shrugged.

"Or practice."

Abbott nodded. "Let's find out if the panty pervert ever played doctor. Ian, go through the hanging cases over the year. See if any others have puncture wounds."

"We'll track down Siren Song and get an employee and client list," Jack said. "I can't imagine they'll fork over their clients without a subpoena, so we'll get that started, too."

"And we'll talk to tenants, including the three women who filed a complaint. Somebody knows where Taylor hangs." Noah winced. "No pun intended."

Faye stuck her head in the door. "Noah, call on one. The woman said it was urgent."

Noah pulled Abbott's phone to the edge of the desk. "Webster."

"This is Eve Wilson. You need to come to 5492 Red Barn Lane. It's in Woodfield."

Eve? Her voice didn't falter, but he heard the underlying fear. "What's wrong?"

"There's a woman here. She's dead. She's hanging from her bedroom ceiling."

His heart sank, both for the newest victim and for Eve's now undeniable connection. "Are you in the house?"

"No. I'm looking through the back window. Her name is Christy Lewis."

"Did you know her from work, too?"

"Yes," she said, resigned. "Just hurry. Please." And she hung up.

Noah stood. "Victim number three."

"I'll get my team out there," Micki said.

"I'll meet you there," Ian said. "I want to see this scene myself."

Carleton already stood, buttoning his coat. "So do I. I'll follow you up, Ian."

Jack put on his hat. "Then let's go."

Abbott waved them out, then pointed at Noah. "You stay. Close the door."

Noah obeyed, knowing what was coming and dreading it.

"Who, how, and why?" Abbott asked.

"Eve Wilson," Noah said dully.

Abbott did a double take. "From Sal's?"

"Yeah. She was at Martha's today. Said she knew Martha from work. She just said the same thing about this victim."

Abbott still looked stunned. "I never would have picked her for a phone sex jockey. So she knows something. Find out what it is. I'll send a squad car to the address, just in case this guy is still around. And to make sure Miss Wilson doesn't leave."

Monday, February 22, 4:55 p.m.

Eve sat in the back of a police cruiser, staring at the handcuffs on her wrists, trying to stay calm and not think about the woman hanging from a rope inside the house.

She hoped somebody's wires got crossed, because she'd been cuffed and pushed into her current seating assignment. It had taken a lot of years, but she'd finally grown accustomed to a casual touch from a friend, or a stranger in passing. But this . . . the cops had put their hands on her. *Pushed me.* For a moment she'd been eighteen again and terrified, without enough air to breathe.

Luckily she'd breathed her way through enough panic attacks to know how to control the fear. She was still rattled, but she no longer needed a paper bag to breathe into.

She'd gotten a text off to Callie before the cops had arrived so somebody knew where she was. Then she'd been surrounded by cruisers, ambulances, flashing lights. For Christy, Eve thought, the memory of her empty eyes still fresh. And terrifying.

"Oh for God's sake. You *cuffed* her? You weren't supposed to arrest her."

Noah Webster. She looked up through the window and met his eyes beneath the brim of his hat. She said nothing as he opened the rear door and unlocked her cuffs.

"I'm sorry, Eve. A little miscommunication there."

Eve rubbed her wrists gingerly. "Have you seen her?"

"Your friend? Not yet. Come." He took her arm and urged her to her feet.

Eve yanked away, panic still bubbling too close to the surface. "Where?"

"To my car. It has dark windows. I don't want the press taking pictures of you."

She followed, but when he opened the passenger door the panic boiled up and over, closing her throat. *Didn't your parents teach you not to get into cars with strange men?*

It was *his* voice. Winters, the man who'd left her for dead, five years, eleven months, and eight days ago. His voice taunted when she was panicked. Or stood next to a man's car. Even a man she trusted.

"Are you all right?" Webster asked.

"I'm fine. Fine," she repeated focusing on Noah's voice. He was real, in the here and now. She forced herself to get into his car, flinching when he slammed her door.

"I need you to listen," he said when he'd slid behind the wheel. He stared straight ahead, his jaw hard. "We know about your work."

She forced her face to remain composed. *How did he know?* "Really," she said.

"Really," he repeated tautly. "You might be in danger. Stay here while I check."

The word "danger" gave her pause. "Don't cuff me again. Please."

"I don't plan to."

"How did you find out about my work?"

He looked at her then. "I'll ask the questions for now. When did you arrive?"

There was disapproval in his eyes. Were it Donner, she'd understand. But Webster had no cause to disapprove of anything she'd done. She'd broken the rules, not the law. "About three minutes before I called you," she said stiffly.

"How did you know to come here?"

"Christy didn't show up to work today. I was worried."

"So you knew her well?"

"Well enough." Which was true. Martha had been all about the merchandise when she came into Eve's Pandora store in Shadowland. She came to buy face upgrades for her Desiree avatar, while Christy's Gwenivere had come to chat. Martha had been all business. Christy had just seemed lonely. Within a few visits, Christy, through her avatar, had blurted her whole real-world life story, including where she'd worked.

And now she's dead. "Her eyes." Eve swallowed hard. "They looked unnatural."

"I know. Do you know if Martha or Christy had problems with anyone from work?"

"Besides the one who killed them?" she asked sharply, then looked down at her hands. "No, I don't know of anyone who would have done this. I wish I could help you."

"So do I. So far you're our only connection between three dead women."

Eve's chin jerked up. "Three?"

"Yes. The other was Samantha Altman."

Eve tried to see the participant list in her mind. They had over five hundred test subjects. Samantha Altman was not a name she remembered. "I don't know her."

"She didn't *work* with you?" he asked, still disapproving. Disappointed.

"I don't think so. If I knew, I'd tell you." She met his angry eyes. "I swear."

That seemed to satisfy him, temporarily at least. "Stay here. I'll tell the officers to keep any press away. You're our one link right now. I don't want any of this leaking."

"Don't worry," she said grimly. "I'm in no hurry to tell."

He nodded and touched the brim of his hat. "I'll be back."

Frowning, she watched him go. *What did he know? How had he known?* And who was Samantha Altman? Quickly she pulled her cell from her pocket and dialed Ethan.

"I can't talk long. I don't want them to see me calling you."

"Who is 'them,' Eve?"

"The police. It's bad. Christy Lewis is dead. And she's not the first."

There was shocked silence on the other end. "Oh my God. Are you all right?"

"Yeah, if you don't count the fact that I've been cuffed and questioned."

"They *cuffed* you?" he whispered fiercely, as if he didn't want Dana to overhear him.

"Detective Webster took off the cuffs. It was a mistake. The cops that first got here weren't supposed to do that. Did you keep a copy of that file you sent me?"

"Eve," Ethan warned. "What the hell is this all about?"

"I really don't know. If anybody catches me talking to you, I'm asking you to get me an attorney. I probably won't need one, but it's a believable story. Do you have the file?"

"Yes."

"See if there is a Samantha Altman on the participant list."

There was a short silence as he searched. "No Altman on the list."

"I didn't think so. Three women are dead. Two were in my study, Altman wasn't. They think I'm their only link, but I can't be."

"Don't say anything else until we get you an attorney," Ethan said firmly.

"I'm not a suspect, Ethan. They're worried I'll be a victim."

"And that's supposed to make me feel better?" he gritted.

Two CSU vans had just pulled up, along with an SUV from the ME's office, followed by a sleek Mercedes. "Not really. If I get arrested, you'll be my one phone call, okay?"

"And until then?" Ethan demanded.

"Until then, I guess we wait. I gotta go. Don't worry. I'm perfectly safe here."

Monday, February 22, 5:10 p.m.

Noah stared. It was déjà vu all over again. *Again*. Christy Lewis hung from a rope on a hook in her bedroom. Her dress was the same style as Martha's and Samantha's, as were her shoes. One shoe lay on its side while the other stood straight up. The makeup, the upholstered stool, the open window . . . Everything was the same.

"My God," Ian murmured. He walked around the victim. "This is . . . unreal."

Carleton had followed him in. "It certainly is . . . except it's very real."

"Can you get a time of death, Ian?" Noah asked wearily.

"Not right now. She's got the same petachiae in her eyes, the rope's in the same position. He's got this down to a science." Shaking his head, Ian went to work.

"Did you find her?" Jack asked, and Noah knew he meant Eve.

"Yeah. Damn locals had her cuffed in the back of their cruiser."

Micki looked up from taking pictures, her brow creased in an angry frown. "You unlocked her, didn't you?" she demanded. She'd been floored when Noah had told her the caller was Eve Wilson. She'd been outraged when Noah had told her Eve worked with Martha Brisbane for Siren Song. *You must have made a mistake*, she'd said, so adamantly Noah had wondered all the way up here what Micki Ridgewell knew.

"Of course I unlocked the cuffs." Noah studied Micki's face. "Why?"

Micki shook her head. "She's just been through a lot, that's all."

Noah knew Micki well enough to know that's all she'd say. He'd look it up later.

"This feels like Groundhog Day," Jack said quietly.

Noah looked up into Christy Lewis's "unnatural" eyes. They were glued open, just as the others had been. "I know."

"Oh God." Ian straightened abruptly and looked around the room, alarm on his face.

"What?" Noah looked around as well, but saw nothing out of the ordinary. Nothing he hadn't seen twice before anyway.

"Look," Ian said, then lifted the skirt away from Christy Lewis's legs.

Rope burns around her ankles. "He tied her," Noah said, then saw what Ian was pointing to. He cringed, horrified. Twin pricks on the side of her foot. "Oh my God."

Jack bolted back a step, going pale. "*Fuck*. A goddamn snake. I hate snakes."

"They're more afraid of us," Micki said, then her lips twitched. "Maybe not of Jack."

"From the necrosis around the bite, it was venomous," Ian said.

Jack paled even more. "F—" He couldn't even get the oath out.

"Jack?" Carleton turned to study Jack's face. "Are you all right?"

"Yes," Jack managed, but his rapid shallow breathing and pallor said no.

Carleton gave Micki a look of reproof. "It's not funny," he said seriously.

Micki took pity on Jack. "Everybody out until we know the house is clear," she said.

Jack didn't have to be told again. "Bye. Meet you by the car."

Carleton checked his watch. "Luckily I have a patient appointment at 6:30, so I'll leave you all to your snake hunting." He took a last look at the victim. "This killer is a fascinating personality. I don't think I've ever read anything like this in the literature. I'll do some in-depth research tonight. Consult with my colleagues."

"Can you check on Jack?" Micki asked. "I'm feeling a little bad for laughing at him."

Carleton nodded, a frown of reproach on his face. "I will. And you should."

"I'll wait outside with Jack," Noah said when Carleton and Ian had gone, leaving just himself and Micki. And the victim, of course. He thought of Eve Wilson, sitting outside in his car. "And I want to know how Eve connects to it all. What do you know, Mick?"

"What happened to her, in Chicago . . . was bad. Any more needs to come from her."

"Suggestions?"

Micki's eyes shadowed. "If you run into a wall, call Olivia Sutherland."

"Olivia?" She was one of their homicide detectives. "How does she connect?"

"She's a friend of Eve's family. Just . . . be kind. And keep Jack muzzled."

Chapter Six

Detective Olivia Sutherland's eyes were tearing over her partner's dinner. "Jennie's going to kill you when I tell her what you've been eating." She waved the air between them. "Not that I need to. Those onions will do it for me."

"She's out of town," Kane said. "Back on Thursday." He waggled his brows in a way that always made her laugh. "Could be worse. Could be sardines."

"God, I'm glad you gave that up." She shuddered. "I'd forgotten about those."

"What are you doing for dinner?"

"After that thing, I have no appetite. I got a few pounds left to lose anyway."

"You're fine." Which was what he always said, but Olivia knew differently. She'd gained a little weight after some surgery a few years back and she still wasn't back to top condition. She'd expected her metabolism would slow down, but she never dreamed it would happen at thirty-one. And of course Kane could eat whatever he wanted and never gain a damn ounce. It wasn't fair. And it was disrupting her job.

"Which was why I lost that creep this afternoon," she muttered. To be outrun by a teenager was one thing, but to lose a middle-aged dealer whose primary exercise was the heavy breathing he did while snorting coke . . . She was still kicking herself.

"Liv, he caught a ride. No way he could have outrun you like that. He's probably in the wind," Kane said, speaking of the DA's star witness, the dealer who'd given her the slip. "We wait until he pops his head up again. DA doesn't need him till next week."

"You're right," she murmured, then answered her cell phone, knowing it was Abbott as soon as she heard the opening bars from "Bad to the Bone." "Sutherland."

"I need you two on this hanger case. We need to find one Cassandra Lee. She runs a phone sex operation called Siren Song."

"We're looking for Dustin Hanks," she said. "DA needs him in court."

"This is more important. Faye's waiting with the addresses we have for this Lee."

Olivia handed the phone to Kane. "It's Faye. We're being pulled into Webster's hanger case. And try not to get onions in my phone."

Monday, February 22, 6:45 p.m.

At least they hadn't cuffed her again. Eve sat alone in the interview room at the precinct. It had been almost an hour. A cup of coffee sat untouched, its aroma taunting her churning stomach. All she could see in her mind was Christy Lewis. Hanging there.

Three women were dead. Somebody killed them. *And they think I know who.*

You have to tell them, Eve. You have to tell them everything.

Deliberately Eve turned her head and stared at what she knew was a two-way mirror. Her own eyes stared back, dark and angry. "Fine," she muttered. "I will."

"Excuse me?" The door opened and Webster came through it. Jack Phelps was right behind him. Jack had spoken. "We missed that."

"You were watching me? All this time?"

"No. We came in just as you spoke." Webster put a bag on the table. "A sandwich."

She pushed it away. "I can't eat. But thank you."

Webster sat across the table. "We've been trying to get in touch with your boss."

Eve kept her face expressionless, but her stomach turned over. Donner was going to shit a ring. When this had been about suicide, it had been possible a discipline committee would have taken her side over his. But it wasn't about suicide or Martha's state of mind. She was a lowly grad student who'd broken double-blind. *I'm on my own.*

The help she'd give the police would be at her own professional peril. "My boss."

Webster's eyes were steady as he studied her. Something had changed from when he'd first removed her cuffs and placed her in his car back at Christy's house. He'd been disapproving then. Now, she saw gentleness. And concern. And compassion.

Dammit. He knew. She could always tell when they knew. No one in the bar ever asked, unless they were drunk, and Sal would kick their asses out of the place. But when they found out, they'd always look, and they'd whisper.

"Yes," he said, "your boss. We need a personnel list."

Eve frowned. "Why?"

"Because we need to know who's in danger there."

A personnel list? That didn't make any sense. She was about to tell him so when the door opened and a well-dressed man in his mid-thirties entered.

"Don't say a word," he cautioned. It was Callie's defense attorney date. "I'm Matthew Nillson. I've been retained as Eve's attorney. May I speak with my client?"

"When did you call a lawyer?" Webster asked.

Eve shrugged, her eyes wide. "I didn't."

Matt shot her a warning look. "Make sure you turn the speaker off, Detective." When they were gone, Matt sat. "Do you know the meaning of 'Don't say a word'?"

She ignored that, going for the obvious issue. "I can't afford to pay you."

"It's okay. I do pro bono every so often. Callie called me. She drove to the scene, but the police said you'd been taken away. She was very upset."

"I didn't mean to scare her. Look, Matt, I really appreciate you coming, but I don't think I need an attorney. After today I'll need a new career, but not an attorney."

"Callie said you'd say you didn't need me. Did they let you keep your cell phone?"

Eve sighed. "No."

He nodded, as if that were all the proof he needed. "Tell me your story, Eve. Let me decide if you need me or not."

Eve considered it. "You're my lawyer, right? So everything we say is privileged."

He lifted his brows. "With a few exceptions."

"I didn't kill anybody. But, if you can secure anonymity for my testimony, that would be a big help. So. From the beginning. Two years ago I got into grad school . . ."

* * *

Monday, February 22, 7:00 p.m.

Abbott, Jack, and Noah stood at the mirror, watching Eve in the interview room with Matthew Nillson, the speaker turned off. "I want to know what she knows," Abbott said. "Damn attorneys."

"She's probably worried she's in trouble for being a phone sex provider," Jack said. "We should have questioned her in the car."

"Why didn't you?" Abbott asked, annoyed.

"I wanted to," Jack said. "Mr. White Knight here wouldn't let me say a damn word."

Noah glared at him before returning his attention to Eve. "I wanted to know what I was dealing with." Now he did. And it was worse than he'd ever imagined.

Abbott blew out a breath. "Now she's lawyered up."

"I don't think she killed any of these women, Bruce," Noah said. "Do you?"

"I don't want to. But until she tells us what she knows, she's a suspect. Got it?"

Noah opened his mouth to protest, then closed it. "Got it."

"So what are we dealing with?" Abbott asked.

Noah didn't take his eyes off her face, not wanting to remember all the things he'd just read about Evelyn Jayne Wilson, knowing he'd never be able to forget. "She was assaulted, almost six years ago, left for dead. In fact she did die, twice, on the way to the hospital." Bile burned his throat, thinking of what Eve had endured. Stabbed, strangled. Assaulted. "She recovered, some. Then two years later, she was kidnapped."

Abbott's eyes widened. "Same perp?"

"No, different one. She was working for a shelter aiding

battered women escaping their abusers. Dangerous stuff. You remember that woman in Chicago a few years back? The one that kidnapped a deaf kid, then killed something like a dozen people?"

"Yeah," Abbott said slowly and pointed to Eve. "You mean she . . ."

"Was kidnapped by this killer, too. The Chicago cops credit Eve with saving the kidnapped boy's life. She didn't kill these women, Bruce."

Abbott sighed heavily. "But she knows who did."

"She knows something. I think if she knew who did it, she would have already told us."

"See if you can get her to talk about Siren Song, at least to tell us where we can find the owner, Cassandra Lee. I've got Sutherland and Kane looking for her."

"And Sutherland and Kane found her." Olivia Sutherland entered the observation room from the hall. "And lost her again. Faye said I'd find you here. Cassandra Lee lives in Uptown. By the time Kane and I got down there, she'd left. Her doorman said he hailed her a cab. He said he didn't hear where she told the cab to go."

"Did you believe him?" Noah asked.

Olivia shrugged. In her early thirties, she was blonde, graceful, and a damn good cop. Micki said Olivia was Eve's family friend. Noah had questions, but he'd save them.

"No," she said, "but we couldn't prove he was lying. Kane's pulling her credit cards to try to track her. We alerted area airports, bus stations, and rental car facilities." She started, staring at the mirror. "What's Eve Wilson doing here?"

"She found the last victim," Noah said. "She called me."

Olivia's lips closed tightly.

"What?" Abbott demanded.

"She called me, too," Olivia said. "Earlier this afternoon. She left a message on my phone at my desk. I was just about to call her back. How does she know the victim?"

"Vic*tims*," Abbott said. "She knew Martha and Christy. From Siren Song."

"No way. No how. Eve is not mixed up with sex ops. Let me talk to her."

"That's her lawyer," Jack said. "Good luck."

Olivia knocked on the window and Matthew Nillson came out to the observation room. "I'm a family friend. I'm going to talk to her."

Olivia started to push past, but Nillson stopped her. "My client wants to talk to you all, too, but she's afraid of the impact it will have on her work."

"What impact?" Jack asked. "Guys call, get off, she gets paid. Where's the impact?"

Nillson stared at him. "What are you talking about?"

"Your client," Abbott said. "She works for a company called Siren Song. They provide phone sex services."

Nillson was still staring. "And you think Eve works for them?"

"She knew Martha Brisbane from work," Noah said. "Martha worked for Siren Song."

"We have epic misunderstanding here," Nillson said. "Eve's a grad student working on her master's in psychology. She knows Martha and Christy through her duties there. She thought it was strange that you asked for a personnel list. Now that makes sense."

"So Eve doesn't work for Siren Song?" Abbott asked carefully.

Thank God. When Noah saw her at Martha's, he'd thought it was fate. *Maybe it was.*

Nillson shook his head. "Um, no. She does not work for Siren Song."

"Told you," Olivia said with satisfaction. "So why did she want a lawyer?"

"Because she's found herself in a corner. She's seen information she shouldn't have seen. Information that led her to two of the victims. She's worried that if her role in helping you comes out, she'll be expelled. She'd like to be a confidential informant."

"A CI?" She was staring into the mirror, but Noah got the impression she wasn't looking at them, but at herself. He'd watched her tending bar, watching everyone else so cautiously. Knowing about her background, her innate caution made perfect sense.

He'd watched her, wishing he was a different man, wanting to shield her from himself. Now she needed shielding from whatever danger she'd stumbled into.

Noah cleared his throat. "We can proceed on a CI basis, right, Bruce?"

Abbott was also watching Eve, thoughtfully. He nodded. "Okay. For now."

"Then, let's begin," Matthew said. "She has a hell of a story for you."

Monday, February 22, 7:20 p.m.

Eve was relieved when Olivia came through the door. Webster and Phelps followed, along with Abbott, their captain. Matt closed the door as Olivia took the seat next to her.

"They've agreed to keep your role confidential," Matt said taking his seat.

Eve nodded, still guarded. "I appreciate that."

Webster sat across from her. Again, something was different. Where she'd seen anger and compassion, now his eyes flickered with relief. Matt looked almost amused.

Abbott reached across the table to shake her hand. "I'm Captain Abbott."

"I know. Vodka, straight up."

"We're very interested to hear your story," Abbott said.

Jack Phelps hadn't said anything at all, which was highly uncharacteristic. He stood off to the side, back against the wall, watching. He seemed . . . disappointed.

Eve glanced at Olivia. "What just happened?"

Olivia's lips twitched. "I'll tell you later. It'll make your day."

Webster looked uncomfortable. "We're ready to listen."

Eve met his eyes, again sensing she could trust him. Six years had taught her a great deal about who she could trust. Webster was the real deal. "I wanted to tell you earlier, but I wasn't sure you'd believe me. I'm not sure I believe me. I'm a grad student. I've wanted to become a therapist for a long time. To help victims of violent crime."

Webster nodded. "I understand."

She was certain that he now did. "I'll tell you what I know. But first, can you tell me when Christy died?" *Please say it was before I met you on Martha's doorstep.* She'd been rehashing that moment in her mind, hoping her selfish desire to keep her secret hadn't cost Christy Lewis her life.

"The ME thinks it was sometime early this morning," Webster said kindly.

Relief had her shoulders slumping. "Thank you. All

right. My thesis is on the use of the virtual world to improve self-esteem."

"Virtual world?" Abbott asked with a frown.

"RPG. Role play games," Eve added when he still frowned. "Like Shadowland."

"It's a computer game," Olivia said.

"It's more than a game," Eve said. "It's a community. You can meet people, have a job, buy property. All with complete anonymity. At least that's how it's supposed to be."

"Their motto is 'Sometimes you want to go where no one knows your name,'" Jack said. "I've played. A little."

"Well, a lot of people can't play 'a little.' Martha couldn't. That's why we picked her for my study. I wanted to tap the potential of the virtual world as a teaching tool. Like a big flight simulator, only to teach life skills, socialization. I wanted to help people who couldn't function in the real world to . . . practice in the virtual world."

"So a person who was socially clueless could learn to interact without the fear of rejection," Webster said.

"Yes. I want to help these people leave the virtual world and make lives for themselves in the real one. This is important to me. I've worked hard to get here, to get into grad school, and I didn't want to lose it. Which is why I didn't tell you earlier."

"All right," Webster said. "So where do Martha and Christy fit in?"

"We recruited subjects for my study. People who'd never played before, like Christy Lewis. People who dabbled, like Detective Phelps. And what we called our 'ultra-users,' like Martha Brisbane. Martha averaged eighteen hours a day in Shadowland."

"Eighteen hours?" Abbott said, shaking his head. "How did she have a life?"

"I wondered how Martha made a living, because she was in the game all the time."

At that Webster actually blushed. Eve glanced around, only to find everyone in the room casting their eyes everywhere but at her. "Okay, what did I miss?"

Olivia sighed. "Martha was a phone sex operator, Eve. When you told Detective Webster that you knew her from her work . . ."

Eve's mouth fell open. "That explains a lot." She felt her own cheek heat and knew her face was aflame, leaving her scar starkly white. "For the record, I don't do . . . that."

Webster cleared his throat. "I'm sorry we thought so."

A hysterical giggle bubbled up and she shoved it back. "Okay. Moving right along."

"Your study," Olivia prompted.

"Our subjects do exercises to increase self-awareness. Like find three people with whom you have something in common. It started out by them finding people that looked like them. Or their avatars. Later, they dug deeper for hobbies and personal interests."

"Avatars?" Abbott asked, then shrugged. "Sorry. I'm old."

Eve smiled at him. "No, you're not. An avatar is like a game piece. Like when you play Monopoly, you're always the . . . ?"

"Shoe," he said.

"I'm the iron," she confided and Abbott smiled back. "An avatar is what you look like in the virtual world. Martha was a sex goddess named Desiree. Christy was a former Miss Universe and champion ballroom dancer named Gwenivere."

"Who are you?" Webster asked softly and she started, not expecting the question.

"Me? Oh, lots of different people," she evaded. "But for the purposes of this study, I started as Pandora. I own a shop called Façades Face Emporium. I sell avatars."

"Sell?" Abbott leaned forward, interest in his eyes. "You sell things in this world?"

"You can sell all kinds of things. When you enter the game you can design your own avatar, but it's from a template. If you want anything more unique, you pay someone. I don't charge a lot for my avatars, which is why I get a lot of business, especially with people new to the World."

"Like many of your test subjects," Webster said.

"Exactly."

"You were watching them," Jack said. "As Pandora."

Eve nodded. "Yes. That's where I get into trouble."

"Why were you watching them?" Webster asked.

"My concern was having subjects abuse Shadowland. The ultra-users did, but they were our control. I worried that people who had full lives in the real world would be sucked in, so I monitored usage. We also measured personality changes. Mood swings, changes in sleep, missing work. And suicidal tendencies."

"Oh." Webster leaned back, understanding in his eyes. "You read Martha committed suicide. You thought it had something to do with your study. With the game."

"That was my fear. I'd wanted to test subjects monthly for mood changes, but my advisor wouldn't approve that frequency. We tested every three months instead. I was, and still am, worried that that's not often enough."

"So you monitored them from the inside," Abbott said. "Clever."

"And against the rules, Captain. I was only supposed to know these people by a number. I got worried when a few of them started spending huge hours in the World. It was like recruiting people for a gambling study and watching them become overnight addicts. It was taking over their lives."

"So you went undercover," Olivia said.

Eve nodded. "I opened Façades and waited for people to come to me. It was the least intrusive method I could conceive. I could chat with them, gauge their moods, and they didn't know who I was. Martha's Desiree was one of my best customers. She was an obsessive face upgrader. Then about a week ago, Desiree disappeared."

"What did you do?" Webster asked.

"Worried. Hoped Martha had gone on a real-world vacation, but I knew she hadn't. She was hard-core. And she'd been like that for months before the study began."

Webster frowned. "How long had she been a gamer, in total?"

"I'd have to check my notes, but maybe a year?"

Webster looked over his shoulder at Phelps. "It's when everything changed for her."

Phelps was nodding. "The mess in her apartment, missing her bills. The fights with her mother. Makes sense. So Martha disappeared. Then what?"

"I went looking for her. I didn't find Martha, but I did find Christy. Every single night Christy would go to the club. It's called The Ninth Circle."

"Of hell?" Webster winced. "Lovely."

"It's a dance club, a social center. Christy's Gwenivere was a party girl. I'd use Greer—that's another of my avatars—to check on her and my other red-zones, the subjects I most worried about."

"How many red-zones do you have?" Webster asked.

"Right now, five more, with another dozen brewing. I just checked on Christy last night, when I got home from Sal's. She was dancing and flirting, same old."

"So how did you know who these people were in real life?" Jack asked.

"This is where I really get into trouble. I broke double-blind."

The detectives glanced at one another, their confusion clear.

"Double-blind means I don't know who they are and they don't know which group they're in. It's supposed to be sacrosanct."

"But you peeked," Olivia murmured.

"Big time." Eve rubbed a tight cord in the back of her neck. "I broke in, located the test numbers of the subjects I was most concerned about, and their real-world names."

"And real-world addresses?" Webster asked sharply.

Eve closed her eyes, trying to figure out how to keep Ethan's involvement secret. "Not until today. I needed to know where to find Christy. I'd just come from Martha's. You said she'd been murdered. And here's where it gets incredibly unbelievable."

Eve looked at Webster. "I'd set a Google Alert for Martha. This morning it popped up, with an article saying she'd committed suicide. I didn't know what to do. I ended up going to my advisor. I told him about Martha."

"You admitted you broke the double-blind?" Webster asked. "That was brave."

"It was the right thing to do," she said and saw respect in his eyes. "I couldn't let anyone else's life be ruined by this study. But my advisor got angry. I gave him a printout of the article about Martha. He . . . shredded it and told me I'd never seen it."

"Bastard," Abbott murmured.

"Technically, he was right. Morally he wasn't. I knew where Christy worked. She'd told me about her job when she came to Pandora's. Christy was lonely. She just wanted to talk. She was worried about getting fired for being on-line so much, but couldn't stop."

"She was addicted," Webster said quietly and Eve nodded sadly.

"I went to see her in real life, but she hadn't come to work. I thought she was home, playing. I thought if I couldn't find Christy, I should at least pay my respects to Martha. That's when I saw you, Detective Webster."

"And when you called me?" Olivia asked.

"Not yet. I went home, got online." Eve felt her heart start racing all over again. "I went to Christy's house, in the World. There was a black wreath on the door and . . ." She swallowed hard. "She was hanging. And her shoes had fallen off."

"How?" Webster asked, his eyes narrowed.

"The same way they were in the real world. I almost called 911, but it sounded too crazy. So I called Olivia here at the station. I didn't have her cell."

"That'll change," Olivia said. "My sister will kick my ass if anything happens to you."

Eve's smile was wan. "Can't have that. I figured you could get her address, that you could check on her and make sure she was okay. I didn't think you'd think I was crazy."

"How *did* you find Christy's address?" Webster asked, more quietly this time.

"Don't answer that," Matt said, then lifted his brows at Webster's scowl. "For now."

"I went to see Christy," Eve said, "hoping it was a sick joke. But it wasn't."

"What about Martha's door?" Webster asked. "Did it have a black wreath, too?"

"I didn't check today. I was too rattled. But it didn't as of yesterday."

"Let's check when we're done here," Webster said. "What about Samantha Altman?"

"She may live in Shadowland, but she wasn't in my study. I'm sorry."

"How do you know?" Webster pressed, and Matt Nillson stepped in.

"All you need to know is that Eve checked the list and Altman wasn't there."

Webster shook his head. "Two of my victims were in her study. Not a coincidence."

"That's exactly what it is. Hear me out," Eve added. "Two victims spent inordinate amounts of time in the virtual world. Your third might have, too, but not as part of my study. Whoever killed them knew Christy played, because he simmed the crime scene."

"Simmed?" Abbott said.

"I'm sorry, Captain. Simulated. Maybe he knew all three from the World. Maybe he preyed on them there." That Christy wouldn't have been there except for her study was something Eve couldn't dwell on right now. The guilt would come later.

Webster was shaking his head. "What are the odds that he'd meet two of your test subjects at random, Eve?"

"Pretty high, if he's local. We required our subjects to come in for evaluations. They had to be local. We stacked the deck, geographically speaking. If he was looking for women from the Cities, he would have had a larger-than-average pool to choose from."

"That does make sense," Webster admitted.

"And we don't even know if Samantha Altman was a player," Abbott said.

"Gamer," Eve murmured.

"Gamer," Abbott repeated. "Until we find differently, Samantha was not a *gamer.*"

"The other connection," Jack said, "could be Siren Song."

"Or something you don't know yet," Abbott said. "For now, we assume nothing."

"At least we know he met Christy in this Shadowland," Webster said. "We need to use that to find him. Will you help us, Eve?"

"Of course. Tell me what you need me to do."

Monday, February 22, 7:45 p.m.

Liza had held her tears until she'd made it home from the police station. Sitting at her kitchen table, she looked again at the paper the officer had given her. She'd gone to file a missing person report and the officer had put the information in the computer.

Then he'd looked at her with a frown. "You said your sister cleaned buildings."

"She does," Liza had insisted, but he'd shaken his head.

"Afraid not." He'd turned his monitor so she could see for herself.

She was still . . . stunned, two hours later. A mug shot.

SOLICITATION, the charge read. "We picked Lindsay up for hooking two months ago. You didn't know?"

Lindsay had chosen to . . . sell herself. And now she was missing. *I have to find her.*

She didn't have the first idea of where to begin looking. She'd figure it out. She'd find some hookers, start asking questions. Somebody must know her sister. Somebody must have seen her. *I have to know.*

Lindsay could be alive somewhere, hurt. *Needing me. I have to try.*

Chapter Seven

Monday, February 22, 8:15 p.m.

Amazing." Abbott watched as Eve sat at his desk showing them Shadowland.

Noah sat on Eve's right, more interested in the focus in her face. She was giving them what she knew in a professional way. Well, almost everything she knew.

Her attorney sat at the round table across from Abbott's desk, as did Olivia, two people who wanted to protect Eve Wilson. *So I'm not the only one.*

She glanced at him from the corner of her eye. "Can you see the screen, Detective?"

She didn't like to be watched. "Yes. Can you show us your Pandora avatar shop?"

"I thought we were waiting for Detective Phelps."

"He's gone back to the crime scene. He'll join us if he's able."

"All right." She typed in a few commands. "Welcome to Façades Face Emporium."

Abbott let out a low whistle. "All those faces. That's just damn creepy."

One side of her mouth lifted. Noah had always thought she'd conjured her Mona Lisa smile. Now he knew a monster had cut her face, damaging nerves on one side.

"Like an old Vincent Price flick," she said. She clicked

her mouse, bringing up a female avatar with blonde hair and a sweet face. "Meet Pandora. She runs the shop."

Pandora. She'd known all of this would bring her grief, but she'd done it anyway.

"Customers come in, try on faces," she said. "We chat. It's almost . . . real."

"Indeed," Abbott said. "Show me Martha Brisbane's face."

"Here are Desiree's last six faces, top quality. Martha had Shadowbucks to burn."

"Where did she get it?" Noah asked. The faces were ethereal. Beautiful.

"I don't know. Most serious gamers keep a balance sheet. It would be on her PC."

Micki had found nothing on Martha's computer. Noah hoped Christy's wasn't wiped.

"What do you do with the money you earn, Eve?" Olivia asked from the round table.

"Mostly pay the rent. Façades is on the Strip. Location, location, location. What's left, Pandora donates to virtual charity." Again the half smile. "She's a community activist."

As was Eve. "You designed *all* these faces?" Noah asked and she nodded.

"I wanted to be an artist, long time ago. But my hand was damaged, so I got into graphic design. Drawing faces was much easier with a mouse than a pen."

That she'd begun creating faces when hers was scarred was insight he didn't think she'd want him to pick up. "You're very good," he said and her cheeks pinked.

"Thank you. I've studied faces for a long time. People make instant decisions about whom to trust, and facial features are key. I track the faces my customers choose with what kind of character they become. Kind of a side psychology hobby. Where to next?"

"Martha's virtual house first," Noah said.

"Let's get Greer." A redhead appeared, very buxom and very sparsely clothed.

Abbott choked on a laugh. "Well, nobody's gonna be able to describe her face."

"That was the idea," she said, embarrassed, then rolled her eyes. "Geeze."

Noah bit back a smile. "I got the meaning behind Pandora. Why Greer?"

She shrugged self-consciously. "It means 'guardian' or 'protector.'"

"I see." And what he saw, he liked. Very much. *Fate*, he thought. *Maybe*.

A cell phone rang. "Mine," Olivia said. "Miss Lee, Siren Song, just checked in for her flight to Vancouver. I'm meeting Kane at the airport. You'll bring me up to speed?"

"Of course," Noah said. "Call us when you get Miss Lee."

"Thanks, Olivia," Eve called. "This is the trendy part of the city," she said as Greer strode confidently down a crowded street. "Martha's Desiree lived well."

"Is it always dark outside?" Abbott asked.

"No. It runs on real time. If you work real-world days, you play in virtual-world nights."

"Or you can spend eighteen hours a day online like Martha did," Noah said.

"Too many do." Eve walked Greer down a hallway. "There's Martha's black wreath."

It spanned the width of the door. "This wasn't there yesterday?" Noah asked.

"No. You want me to go inside?"

"Depends," Noah said dryly. "Do you need a virtual warrant?"

Eve smiled. "I have connections. If I need a warrant later, I can get one."

"Then by all means." But levity vanished when Greer opened the door and he stared, stunned. "Damn. It's just like the real scene. Down to the shoes."

Eve zoomed in on the avatar's face. "Whoever did this accessed Martha's online file. He made up her Desiree face like a hooker's, which means he edited her avatar."

"I thought it was your avatar," Abbott said. "Your design."

"Some designers lock their code so clients can't alter anything. I leave mine open."

"Don't your customers go in and edit themselves?" Noah asked.

"Sometimes. Mostly they just change their dress colors. Whoever changed Desiree's face was in Martha's file and may have left something behind. Did you find her computer?"

"Yeah, but it was wiped," Noah said. "We're trying to lift data from the drive."

"That would be a way," she murmured, emphasizing the *a*.

Noah leaned forward a hair. "There's another way?"

She leaned back a hair. "Well, sure. You can ask ShadowCo nicely to let you into her file or . . . your forensic people can hack their way in from another computer."

"You wouldn't know how to do that, would you, Eve?" Abbott asked.

"Eve," Matthew warned from his seat at the table.

Noah had almost forgotten he was there. He wondered how to make him leave.

Eve smiled wryly. "It's really not that hard. High school kids do it all the time."

She hadn't denied hacking, Noah noted. "Take us to the club. Ninth Circle."

The club was a neon castle where flames burst from the turrets. Greer pushed her way in, stride confident. Eve moved that way, tall and sure of her own space. He wondered how she'd managed that given her past.

"The band sucks," he said, wincing at the screeching noise.

"True. But nobody comes here for the music. What do you want to see?"

"Do you see who Christy was dancing with last night?" Noah asked.

She searched the room bursting with gyrating avatars. "No. He was one of Claudio's. Claudio runs the most exclusive avatar shop in Shadowland. But the dancer-guy's not here now. And I never spoke to him so I don't know his screen name."

"Write down a description," Abbott said. "We can track him through his registration."

"Maybe," Eve said doubtfully. "If he used his real name. Hardly anyone does. The only place you'll find real personal info is through the banks and money exchanges."

"Follow the virtual money," Noah said. "I guess that's true everywhere."

She logged off. "I'll get on later from home. If I see him, I'll call you right away."

"Don't approach him," Noah said. "We'll take it from here."

She nodded, her dark eyes serious. "Of course."

He knew she lied, but didn't care. Let her hack in. It would save them a lot of time.

Matthew Nillson had also risen. "I'll take you home, Eve."

I don't think so, Noah thought. He thought about the flash of hunger he'd seen in her eyes the night before. That their paths had crossed today could be no accident.

"I'd prefer if someone could take me to my car," she said. "It's still up at Christy's."

"Then I'll take you. It's still a crime scene," Noah said when Nillson started to object.

"It's okay," Eve said to Nillson. "I'll be careful of what I say."

"For the record, I'm telling you it's not wise," he said and she smiled, then winked.

"Thanks for helping me. I'll give Callie a good report. I'm ready, Detective. Let's go."

Monday, February 22, 9:00 p.m.

Webster's inside source had been at Christy Lewis's house and in all the excitement had dropped her keys. Careless of her, he thought as he crept up the three flights of stairs to her apartment. She wasn't home now, but she'd be back. He could wait.

She'd have to catch a ride with someone else as she had no car key. He doubted Eve was as foolish as Christy, who'd kept keys under her doormat and under her car.

He hoped whoever brought Eve home would just drop her off at the front entrance downstairs, where he would be waiting. He hoped she'd be alone, for her companion's sake and his own. He'd killed two at a time before, but it was logistically more difficult.

It would look as if she'd left town for a few days. Finding a dead body could be so stressful, after all. He wanted Eve silenced. He wanted no connection between her thesis and his six victims. She shouldn't know of any connection. She shouldn't know Christy was a participant in her study. And maybe she didn't, but he wouldn't count on it.

He opened her front door and slipped inside. She was tidy, but her roof leaked. If he had to listen to that constant dripping into pots, it would certainly make him insane.

Eve wouldn't have to worry about the dripping for much longer. The gun in his pocket would ensure her compliance as he forced her into his SUV. The syringe in his other pocket would keep her quiet during transport. Disposal in his pit would ensure no one would ever find her. And whatever happened in between . . . Icing on the cake.

To his surprise he saw her laptop on the arm of a stuffed chair. He hadn't expected she'd leave it behind. He'd definitely be taking that with him. But there should be more. Papers. Notes. He needed everything connecting to her thesis. He was searching her desk when he heard a door slam below. *Damn.* He'd wanted to catch her downstairs.

"Evie?" A man was coming. Footsteps pounded as the man ran up the stairs. "Evie?"

Her door stood ajar and there was no time to close it. He darted into the coat closet empty-handed, listening, pulse racing. *I should have grabbed the laptop first and run.*

"Evie?" The man pushed the front door open. Through a crack in the closet door he watched him come into the living room and stop a foot from where he hid. All he could hear was the pounding of his own heart as he lifted his eyes, higher, assessing the stranger. The man was big, far too big to overpower long enough to get a syringe in his neck. *Shoot him. Now.* But that would leave quite a mess and getting that gorilla body down three flights of stairs would be difficult to say the least.

Perspiration beaded his forehead and he stood poised, his finger on the trigger.

"Evie. You left your door unlocked. *Again.*" The man's annoyance became fear and he rushed back to the bedroom. *"Evie?"*

Get the laptop. He slipped from the closet and took a step toward the stuffed chair when he heard footsteps returning. *Damn.* Leaving the laptop, he ran through the door and down the first flight as Eve's visitor came rushing back to the living room.

He crept down the remaining stairs and climbed into his SUV, adrenaline pumping. A red pickup truck was parked on the street. It had not been there when he went in.

He brought up a license plate lookup site on his Black-Berry and keyed in the man's Illinois plate. His name was David Hunter. *Means nothing to me. Maybe he'll go away.*

He certainly hoped so, because if not, he'd have to get rid of him, too. Because eliminating Eve was of paramount importance. She knew far too much.

Monday, February 22, 9:15 p.m.

"I can bring you back tomorrow, and you can search for your keys in the daylight," Webster said as he pulled away from Christy's house.

"I must have dropped them when I got cuffed."

He hesitated. "They didn't hurt you, did they?"

Treating her carefully was a common reaction of people on learning of her assault. Normally it annoyed, but tonight, coming from him . . . it hurt.

"No," she said sharply, then sighed. "I can always tell when someone knows what happened. That you found out is okay, but it's not okay to treat me like I'm broken, because I'm not." She smiled to soften her words. "Everyone wants to know about my scar, and the evil villains, and what it was like to die, and did I see bright lights and God. You've got questions. Stop tiptoeing around and ask them."

He shot her one of his unreadable glances before returning his eyes to the road. The minutes ticked by as she waited for him to ask what he really wanted to know, but he didn't. Instead the air between them grew heavy. Charged. Dangerous, even.

Which seemed dichotomous as she actually felt safer right here, right now, with him, than she had in years. The danger was the same she sensed every time she watched him framed in Sal's doorway. That feeling of standing on the edge. A precipice.

Of putting out her foot and feeling only air.

Hot, heavy air. It was intoxicating. Her skin tingled and her body throbbed even as she told herself it *wasn't going to happen.* Still, it compelled her to ask what she'd wanted to know for a year. "Why do you come to a bar and drink tonic water?"

He started. "What?"

"I've filled your drink order for a year. You never drink anything but water. Why?"

"Because I'm a recovering alcoholic," he said, then glanced over, as if surprised he'd told her. "That's not in my personnel jacket."

"Bartenders don't tell. But that wasn't really my question. Why come to Sal's at all?"

She knew, but felt a perverse need to hear him say it out loud. *That's cruel, Eve. Making him admit he wants you might make you feel better, stronger, but it'll hurt him. You can't give him what he needs. You can't give any man what he needs. So let it go.*

His jaw tightened. "I guess I like to people watch."

"So do I. Now, your partner, on the other hand . . . Jack's not a watcher."

"He's a live wire," Webster murmured. "Life of the party."

"That's what he wants everyone to believe. But I think he's alone, even in a crowd."

"I don't think he'd like to hear that." But he agreed, she could tell.

"I'm sure he wouldn't. But I can see it in his eyes, every time he hits on me when he fetches your tonic water for you."

His hands tightened on the wheel. "You want me to tell him to stop hitting on you?"

End this right now, Eve. Don't hurt him. "It doesn't really matter, the result would be the same. I'm not . . . available. For anyone." It was as kind as she could make it.

He blew out a long breath. "I see."

She could see he did. "I'm sorry, Noah," she said softly. And she was. Very much so.

He kneaded the steering wheel. "I never would have said anything to you."

"I know. And I'm flattered, but I didn't want you wondering. You're too nice for that."

His smile was grim. "Sometimes," he said cryptically. "I'm ready to ask my question."

She studied his profile, clinically, she told herself. But it wasn't true. Normally she clenched her hands to keep from touching her own scar, but at this moment she did so to keep from touching his face. Just a few feet away. His cheeks were stubbled and she wondered how that would feel. Against her fingertips. Against her own cheek.

That she'd never find out was a bitter pill to swallow. "So ask."

He turned to look at her, his eyes intense. "Why are you not available for anyone?"

Her chest hurt, but she kept her face impassive. "If I told you that was too personal?"

"Then I'd accept that. I understand about keeping secrets to yourself."

But he'd told her a secret and she felt compelled to do the same. "I lied," she said simply. "I am broken. Therefore, unavailable."

A muscle twitched in his taut jaw. "I don't believe that."

Her throat grew tight. "You don't know me."

He was quiet for a beat. "That's fair. But that can change. Let me know you."

"Do you know how much I wish that was possible?" she said, very quietly. Her voice trembled and she firmed it. "But it's not. I'd appreciate if you would accept that. I'll be happy to help you in any way I can with this case. But it has to end there. I'm sorry."

She watched him swallow, his jaw clench. "All right," he said finally, harshly. "Then tell me about the women in your study who become addicted to this virtual world."

"Why?"

"Because your study is the link, Eve. Whoever killed at least two of these women hunted them in your game. He understands them, or that part of them at least. To catch

him, I have to think like him. So help me see the victims
the way he does."

She almost smiled. In helping him understand his victims, she'd be sharing a great deal of herself. And she was
certain he knew that. "All right. That I can do."

Monday, February 22, 10:00 p.m.

Bitch. He backed away from the blinged-out, bleached-
blonde bimbo avatar, tempted for a brief moment to abandon his plan and take her out next, wherever she lived.

Drop dead, she'd said. Women were rude when they
thought they were anonymous. He hadn't wanted to buy
her a drink. It was just his way of keeping his avatar moving. In Ninth Circle, the avatar that stopped got attention.
He did not want attention.

He was furious that he'd missed Eve, more furious that
he'd been forced to run. He'd logged in to Shadowland before he'd properly calmed down. That was a good way to
make a mistake. He couldn't afford any mistakes.

The cops knew Eve, so they knew about Shadowland.
Right now there wasn't much they could do about that. No
one knew he was here and if they did, no one knew who
he was. Importantly, no one knew who he'd target next.

The blonde bitch wasn't on his list. He made his way
through the crowd, searching for the one he'd come to see.
Rachel Ward. He'd been looking forward to this one.

Rachel married young, but never reached her fifth anni-
versary. She'd botched it all, having affairs while her husband drove a truck to support them. The husband found
out and, appropriately angry, had set fire to the motel in
which Rachel met her lovers.

Her lover was killed. Rachel had nearly died of smoke inhalation. Now, five years later, Rachel's husband sat in prison and she had a very understandable fear of fire.

Rachel worked hard all day. But at night, she played—in the virtual world. She was Delilah, a cabaret dancer performing four times a week at the Casino Royale. Tonight she was off, which meant he'd find her here, in Ninth Circle. She'd go "home" with whoever was first to buy her a drink. He'd been first a few times.

She'd fallen for the sweet virtual pillow talk afterward. He was shy, he'd told her, with women in general. It was why he'd never had a real date, why he worked all the time, on the road five nights a week, filling his lonely nights in cheap motel rooms with virtual dancing and virtual sex. She'd pitied him. She was lonely, too, she said. And needy.

He guessed so. Five years was a long time to be celibate when she'd been such a whore, and virtual sex had to pale in comparison to the real thing.

If you're ever near Minneapolis, give me a shout, she'd said. *We'll have a drink. Maybe do some real dancing.* Tonight he'd give her that shout. He'd tell her he was coming to the Twin Cities on business, but for only one night. Tomorrow night.

That would give him time to pull everything he needed together.

She set the virtual dance floor on fire, but tomorrow it was Rachel who would burn.

He glanced up, startled by the beam of headlights. He closed his laptop, hoping the driver had not seen the glow of his screen. It was Noah Webster. Driving Eve home.

He glanced at his clock, surprised by how much time had passed. He'd thought he had been in the game for only a few minutes, but the software ran slower, took longer when he used his wireless card. *I shouldn't have been searching for Rachel. I should have been watching for Eve.*

With that man still in her apartment, his only chance to grab Eve would have been at the downstairs door as she went inside. Now she was already home, and, as expected, she was not alone. Unfortunately, he doubted Webster would just drop her off and drive away. Webster was too much the white knight, he thought bitterly.

There would be no opportunity tonight, unless he shot her from where he sat, but he'd have to take out Webster first. He hated to do that. Not that he was averse to killing a cop, of course. *But if Webster dies now, his death will overshadow my case.* The press would be sympathetic to a cop killed in the line of duty and all the wonderful outrage he was about to whip up would be gone before it started.

There wasn't much choice. To get to Eve tonight, he had to go through Webster.

Unless he waited. He had her keys. He could return to her apartment once the guy with the pickup truck left. He frowned. If he left. Hunter might sleep over. He might be Eve's boyfriend. So be it. If Hunter didn't leave, he'd kill them both. He'd wait until Hunter was asleep. Horizontal. Once Hunter was out of the way, transporting Eve to his basement would be much easier.

He liked that idea better. Better to save cop killings for the end, when the public would think they'd gotten what they deserved. He slid his laptop into its case, put his SUV in gear, and drove away. He'd be back later.

*   *   *

Monday, February 22, 10:00 p.m.

Harvey Farmer stopped his car a block behind Webster's. The detectives had split up, so he and Dell had as well. Dell was following Phelps. Harvey wasn't sure that was always such a good idea. The boy had a hair-trigger temper. He hoped his surviving son had grown enough sense not to kill Phelps before they had the information to ruin them.

Harvey wanted Phelps ruined, then dead. *No martyred cops on my watch.*

He'd followed Webster from the station to the crime scene and now here, the home of the woman who'd been searching the scene for her keys, which she had not found. He wondered how she fit. It was the second time today he'd seen her with Webster.

He hadn't noticed Webster with any women and he'd been watching him for a long time. He coached pee-wee basketball on Saturdays and on Sundays had dinner with his cop cousin. Mondays he went to Sal's, and Tuesdays he hit his AA meeting downtown.

That Webster would have a woman made Harvey clench his teeth. His son had planned to raise a family, but VJ would never get that chance. Webster and Phelps had stolen one son's life. Sent Dell into a depression that had the boy half crazy.

Me, too. He hadn't had decent sleep in a year. But it would be worth it. Webster hadn't misstepped, but he would. He had before. It was a matter of time.

He hid his face as a black SUV slid by. He didn't want any notice until he was ready.

*   *   *

Monday, February 22, 10:00 p.m.

Noah had listened as she'd talked about the women she'd known as Gwenivere and Desiree and now he better understood the victims, and Eve. They weren't so different, he and Eve. But she wasn't ready to hear that. Yet.

"Thank you. Comparing the victims' attraction to the virtual world to an addiction puts it in terms I can better understand," he said and she sighed, just a little.

"When we can't meet our needs with what we possess, some of us look for escape, rather than try to change what's keeping us from what we crave. Change is hard."

"And addiction is a means, or perhaps the consequence of escape," he said.

"True. People get sucked in to Shadowland because what they find there meets their needs. Excitement. Attention. Love. Escape from a real world they can't deal with." She shrugged. "A lot of the same reasons people drink or do drugs."

There was so much more he wanted to hear her tell him. But it was late and she was pulling on her gloves. "How will you get in without your keys?"

"My friend Callie has a set. I texted her to bring them over. She should only be a few minutes, so you can go if you want. I'll be fine."

Noah bit back his impatience. "Eve, even if Samantha Altman wasn't in your study, you are connected to two dead women. How do you know you're not a target?"

"I guess I don't," she said, but she clearly didn't believe she was.

"That doesn't seem to worry you as much as it should."

She drummed her fingers on her knee. "Well, I've been thinking."

"Why am I not surprised?" he asked and she smiled wryly.

"Just listen. Let's assume he met all three victims in Shadowland. He chats them up. Sometimes people forget they're playing a role. They get caught up and become themselves again. Christy did when she came to Façades. She probably did with him, too. He finds where they live, landmarks around their house where people hang out. You hear of kids being targeted online like this, but adults forget they're vulnerable, too."

"Okay. He finds out where they live or he lures them to a meeting place."

"Exactly. 'You like sunsets, I like sunsets. You like long walks on a snowy day, me, too. We have so much in common, let's meet IRL.'"

"IRL?"

"In real life. So they meet and the women either take him home or he follows them. He could be local or he could be hitting women all over the country."

"That makes me feel better," Noah said sarcastically and her dark eyes flashed.

"I'm not trying to make you feel better. I'm trying to keep from having another woman's blood on my hands."

"So you *do* believe your study is involved."

"Only because that's why Christy was in Shadowland to begin with. Martha was there before I started my study and Samantha wasn't in my study at all. The point is, he's probably making contact with them. I'm not planning to meet anyone I meet online, so I'm safe. So don't worry. You worry too much."

"So do you, Greer the Guardian," he said softly and her cheeks heated prettily.

He wished he could touch, but knew she'd pull away.

Last night he'd been prepared to walk away, for her own good. Now . . . this was a sign too bold to ignore.

They were at a crossroads, he and Eve. She meant to walk on alone. He didn't. But he wouldn't push tonight. She'd said no, after all.

"Touché." She got out of the car. "Thanks for the ride home. You can go. I'll be fine."

"Don't be stup—" He caught himself. "Stubborn," he amended, then frowned when a shadow moved across a third-floor lighted window. "Do you have a roommate?"

She looked up at the window, worried. "No. If I did, I'd have knocked on the door."

"Then come, but stay downstairs." He ran up the stairs, tried the doorknob, hand on his gun, stepping back when the door opened. A man stood, wearing nothing but faded jeans and a towel around his neck. Steel-gray eyes flicked to Noah's gun, then back up.

"Can I help you?" he asked calmly, but his fists gripped the ends of his towel.

I'm not available, she'd said. Now Noah saw why. People called Jack handsome. Jack had nothin' on this guy, he thought bitterly. "Who are you? How did you get in?"

The man's perfect jaw clenched. "I'm a friend of the woman who lives here."

I'll just bet you are. "Do us both a favor and don't move." Noah took another step back, not taking his eyes from the man. "Eve," he called loudly. "Come up, please."

She took the stairs at a fast jog, then paused when she reached her landing. "Oh my God. *David?*" She flew past Noah, throwing her arms around Mr. Perfect, who spun her around. When he set her on her feet, it was like Noah wasn't there.

"Let me look at you," David said and tipped her chin

up. "Wow. You look good, kid. Really good. You can barely see . . ." He trailed off when her smile dimmed. "I'm sorry."

"It's okay. I had a hell of a plastic surgeon." Her smile returned. "Why are you here?"

"And how did you get in?" Noah repeated carefully.

Eve frowned up at David. "Yeah. How *did* you get in?"

David frowned back. "You left your door unlocked. *Again.*"

She shook her head, her face gone pale. "No. I didn't. I don't do that anymore. Ever."

"It was open when I got here. You have to be more careful, Evie."

"You did leave in a hurry," Noah said quietly.

"But I always lock my door. Oh my God. My computer—"

"Is still here," David said calmly and Eve drew a deep breath of relief.

"So what are you doing here?" Noah asked.

David lifted his brows. "Fixing her roof. Who are you again?"

"This is Detective Webster," she said, still anxious. "Detective, this is my old friend from Chicago, David Hunter."

Noah shook his hand, even though he didn't want to. "You came all the way from Chicago to fix her roof?" he asked, annoyed that he sounded so . . . annoyed.

"She left me a message asking how she could do it herself. I had a few days off and didn't want her climbing the roof. Look, I'm freezing. Why don't you come in?"

"It's okay. I've got to get back. Can I talk to Eve for a minute, privately?" He waited until the door was closed. "Does he come often to do home repairs?"

"He's never visited before." Eve looked at her door thoughtfully. "I think there's more to it, but I'll take a fixed roof for now. It's been a long day. Go home. I'm fine here."

He could see that. "You have my cell. And if you go back into Shadowland—"

"Greer will not approach the avatar that was talking to Christy's Gwenivere last night, and I will call you right away. Nor will I make any dates with avatars. I got it. I'm fine."

"All right." He was halfway to street level when she called his name. She looked over the rail, her dark eyes now troubled.

"I'm not with David. It changes nothing, but I didn't want you to think I'd lied to you."

He nodded hard. "I'll be in touch. Lock your door."

Monday, February 22, 10:20 p.m.

David was on her land line when she got back. "A cop brought her home." He gave her a stern look. "It's Ethan."

She winced. "Ooh. I forgot to call him back."

"Yeah. You did." He handed her the phone. "He wants to talk to you."

"Do you know how worried I've been?" Ethan's words were thundered in a whisper. Which meant he still hadn't told Dana. At least there was that.

"I'm sorry. Ethan, I just finished with the police and I haven't eaten all day. Can I call you in a little while? I'm going to need some advice on hacking anyway."

Ethan's sigh was weary. "Call my cell, not the house phone. All the kids are in bed."

David was buttoning his shirt when she hung up, his

eyes narrowed. "I'll make you dinner while you tell me what the *hell* is going on."

The sight of David in a kitchen brought back memories. "You used to cook for me."

He stilled, then resumed his search of her fridge. "While we waited for Dana to come home from the bus station," he said quietly.

Eve's guardian had picked up many a terrified woman from the bus station in the middle of the night, risking the ire of the abusive husbands that had driven them to flee. David had worried about Dana all the time, but that hadn't stopped him from supporting her efforts. Anything that needed doing around their shelter, David had attended to.

He'd been in love with Dana. Probably still was. To Eve's knowledge he'd never said a word. And then Ethan had come along and Dana had fallen like a rock. It had to be hard for David, watching Dana's family grow.

He set peppers and onions on a cutting board. "Where are your knives?"

"On that top shelf in the lockbox. Key's taped to the bottom of the box."

He looked over his shoulder, concerned. "You still dreaming?"

She shrugged, not wanting to talk about that. "Now and then. How did you know to call Ethan?"

"I was scared shitless. I did a redial on your phone and who should answer but Ethan, totally frantic. You were sitting in a police car and some woman was dead."

"I should have called him."

"Yeah, you should have. But I guess you were a little busy."

Eve watched David dice vegetables faster than a chef. "Why are you here? Really?"

"Dana used to climb on the roof. I didn't want you doing the same and breaking your fool neck. I dumped all the water out of your pots, by the way. They were overflowing."

"Thanks. For emptying my pots and for dropping everything to come out and help me. But a phone call would have sufficed. I probably wouldn't have gone on the roof."

"I had a few days off. Thought I'd get away. I'll start patching tomorrow."

Her eyes fell on the calendar on her fridge, with the big circle around Thursday. "Dana's baby shower is Thursday night," she said quietly. "At your mom's house."

His wide shoulders sagged and she knew she was right. Dana's family and David's were close. Major holidays and special occasions were spent together. To Eve's knowledge Dana had no clue how David had felt all these years. It must have been torture for him.

"So," she said briskly, "what do you know about a game called Shadowland?"

He slid the vegetables into a skillet. "Sometimes you wanna go where no one knows your name," he said, then turned to her with a grin that didn't reach his eyes.

She was genuinely shocked. "You play?"

"Here and there, between calls at the firehouse. It passes the time."

"Well then, David, dear, do I have a story for you."

Chapter Eight

Monday, February 22, 10:45 p.m.

Micki and Jack were in Abbott's office when Noah got back. Jack and Micki were reviewing case notes and Abbott was absorbed in his computer screen. "What's with Abbott?"

"He's playing the game," Jack said. "Shadowland sucked him in."

"I am not sucked in," Abbott retorted. "I am investigating Ninth Circle."

On Abbott's screen a male avatar mingled. "That's you?" Noah asked

"It is. I'll never attract a looker like Eve's Greer, although that's probably for the best. My wife wouldn't like that too much."

"Where did you get the avatar?" Noah asked.

"Bought it from Pandora's website in the game."

Noah blinked. "You? I thought you were clueless."

"I wanted Eve to think so. But everything she told us was spot on. Our killer doesn't have to have a lot of technical know-how. It is an amazing place, though."

Shaking his head, Noah went back to the table. "That's too weird," he murmured.

"I know," Micki whispered. "I think he's been playing dumb all these years, making me explain things. I've got his number now."

"I can hear well, too," Abbott called and Micki rolled her eyes.

"What do we know?" Noah asked.

"We found the snake," Jack said with a grimace. "What was left of it."

"Timber rattler," Micki said. "Outside in the snow. The head had been shot off."

"I thought the timber rattler was endangered," Noah said.

"It's threatened," Micki said. "Rarely found this time of year. They hibernate in the wild. I'm thinking this was likely a specimen. We're making calls to the zoos and universities. So far nobody's missing one, but hopefully we'll be able to track it down."

"But why?" Noah pressed. "Everything else was the same, except the snake bite."

"Because he's fucking *nuts*?" Jack asked.

"Fucking nuts and knows forensics," Micki said. "So far no prints, hairs, nothing."

The phone rang and the three of them went silent when Abbott picked up.

"Olivia," he said, then sighed as he listened. "They got the Siren Song employee list," he said when he hung up. "Cassandra Lee was cooperative when she heard the news."

Noah sighed. "Christy and Samantha weren't on the list, were they?"

"No. Web, get the list of participants in Eve's study and figure out how Samantha Altman links. Micki, do we have anything from Martha's hard drive?"

"Not yet," she admitted. "Whoever wiped it, did good. It's like she never used it."

Noah went still. "Mick, do you have those photos of Martha's messy apartment?"

"In my folder." Micki spread the photos on the table.

"Dammit. She had two monitors on her desk before," Noah said, tapping one of the photos. "We only found one. And her computer in the picture is high end. We took a cheap one. I wondered why a consultant would have such a cheap PC."

Micki scowled. "I've wasted time searching the hard drive of a decoy computer."

"This guy is very good," Jack said thoughtfully. "Very smart."

"He took Martha's computer because he knew we'd find evidence of Shadowland on her hard drive and in her Internet cache," Micki said. "We'd be able to follow her movements and maybe even who she talked to in the World."

Abbott looked grim. "Then it's important. We need access to Martha's and Christy's game files. Someone altered their avatars. We find out who, we find our man."

"You want to hack or ask to be admitted through the front door?" she asked.

"Front door," Abbott said. "Jack, kick up the search for the panty pervert, Taylor Kobrecki. Right now he's the closest thing we have to a suspect. Noah, get a list of Eve's test subjects and everyone meet back here at 8:00 a.m."

Monday, February 22, 11:15 p.m.

"You can go home, you know," Eve said to Callie, who'd arrived with Eve's keys shortly after Noah Webster had departed. "David's back from the corner store."

"Yes, he is." Callie watched David whipping a cream

sauce with a wire whisk. "I'm hoping when he finishes dinner he does something that makes him hot and sweaty."

Eve sighed. Women everywhere had the same reaction to David. She might have, too, had they met under different circumstances. Instead David had been a man she'd learned to trust when her world had been a very dark and scary place.

"Leave him alone. I want my dinner."

"Fine. So why did he just bring you two disposable cell phones?"

"He was going out for heavy cream for his sauce anyway. Mine had curdled."

"Don't be a smartass. I got you a lawyer. The least you can do is give me a hint."

"I appreciate you sending Matt, and he did a great job, but I don't want to put you in a bad position. The less you know, the better for you. Just go home. Please?"

"You're not making me feel better and I'm not going home. At least let me help."

"You didn't cause this, Cal. You shouldn't have to be involved."

"You didn't cause this either. You didn't force these women to play your game."

Eve thought of Christy Lewis, who'd never heard of role play games before she'd seen their ad for test subjects in the local paper. "Yeah, Cal, I kind of did."

"Good God. Who taught you to shoulder the burden of every person you meet?"

"I know who," David said dryly from the kitchen. "You can't fight it, Callie. It was hardwired into her by one of the best."

"Thank you," Eve said, touched, and he smiled back, but his eyes were troubled.

"Callie's right, Evie. None of this is your fault. Let the police do their jobs."

"I am. Mostly." She toggled her laptop screen to Ninth Circle. "He could be there, hunting his next victim. I can't just stand by. I have to do something."

David shook his head helplessly. "God, it's like a Dana echo in here."

"Thank you," she said again and he scowled.

"*That* wasn't a compliment," he said. "So what are you doing that you shouldn't be?"

"Reading blogs of ShadowCo people. You can learn a lot from employee blog rants."

"What do you want to learn from ShadowCo's angry employees?" Callie asked.

"I want a contact in the company. So I can hack in."

Callie nodded. "That's what I expected you to do. Can I watch?"

Eve laughed. "Sure. If I'm lucky this marketing guy who ranted about his boss, who works him like a slave, will still be in the office."

"At this time of night?" David asked.

"If it's anything like law firms," Callie said, "people will work until midnight."

"Besides, they're in Seattle," Eve added. "This blog is from a marketing genius who included his title and phone number at the end of his rant about the multi-million-dollar bonus given to ShadowCo's CEO."

"I don't know why people are so stupid as to blog about their bosses," Callie said. "Anyone in the world can see it once it posts. Idiots."

"Well, this idiot's name is Clayton Johnson." Using the disposable cell, Eve dialed.

The phone rang six times. "Johnson," he said, clipped and annoyed. Perfect.

"Mr. Johnson," Eve said, "my name is Gillian Townsend. I'm with Attenborough IT Services. We're contracted to support your company network systems."

"So?" Johnson asked impatiently. "I don't have time—"

Eve broke in before he could hang up. "We're doing server maintenance and I can see you're still logged in. In a few minutes, we'll be shutting down your server."

"No," he said angrily. "I have a report to finish and I need—"

"It's all right, sir. We're shutting down your server and immediately starting up the backup. I can validate your account on my end so that you won't have any down time."

"Oh." He sounded mollified. "Well, all right."

"What's your user name and password, please?" She looked up to find Callie staring at her like she'd grown two heads. David just looked resigned.

"JohnsonCL and sonicsrule, all one word," Johnson said.

Eve smiled. "Thank you. You won't see even a blip in your service. Be sure to change your password first thing in the morning, okay?"

"Okay. Thanks."

"My pleasure. Have a good evening." Eve hung up. "That's how it's done."

Callie looked stunned. "You lied to that man."

"Yes I did. And he gave a complete stranger his password and user name."

"You *lied* to that man," Callie repeated. "With the cell phone David bought you."

"Why do you think she wanted an untraceable phone?" David asked. "But, Evie, that Johnson guy was just an innocent bystander. You could get him fired."

"That's why I told him to change his password. If he does, he'll appear like he was security-conscious. Don't worry. Once this is over, I'll tell Ethan and he can pay a sales call to ShadowCo and show them the huge holes in their network security."

David blinked. "*This* is what Ethan does for a living?"

"Sometimes. I used to hack for him part-time when I lived in Chicago. It's a good way to get his consulting foot in the door. A company's biggest vulnerability is often its people. Ethan shows them the security hole and offers to patch it up."

"That's . . ." David shook his head. "That's dishonest."

"It would be if he used their servers for personal gain. He doesn't. He's a white hat."

Callie's lips twitched. "A white hat?"

Eve nodded. "That's what they're called, I swear. As opposed to black hats who hack in with malicious intent. If a business tells Ethan they don't want his services, he tells them where the hole was anyway. Most likely a high school kid's already found it."

"Don't these companies get mad that you hacked?" Callie asked.

"Usually they want the hole patched before the big cheese finds out. In the end, everybody wins. How would you like it if your bank's server had a security hole?"

"They wouldn't," David declared, then his features shifted uneasily. "Do they?"

"Remember when Ethan and Dana put the downpayment on the house for all their fosters? That downpayment was a retainer from your bank, buddy. Some hacker had already breached their system. They said they wished Ethan had breached it first."

"It's still dishonest," he grumbled, but without heat. He brought her a plate of pasta and cream sauce, then perched on the arm of her chair. "So you're in?"

"Not yet. Johnson was a little fish. As a marketing guy, his access rights are diddly. I need to elevate my privileges so that I can get into the client files. That'll take time."

"Why didn't you start with somebody with better access?" David asked.

"Like an IT person? Because they probably would have called the cops on me."

"Will you call anybody else?" Callie asked, fascinated.

"Not tonight. I'm going to run exploits until I find another, better hole."

"English," David murmured.

"Exploits are codes, scripts hackers use to find security holes. Hackers see network security as one big Rubik's Cube. It's there to be breached, a puzzle to be solved."

"Like mountain climbers scale Everest because it's there," Callie said.

"Absolutely. They create code that basically knocks on the walls of network security until it finds a loose brick. Knock the loose brick through and you're in."

"It's part of the game," David said. "Hackers make holes, businesses patch them."

Eve smiled at him. "Kind of like roofs. Some hackers look for loose bricks for nefarious reasons, like they want credit card info. But some do it just because it's there. They share their code because it gives them status. Hopefully one of these scripts will find a ShadowCo hole. Then I can get into Martha and Christy's files and check their movements, who they talked to, and importantly, how their avatars were altered."

"And then you'll hand it over to Detective Webster," David said.

"I promise. It'll take the cops days to get a warrant for ShadowCo files. I can access them in a day. Then they stop the killer and I don't have any more deaths on my conscience." She set the scripts to run, toggled back to Ninth Circle, and dug into her pasta. "And don't tell me they're not on my head. Because they are."

Neither of them corrected her, either because they knew she wouldn't listen or because they knew she was right. Eve patted Callie's arm. "Go home. David's here and I'll be fine."

"You won't leave her?" Callie asked. "Because even if she's not worried about that psycho coming after her, I am."

"I'll sleep on the sofa. If I can sleep on that ratty couch in the firehouse, I can sleep anywhere. Come on, Callie. It's late. I'll fix you a plate and walk you down to your car."

They were gone and it was quiet. Except for the dripping. She turned up the volume of the Ninth Circle band. It was the lesser of two evils, but just barely.

She searched the bar once again for the handsome avatar, then turned to her list of red-zones. There were still five, three of which were women. Rachel Ward, Natalie Clooney, and Kathy Kirk. She knew them only by their avatars—Rachel's cabaret dancer, Natalie's poker queen, and Kathy's real estate mogul.

Who they were in real life Eve didn't yet know. That was about to change. But first she wanted to be sure they were still present. She spotted Kathy's avatar on her bar stool, negotiating a land deal. Natalie's hung at the casino, as did Rachel's on the nights she was dancing. But on Mondays, Rachel hung at Ninth Circle with everyone else.

Eve was looking for Rachel, when a sharp knock startled her. She set her laptop aside and got up to let David back in. "Remind me to make you a key."

The words were out before the man on her welcome mat registered in her mind.

Noah Webster's face was shadowed by his hat brim, but she could see the wry humor in his eyes. "I'm flattered," he said. "But it's a little soon for that, don't you think?"

A disturbing little thrill raced down her spine. "I . . . I thought you were my friend."

"Now I'm hurt," he said mildly. "I haven't even told you why I'm here."

"I didn't mean . . ." Flustered, she looked down at her feet, got her composure, then looked back up to find him staring in that unsettling way of his. "Come in."

Webster slipped his hat from his head in a gesture she found endearing. "I saw your friend downstairs. He was looking under the hood of Callie's car. It wouldn't start."

"Callie drives a bigger hunk of junk than I do. David will find the problem."

Webster's dark brows knitted slightly. "So your friend fixes cars and roofs?"

"David does a little bit of everything," she said. "He's a fireman, too. And he cooks."

"All that," Webster said sourly and she had to chuckle.

"I've never met a woman who could resist him," she said lightly.

"Except you?" he said, too seriously, and something twisted in her stomach.

"Except me." David had earned her trust. But to fall for a man on the basis of his pleasing face? Never again. She required actions before she trusted a man now. But she'd trusted Webster, almost at first sight. To deny it would be an outright lie.

And Noah Webster had a very pleasing face. It was a bothersome admission.

"What brings you back, Detective?"

His eyes left hers and too late she remembered she'd left the disposable phone out in plain sight. He walked to her chair, picked it up. "Untraceable cell phone?"

"It's not a crime to own a prepaid phone," she said blandly, but she tensed. A bit.

"No, it's not. But, hypothetically speaking, if you learned anything, you'd tell me?"

"You'd be the first call I made. Hypothetically speaking."

"Of course." He looked at her laptop. "Did you see the guy who talked to Christy?"

"Not yet. I've been checking off and on since I got home." She didn't want him looking too closely at her screen. "Have a seat, Detective. I'll put coffee on."

But again, it was too late. "Who is this, Eve?" He pointed at the panel in the top left of her screen, the one that showed her active avatar. "Did Greer take the night off?"

She'd indeed given Greer the night off, resurrecting an avatar she hadn't used in a very long time. "I needed to get her appropriate clothing. Didn't want her to catch cold."

He sat in her chair, pulled her computer to his lap. "And here I thought you'd created a new avatar so that you could approach this dancer without breaking your word to me."

Eve sat on the sofa. "I'm not that clever."

He didn't smile. "Uh-huh. So who is this new face of Eve?"

Eve took her computer, set it aside. "What happened? Why did you come back?"

He glared at her laptop, eyes flashing with annoyance. "I need your participant list."

"I expected you'd ask once Matt Nillson was gone. He'd have a cow, you know."

"I won't say where I got it. I promise."

"I'd planned to bring it to you tomorrow anyway. Wait here. I'll be back."

Noah watched her head to her bedroom, laptop under her arm, then checked the phone. Her only call was to a 206 area code, same as ShadowCo. He knew this because he'd looked it up for his warrant request.

Eve was planning to hack into Shadowland, if she hadn't done so already. *In her place I'd do the same.* He put the phone back and considered her computer.

He'd caught a look at her new avatar. Dark, sleek, and dangerous—of a different style than her other designs, although the face had been disturbingly familiar. He knew he'd looked at a much younger Eve, before she'd met the man who'd left her for dead.

The new avatar's name was Nemesis. Noah knew Eve well enough by now to know that meant something. On his own cell, he did a quick Internet search. *Nemesis, the goddess of divine retribution.* Eve was planning to kick some virtual ass. That shouldn't arouse him, but he'd be lying if he denied it did.

Eve reappeared, a stack of papers in one hand. "It took a few minutes to print."

He took the stack. "How many people are in this study, anyway?"

"Five hundred, but you don't have to check them all." She leaned close to point at a page, but didn't touch him. He thought of how she'd thrown her arms around Hunter and felt a tug of jealousy. It was irrational, and embarrassing, but it was there.

"We have three groups," she was saying. "Group C is the one you want to focus on."

"They're in Shadowland."

"Where they do self-esteem exercises. They're broken into three subgroups—those who never played until this study, who played a few hours a month, and who played a few hours a week. They fill out diaries with their usage, but I can check their online time. The heavy users almost always lie, understating their usage."

"Like Martha."

"Actually she was honest about her habits." She pointed. "These are the top users."

"Martha and Christy are still on the list," he noted.

"I'm not supposed to know I should take them off," she said quietly. "And that sucks."

There was guilt in her tone and Noah wanted to alleviate it if he could. "When would they have been missed from the study? If you hadn't been keeping track?"

"In a few weeks, when they had to come back for their personality evals."

"Then you did good." He met her eyes. "You couldn't have stopped these murders. But you might have saved his next victim by doing everything you've done. Don't let your guilt overshadow your contribution." He smiled. "No pun intended."

"Thank you. That helps a lot more than being told it's not my fault."

He held her eyes a moment longer before she looked away, but in that moment he saw an unguarded loneliness that squeezed at his heart. Trina's words came back to hit him like a ton of bricks. *You don't deserve to be alone forever.* And he finally admitted he didn't want to be. That he'd give anything to have somebody again.

"One more question. You want people to have meaningful lives in the real world."

Her glance up was nervous, fleeting. "Yes, so?"

"So, what good is living in the real world if you have to live alone, unavailable?"

She flinched and he knew he'd overstepped, but didn't care. She walked to her front door and opened it wide, not looking at him. "Call me if you need anything else."

He stood looking at her for a few seconds before walking through the door. It closed sharply behind him and he heard the click of her deadbolt. With a sigh he walked down a flight of stairs, only to find David Hunter sitting on one of the steps, looking very cold.

"Is everything all right?"

Hunter stood. "I figured you two needed to talk about whatever happened tonight."

Noah narrowed his eyes. "She didn't tell you?"

"She witnessed a crime and gave her statement. Why? Is Evie in trouble?"

"No, she's not." Noah walked down another flight before he turned and looked back up. Hunter was watching him, his expression purposefully bland.

"Is everything all right, Detective?" Hunter asked cordially.

"No." Noah studied Hunter's near-perfect face. "You knew her, in Chicago."

"Yes." The single word was clipped and laced with warning.

"I read about what happened to her four years ago, with that kidnapping and the boy she saved. And what happened two years before that."

Hunter's jaw had tightened. "Is there a question in there, Detective?"

Yes, but he'd be damned if he knew what it was. "She has a disposable cell phone in her apartment," he said and Hunter's expression smoothed.

"I know. I bought it tonight. I left the charger for my cell back in Chicago and my phone is dead. The prepaid will keep me going until I get home."

The man's gray eyes didn't flicker an iota as he lied. "Look, I know Eve's going to hack into Shadowland's system. When she does, can you make sure she calls me?"

Hunter's lips thinned. "Why, so you can cuff her again?"

"I didn't do that, and I uncuffed her as soon as I got there. I want her to call me because she doesn't think she's in danger. I won't take the chance that she's wrong."

Now Hunter's eyes flickered, but with worry. "I'll make sure she calls you."

"Thanks." Noah hesitated. "Why did you really come, Hunter?"

"To fix her roof. Evie's like my kid sister. There's not a lot I wouldn't do for her."

A sense of relief loosened the knots in his gut. "Thanks. See you around."

"Detective," Hunter called after him, "weren't you wearing a hat when you got here?"

Noah nodded. "I thought I'd come back for it tomorrow."

Hunter hesitated. "Don't hurt her," he said quietly. "She's been through enough."

"I wouldn't dream of it."

Eve let David back in, still feeling unsettled. Angry. She'd tried to be honest but kind to Noah, but he did not respect boundaries. She locked her deadbolt, her frown deepening. "I know I locked my door this afternoon. I can picture it in my mind."

"You were rattled," David said. "You still are."

"Of course I am," she said irritably. "Two women I recruited to my study are dead."

He studied her face shrewdly. "And Noah Webster cares for you."

Eve sighed. "I know. I wish he didn't. I tried to tell him to go away."

"Now why would you do a foolish thing like that, Evie?" David asked gently.

"Not gonna happen." She sat in her chair and grabbed her pasta, now cold.

"Which? You and Webster or you and me talking about you and Webster?"

So what good is *it to live in the real world all alone?*
"Yes. Either. Both."

He shrugged. "All right. Any of your scripts finding loose bricks in ShadowCo?"

She opened her laptop. "Not yet."

"Then I'll make coffee. I guess it's going to be a long night." He puttered in the kitchen, then returned holding two cups, and it was then she noticed what looked like a walkie-talkie hanging from his belt. A baby pink walkie-talkie.

"What the hell is that?" she demanded when he put a steaming mug in her hand.

He lifted a dark brow. "Coffee."

She rolled her eyes. "No, *that*. What the hell is *that*?" She pointed to the device.

"Oh, this." He unclipped it from his belt and turned it toward her, showing her a small screen that was murky and dark. "Baby monitor. This is the receiver."

He put the receiver on her lamp table, then sat on her old sofa and pulled his laptop from a backpack as if nothing was strange about a grown man having a pink baby monitor when there were no babies in the house. *And never would be.*

"Why? And where did you get it?"

"It was going to be Dana's baby shower gift. I've had it in my truck for a week."

Eve studied the receiver, fascinated. "Where's the camera?"

"It comes with two. One is above your front door and one is outside the building door, downstairs. Wireless, range is almost four hundred feet. Infrared night-vision."

"Freaking cool. When did you install it?"

"One after I walked Callie to her car and the other just now, after Webster left. I activated the receiver while the coffee brewed. It's not rocket science."

"What did Webster say to you?" she asked, her eyes narrowed.

"What I already knew. That you don't think you're in danger, but he thinks you are." He took a sip of his coffee, his eyes not leaving hers. "And that he's interested in you."

Briefly Eve closed her eyes. "David, please." He made no apology and she sighed, turning her focus back to the camera. "If I were in danger and some killer did come after me, a baby pink camera would tip him off, don't you think?" she said and he frowned.

"Give me some credit, Evie. I put the one downstairs where it couldn't be seen. And if he comes close enough to take the camera out, we'd get his face." He connected a video cord from his laptop to the receiver. "We've got streaming video and an alarm that screeches if either camera is disconnected. Gotta love it."

"On a *baby monitor*? You've got to be kidding."

"All for under three hundred bucks. Technology meets parental paranoia," he said, then shrugged. "And my paranoia, too. I thought it would give Dana a little peace of mind to have the cameras versus the old audio monitor. She has all those foster kids, coming and going. Most are good kids, but all it would take would be one bad one."

Eve's throat tightened. *He still loves her.* What a waste of a life. Of a good heart. "Amazingly thoughtful," she said roughly. "A little used by the time she gets it, but . . ."

He didn't smile. "I'll get her another. Tomorrow I'll install something less noticeable for you than a baby pink camera, but it'll work for tonight. A woman living alone should be careful. A woman living alone who's tied to two dead women should be terrified."

Alone pierced like an arrow so that she almost didn't hear the rest. "I have a gun."

"Then give it to me. If anyone comes through your door tonight, I want to be ready."

A chill chased over her skin. "You're serious."

"About your safety? Deadly serious. Now drink your coffee before it gets cold."

Tuesday, February 23, 12:35 a.m.

Noah quietly let himself into his house, considering the way he'd left Eve, and the fine line between pursuit and harassment. He didn't want to cause her pain, stress, grief, any of those bad things. Just yesterday he'd been all set to protect her from himself. But she'd said she didn't want to be protected. He wanted to believe her.

She'd said she was broken. That he didn't want to believe, but understood. He sat down on the edge of his bed. Out of habit he picked up the photo he'd held so many times and remembered how broken he'd felt when he lost Susan and the baby.

He thought about how he'd handled his grief, compared it to how Eve had coped. They really weren't that different. They'd both hidden, escaping reality, Noah into the bottle, Eve into the virtual world. They'd both set themselves free.

And for what? To work. To protect the innocent. He thought of Eve's Nemesis avatar. He put the picture back, and got ready for bed, wondering how Eve punished the guilty in her world. She'd told him that some of her red-zone cases had relationships in Shadowland that spanned from the casual one-night stand to marriages.

His knee-jerk reaction was to wonder what possible satisfaction a man could have in a pretend relationship. Then he considered the relationships he'd had over the years. They'd been cordial, but empty, and when they were over, he'd walked away as had the woman, whichever woman it had been at the time. He'd missed the sex and the occasional benefit of sharing a meal, but other than that, there'd been nothing.

Pretend relationships were a relative thing.

And now, sitting in his silent house, on the edge of his empty bed, he understood the lure of a virtual relationship. If one was lonely, sometimes a conversation could mean more than a quick roll across the sheets. He smiled grimly. Well, at least *as* much.

He stretched out in his empty bed, but again, sleep would not come. He tossed and turned. And when he finally did fall asleep, he dreamed again, this time of Eve in an ambulance, while paramedics brought her back from death with the paddles.

His eyes opened and he stared at his ceiling. That wasn't a dream. He'd read it online in a newspaper archive. She'd died twice on the way to the hospital after having been discovered by her guardian, Dana Dupinsky, who saved her life.

Greer the Guardian. The name took on new meaning. Eve's real-life guardian had protected battered women and in working with her, so had Eve. Now she protected the subjects in her study who were being stalked by a man they thought was fantasy.

Noah's sigh echoed off the walls of his empty room. He'd been given the role of guardian and protector once, so long ago now. He'd failed his family, abysmally.

And now you're alone. He did, however, have purpose. He had a badge. He'd catch this killer, then he'd do the paperwork and move on to the next homicide.

A depressing future. He'd been sober for ten years, but at this moment wanted a drink so badly he could taste it. He rolled over, grabbed his phone, hesitated.

I hurt Brock last night. He couldn't do that again. Wouldn't.

The phone in his hand rang, startling him. It was Brock. "What's wrong?" Noah asked.

"Nothing. I, uh, didn't see you at Sal's tonight and I got worried."

"I'm working a case. Besides, I said I wasn't going back," Noah added, annoyed.

"Well, forgive me if I doubted you really meant it this time," Brock flung back. "Eve wasn't behind the bar tonight. Sal said she had an emergency."

Subtlety had never been Brock's strong suit. "I know. She was with me."

"That's good then," Brock said cautiously. "Isn't it?"

Noah's temper flared. "No. She's got a goddamn target on her head. And she wasn't *with* me. In fact she told me she wasn't with anyone, including me."

"Ouch. You need another bout in the ring?"

Noah thought of the harm he'd wreaked the night before. "No, but can you meet me for coffee? I need to get out of my house." *Out of this empty shell of a house.*

"Of course," Brock said. "Usual place?"

"Yeah. In a half hour?"

Tuesday, February 23, 2:00 a.m.

That Hunter guy was still there. Sipping coffee in the frozen seat of his SUV, he glared at the red pickup truck with Illinois plates from a block away. They'd turned out the lights in the living room. It appeared David Hunter was staying the night. No matter. It would be easier to shoot him in bed anyway.

Webster had come, then gone again. *What did Eve tell him? What did she know?*

It doesn't matter, he told himself. *Even if she knows*

about Shadowland, she can't know about me. Still, the clock inside his mind was ticking. He needed to move.

But carefully. Hunter had hidden something behind the bush next to the door to Eve's building. *Let's see what it was, shall we?*

He approached from the side of the building, grimacing when snow went in his shoes, wet and freezing. Another pair of shoes, ruined. He came up on the bush, his head down, the lapels of his coat pulled around his face.

Whatever it was, it was pink. He picked it up then furiously turned it lens down, grateful he hadn't approached from the front. *Stay calm.* The camera had not captured his face, only his thumb as he'd grasped it. And he was wearing gloves. *It's all right.*

He placed the camera in the snow and ground it under the sole of his shoe. *What the hell kind of surveillance camera comes in pink?*

He'd put his hand on the downstairs building door when he heard something inside. Footsteps, muted murmurs. Someone was coming. Hunter and Eve. *So? Kill them.*

Finger on the trigger, he retreated to the shadows, waiting for them to emerge. But they did not. He crept as close as he dared. Through the door's leaded-glass side panels he could hear arguing in loud whispers, but he could see no one.

"Call 911." It was Hunter. "Just do it. For God's sake."

"Okay, okay, I'm dialing, but don't go out there. David. *No.*"

"I thought you said it was just a dog," Hunter hissed. "Stand back and let go."

"Maybe it is. If it's not, I don't want you hurt. Hello? We may have an intruder outside." She gave the address. "Yes, I'll stay on the line . . . No, we won't go outside."

"Give me your phone and take mine," Hunter demanded. "Call Webster and tell him to get his ass over here. I'll hold with 911."

He couldn't see them unless he stood straight in front of the leaded glass, where he could be seen as well. If they took even a few steps toward the stairs, they'd be in range. *Just shoot the glass, break the window, then you can see.*

And wake the neighborhood? That would be the best way to get caught. The police were on their way. *Dammit.* He was running away for the second time tonight. Hating Hunter, he crept back the way he'd come, destroying his footprints as he did so.

Unfortunately, now Eve would be watched all the time. Protected. He had to lure her away. Climbing into his SUV, he was two blocks away when he saw the cruiser in his rearview. He gripped his steering wheel and twisted viciously. It should have been Eve's throat in his hands.

He jammed one hand into his coat pocket and felt the syringe that had been meant for Eve. His mind was racing. He'd been all primed. Ready. *I'll never sleep tonight. Just one. One to take off the edge.*

He turned the SUV toward the city. He knew where to find what he wanted.

Chapter Nine

Tuesday, February 23, 2:25 a.m.

Noah received Eve's call as he and Brock had finally gotten around to the topic he'd really wanted to discuss. Eve. He'd sent Brock back to Trina and a warm bed and with a combination of dread and anticipation, he'd come back here. Again. For the third time in one night.

Noah looked up at the pink camera over her door. There would be an interesting story to that. The door was opened by the officer who'd responded to the 911. Eve was sitting in her chair, arms around her knees. She met his eyes with weary resignation.

"Thank you for coming," she said. "David made me call."

Hunter was on the sofa, arms crossed tightly over his chest. "Damn straight I did."

"Who put up the pink camera?" Noah asked.

"I did," Hunter said grimly.

"Why are you here, Detective?" the older officer said. "This isn't a homicide."

Noah flicked a glance at Eve. "It's personal. Did you find evidence of an intruder?"

"Somebody was out there," the younger cop said. "Footprints were wiped out. One of the other cameras was pushed into the mud. Should we go door to door?"

"CSU will check the perimeter at first light. We may do door to door then. Send me a copy of your report." The cops left and Noah closed the door. "What happened?"

Hunter told the story while Noah examined the pink video receiver.

"The system triggers an alarm," Hunter finished, "if the camera loses a signal. When the guy ground it into the mud, the alarm woke me up." He hesitated. "Eve has a registered gun. She'd given it to me. I started down the stairs, but she followed."

"It's my apartment," Eve said stubbornly. "My problem and my goddamned gun."

Hunter shook his head. "And that's it. We didn't hear him or see him."

Noah met Hunter's grim eyes. "Good thinking. And fast action."

Hunter shook his head again. "I should have gone out after him."

Noah watched Eve roll her eyes, but she said nothing. "We don't know if this guy is armed," Noah said. "We've got three dead. We can't be taking chances."

"Told you so," Eve muttered.

Hunter made an annoyed sound in his throat. "Now what?"

"Now we watch Eve like a hawk," Noah said. "Eve, you don't go anywhere by yourself until we know exactly who and what we're dealing with."

"Told you so," Hunter muttered and Noah knew a small moment of relief. If nothing else, these two behaved like brother and sister.

She rose, briskly. "David made coffee. Do you want some to go?"

He realized for her, none of this had changed anything

personal. "No thanks. I've had enough coffee tonight. Don't go anywhere alone."

"She won't," Hunter said flatly, then softened his tone. "Thank you for coming."

"Yes," Eve said, not meeting Noah's eyes. "Thank you. I'm tired. David, can you see Detective Webster out?" Without waiting for an answer she went back to her room.

Hunter puffed out his cheeks. "Well."

Noah frowned. "Well? Well what? What's that supposed to mean?"

"That you're under her skin." He walked him to the door. "Give her time."

"I have lots of that," Noah murmured, then narrowed his eyes. "Why pink?"

"It was a baby shower present. Do you know a Detective Sutherland?"

Noah was surprised at the sudden topic change. "Olivia? Damn fine cop. Why?"

"Her sister Mia's one of my best friends," he said. "Another damn fine cop. Olivia and I were both in Mia's wedding. When you see her, tell her I said hi."

"I will. And, I meant it. That was good thinking. You may have saved Eve's life."

Hunter's eyes hardened. "This guy knows Eve's involved. How does he know?"

"I was wondering the same thing," Noah said grimly. "Keep me on speed dial."

"I will. Don't forget your hat."

"I'll leave it here for a while." If it was here, he had an excuse to return. "Thanks."

Tuesday, February 23, 2:25 a.m.

Lindsay never would have wanted her to see this side of humanity. *Too late, sis*, Liza thought dully, as she waited for a bus to the next neighborhood. She'd been searching for three hours and she was already ready to give up. Most of the prostitutes hung out in bars and hotels this time of year. The bars wouldn't let her in because she wasn't twenty-one. And nobody in the hotels had seen Lindsay.

A well-intentioned bouncer had let her into one of the bars long enough to get warm. A waitress gave her a coffee. Neither had seen Lindsay. In her pocket was the napkin on which the bouncer had written directions to another place she might look. She had enough change for bus fare there and bus fare home.

And if you find nothing? Then what?

I don't know.

Numbly she watched as a girl came out of the bar she'd just left, picking her way over the ice in five-inch stiletto heels. The girl's legs were bare, her short skirt barely covering her butt, her wig teased big. She pranced to the end of the block and leaned against a light pole. A minute later a black SUV slid to a stop, rolled down its window.

"Don't do it," Liza murmured, as if words could help. The girl climbed up into the SUV and it did a U-turn in the street, headed back the way it had come.

Tuesday, February 23, 3:25 a.m.

He drew a deep breath, the climax shuddering through him. Slowly he released the hooker's throat. He relaxed, lowering his body to sit on the body he straddled, his seed glistening on her skin. Under her wig she'd had short dark hair and a long neck and as he'd choked the life out of her, he'd imagined her face was Eve Wilson's.

It should be Eve lying here, on this disgusting, foul-smelling bed. Dead, her open eyes staring at nothing at all. It was supposed to have been Eve. But it wasn't.

But the words he'd whispered in the hooker's ear as she'd slid into her little ketamine stupor would drive terror into Eve's heart when she finally lay here beneath him on this bed. *Twine around your throat, pulling tighter, you can't breathe. You're going to die.*

The hooker had awakened, gasping for air, thinking she was being strangled. Then, she really was. He did love it when fantasy met reality with such perfection.

He climbed off the girl, yanked on the concrete slab, and winced. The girl from Sunday wasn't quite done yet. He stared into the pit for a moment, troubled. Two days. He'd never gone only two days between kills.

He had to be more careful, he thought as he dragged the hooker's body from the bed, rolling her into the pit. He'd never gone to the same street twice, but he had to-night. It was like he'd been on autopilot as he'd driven away from Eve's.

It was the stress. When this was over and he was done, he'd go back to his old way. Things would be normal again. He donned his protective gear, performed his duties, toss-ing the girl's clothing in after her. When he was finished, he pulled the slab closed and picked up the girl's cheap stilettos, carefully placing them heel out on the shelf next to Christy Lewis's very expensive Manolos.

He stood back, surveyed his collection. It was a veri-table time capsule of women's shoe fashions spanning nearly thirty years. Most were, of course, on the most flamboyant fringe of fashion, the shoes no respectable woman would be caught dead wearing. Most were small sizes, as his victims had been. It was a more efficient use of his energy that way. Smaller victims were more easily overpowered. More easily transported. Leaving all his energy for what happened in this room, as it should be.

There were exceptions. His eyes lowered to the bottom shelf, far left. Next to the worn pair of work boots he'd removed from the man who'd dug his pit were a pair of scuffed pumps, black, size eleven. They were plain. Ugly. Matronly, even. They'd been out of style thirty years ago. Which was why they'd been relegated to the church charity bin.

He remembered her digging them from the bin along with the articles of clothing that had been too worn to make decent rags. A few dresses for herself. Trousers for her sons that would be too short for the older, and far too large for the younger. But she didn't care. Didn't care that everyone knew every stitch she wore was fished from the charity bin. Didn't care that her sons were laughingstocks of the entire town.

She'd had no pride. No shame. Nothing but a selfish, unquenchable thirst. He carefully took one of the pumps from the shelf, studied it, remembering. They were scuffed because she'd fallen down all the time.

She'd fallen down all the time because she was drunk. As were the constant stream of paramours she entertained to earn her next bottle. Except a few of them hadn't been as drunk as she. And a few of them had come with a different price in mind for that next bottle.

His hand clenched into a fist and he abruptly relaxed it.

No point in damaging the most valuable of his souvenirs. He remembered the day he'd taken these shoes from her feet, minutes after he'd taken his hands from her throat.

Seconds after he'd taken her miserable life.

He remembered the sight of her swinging from the tree outside the rusted-out trailer she'd had the nerve to call their home. No pride. No shame. Now, no life.

He'd chosen the branch carefully. She'd been a tall woman. That she hadn't passed those genes to him had often struck her as funny.

He'd laughed about it himself as he'd hoisted her up, left her feet dangling. It had taken more energy than he'd expected, but it had been worth it. Of course tying the noose had been no problem. He'd had months to practice the technique. There hadn't been much else to do, in juvenile detention. Not much more to do than watch his own back and dream of his hands around her throat.

He'd expected the moral satisfaction, even the thrill as she drew her last breath. What he hadn't expected was the pure, sexual release. It had caught him off-guard, that first time. He lifted his eyes, surveyed his collection. He'd known to expect it every time that followed.

He looked back at the shoe in his hand. He'd strung her up and left her swinging. No one had questioned that she'd killed herself. Everyone had been relieved that she was finally gone. His only regret was that she'd been dressed in the cast-off Sunday dress she'd pulled from the church charity bin and not like the whore she was. And that he hadn't had his pit then. He would have enjoyed walking over her any time he chose.

He placed the shoe back on the shelf, straightened it neatly. The next pair of shoes he placed on the shelf would be Rachel Ward's, victim five of his six, who'd already agreed to meet him tomorrow night. Tonight, he amended.

But the next body into the pit would be Eve's. Eventually, he'd have her here. She'd be silenced, her worst fear realized. She'd almost died twice. Third time was a charm.

Tuesday, February 23, 4:30 a.m.

Harvey Farmer sat drumming his fingers on his kitchen table when Dell returned, looking cold and tired. "Where have you been?" Harvey snapped.

"Following Jack Phelps, just like we agreed." There was attitude in his son's voice that Harvey did not like and he smelled like perfume. Again.

"And what did Phelps do?"

"Went to a bar, then sat outside for a few hours waiting for some guys to come out."

Harvey's brows lifted, sniffing a break. "Guys? Really?"

"No, not like that. Phelps is very much into women. He was waiting for these guys to come out so he could write down their license plates. I guess they're suspects." Dell dragged his palms down his face. "This plan of yours isn't working."

"It will. Be patient." He jumped when Dell's hand slammed down on the table.

"I'm done being patient. How long have you followed them, hoping they stumble?"

Harvey cocked his jaw. "Since I put your brother in the ground."

"And so far? Nothin'."

"Not nothing. Pages of notes on what they've done, who

they've seen . . . You've been at this three weeks." *Fired by the article that made my son's murderers look like gods.* Harvey had welcomed Dell's rage. Now he needed to harness it before Dell did something wild. "They're on a big case. They'll be under pressure to make an arrest."

Dell scoffed. "They couldn't find a crook if they tripped over him."

"Exactly. When they can't arrest somebody, they'll find a scapegoat."

"Like VJ," Dell murmured.

"Like VJ," Harvey repeated. "Here are the pictures I took of Webster tonight." He handed the memory card from his camera to Dell. "Group them with the ones you took of Phelps and print them out. We'll regroup in the morning."

Tuesday, February 23, 6:45 a.m.

"You're here early," Jack said, dropping into his chair.

"I had a busy night. Somebody tried to break into Eve's place last night."

Jack's eyes narrowed. "Why didn't you call me?"

"I tried. Left you a message on your cell. Figured you were just sound asleep. If the unis had found anything, I'd have called your home phone and woke you up."

Jack frowned at his cell phone. "There is no call from you in my log."

Noah wanted to tell him to cut the bullshit, but didn't have the energy. "Maybe you need a new phone," he said wearily. "I asked Micki to check the area around Eve's apartment this morning. We'll see what she finds. Is one of those for me?"

Jack had two full cups from his favorite coffee house. "They were both for me, but you look like you need it more." He slid a cup across their desks. "What's that?"

"Eve's test participants. I'm comparing them against the suicide reports."

"She gave you the list?"

"I didn't have to ask twice. So far, no matches. That's the good news."

"Bad news is you've got a long list and we don't know who he's targeting next."

"It's not that bad. Eve separated out the heavy users. If he's luring them to meet him somewhere, it stands to reason that he'd have a better chance of encountering them in the virtual world the more frequently they play."

"Makes sense to me."

Noah sat back, pushing the list away for a little while. "So why are you here early?"

"I found Taylor Kobrecki's pals at a bar last night. The bar was the first number on Kobrecki's grandmother's LUDs. She called the minute you left her yesterday."

"I bet his pals say they haven't seen him in weeks and Taylor would never hurt a fly."

"Almost word for word. When I asked their names, they gave me every crank-call name in the book, so I waited for them to leave and copied down license plates. I'll run their addresses. One of them could be hiding him." Jack tossed his hat to his desk. "Although if Kobrecki's IQ is anywhere near his Neanderthal pals', there's no way in hell he's smart enough to have pulled this off."

"Did you talk to any of the women who filed complaints about him?"

"Two of the three. Both caught him staring in the bedroom window. Both filed a complaint and suddenly things started breaking in their respective apartments. Finally both moved out, saying Mrs. Kobrecki would lie like a rug to protect her grandson."

"So he's a peeper and a sniffer. Could he have moved to murder? It's a big step."

Jack shrugged. "Like I said, based on the friends he hangs with, I don't think he's got the brains. But we'll keep looking for him, if for no other reason than to cross him off."

"Speaking of lists, I need to get back to this one. We're going to have to decide if we begin contacting the heavy users on Eve's list or not. If we do, Eve will bear the brunt."

"And if we don't," Jack said seriously, "we could find one of them hanging from a rope. There's really no choice, Web."

"I know," Noah said. "And Eve knows that, too."

"Give me half of the names," Jack said. "I think our time is better spent identifying potential victims than tracking Taylor Kobrecki."

"You're right." Noah gave him half the stack. "Focus on the heavy users."

They worked for twenty minutes in silence, and then Jack spoke in a strained tone. "Web, I think I found Samantha Altman."

Noah's head jerked up. "What? Eve said she wasn't on the list."

"She wasn't, not as Samantha Altman." Jack handed Noah a single sheet across their desks. "I put a check next to her name."

"Samantha Porter," Noah read, then he remembered. "She'd just gotten divorced. Porter was her married name, but she'd gone back to Altman."

"But when she signed up for this study, she was still Samantha Porter."

"Eve's got her in the lightest user group. Zero to five hours a week."

"Samantha couldn't play if she was dead," Jack said dryly, then he frowned when Noah picked up the phone. "What are you doing?"

"Calling Eve."

"At this hour?"

"She won't mind."

"Noah?" Her voice was husky with sleep and he pushed the distracting mental image of her snug in bed from his mind. "What's happened?"

"We found Samantha Altman, the first victim, on the list you gave me last night."

He heard the creak of bedsprings. "That's impossible. I checked myself. Twice."

"She'd just gotten divorced and Altman was her maiden name. She'd registered with you as Samantha Porter. She was in the light user group."

There was a pause, then a quiet sigh. "Because she was dead. She would have been at the zero end of zero to five hours a week. Oh God."

"Can you check her usage history, find out when she stopped playing?"

"Already checking. Hold on . . . Two weeks ago she went from six hours a day to nothing. I must have seen this. How did I miss this?"

"If you had seen it, you just would have thought she'd lost interest in the study."

"You're right." She drew a breath. "Hysterics won't help. What do you need?"

Noah's respect for her ratcheted up. "I take it you never saw the avatar who was with Christy Sunday night."

"He wasn't on." She went quiet. "I'd convinced myself that a local killer trolling for local women was more likely to find my test subjects as we'd geographically stacked the deck. But now, three for three . . . Somebody has access to our subject list."

"Jack is here. I'm going to put you on speaker. Who has access, Eve?"

"Jeremy Lyons. He's Dr. Donner's secretary. He typed the names in. And anybody who has access to Jeremy's office. Jeremy keeps his user name and password on a sticky note under his desk blotter. If his computer is on, you can get in."

"So anybody wanting the files would have to physically go to his office?"

"Well, no. If you connect to the university's server from an outside line, you could also get in." She hesitated. "With Jeremy's password, that's pretty easy to do."

Which was how she'd found Christy's address. "Who had access to his office?"

"Anybody who enters the building. Jeremy takes a lot of bathroom breaks and leaves his computer unattended. Anybody who knew about the study could have managed it."

This wasn't what he'd wanted to hear. "Which includes who?"

"Dr. Donner, the committee that approved my thesis proposal, any of the members of the study itself, most of the grad students in the department, and ShadowCo."

Noah frowned. "Why ShadowCo?"

"They sponsored my research. Not a huge stipend, but

enough so that their PR people could say they put money toward responsible use of role play games."

"In other words," Jack said, "a helluva lot of people."

"Well, maybe somebody saw him with Christy on Monday night," Noah said. "If he broke into her house, we should have seen evidence of forced entry. If he lured her out, hopefully somebody saw them. Does Shadowland keep track of conversations?"

"It's up to the individual. A lot of gamers don't want anyone to know where they've gone or who they've met. Anonymity is a benefit of the game."

"If the user does choose to save the conversations, where do they go?" Jack asked.

"They're saved to the gamer's hard drive. I suppose ShadowCo may store them on their servers, but that seems unlikely given the volume of conversations. It would be like if the wireless companies kept track of each individual text message or IM. They don't because they simply don't have the capacity. Did you get Christy's computer?"

"Yes, but it's . . . unlikely that we'll find anything on it." Especially if the killer had switched Christy's computer as he'd done with Martha's.

"We may have to resort to old-fashioned detective work," Jack said with a wry smile.

Noah didn't feel much like smiling back. "Eve, for now, I'd like a list of anyone you know who could have accessed the files. We'll start with alibis for Donner, Lyons, and the grad students. I'll be in touch." Noah hung up and leaned back in his chair. "Well?"

Jack lifted his brows. "I was right. She would have been great at phone sex."

Noah gritted his teeth, irritated. "Jack."

"You have no sense of humor," Jack said and Noah gritted his teeth harder.

"Christy Lewis. She's online chatting up avatars around midnight Monday morning. She's gotta be dead before nine o'clock, because she doesn't show up for work."

Jack grimaced. "And there's a snake involved."

Noah took the lid off the coffee cup Jack had brought him and stirred in his normal four packs of sugar. "We can't forget about the snake. Why use a snake?"

"'Cause he's a sick bastard. You don't need all that sugar. This coffee is good."

Sugar had become his vice when he'd quit the booze. "Habit. Okay, so we know he's a sick bastard. He's killed three women. Still, why the snake?"

"Maybe Ian can tell us more after he finishes the autopsy."

Noah stood up. "He said he'd do it last night. Let's find out if he's done."

Tuesday, February 23, 6:45 a.m.

Liza cooked the last egg they had. They were always low on food, but she'd been afraid to spend any money until Lindsay came home. *If she ever comes home.* The police weren't looking for her. Nobody was looking for her, *nobody except me.*

She closed her eyes, so tired. She'd covered miles the night before, only to come up empty-handed. No one had seen Lindsay. *She's dead.*

A wave of grief washed over her. *Don't give up.* If Lindsay was lying in an alley somewhere, hurt, she was frozen by now. *Don't give up.*

She lifted her chin. She had an English exam today. When Lindsay did return, she'd kick Liza's butt for failing a test and losing her chance for a scholarship.

She went back to her room to get ready for school.

Tuesday, February 23, 7:25 a.m.

Noah and Jack found Ian at his desk, typing a report. "I was going to bring a report to Abbott's 8:00 a.m. meeting," Ian said. "You didn't have to come down."

"We're stuck on the snake," Noah said. "We don't know why he used it and were hoping you found something that would shine some light on it."

"Because he's a sick bastard?" Ian said sourly.

"Told you so," Jack said.

"I was hoping for a more scientific explanation," Noah said. "Anything, Ian?"

"Plenty." He pulled the sheet from Christy's body. "She has the same puncture on her neck and was positive for ketamine, just like Martha. Unlike Martha, Christy was restrained at her ankles. The rope burns are only on the front, bruising on the back."

"She was tied to a chair," Noah said.

"I think so. There is also swelling in her elbows." Ian looked up, his eyes weary. "We see that elbow swelling when the arms are kept crossed over the torso for long periods of time, like this." He demonstrated. "But there's no evidence of arm or wrist restraint."

Jack frowned. "Straitjacket?"

"It makes sense," Ian said. "A straitjacket will immobilize without leaving marks. I found bruising between her shoulder blades, same height as the chairs around her dining room table. I think she struggled, repeatedly rocking back against the chair."

"Trying to get away from the snake," Jack said, horror in his voice.

Noah cringed at the thought. "He tied her to a chair and set a rattlesnake on her?"

Jack looked ill. "If she struggled, she wasn't sedated. Why the ketamine?"

"Good question. Perhaps he sedated her before, to get the jacket on her," Ian said. "Officially, strangulation was once again the cause of death."

"He terrified her," Noah murmured. "Why? Other than the fact he is a sick bastard?"

"Sometimes it's just because they can," Jack said.

Noah sighed. "True. But why a snake? How did he know that would scare her?"

"Most people are afraid of snakes," Jack said thinly. "It's a common phobia."

"I suppose. Still doesn't feel right. What else, Ian?"

Ian shrugged. "She ate waffles a few hours before she died, with maple syrup."

"And time of death would have been when?" Noah asked.

"Sometime between five and six yesterday morning."

Noah did the math. "So she ate waffles around 3:00 or 4:00 a.m. She either made them in her own kitchen or she went out."

"I didn't see any evidence that she cooked," Jack said. "I think she went out. And at that time of the morning, there aren't many places that serve. This is a good break."

"So we take her photo to the all-night diners and waffle houses around town."

"She also filled her tank with gas. There were traces of hydrocarbons on her hands."

"A waffle house near a gas station," Noah mused. "When will you get Samantha?"

"Sometime after eight. Since I've given you my prelim, I'll stay here and start on Samantha Altman's autopsy as soon as she arrives. I'll be in touch."

Tuesday, February 23, 7:45 a.m.

Eve was frying eggs when David stumbled into her kitchen, rubbing his eyes.

"You need a new couch, Evie. I could feel every spring."

She handed him a cup of coffee. "I know. I got it from a yard sale."

"Yeah, I noticed. Nice to have someone cook for me occasionally."

She put their plates on the table. "Don't any of those other firemen cook?"

"Out of a Hamburger Helper box. Hey, these are pretty good."

"Even I can fry an egg. So, you gonna fix my roof today?"

"If it stays dry. Who was that on the phone earlier?"

Eve picked at her breakfast. "Noah Webster. They found the first murdered woman on my list. She'd signed up under her married name, but got divorced. Three for three."

David sighed. "Sucks, kid. But you still aren't responsible."

"Neither Samantha nor Christy had played Shadowland before we placed our recruiting ad. They were there to be preyed upon because they signed up for my study."

"And if you'd asked them to take a daily walk in the park and they'd been mugged? Would that have been your fault, too?"

He was right, but that didn't make it any easier. "No."

He set back to work on his breakfast. "You break into Shadowland yet?"

"Not yet. I upped my network privileges, but I still haven't got the keys to the kingdom. I'm a lot closer though. Shouldn't take too much longer."

"So you're going to stay here all day to work on that, right?"

"No. I'm not going to stay here all day so you can watch over me. But thanks."

He frowned. "Then where will you be today?"

"On campus. Somebody's gotten access to our study files. It's the only way he could have picked all three women."

His frown deepened. "And what will you do should you find this person?"

"Don't worry. I'm not planning to make any citizen's arrests. I'll call Webster."

"And what if he comes after you when you're alone on campus? What then?"

"I'm licensed to carry a concealed. I never leave the house without my gun in my computer bag. Except for yesterday." She bit at her lip. "I was so rattled over seeing Christy hanging like that, I forgot a lot of things."

"Considering you were cuffed and questioned, it's probably good you didn't have your gun with you. I'll drive you to school. Let me know when you're ready to leave."

* * *

Tuesday, February 23, 8:05 a.m.

Abbott tossed the morning *Mirror* on the table. "That punk reporter Buckland was at your scene last night," he snapped. "What happened to securing the perimeter?"

Jack frowned. "I didn't see Kurt Buckland there yesterday."

Micki pulled the paper closer to where she and Carleton Pierce sat. "I didn't either, and Christy's house is pretty remote. We would have seen his car if he'd driven up. Must have parked a ways off and used a telephoto."

Noah scanned the front-page article whose headline screamed RED DRESS KILLER and in smaller caps, THREE WOMEN DEAD. "He's named all three women, including Samantha. Here's a quote from her mother. 'We knew our daughter could never have killed herself.'" He passed the paper to Jack. "I bet he was following us yesterday when we went to see Samantha's mother."

"Asshole reporter even added the part about the snake," Jack said, pushing the paper away in disgust. "We would have held that back."

"Find out where he was hiding," Abbott said grimly. "I want to know how he knew about the red dresses and the snake *and* I want him kept away from our crime scenes."

Carleton looked uncomfortable. "Are you sure that's the best approach? It'll just make him more determined. Maybe he would make a better ally."

Abbott scowled. "I'm not embedding any media in my teams."

"I didn't say strap him to your chest like a papoose, Bruce," Carleton said mildly. "I'm familiar with minds like his. If you deny him access, he'll go on the offensive."

"The doc's right," Jack said. "I'd rather control what

this Buckland guy knows. On the bright side, at least he didn't know about the connection."

Carleton looked around the table. "And that would be?"

"Ever hear of a computer game called Shadowland?" Noah asked before Jack could mention Eve. Noah wasn't sure Carleton would be allowed to keep her involvement from her faculty advisor. Ethically Carleton might have to tell.

"I never got into computer games," Carleton said. "But I take it that the victims did."

"Big time," Jack said. "Hours a day."

"I have a few patients who have game addictions. They talk about a Worlds of War."

"Warcraft," Jack corrected. "Similar principle."

"We found that all three women were participating in a psychological study at one of the local universities," Abbott added and Noah wanted to protest, but it was too late.

Carleton's brows shot up. "How did you find this out?"

"Confidential informant," Noah said.

"Does this informant have a name that you'd care to share with the team?" Carleton asked quietly, but he was angry and Noah supposed he had a right to be.

Abbott nodded. "Yes. If it comes down to it, we'll tell you."

"For now," Noah added, "we don't want to put you in the spot of having to report it."

"Pesky ethics," Carleton said tightly, his smile forced. "Fine. For now. So . . . obviously somebody besides your CI knows about this study. Do you know who?"

"We're investigating that today," Noah said. "Your profile would be a big help."

"I'm not so sure it's accurate anymore. Knowing about

the computer game could make a difference. Knowing there is a link to a psychological study makes an even bigger difference." Carleton's voice was sharper than Noah had ever heard it. "It's possible I wasted five hours of my night on a profile that is completely meaningless."

Noah closed his eyes. "I'm sorry, Carleton. I didn't think about that."

"I guess not," Carleton replied. He pressed his fingertips to his temples, then lifted his head. The anger was gone, but the irritation was still there. "Tell me what you can."

Tuesday, February 23, 8:45 a.m.

"Excuse me. I'm looking for Eve Wilson."

Dr. Donner's odious secretary, Jeremy Lyons, pointed. "She sits back there."

Eve closed her laptop quickly. *Dammit.* She'd been so close to getting into Martha Brisbane's Shadowland file, but a man was coming her way. He was clean-cut, well dressed, but there was an arrogant gleam in his eye. Eve instantly did not trust him.

"Miss Wilson." He held out his hand. "I'm Kurt Buckland, with the *Mirror.*"

She shook his hand reluctantly. "Mr. Buckland. I'm rather busy at the moment."

He ignored her. "So tell me how you knew the three murdered women."

Years of maintaining the secrets of Dana's shelter had taught her how not to react. But it was hard. She blinked. "Murder? You have the wrong woman, Mr. Buckland."

"You drive an old Mazda. Blue with a dented fender. Yes?"

"Yes. But I still don't know what you're talking about."

"Your car still sits in front of Christy Lewis's house. You were at Martha Brisbane's apartment." He handed her another photo. It was her with Noah and her heart sank.

He knew. Soon everyone would know that her study had lured these women to their deaths. Their killer would know they knew and the police would lose any advantage.

"You spoke with the detective," he said. "I want to know what he said."

Even as her heart pounded, she was relieved. The intruder last night was this reporter. Not a killer. "Talk to Detective Webster." She swiveled in her chair, hoping he would leave.

Instead he leaned against her cubicle wall. "So. What *was* it like to die? Twice? Did you see bright white lights? God? Angels? Or was it hellfire and brimstone?"

Fury bubbled, but she kept her cool. "Use your imagination. It's what you're good at."

"I'll pick God and angels. So, when that man strangled you, did it hurt?"

It had. It still did, in her worst nightmares. Worse, it shamed her. *No more.*

Slowly she stood, damned if she'd be victimized again. "Yes, it hurt very much. I have a scar from where he wound twine around my throat. Would you like to see it?" She unfastened the leather choker she always wore, leaned forward, chin high. "Would you like to touch it? So that you can more accurately describe it to your readers?"

His eyes flashed. "You can't bluff. I get what I want, or

I will print your personal story. Tell me about these three murdered women and your privacy will remain intact."

She smiled at him, a full smile that accentuated the dead side of her face. It looked creepy, she knew. Phantom of the Opera creepy. She'd perfected her half smile so she wouldn't see the disgust she saw on Kurt Buckland's face at this moment.

"You've already breached my privacy," she said loudly. "Everyone in this room is googling me. They'll be too polite to come and ask about it to my face. But they'll talk among themselves. Bad move, raising your voice like that. You just lost your leverage."

"The rest of my readers won't be so polite," he snapped. "They'll point and stare."

Eve laced her fingers loosely even though her insides were so taut she thought she'd break in two. "If you want a story, talk to Webster. You won't get shit from me."

He drew himself up tall and put his smile back on. "I'll make sure you get a copy of tomorrow's paper. For your scrapbook. You can paste a clipping next to this one."

He tossed a photocopy of a murky newspaper photo to her desk and her taut insides shattered. *That's me.* The day she'd been released from the hospital, almost six years ago. The face was horrifically scarred, the eyes wide and terrified. Eve felt the pain, all over again. But she'd made it through then. She was stronger now.

"One last chance," he said quietly. "Nobody else has to see that."

Eve made herself touch it. Keeping her hands steady, she brushed past Buckland, walked straight to the bulletin board and pinned the picture in the middle with a tack. Then she turned, her half smile in place. "I'm not afraid of you. Leave. Now."

One of the other students rose from his cubicle. Jose was built like a brick, and now he put one of his beefy hands on Eve's shoulder. "The lady said leave."

"And stay away from my apartment," Eve added, "or I'll get a restraining order."

Buckland glared. "I haven't been near your damn apartment."

"Save it for the judge. Stay. Away. From me." With a final glower, Buckland walked away and Eve let out a breath. "Thanks, Jose. I owe you one."

He took the horrible picture down. "You want me to shred this?"

Eve took it from his hands. "No. I think I'll keep it."

He took the choker from her stiff fingers and fastened it around her neck. Eve turned to thank him but something in his eyes gave her pause. "You already knew, didn't you?"

He shrugged. "I was doing research last year for Abnormal."

The class she was taking now. "The mind of serial killers," she murmured.

"I found articles on Rob Winters." She winced and he grimaced. "I'm sorry, Eve."

"It's okay. Really." She made herself smile. "It's not like we can go around calling him 'He who should not be named.' That's kind of long."

His lips twitched. "I think that's copyrighted, anyway." He sobered, kindly. "None of us knew what to say, so we decided not to say anything. It's your business. Your life."

"Which I think I just took a little more back of this morning." And it made her proud.

Her elation was short-lived. Donner's assistant was watching her with ill-disguised curiosity from behind his

round spectacles. She'd waited all morning for Jeremy
Lyons to take his break so she could download the study
files from his PC. She didn't want access traced to her
own laptop and she wouldn't dig Ethan in any deeper than
he was.

But Jeremy had stubbornly stayed and soon Donner would return from the class he was teaching. After
Buckland, Eve wasn't sure she had the energy left to
stand up to Donner, too. Donner would demand to
know what she'd done, why she'd told the police about
Martha when he'd all but commanded her to forget
Martha's name.

Besides, Donner had access to the list. As did Jeremy. *They could be involved.* She'd thought it a hundred times since talking with Noah that morning, but
it was no easier to believe. Donner was an academic,
Lyons an annoying weasel. Neither of them looked
like killers.

But then, neither had Rob Winters when she'd first met
him. "Jose, can you divert Jeremy? I need to get out of
here and I don't want to deal with him."

Jose's eyes narrowed. "I hate that little troll. Just leave
him to me."

Jose blocked Jeremy's view and Eve sailed by without detection, but once outside the building, the bubble
of accomplishment popped. *I don't have my car.* And
then Jeremy was running out of the psych building,
followed by Jose. Instinctively, Eve ducked around
the corner, into the alley between their building and
the next. From here she could listen and see without
being seen.

"Where is she? Dammit," Jeremy said angrily.

"She's gone home," Jose said. "Let her be."

Jeremy looked afraid, and the hairs on Eve's neck lifted. "I'm so dead," he muttered.

It could have been simply an overused phrase, but Eve was taking no chances. Sticking to the alleys, behind and between the buildings, she began to run, her cell phone in her hand.

Chapter Ten

So this is all being done within a game?" Carleton asked incredulously. "This is . . . amazing. And certainly changes the nature of my profile."

"How so?" Noah asked.

"There's a level of intelligence, of order that I've never seen before. You say he's able to go in and change these game characters—"

"Avatars," Jack inserted.

"Avatars," Carleton repeated. "He's got technical skills or he's able to learn them quickly. And then there's the cruelty. I have to tell you, I haven't been able to get that victim from yesterday out of my mind. That he went to the danger and effort of locating a highly venomous snake, immobilized her . . . I don't even want to imagine what that poor woman went through. I have patients with snake phobias and they are very real."

Micki glanced at Jack, looking chastised. "We're still trying to find out where he got the snake. But why only the snake with Christy? Why change his MO now?"

"And how will he change it the next time?" Jack asked grimly.

"I don't want a next time," Abbott said. "Micki, anything else from the scene?"

"Yeah." Again the cautious look at Jack. "The snake had just ingested a mouse."

Jack grimaced. "Oh God."

"It hadn't digested it yet. It must have swallowed it right before the killer blew its head off. We found a puncture in the mouse. It had been dosed with ketamine as well."

"Why?" Jack mouthed the word.

Remembering the snake bite on Christy's foot, Noah knew why. It made him ill.

"The mouse would have remained alive, warm-blooded," Noah said. "Attractive to the snake. The mouse just wouldn't have been able to run away."

"The mouse was bait," Carleton said, his voice thin and horrified. "Dear God."

Abbott cleared his throat. "Keep the mouse out of the paper."

Jack pulled his palms down his face. "I don't want to think about that. Give me a few minutes to pull up the all-night waffle houses in the area and we can roll."

"Christy Lewis's last meal was waffles," Noah explained. "We figure she ate it in the middle of the night, so we're off to check the twenty-four-hour waffle houses and diners."

Faye, their admin, stuck her head in the door. "Call from Ramsey in the DA's office, Captain. You got your search warrant for that apartment next to the Brisbane woman."

"Thanks," Abbott said. "I'll have Sutherland and Kane do the search. What about Taylor Kobrecki? Do we know any more about him?"

"I met his best pals," Jack said. "He might be hiding with one of them."

"I'll have them checked. We will hold a press confer-

ence this morning. We have flyers made up with the victims' photos to give to the press. If somebody saw them
the night they died, we can start retracing their steps."

"What about warning potential victims?" Micki asked.

"Do we even know who to warn?" Carleton asked.

"We know who the study's heavy users are," Jack said.
"They're the likely targets."

"Wait." Carleton held up his hand. "How do we know
who the heavy users are?"

"Our CI gave us a list of study participants, organized
by usage patterns. Jack and I will dig up contact info on
the heavy users, but which he'll target next is anybody's
guess."

Abbott hesitated. "How many people are on the list?"

"Five hundred," Noah said, "but only sixty that are both
women and heavy users. Five ultra-users, like Martha."

"Give me the list," Abbott said. "Let me think
about it."

"We're off to interview the study supervising professor.
He and his assistant have direct access to the list. Then
we'll check waffle houses." Noah had pushed away from
the table when his cell phone rang. *Eve.* "What's happened?" he asked in a quiet voice.

"Do you know a reporter named Buckland?" she asked,
her voice strained.

His heart sank. "Yes. I assume you do, too. How did he
find you?"

"He saw my car at Christy's. He paid me a visit today.
He may be a problem."

"Buckland's already a problem. What did he say?"

"Oh, lots of things, but mostly he wanted to know about
the murders. I didn't tell him anything. Listen, I need my
car. Is it possible someone could drive me up to get it?"

Noah frowned at the breathlessness in her voice. "Are you running?"

"Kind of. Dr. Donner's assistant is out looking for me."

"Define 'out looking for me.'"

"When Buckland left, so did I. Donner's assistant followed me outside. He's checking buildings and cars, definitely looking for me." There was fear in her voice. "I'm sticking to the alleys. Noah, this is like something out of a bad Jason movie. This is insane."

It certainly was. "Can you get to the Deli?" It was a combination coffee house and sandwich shop near the campus. Next to Sal's, it was a favorite cop haunt.

"Yeah. I'll meet you there."

"We'll have a couple of officers there. You don't have to sit with them, but they'll be watching. Wait for me." He turned back to the team. "Our CI's run into some trouble."

Jack was buttoning his coat. "I like the Deli. They have fantastic pastrami."

"Wait." Carleton stood. "I know you're trying to keep your CI safe, and presumably employed. But I'm not the ethics police. I won't turn him in. I may even be able to help."

Noah was listening. "How?"

"If I don't know who's running your CI's study, I'll know somebody who does. If your CI is running into trouble, I may be able to smooth the way with his boss."

Noah nodded. "Right now the issue seems to be with the boss's assistant, but I'll tell the CI you've offered to help. Thanks, Carleton. Really."

"We'll give you all the info soon," Abbott added. "It's not that we don't trust you."

Noah knew this had to be particularly awkward for Abbott. He and Carleton Pierce went way back. They all did.

They'd used Carleton's profiles to solve dozens of homicide cases over the years. But they'd promised Eve.

"I know that, Bruce. I don't like it, but you obviously believe I'll have a conflict of interest with this and I have to respect that. I'd offer to find another psychologist to do the profile, but you'd have the same issue with whoever had my role. Besides, this is a fascinating personality. I don't want to miss the opportunity to study him."

"I'd prefer it if you were studying him from closer range," Abbott said dryly. "Like with him behind bars. Go," he said, waving Noah and Jack toward the door. "I'll have a squad car sent to the Deli. Call me when the situation's clear."

Tuesday, February 23, 9:30 a.m.

Eve bought a coffee and blindly grabbed a magazine from the rack, trying to blend in with the other coffee-breakers. The Deli may have been just a sandwich joint in the past, but now it was an upscale bistro where students and professors—and cops—came to meet, greet, see, and be seen. *Kind of like Ninth Circle, without the bad band.*

"Now, he's something," the guy behind the counter said. Eve looked down, grimly unsurprised to see the face of Jack Phelps staring up at her. She'd "blindly" grabbed *MSP*. A Freudian slip. *Yeah, right.* The barista winked. "He can book me any day."

"Yeah. He's something." Now Jack's partner . . . was something else. Eve wished she knew what. She had told him she didn't want him, told herself she couldn't have him, but when she got scared, Noah's had been the first number she'd dialed.

With a quiet sigh, she sat behind two officers who casually sipped their coffee. They might be the cops Noah sent or they might really be on break. Either way, she felt safer close by.

She flipped pages until she found herself looking at the picture of Noah Webster as she had before, so many times. Jack's face was something. Noah, though . . . His face was rugged, hard. *Thuggish* was the word that always came to mind.

Dangerous. But his green eyes could be warm. *And he makes me feel safe.*

The bell on the Deli's door jingled and she lifted her eyes to see Jeremy entering, searching the room. He came straight toward her table, giving her only a moment to debate asking the cops behind her for help should she need it.

If you do, you'll be admitting working with them. She wanted to delay that as long as she could, for the sake of Noah's investigation. The longer the Shadowland connection went undisclosed, the longer Noah would have to hunt a three-time killer.

"Can I join you?" Jeremy asked, breathing hard. "Thank you." He sat, without giving her time to say no, then took off his glasses, wiping away the condensation that had formed by coming into the warmth from the cold. "You're a hard woman to catch, Eve."

She dug deep, found a tone that felt right. One that was wounded, but still bristling from her altercation with Kurt Buckland. "I didn't realize you were looking for me."

"Donner told me to watch, that you might go to the press. You little conniving bitch."

To the press. Not to the cops. Donner had immediately assumed she'd grab notoriety versus doing the right thing.

Why am I not surprised? "I didn't go to the press. That guy came to me. And in case you missed it, I didn't cooperate with him."

"A very convincing act, but as you came here to meet him it's not going to fly."

Eve shook her head. "What are you talking about?"

He pointed behind her. "Your reporter." Eve was stunned to see Buckland watching with a smug smile. *How long had he been there?* "You'll be thrown out of the program for this," Jeremy said with satisfaction. "You never should have been here anyway."

She turned back to Jeremy, shaken, but hoping it didn't show. "Why not?"

"Most of your undergrad work was online. Your degree's from a state school."

She tried to focus on the weasel in front of her versus the snake behind her. "So?"

"*So* you got in because you're a little victim, not because you were qualified."

There was venom in the man's voice, jealousy in his eyes. "And you are qualified?"

His jaw cocked. "Hell of a lot more than you."

And then she understood. "You didn't make the cut. That's why you're Donner's office assistant and not his graduate assistant."

A muscle in his cheek twitched. "I made the cut. But they let you in instead just because some guy slashed you. They thought you'd bring an 'interesting point of view.' "

That she'd been admitted on something other than her own merit stung. Buckland's observing them made it worse. But Jeremy was no longer talking about the cops. *Where are you, Noah?* "How would you possibly know that, Jeremy?" she asked.

"I know everything," he spat contemptuously. "I see everything. I know every medical fact, your grades, your favorite color, and that you hate beets and heights. I can see it all."

I can see it all . . . Her grades, likes, dislikes . . . *Sonofabitch. He hacked into my file.* Eve didn't know whether to laugh at the irony or be angry. In the end she did neither, opting for a weariness that was not an act. "I did not call that reporter today, so you can go back and tell Dr. Donner that whatever he was worried I'd say, I didn't."

Jeremy shrugged. "I'm not leaving until Donner gets here. If you didn't tell the press, then you told the cops. Otherwise, you wouldn't have been with them last night."

That was the first logical leap he'd made. "Donner's coming here? Why?"

"To escort you back to his office, where he'll formally kick you out of the program."

Alarms went off in her head. Donner was coming. *For me.* "Which would open up a spot for you?" she asked, forcing a smile.

He nodded, graciously. "Yes."

She kept her tone friendly. "So you think I went to the cops about . . . what?"

"Don't know," Jeremy admitted. His eyes dropped to the magazine. "That's Webster, isn't it? The cop that reporter saw you with."

Indeed it was. And *that* was Webster, getting out of his car on the curb. He'd be coming through the Deli door in about ten seconds and would validate everything Jeremy and Buckland suspected. The seconds ticked and she made a decision.

There was a way to explain away her presence at both Christy's and Martha's homes yesterday, hopefully

shutting down both Buckland and Jeremy. She just prayed
Webster would understand and play along.

She smiled proudly, running her thumb over the small
photo. "Yes, that's my Noah. I think *he* should have been
on the cover, but I *am* a little biased." She stood, waving
broadly as the doorbell dinged and Noah came in. "Noah,
honey, I'm over here."

Webster's eyes flicked down to the stunned face of Jeremy Lyons, then without missing a beat, he approached,
his smile warm. Her heart thumped hard in her ears, harder
in her chest. She knew what she needed to do. Channeling
Greer and every imaginary character she'd ever created,
she reached both arms up around his neck and pulled his
faced down for a hard kiss on the lips, making it linger a
few seconds longer than might have been appropriate.

His arms came around her naturally, as if they'd done
this a thousand times. He was rock solid, just as she'd
known he'd be. But his lips were far softer than she'd expected. And sweeter. And hotter. *What have I done?*

She eased back, rocked to the soles of her feet. There
had been a split second of shock in his green eyes, quickly
obliterated by a flare of desire. It was still there, tempered
by his control.

Remembering what she had to do, she slipped her arm
around his waist and turned back to Jeremy, whose mouth
had fallen open. "Noah, I want you to meet Jeremy Lyons.
He works for my graduate advisor, Dr. Donner."

Noah shook Jeremy's hand. "Nice to meet you," he said,
then put his arm around her shoulders, lightly squeezing.

"Likewise," Jeremy murmured.

"So, Jeremy, now you know. We hoped to keep it to ourselves a little longer. You know how people talk. But . . ."
Eve shrugged. "I guess the cat's out of the bag, Web."

"We knew we couldn't keep it a secret forever," Webster said, his voice a soft caress that sent shivers racing across her skin and she had to remind herself that none of this was real. It was as imaginary as any relationship in Shadowland.

You can't have him, so don't dream. But she would dream, because now she knew what it was like to hold him, to feel his body against hers. *What have I done?*

Noah cleared his throat. "I'm sorry, I can't stay, babe. I've got to get back to work."

"Oh," she said feigning disappointment. "I understand." But when her smile faltered, it was sincere. "Then, can you take me home? I had kind of a difficult morning."

Webster rested his cheek against the top of her head and for just a moment more Eve held on to the dream, leaning into him. "Sure," he said quietly. "Let's go."

She gathered her things and walked away, Webster's arm still tight around her shoulders. The cold air on her hot face felt good and she let out a long sigh of relief. Phelps was sitting in the front passenger seat, eyes wide, obviously having seen it all.

Webster opened the back door, and only then did he relinquish his hold. "You'd better make me that key after all," he murmured, surprising a snort of laughter from her.

"Babe?" she asked, and he smiled wryly.

"I panicked. Now, buckle up," he said and closed the door.

Jack waited until they'd cleared the first intersection before twisting around to stare at her, then at Webster. "And that was . . . ?"

Really nice, Eve thought, resisting the urge to lick her lips to see if she could still taste him. *A dream.* "Damage control," she murmured. "It's been an eventful morning."

Tuesday, February 23, 9:55 a.m.

Noah's heart had not stopped pounding. First he'd feared for her safety, then she'd rocked him with a kiss she'd called "damage control."

Now it pounded with helpless rage as his hands twisted the wheel, wishing it was the reporter's neck as she relayed the details of Buckland's visit. "He threatened you?" he asked ominously, and in his rearview he could see her grow wary.

"I dealt with it," she said. "Whatever hold he thought he had over me, he doesn't."

And for that, he was fiercely proud of her. "It doesn't matter. He had no right." No right to extort her with her own assault. It was as if she'd been victimized a second time.

"You're not helping," she said softly and she was right.

"I'm sorry." But he wasn't sorry, not really.

"At any rate," she said, "Buckland's been following you to your crime scenes. He followed me to the coffee shop."

"He was there?" Jack asked. "Just now?"

"Yeah. I guess he thought I'd meet you, to warn you about the pictures. I didn't want him to think he was right. So I . . . did what I thought I needed to do."

Damage control, Noah thought bitterly. "I understand."

"Hopefully Buckland and Jeremy don't think I'm part of your case anymore. But you need to watch out. Buckland wants his story and he'll keep following you till he gets it."

"He's following us now," Jack said. "Has been since we left the Deli."

Noah checked his rearview again, focusing on the traffic behind him instead of the woman in the backseat. A dark Subaru was maintaining a safe distance. "Sonofabitch."

"You gotta hand it to the man for persistence," she said, wry amusement in her voice. "Are we going to lose him in a mad dash? Is that why you told me to buckle up?"

Noah chuckled in spite of the anger churning in his gut. "Sorry. It's against regs."

"Well, damn," she said. "I haven't had a good mad dash in years."

Jack twisted in his seat so he could look back at her. "If I promised you a mad dash, would you kiss me like that?" There was something harsh and almost demeaning in Jack's tone and Noah shot him a furious glare.

In the rearview, Eve's smile disappeared and she looked away, embarrassed. "No."

"Jack," Noah gritted.

Jack settled in his seat with a sarcastic sigh. "Can't blame a man for trying, Web."

Noah bit his tongue. *Focus on the case, not flattening Jack's pretty face.*

Eve must have thought the same. "Now what? I tried to confuse things by insinuating that I was there to meet Noah, but I don't know if I convinced him."

"You sure as hell convinced me," Jack said blandly.

"*Jack*," Noah muttered between his teeth. *But she sure as hell convinced me, too*, he thought. And he was already wishing for another demonstration.

"You convinced every guy in the place," Jack added as if Noah hadn't spoken.

"Do you *mind*?" Eve shook her head angrily. "This is serious, Detective."

"It's his way," Noah said flatly. "How easy will it be to connect you to Shadowland?"

"Pretty easy," she said. "All the grad students know it's part of my thesis, although after this morning I don't think they'll talk to Buckland."

"That's good," Noah said. He nearly asked her if she'd gotten into the Shadowland network, but he knew she'd have told him if she had. "Now, what do we do with you?"

"I have a good idea," Jack muttered, and Noah clenched his teeth so hard they hurt.

I am so going to turn you in. He should have done it years ago. Why he hadn't was a mystery to many, he knew. He was aware of the talk, the betting pool, but like a fool, he'd hoped Jack would get his life back together. *I did, after all.*

"What do you mean?" Eve asked warily. Apparently she hadn't heard Jack's mutter.

"That if Buckland knows you're involved, it's just a matter of time before he prints it."

"He's printed just about everything else," Jack said sourly.

"Like what?" she demanded. "What did he print?"

Noah hesitated. "That they wore red dresses and the killer used a snake on Christy."

"A snake?" She looked confused. "Like, a real snake?"

"A real rattlesnake," Jack said grimly. "It bit her."

"Did he do that to Martha?" she asked, troubled.

"No," Noah said. "And we're not sure why."

"Did he sexually assault these women?" she asked.

Jack frowned. "Why do you want to know?"

"Did he?" she insisted and Jack shook his head, disgruntled.

"No, he didn't."

"So he meets them in the virtual world, attacks them in

their own homes, strangles them, then stages a hanging. And now he uses a snake, a common phobia."

Noah glanced at her again in the rearview. She'd become very quiet, her expression contemplative. "Do *you* know why he used the snake, Eve?"

"Maybe. Something Jeremy said today just struck me. He was on a diatribe, telling me why I didn't belong at Marshall, throwing out things he had no business knowing."

"Like?" Noah prodded gently.

"My favorite color and that I don't like beets. Or heights." She said the last words slowly. "I'm trying to remember who I told that to. The only thing I can think of is that I filled out a questionnaire when I was first admitted to the program. We did something similar with our study, asked all the things they love, hate, things that comfort, scare them . . ."

Noah got it. "If he has the files, he would have seen Christy's questionnaire."

Eve nodded. "And if she wrote she was afraid of snakes, he would have known. Did Martha's autopsy show anything odd?"

"Her blue lungs," Jack murmured.

"She had blue lungs?" Eve asked. "Why?"

"The ME thinks her killer shoved her face in a toilet," Noah said. "We need to see those study files, Eve. We need to know what these participants said they feared, and as soon as we request the subpoena, your role in this will come out."

"I know." She hesitated. "I can get the files for you faster."

Jack frowned. "And more secretly?" he asked pointedly. "And more *safely* for you?"

Noah glared at him yet again. *"Jack."*

"No, you listen. Anything she gets by hacking is poisoned fruit. The DA will throw any arrests out like yesterday's garbage and us with it. No hacking. We do it by the book."

There was an anger in his partner's voice that Noah wasn't sure he'd heard before, but before he could get closer to its cause, Eve spoke, calmly, coolly.

"My role in all this will come out, Detective Phelps. That's a given at this point. I'll be taken before the committee and probably thrown out of the program. If that happens, I'll be blackballed from any other program. I think it's safe to say my career is over, so secrecy—and safety—for myself isn't my main concern."

"So what is your main concern?" Jack asked, his voice also cool.

"That you not show your hand to this monster too soon. If he knows you know his MO, he'll change it. He will kill again. It gives him . . . pleasure."

A shiver went down Noah's spine, not from her words, but from the way she said them, almost as if she were in a trance. "How do you know that it gives him pleasure?"

She looked away, the spell broken. "It just makes sense. Get your subpoena for the files if you like. I don't know what the file names are, but I can get you a description. That should speed your warrant. Now, if you wouldn't mind, I'd like to go home."

*   *   *

Tuesday, February 23, 10:35 a.m.

"You didn't have to walk me up, Detective," Eve said as she let herself in.

Noah followed her inside her apartment, closing the door behind him. She'd become formal again. He'd liked it much better when she'd relaxed her guard and wondered how to get her to do it again. "Yes, I did. Where's Hunter?"

"Probably buying roofing supplies." Her smile was brittle. "I'm fine, as you can see. Your partner is waiting for you, so go." She went to the window and stood, eyes closed.

"I'll go in a minute." He stood behind her, wanting to touch, but knowing she didn't want him to. "I know you weren't offering to get us access to protect yourself."

"Don't be so sure your partner wasn't right," she murmured. "Maybe I was."

He gave in to the need to touch her, grasping her shoulders gently. She tensed, but her face reflected in the window remained unmoving. He kneaded, wishing he could turn her around and kiss her again. She'd know it was real this time.

But he didn't, instead dropping his hands to his sides. "I don't want you here alone."

She shrugged. "It's much more likely Buckland was here last night, and not your killer. He'd been following you and latched on to me."

"Still, if Buckland prints your name, the man who killed three women will know you are involved. Then he may come after you."

Her mouth firmed, her chin lifted. "I hope he does. I'll be ready for him."

Alarm had him frowning. "Eve, this isn't the virtual world where you can kick ass as Nemesis or Greer. This is real. He's killed three times. He won't blink at four."

"Which is why as Eve," she said, with a calm that rattled him, "I have a very real gun and I know how to use it. It goes with the whole survivor thing."

He knew he should go, but didn't. "What else goes with the survivor thing?"

"Different things. I wasn't always like I am now. I sat in the dark for two years after my assault. Never looked in mirrors and didn't leave the house unless I had to, and when I did it was under an inch of makeup because I was afraid."

"Of?" he asked softly.

"Of the way people looked at me. I was young, before. Pretty. Then, I was a freak. Scarred. People stared in horror, grateful it hadn't happened to them, scared that it could. Nobody looked me in the eye. Once I made a child cry, he was so afraid of me."

She'd dropped her eyes, shame in her voice and Noah's heart squeezed so hard it hurt. But there was nothing he could say that she'd want to hear, so he stood, helplessly listening. After a moment she lifted her gaze, meeting his reflected in the glass.

"My world was in the computer. It kept me connected to people, and in many ways it kept me sane. When I finally got the courage to come out of the dark, helping people to break free like I did became more than a wish. It became my purpose. People need purpose, Noah. That's a survivor thing, too."

"I know," he murmured. And he did know. "But I don't want you to get caught."

"I'm going to get caught, Noah. I'll have to give up

what makes me get up in the morning." She swallowed hard. "And it's killing me. But if I stand by and do nothing, I slide back into the dark. I can feel it, always there at my back, luring me back to where it's safe. But even though it's safe, it's not right. I can't expect you to understand that."

But he did, more than she knew. In his mind he could see himself clawing his way out of the bottle. Out of the dark. Trying to escape the demons that had driven him there. Every day he had to renew that resolution. Every day he staved off the dark.

One day at a time had always seemed like a corny metaphor. Until it became his life. "I do understand." He made himself smile. "It's why I drink tonic water."

She drew a quick breath, her eyes widening. "I'm sorry. I didn't think."

He brushed his palm down her arm, just once. "I didn't want you to. But you're not alone and I do understand. Will you keep trying to get into the Shadowland files?"

"Do you want me to?" she asked and he carefully considered his answer. She had a purpose and he suspected she'd sacrifice a great deal to keep that purpose alive. But right now, he was more concerned about keeping her alive. And out of jail.

"What I want is to stop this guy before he kills anyone else. Including you. But I don't want you to break the law. Jack is right on that. Nothing you give us that's a product of an illegal enterprise can be used in court. We could catch him, but have to let him go. And, Eve, if you did something illegal, I couldn't protect you either."

"I don't expect you to." She turned suddenly, looking up with eyes that were almost black. Intense. He couldn't have turned away had he tried. "Do you want me to stop?"

Desire surged through him like a storm and he tightened his hands into fists to keep them to himself. *This is not the time, Webster. Focus.* "Are you close?"

Her dark eyes flashed dangerously. She felt it too. "Very."

He made himself think of Martha and Christy and Samantha. He thought of Eve, drawn into this mess because she couldn't, wouldn't look away. Then he thought of the other names on her list and wondered who would be next because a killer was playing a damned game. "No," he whispered hoarsely. "I don't want you to stop."

She settled. "All right then. I'll call you when I have something I think you can use."

Cautiously he lifted his hand to touch her cheek. "Earlier, in the Deli . . ."

Her cheek grew flushed beneath his fingertips. "It won't happen again."

"Yes, it will. And when it does, it won't be an act. For either of us." He took a step back, dropping his hand from her face. "I need to go."

She nodded, unsteadily, making his blood churn. "Don't forget your hat."

Noah took his hat from the bookshelf where he'd left it the night before. Questions filled his mind, too many to ask. But she'd opened the door to her life and he'd ask a question before she closed it again. "I read about what happened to you six years ago. But I couldn't find anything about why. Why did that man try to kill you?"

"To get to his wife and his son. They'd run away because he'd beaten them for years. I knew them, loved them both. I didn't know who he was at first, but figured it out. I was afraid he'd find Caroline and Tom and make their lives a living hell all over again."

"So he was trying to stop you from warning them?"

"Partly, yes. But he had a gun. He could have just shot me and finished the job. Mercifully. But he didn't." She swallowed hard. "Instead, he stabbed me eight times. Slashed my face open. Nearly filleted my hand. Then he strangled me."

"Because it gave him pleasure," Noah said grimly.

"Yes." She crossed her arms over her chest, body language screaming volumes. "I know the kind of monster you're seeking, Noah. I stared mine in the eyes as he pulled that twine tighter around my throat. Yours won't stop. He won't stop until you stop him."

"And you?" He had to force the words from his tight throat. "Until you stop him?"

Her eyes were dark. Stark. So incredibly alone. "I didn't stop my monster. In my dreams he comes back, again and again. I'd do almost anything to stop yours."

He nodded hard. "Lock your door." He waited until he heard the deadbolt slide into place, then went back to the car where Jack was drumming his fingers impatiently.

"Are we ready to go to work now?" he asked acidly.

"In a minute." Noah dialed Abbott. "It's Web. Eve's fine, but she's had Buckland from the *Mirror* and her advisor's secretary on her ass."

"Where's her ass now?" Abbott asked dryly.

"We just took her home. We're going to Marshall to talk to Lyons and Donner, then work the waffle houses. Has Faye run checks on Jeremy Lyons and Donald Donner?"

"I'll check and call you," Abbott said.

Noah made himself say it. "We need to make a formal request to the university for their subject files. Eve said each participant listed their worst fear on a questionnaire."

"The snake," Abbott said. "That actually makes sense.

As soon as we make the request, Eve's going to be the first person they look to for the leak."

"She knows that. She's prepared to take the consequences."

Abbott sighed. "Maybe Carleton can help her so this doesn't damage her too much."

"Damage control," Noah murmured, fighting the urge to lick his lips. "I hope so."

Jack's jaw was tight when he'd hung up. "*Now* we get to work?"

Noah took one last look in his rearview before putting the car into gear. "Yes."

Tuesday, February 23, 10:45 a.m.

Frowning, Harvey watched Webster and Phelps drive away. "Who lives here?"

Dell was busily inputting the address into the property tax website he'd brought up on his BlackBerry. "Deed's held by a Myron Daulton."

"Webster was here three times last night. She's important. I got a picture of Webster walking her inside. Unfortunately, he didn't touch her, today or last night."

Dell snorted. "He sure did at that coffee place. Take a look."

Harvey looked at Dell's camera display where Noah Webster and the woman were locked in a passionate embrace. "Webster is using taxpayers' vehicles on taxpayers' time to drive his lady friend around. But that's not nearly enough."

"No," Dell murmured. "It's not. Not nearly enough."

"Dell. Remember our plan."

Dell smiled slightly. "Of course. The plan that's working so well."

Harvey's hand was slapping Dell's mouth before he knew it. "Watch your mouth."

Dell touched the corner of his lip. "Whatever you say, Pop." But his eyes were hard and angry and Harvey wondered how much longer he'd be able to control his own son.

"Which way are they headed now?" Harvey asked.

Dell checked the navsat screen he held. Planting a tracking device under each of the detectives' cars had been Dell's idea, and a damn good one. "Toward the city."

"Then follow. I'm right behind you." Dell got out of the Subaru and went back to his own car while Harvey thought about Webster having a girlfriend. Women were weak. They'd be able to get all kinds of good information out of her with the right inducement.

Tuesday, February 23, 12:15 p.m.

"Thanks." Eve glanced up briefly as David put a sandwich next to her elbow, then returned her eyes to her computer screen. "I appreciate you doing the shopping."

"I thought I'd better, since I'd like to eat while I'm here," he said. "Are you in?"

"Finally. ShadowCo's security is better than average. Took longer than I thought."

"And? What did you find?"

"What I expected. He altered the avatar files on both Martha's Desiree and Christy's Gwenivere. It's how he made their faces look as if they'd been made up. He also changed the rooms in their virtual homes with the rope and the shoes he left behind."

"And so? Can you figure out who he was?"

"Not directly. He made these changes using his victims' user IDs. But both avatars have been changed the same way. If you dig deep enough, the graphics are just lines of code. The code gets kind of clunky, where he changed it."

"Clunky." He gave her an amused look. "So he's an amateur?"

"Perhaps. The code he wrote gets the job done—the avatar's face changed. But a professional programmer would have done it more elegantly."

"Now you sound like Ethan," David commented blandly. "He likes to say 'elegant.' "

"Ethan taught me a lot," she said cautiously. To love Dana could have meant David had to hate Ethan, but Eve knew that wasn't true. Still, she was careful not to lavish too much praise on the man who'd made her guardian happy and her friend miserable.

"Like how to break and enter, virtually. Which can get you arrested in the real world."

"Now you sound like Noah."

"Whose hat is no longer on your bookshelf."

Irritated, she kept her eyes on the screen. "You get the stuff to fix my roof?"

"Ordered it. I pick it up after three. I can take you up to get your car on the way."

"Thank you. I'll pay you for all the supplies." She had enough put aside. She hoped.

"Miss Moneybags," he scoffed gently. "I'll pay for it. You do know you're ultimately helping your landlord?

Once he kicks you out, he'll have an improved roof at no cost."

"But he'll learn that he can't kick people around. That he can't kick me around." Then she understood. "You're helping because you don't want him kicking me around, either."

"Too many people have," he said quietly. "You've pulled yourself out of something that would have broken most people. I'm proud of you." Her throat closed, her eyes filled. There were no words, but she knew he understood. "Get back to your virtual B&E. But I want you to give Webster a chance. That's my price for fixing your roof."

He left her alone, but Eve couldn't focus. She saw Noah's face reflected in the window, worried and understanding. *That's why I drink tonic water.* She wondered what journey had brought him to the place of a recovering alcoholic.

She chided herself for being so selfish that she hadn't seen, or cared for, his feelings. And for just a second she let herself remember how he'd tasted when she'd kissed him. How good she'd felt when his arms wrapped tight around her.

But giving him a chance? No. Not even for David. Because in the end she didn't want to hurt Noah Webster or any other nice guy who was looking for a future, because in the end, there would be none. *Not with me.* That was Eve's reality.

She blinked, clearing her eyes so that she could see her screen. For Noah, she had to be careful. After he'd left, she'd called Ethan and at his direction had taken precautions, routing through a dozen proxy servers to make tracing her online movement difficult. But ShadowCo could still find her, and the blame might fall on Noah.

And that wouldn't do at all because Noah was a good man. There had to be a way to stop this monster. Just knowing he'd been in Shadowland, messing around with avatars, wasn't good enough. She had to use what she knew to make him show his face in the real world. It wouldn't be easy. Noah's monster was very smart, so far staying one step ahead of them. *I'll just have to be smarter.*

Tuesday, February 23, 2:30 p.m.

Liza sneaked out the ditching exit, the first time she'd ever ditched class. It wasn't like it was real class, just a stupid assembly with a stupid jock. It was making her crazy, sitting in a stupid assembly when she could be looking for Lindsay. So she left.

"Hey, girl, you gotta light?"

She jerked around, startled. A kid was standing by the door, hunched over, hands in his pockets. "No. I'm sorry." Unsteadily, she kept going. Too little sleep and no food had her light-headed. She had only a few dollars left and she needed them for bus fare.

The city bus stop was up a block, so she put her head down against the wind and started walking. The next thing she knew she was on her butt, her bookbag spilled, and her papers blowing away.

"I'm so sorry. Let me help you." It was a really tall boy. No, older. College maybe. He gathered her papers and brought them to her. "Some of them got a little dirty."

"It's okay. Thank you." She shoved the papers back in her bag and stood, stumbling at the next little dizzy spell. *Note to self. Need to eat.*

"Are you okay?"

She looked up. Way up. Liza was five-ten, so this guy had to be six-six. "I'm fine."

He frowned, studying her face. "You don't look fine. You look pale."

"I'm *fine*. Really." Then she huffed, frustrated as the city bus pulled away. "Except now I've missed my bus. The next one isn't for twenty minutes." *Wasted time. Dammit.*

She started walking fast and he walked beside her, ambling easily. "Did you come out of the smoker's door?" he asked.

She glared up at him. "Are you gonna turn me in?"

"No. But, well, why are you ditching? You don't look like the type."

"And what *type* is that?" she asked between her teeth, thinking of the way that officer had dismissed Lindsay as a missing person because she was a . . . prostitute.

"The type to take AP English. Your paper on *Heart of Darkness*," he added. "Most advanced students I knew would never ditch class. Plus, your eyes are red. You've been crying."

"Allergies," she snapped.

"In February?" He shook his head. "Try again."

"I have someplace to go." She glared up at him again. "Do you mind?"

"Where are you going?"

Liza rolled her eyes. "None of your business."

"Well, I feel bad that you missed your bus. Can I give you a lift?"

She stared up at him, appalled. "No. If you don't leave me alone, I'm going to call the cops. In fact, I'm going to the police station now and I'll just report you."

"Are you going to the police station because of your sister?"

Liza stopped short. "How did you know that?"

"Just guessed. One of the papers I grabbed was a police report. Barkley, Lindsay. The name on your English paper was Liza Barkley and you look like the mug shot."

Liza shook her head. "What are you? Some kind of CSI wannabe creep?"

He smiled. "No, but you look like you need help and I feel bad that I've kept you from where you're going. You can take a cab to the police station from here."

"Yeah, right." She started walking again, muttering under her breath, "Can't even afford lunch and this idiot wants me to get a cab."

"No, I'll pay for it." He was walking beside her again, holding out a twenty. "Get yourself something to eat while you're at it. You don't look so good."

Liza stopped again and stared at the money in his hand. "You scare me."

"Tell you what," he said when she didn't move. "There's a sandwich place across from that bus stop. I'll buy you some food and you can wait for the bus where it's warm."

She hesitated. "I don't want your charity."

"But you're hungry. Come on." He took the bag from her hand and started walking.

"Hey." She stumbled trying to catch up. "That's my bookbag."

"Liza, trust me as far as that sandwich shop, okay?"

"Like I have a choice?" she asked, and hurried behind him.

True to his word, he went into the sandwich shop and put her bag on the table. "Sit. I'll be back." She obeyed, and a few minutes later he brought two sandwiches and fries. "Eat," he said. Again, she obeyed, ravenous. "Slowly. How long since your last meal?"

"An egg this morning. Before that, lunch yesterday." She said nothing more until she'd eaten her sandwich, fries, and his fries, too.

He was impressed. "Girls usually pick at food like it's a disease. I'm Tom Hunter."

"It's nice to meet you, Tom. Thank you for the food. I was hungry."

"Why did you ditch class?"

Now that she was no longer hungry, she could think. "It was just an assembly. They took us out of class to tell us to stay in school. How stupid is that? And jocks . . . like they know anything about school." He was smiling at her. "What?" she demanded.

"I'm one of the jocks from the assembly. I graduated with a 4.0," he added helpfully.

Liza's face burned. "God. I'm sorry."

"It's okay. Mostly you're right. But that's why I come to the schools. If the kids will listen to me, even one, it's worth it. Why are you going to the police station?"

She studied him. He was handsome, blond with clear blue eyes. A basketball player, she remembered from the assembly announcement. A big-time college player. Some of the boys in class were drooling at the thought of seeing him. "Why do you care?"

He shrugged. "My mom's something of a social worker. It's ingrained. Look, I have a baby sister. Her name is Grace. If she were in trouble, I'd hope someone would help her. I won't hurt you. If nothing else, I'm a damn good listener. So why were you crying, Liza?"

She let out a breath. "My sister's missing." And she told him the whole story, everything except living alone. "Yesterday I got that police report and last night I asked every hooker I could find and nobody knew her. I started thinking today that maybe somebody was arrested with her, in a raid, or maybe somebody bailed her out."

"So you want to know if the police can tell you that?"

"I have to try. Nobody's going to look for a missing hooker. Nobody but me."

He frowned. "You went looking for your sister? Where did you find hookers?"

"Internet. I googled and found where they hang."

He looked pained. "O-kay. I know a few cops. Let's take a cab to the station, see what we can find out."

"The city bus goes to the station. Give me the cop's name and I'll ask him."

"You missed the bus again. But you were eating, so I didn't want you to stop."

She sighed. "You're not going away, are you?"

"Not just yet. Come on, let's go."

Chapter Eleven

Noah stopped in front of the fifth and last waffle house on Jack's list. It was a diner off the interstate, next to a gas station. He hoped this had been Christy's last meal.

They'd missed Donner and Lyons. Neither had been at their desks, nor at home. They'd go back later, now turning their attention to Christy's last movements. Four waffle houses had been busts and his partner had been silently surly.

Noah's patience was fraying around the edges. "Let's just get this done."

But Jack didn't move. He sat, staring at the waffle house. "I'm sorry, Web."

The quiet words were the first his partner had uttered in hours. "About?"

"I was out of line. I knew Eve wasn't trying to save her own skin."

"That apology should go to Eve. I don't understand why you said it in the first place."

"It's not that complicated. I told you I'd been trying to get her attention for months."

"Let me get this straight. *You* are jealous of *me*? You told me to ask her out."

"Thinking she'd say no. I never expected her to fall all over you in less than a day."

"That was just an act." No, it wasn't. *Not for me.* And when Eve was able, she'd say it hadn't been for her either.

Jack opened his car door. "Not from where I was sitting. Let's go."

Noah followed him into the waffle house, forcing his mind to think about killing, not kissing. Jack had Christy's driver's license photo in his hand, showed it to the hostess.

"We're with the police, ma'am," Jack said. "Have you seen this woman?"

"No, but I've seen you." She pointed to the magazine rack. "You're Phelps."

Jack winced. "Can we talk to the manager or some of the other servers?"

"Have a seat, Detectives. Can I get you some coffee?"

"No, ma'am," Noah said. "We'll wait."

The manager hurried out. "I'm Richard Smith. Please come back to my office."

"We're looking for anyone who saw this woman early Monday," Jack said.

"This shift wouldn't have been here during the night. You should come back tonight."

It was what they'd heard four times before. "Thank you, we'll do that," Noah said.

"Or," Smith continued thoughtfully, "we have security video of the cash register."

They'd also heard that four times before, but three of the cameras were pointed toward the cashier, management more concerned about employee theft than robberies. The fourth video quality was so bad they couldn't see anything.

"That would be a big help," Jack said. "Thank you."

Smith went to his computer and began typing. "Sunday between midnight and four?"

Noah and Jack exchanged impressed glances. "You have it digitized?" Noah asked.

"We just invested in a new system about a year ago. There was a robbery next door. A kid was shot pretty bad. They had an old system and you couldn't see the shooter's face. We're open all night, too. All of our people were at risk. So me and the manager next door went in together, got a better system and made sure everybody knew it. So far so good. Nobody's hit us again."

After a few minutes of stopping and starting, Smith looked up. "This might be her."

"It's Christy," Noah said, when he looked at the screen. "Time was 3:24."

"Here's the crew that was on that night, with their phone numbers, in case you can't wait until tonight to interview them. You'll want the original digital video file, I assume."

"Thank you," Noah said, with relief. "Not many shops put this much into security."

Jack's eyes lit. "You have cameras in the parking lot. Here and the gas station?"

"Yes, sir," Smith said proudly. "We sure do. You want video of the same time?"

"Plus two hours on either end, please," Jack said, then turned to Noah. "If somebody followed her home, we'll be able to find them."

* * *

Tuesday, February 23, 5:00 p.m.

"Tom." Olivia stood with a big smile for the young man crossing the bullpen. He was the son of one of her sister Mia's best friends, accompanied by a girl with a sober, terrified look, and Olivia was instantly curious. "You played a great game on Sunday."

"Thanks. We need your help. This is Liza Barkley. Liza, Detective Sutherland."

"Pull up some chairs," Olivia said and listened as Liza told her story, haltingly. Heartbreakingly. "It must have been hard to learn your sister was in the life."

"I am so scared," Liza whispered. "What if one of her . . . customers hurt her?"

Olivia weighed her words. "Liza, you seem too smart for me to try to sugarcoat this. Prostitutes have a high mortality rate. If she's been missing for two days and she hasn't called when she always did before, it's not good. After two days, her trail may be cold."

Liza had gone paler, if possible, but her chin went up. "Do you have a sister?"

"Yes, and I wouldn't take no for an answer either if my sister was in trouble. Let me check for you. I'll find out if she was arrested in a group and who posted her bail, but I want something in return. Your promise you will not go hunting at night." Liza nodded dutifully. "You're going to do it anyway, aren't you?" Olivia asked.

Liza nodded and Olivia sighed.

"Olivia?" Tom asked and she knew what was coming.

"No. I'm not going with you."

"Why not?" Tom asked. "Come on," he wheedled, then shrugged. "Mia would."

Olivia shook her head. "That is a low blow."

"But effective," he said.

"If I can, I'll go with you. Once. But I want your promise, Liza."

Liza nodded. "I promise."

Tuesday, February 23, 5:30 p.m.

Tom took Liza's bag and hailed another cab. "I'm taking you home."

"What if I don't want you to know where I live?"

"Too late. Your address was on the police report. I won't leave the cab. I promise."

Liza believed him. She was too tired not to. "I keep saying thank you."

"Then don't, just get in." He followed her into the cab, gave the driver her address.

"You've helped me, when you didn't need to."

"When I was little, my father knocked my mother around. People helped us when they didn't need to. I learned a long time ago to pay it forward. So stop thanking me."

"Okay." She fixed her gaze out the window and made herself accept the truth. "I think Lindsay's dead. But I can't give up looking for her."

"I understand. What time did you start hunting last night?"

"Eleven."

"My uncle's in town and I'm meeting him for dinner. I can't cancel because he'll get suspicious and I don't think he'd like me hunting hookers with you tonight." He said it under his breath so the driver wouldn't hear. "It'll be eleven or twelve before I'm back in the dorm.

Do not leave without me. I will come and get you in my car. Promise me."

"What about your cop friend? Will Olivia tell?"

"Tell my uncle? No. I think they've only met each other once at a wedding, so, no." He put another twenty in her bookbag. "Get some food. Promise me."

"Tom." Overwhelmed, she had to say it once more. "Thank you."

Tuesday, February 23, 5:50 p.m.

Jack dropped a photo on Abbott's desk. "We think we found him."

Abbott picked up the photo of a clean-cut forty-four-year-old man. "Who is he?"

"His name is Axel Girard," Noah said. "He's an optometrist in Edina. His car followed Christy Lewis's out of the waffle house lot on Monday."

"Does he have a record?" Abbott asked.

"No," Noah said. "Only one speeding ticket years ago. He's a churchgoing man and was volunteer of the year for doing free eye exams in inner-city neighborhoods."

Abbott sighed. "And our killer glues their eyes open."

"Exactly," Jack said and put down a series of time-stamped photos. "Security video shows him waiting in his car for over an hour. When Christy came out, she went to the gas station next door. He moved his car so that he was closer to the shared exit. Christy filled up her tank. She leaves, and a minute later, so does Girard."

"You can't see his face in any of these pics," Abbott said.

Jack showed him a close-up of Girard's Minnesota plate. "But we got his plate."

"Then pick him up. I'll get Ramsey from the DA's office to observe. Good work, both of you." Abbott sat back in his chair and studied Noah's concerned face. "Isn't it?"

Jack scowled. "Web thinks it was too easy."

Noah shrugged. "For such a supposedly smart man, that was a really dumb move."

"Pick him up," Abbott said again. "Then we'll see how smart he is. Noah, wait. We requested the files from Eve's study a few hours ago. Tell her I'm sorry."

Noah nodded. Her life was now officially changed once more. "Okay."

Tuesday, February 23, 6:20 p.m.

"What's the verdict?" Eve asked when David came in, blowing on his cold fingers.

"You've got holes in your roof," he said dryly. "I patched the one over your bed and I'll do the other tomorrow." He perched on the arm of her stuffed chair. "Who is that?"

"Gary," Eve said with a nod toward the avatar on her screen. Gary sat on a bar stool at Ninth Circle looking very out of place and very geeky.

"He's not your usual style."

He was totally vanilla, exactly as Eve had wanted. "He's from the template."

"Why?" David drew the syllable out, suspiciously.

"Because I saw that handsome avatar that was talking to Christy in Ninth Circle the night she was killed.

He was back in Ninth Circle dancing with an avatar I don't know."

"And then you called Detective Webster, just like you promised."

"I did, but got his voicemail." She'd wanted to rush up to the woman dancing with the avatar and warn her. The woman was new, one of Eve's own designs. But she didn't warn her, and it was eating at her. Instead, she waited while Gary kept an eye out.

"So what's up with Gary?"

"I don't want Noah to get in trouble, but I wanted to visit Claudio. Claudio designed the male dancer, so I couldn't go using one of my designs. He'd have spotted me right away and thought I was spying on his new spring line. Claudio is very paranoid."

"Claudio is very pricey," David said.

"Spendy. That's what they say here. Tell me you didn't buy from Claudio."

"Nah, just went for ideas. I spend my Shadowbucks on cars. Really fast cars."

She smiled at him, delighted. "You're a racer?"

"Occasionally. I had to upgrade my computer system. The Monte Carlo expansion pack uses more RAM than my computer came with."

"You should've gone with the poker expansion pack. No additional RAM needed."

"But racing is cooler. Do you play in the casino?"

"Used to. Now I just watch. One of my red-zones lives at the poker table. Awhile back, I was the top winner for weeks. But racing is cooler."

"So why'd you go see Claudio?"

"I thought I'd find out about that avatar, see who he's sold it to."

David looked skeptical. "He won't tell you that, will he?"

"He did. Gary asked for references. Claudio felt sorry for Gary's plainness, and was happy to help him upgrade, giving screen names of clients, two of which bought the dancer. I'll give them to Noah. He needs to call soon. I have to work tonight."

David frowned. "I don't like the idea of you being alone."

"I work in a bar full of cops. I'll be fine. If you're so worried, come with me."

He shook his head. "I'm having dinner with Tom."

Eve frowned. "Not fair. The only time I have the night off, he's at a game."

"Take the night off. It'll be like old times."

It sounded sweet. "I want to, but I can't. I missed last night and I need the money."

"Then I'll drop you off and pick you up at Sal's."

"That'll work. I think I'll call Noah again. Sal's gonna be pissed if I'm late."

Tuesday, February 23, 6:45 p.m.

"This is a mistake." Joan Girard followed as Noah and Jack escorted her husband from their nice Edina home, wringing her hands in helpless misery. "A huge mistake."

"Of course it is." Axel Girard tried to soothe his wife. "Call the lawyer, he'll know what to do. Keep the boys calm. Tell them I'll be home in time to read their bedtime stories."

"Now that's a fairy tale, pal," Jack said caustically. "You shouldn't lie to your kids like that. But then again, what's a little lie after three murders?"

"I'm telling you I have no idea what you're talking about. Joan, go back inside," Girard said, his smile forced. He gestured toward their picture window with his head, where two terrified children cried as their father was taken away.

Jack wasn't gentle as he helped Girard into the back-seat. "Keep your hands where I can see them or I'll have to cuff you in front of the kids. Come on, Web. Let's go."

"Wait." Noah's cell was vibrating for the third time in minutes. "I need to take this."

"Fine. Just hurry." Jack got behind the wheel, turning to watch Axel Girard.

Noah glanced at his caller ID. Eve. "What's happened?"

"I tried to call you before," Eve started.

"This isn't a good time. Can I call you back?"

"No. I have some information and need to leave for work. I don't think you want me to be talking about this in the bar. I found the male avatar. He's in Ninth Circle."

Still outside the car, Noah stared at the man in the backseat. "Right now?"

"Yeah. I'm lookin' right at him."

So am I, Noah thought, but his gut wasn't right. "You're sure it's the same guy?"

"As sure as I can be. You told me not to approach him."

"You mean you didn't? Not even as Nemesis?"

"I didn't want to get you into trouble. But I did get into the user files. The avatars were changed and I have the dates and times the codes were accessed. You ready?"

He pulled his pad from his pocket. *I didn't want to get you into trouble.* Noah cursed himself for not having told her they'd requested the study files. He should have, but he hadn't. *You're a coward.* "Yeah, I'm ready."

She rattled off times and dates, all within the last three days. "He didn't access any of their files until after you discovered Martha's body," she said. "I don't know why. I also have user names for you on the dancer. Don't worry, nobody will know it was me."

Noah wrote it all down. "This is incredible, Eve. Thank you."

There was a half beat of silence. "What's wrong, Noah?"

Everything, he wanted to say. Girard was sitting in the backseat, lips moving. *Praying*, Noah thought. Joan stood on their front porch, crying. Neither of them had been on the computer when they'd arrived. The family had been at the dinner table.

"I'm not sure," he said.

"Look, Noah, this guy is hitting on women in Ninth Circle left and right. If this is the guy, he could be hunting as we speak."

But Girard was not hunting. "Yeah, I know. Do me a favor and call Abbott. Tell him about seeing the avatar. He can go online and monitor."

"He knows how?"

"Ah, he's a quick study. He figured it out. How are you getting to work tonight?"

"I have my car back, but David's scared to let me drive alone, so he's driving me."

"Good for David. You got your keys back, then?"

"No. I looked, but didn't find them. I'm still using the set Callie gave me last night."

"I'll see if CSU found them at the scene," he said. He drew a breath. "Eve . . . we had to request the participant files from the university. I'm sorry."

There was another beat of silence. "I knew you would. It's not your fault, Noah."

"I'm still sorry. I'll stop by Sal's later if I can."

"That's fine," she said, but it was as if all the air had been forced from her lungs. She disconnected and he felt as if all the air had been forced from his lungs, as well.

Jack rolled down his window. "You okay?"

No. "Yeah. I'm coming."

Tuesday, February 23, 7:55 p.m.

"Excuse me, Miss Wilson?" Eve looked up from the drink she was mixing to see a petite redhead perched on a bar stool, her hands folded primly on the bar. Eve had seen her before. She was Trina, married to Noah's cousin Brock, who occasionally sat with Noah as he drank his tonic water. Trina sometimes came in with her girlfriends and they were pretty good tippers, but somehow Eve doubted Trina was here for a drink today. Eve knew when she was being scrutinized. And found wanting.

She smiled, despite the jitters in her stomach. "Chardonnay, right?"

Trina didn't smile back. "Right, but I'm not here to drink tonight. I came to see you. What are your intentions regarding Noah?"

"I don't know what you mean."

"You kissed him today in the Deli. Don't look so surprised," she added dryly. "You of all people should know how the rumor mill churns."

"Cops and firefighters," Eve murmured. "Nosy bastards. No offense intended."

Humor flickered briefly in the woman's brown eyes. "None taken. So?"

"I could say it's none of your business," Eve said.

Trina's eyes narrowed. "But you won't. I care about Noah. He's a good man."

"I know," Eve said quietly.

"And for some reason he cares about you."

"I know," Eve repeated, brushing aside her irritation at *for some reason*. Trina was protecting her family. That Eve understood. "That kiss . . ." *Didn't mean anything*, she wanted to say, but that was a lie. "Was a mistake. I've told Noah I'm not interested."

"*You* kissed *him*, where everyone would see," Trina said, her lips thinning in disapproval. "You never struck me as a tease, Eve."

"I'm not a tease," Eve responded, indignant. But several customers were watching, so she leaned forward. "Talk to Noah. It needs to come from him. It was for his job."

Trina looked taken aback. "You're helping him?" she asked.

"I'm trying. But you don't need to worry. I don't intend to cling when it's all over." Eve's tone was harsh, sardonic. Because clinging was exactly what she wanted to do.

"I see," Trina murmured. "You do realize that you can hurt him?"

Eve swallowed hard. "Yeah. I got that part. I'm doing my best not to."

"And you're not interested? At all?"

God, yes. "No," she said. Firmly.

Trina sat back, all primness gone. "You're as bad a liar as he is."

Eve blinked at her. "Excuse me?"

Trina pulled a bowl of salted peanuts closer. "You want

him. He wants you. He's a good man. You seem to be a good person, too. So what's the problem here?"

Eve shook her head. "Wait. You *want* me to want him?"

"I want you to cling like socks out of the dryer." She popped a few nuts in her mouth while Eve stared. "He's overcome a lot. From what I've read on the Internet, so have you. Two lost souls, both want each other . . . Color me a romantic, but it could work."

Eve's cheeks flamed. "It's not that simple."

Trina's red brows rose. "Why not? You dying? Six months to live?"

Eve coughed. "No," she said, stunned.

"Diseases? Witness protection? Secret husband? Undercover nun?"

Eve shook her head, feeling like she'd been run over by a very small truck. "No."

"Do you like him?" Trina wagged her forefinger in warning. "And don't you lie to me."

"Yes," Eve murmured. "Very much."

"Good. Now we're getting somewhere. So you like him, you want him, and there are no reasonable impediments to a relationship that I can see. Do you like roast beef?"

Eve had given up trying to keep up. "Yes."

"Good. We eat Sundays at five." She pulled a folded piece of paper from her pocket.

Eve saw it held an address, neatly printed. "You planned to invite me all along?"

"Yes." Trina smiled then. "Noah made me promise not to interfere, but I figured that kiss this morning nullified any promises previously rendered. I wanted to talk to you, find out if you were leading him on." She sobered. "You're not. Whatever's bothering you is real. But time is precious and Noah's wasted a lot of years. Figure out how to deal with whatever's keeping you from 'being interested.' See you on Sunday."

And with that she slid off the stool and left, leaving Eve staring after her.

Tuesday, February 23, 7:55 p.m.

"So all we have tying this guy to the murder is his car leaving a parking lot after one of the victims?" ADA Brian Ramsey frowned into the glass separating them from an ashen-faced Axel Girard. "Nothing more?"

"No," Noah said. Either Girard was good or he was telling the truth.

"That's not enough to at least *hold* him?" Jack demanded.

"Not unless you have something physical tying him to the victim or the scene."

Jack huffed in frustration. "Dammit, Brian."

"What about his alibi for Sunday night when the Lewis woman was killed?"

"His wife says he was with her," Jack said sarcastically. "All night. Like we haven't heard that before. Dammit, those pictures don't lie. He was there."

"His car was there," Brian corrected. "That's what the defense will claim."

"He never reported it stolen," Abbott said. "If the wife says he was with her all night, he couldn't have been in the parking lot to begin with. Somebody's lying and those pictures from the diner's surveillance system are clear."

"Crystal clear," Jack added. "Wives always say their husbands were there all night."

Brian grunted his agreement to that. "Noah, you're being awfully quiet."

Noah glanced at Jack, who was glaring at him. They'd had this conversation already and Jack was not a happy partner. Jack was also an uninformed partner. Noah hadn't told him about Eve's call. He'd started to a dozen times, but . . . hadn't.

"I don't think he did it, but I sure as hell don't want to take the chance that I'm wrong. If he did it, I don't want to give him opportunity to kill again."

"What about his alibis for the nights the other two were killed?" Brian pressed.

"Ian's time of death windows are wide on the other two," Noah said. "As best we can pinpoint, Girard was home with his wife."

"We passed out photos of the three victims at our press conference today," Abbott said. "They'll run on newscasts and in the papers. We're hoping to find somebody who saw these women the night they were attacked."

"That's good, but that doesn't help me right now," Brian said.

Noah thought of the dates Eve had given him, when the killer had changed his victims' avatars. If Girard had alibis for those times, other than his wife, he'd be cleared. But if he used the information Eve had given him, Ramsey would want to know where it came from and if it resulted in proving Girard's guilt, they couldn't use it anyway.

And Eve's hacking would be exposed.

Noah blinked hard. Too little sleep and too much worry were fogging his brain.

"Noah?" Abbott prodded. "What are you thinking?"

Noah rubbed his temples, hard. "That we need more information. His car was there, but was he? And if he wasn't, how did his car get there? He's involved somehow, Brian. Can't we keep him here until we figure out how?"

Brian shook his head. "Until you can place him at the scene, you can't hold him."

"Goddammit," Jack spat. He glared at Noah. "You *know* he's going to do it again."

"I know he's going to do it again," Noah spat back, "but *he* might not be *him*."

Brian shrugged. "Cut him loose, guys."

"We'll put an unmarked car on his house," Abbott said. "That's the best we can do for now. Get something physical to connect Girard. But first, take a break and cool off."

"I don't need a break," Jack said, disgusted. "I'm going to the morgue. Maybe Ian's finished with Samantha Altman by now. Maybe he's found something *physical*."

Noah winced when Jack shut the door too hard.

Brian Ramsey was looking at him with concern. "You okay, Web?"

"Too little sleep, too much coffee." And too much worry. "Thanks for coming."

Abbott looked distinctly unhappy. "I'll cut Mr. Girard loose. Noah, go to my office."

Feeling like a kid about to be scolded by the principal, Noah could only obey.

Ten minutes later Abbott closed his office door, a cup of coffee in each hand. "There's a fine line between too much and not enough," he said, handing him a cup.

"Too much and not enough what?" Noah asked and Abbott shrugged.

"You tell me," he said, sitting in his chair. "And I mean that. You better tell me."

Noah's head nodded. His mouth, however, did not cooperate.

"Sometime today," Abbott added sharply. "What's going on between you and Jack?"

"Too much and not enough," Noah muttered, then met his boss's eyes. "Eve."

Abbott looked unsurprised. "Are we talking turf war or cold war?"

Noah laughed, but it wasn't a happy sound. "Both. Jack's been after her for months."

"Yeah, I knew that. I go to Sal's. I've got eyes. And today Eve locks lips with you."

Noah's brows went up. "You know about that, too?"

"Yes," Abbott said, clearly annoyed Noah would even ask the question. "I sent two uniforms to keep an eye *out*. Instead they got an eye *full*. What were you thinking?"

I wasn't. For those few seconds he'd held her, Noah hadn't thought about anything at all. Except that he'd wanted more. He still did.

"It wasn't planned, Bruce. She'd been confronted by her advisor's assistant and that asshole Buckland within the space of an hour. She was trying to keep her involvement . . . secret. Jack accused her of doing so to protect her job."

"And wasn't she?" Abbott asked, and Noah shook his head.

"No. She knows it'll all come out eventually and she'll lose her spot in the program."

"There are other graduate programs."

"She said she'd be blacklisted from those. Anyway,

Jack apologized later, said he was basically jealous. Of me."

"Yeah," Abbott said, again unsurprised.

"Why do I get the impression that you know all and you're just making me dance?"

"Being captain is more than nodding when you bring me information," Abbott said testily. "I know my staff. Personalities have to work. Until this week, yours and Jack's did." His frown softened. "And you didn't see your face last night when she was talking."

"When?" Noah asked, feeling testy himself now.

"Every time she opened her mouth. Do I need to take you off this case?"

"No." Noah drew a breath. "She called you about the male avatar, right?"

"She did. I've been following him off and on." Abbott pointed to his screen. "He's still there, doing the tango. And if he's in there, Girard can't be him. Is that it?"

"Partly, yes. And partly that it just doesn't feel right, Bruce. After all he's done to date, he drove his own car and let it be photographed by security cameras."

"How could he have known he was being photographed?"

"Because there were about a hundred signs all over the goddamned parking lot," Noah snapped, frustrated. "That was the point of the surveillance system. The two store owners wanted everybody to know they were on candid camera. That was the deterrent." He rubbed the back of his neck. "Plus, I just don't think he did it, Bruce. I've been doing this job a long time and I don't think he did it."

"Jack's been doing it a long time, too," Abbott said quietly.

"Don't you think I know that? Don't you think he informed me of that, several times?" Noah pushed his knuckles into his throbbing temples. "There's more I couldn't tell him."

"Because you're not supposed to know."

Noah looked up. "Now you're scaring me."

"I figured this was bound to happen. Eve hacked into ShadowCo's server. What did she find that we can't legally use?"

"Times that the killer logged in and changed the avatars' faces."

Abbott's eyes sparkled with interest. "Times that Axel Girard will need alibis for. Why didn't you tell Jack?"

"Today Eve offered to go onto the university's server to get us the test subjects' files. She said she could do it faster. That's when Jack accused her of trying to keep her job and said we couldn't use the info anyway. About the second thing he was right. But a week ago? He would have grabbed those files as fast as she could have printed them."

"Now you're wondering how much of Jack's sudden moral uprightness is true belief and how much is the fact Eve rejected him. And how much of your willingness to accept illegally gotten information is because you want to catch a killer versus being smitten."

Noah sucked in one cheek. "God, you are scary good."

"That's why they pay me the medium-sized bucks. I'll find out if we can get a warrant for Girard's house and office, including the computers, based on what we know."

"If he is guilty, he'll wipe the evidence tonight. Or he'll destroy it."

"Then we'll have to go the conventional route, request ShadowCo's records, and hope that they cooperate."

"Have they so far?"

Abbott shook his head. "We requested the victims' files and they said that they are 'committed to providing their users with a place where their anonymity remains secure.'"

"Sometimes you want to go where no one knows your name," Noah said.

"Exactly. We'll keep an eye on Mr. Girard tonight, then in the morning the two of you pay him a visit at work. Find out where he was at the times Eve said the killer changed the avatars. We can at least do that."

Noah stood. "Did Olivia and Kane search that apartment next to Martha Brisbane's?"

"They did. It was filled with bags of garbage. Some was Martha's mail."

"Because he made her clean the house." Noah frowned. "Why would he do that?"

"Don't know. I made sure Carleton knew, so he could incorporate it into his profile."

"Were there any papers, documents showing her Shadowland movements?"

"So far no. Olivia and Kane have gone through about half of it. Micki had the carpet vacuumed and all surfaces dusted for prints, but if we find Kobrecki's prints, they'll just say he was doing maintenance. Micki will have a prelim report tomorrow morning."

The thought of Micki reminded Noah he needed to ask if anyone had found Eve's keys. One thought of Eve spurred another. "Eve had some screen name possibilities for that dancing avatar. She thought you might be able to use them in a warrant."

"I already know his name. He's Romeo62."

Noah looked at Abbott's screen. "What happened to your other guy?"

"Ditched him. Meet Lola." Lola was a statuesque raven-haired stunner. "I'm trying to get Romeo to talk to me, ask him to meet me. My guy avatar was a definite liability."

"Better for you to go undercover than Eve." Who wanted to catch this guy for all the right—and wrong—reasons. Either way, Noah wanted her off the playing field.

"I thought so, too. If Girard's innocent, we need to continue the Romeo lead. Work things out with Jack. I won't have you working against each other. Are we clear?"

"Yes, sir."

Tuesday, February 23, 8:45 p.m.

"Miss Wilson?" For the second time that evening Eve found herself summoned. A man stood at the bar, looking out of place in a suit. He was an infrequent customer, but she didn't know his name and for the life of her, could not remember his drink.

She smiled her bartender smile. "Yes, how can I help you?"

"It's more how I can help you. I'm Dr. Carleton Pierce. I'm a psychologist."

Apprehension tickled the back of her neck. "Nice to meet you," she said as he put a piece of paper on the bar. Immediately she recognized her own name. "My thesis abstract."

"I work with Noah Webster. Today I heard an interesting story about a confidential informant. Web was adamant on keeping this person's name secret. He's worried I'll turn him . . . or her . . . in. I wanted you to know that I don't plan to."

Eve's exhale was controlled, her frown confused. "I'm sorry. I'm not following you."

He smiled gently. "I'm really here to help you. It took me five minutes to locate your abstract in the university's online library. Using Shadowland as a training tool has amazing therapeutic potential. But your study has attracted the attention of a dangerous man. I was there, yesterday, at your friend's house. I was shaken. I still am."

A chill raced down Eve's back as she thought of Christy, hanging from that rope. Her eyes . . . "You'll have to talk to Detective Webster, sir. He has all the information."

"Because you gave it to him," Pierce said kindly. "That was very brave, Eve. You could be facing disciplinary action for breaking double-blind, but I think I can stop that. I know Dr. Donner's boss, Dean Jacoby. We're old friends. I can smooth the way."

She studied his face. "Why?" she asked baldly.

"You'll need others throughout your career, Eve. We all do. Colleagues, experts. Mentors. You found yourself in an untenable situation and you did the right thing. I'd hate to see you penalized. You have a great career ahead of you. It would be a travesty for you to lose it all before you even begin."

He took a business card from the pocket of his expensive suit and slid it across the bar. She stared at the card for a moment before putting it in her pocket. Then she met his eyes, remembering her manners. "Thank you. I'll keep it in mind."

He nodded once. "Good," he said and turned to put on his coat and gloves.

"Dr. Pierce, does Detective Webster know you came?"

"No. But as I said, it took less than five minutes to connect the study with you. You will be found out, but I think you knew that before you came forward."

"Yes, I did," she murmured and in his eyes she saw respect.

"Call me when you're ready for me to talk to the dean. But I wouldn't wait too long."

She toyed with the business card in her pocket as he walked away, then sucked in a breath when Sal appeared at her elbow. "Who was that?" Sal asked, frowning.

"Psychologist," Eve answered. "Works with the Hat Squad. Interested in my thesis."

"I see," Sal said stiffly and Eve looked up at him. He looked angry and . . . hurt.

He'd eavesdropped. *No surprise there.* "Go ahead. What did you hear?"

" 'Disciplinary action.' And last night you were with the Hats. What's going on?"

Eve dropped her voice. "Sal, somehow my thesis project is being used to hurt people. I can't tell you any more than that. I'm sorry."

"All right," he said in begrudging acceptance. "So what about disciplinary action?"

"The way I got information was . . . against the rules."

He met her eyes and once more she felt the scrutiny of another. But this was different. This was Sal. "Would you do it again?" he asked quietly.

"In a heartbeat," she said without hesitation. "Less than a heartbeat."

"Good enough for me," he said, then his eyes went sly. "So what about the kiss?"

Eve looked up at the ceiling, flustered. "Oh for God's sake."

"I knew it," Sal said smugly, rubbing his hands together. "I won the pool."

Eve stared at him. "There was a fucking pool?"

"Well, not a fucking pool." Sal snickered. "Just a kissing pool."

I should have known. She controlled the anger that rose, knowing it came from humiliation. "Well, I hope you won a bundle," she said quietly and he sobered quickly.

"Only a beer," he said. "Eve, what's wrong?"

Everything. A business card she was afraid to use, directions to a dinner she was afraid to attend. A good man who wanted her when he shouldn't. A man she wanted, but couldn't have, who'd end up hurt when this was over. A career on life support before it began. And over it all, three dead women, a dangerous man, and the real possibility he could strike again. That he was hunting fish in the very barrel she'd stocked.

A sudden urge to weep grabbed at her throat and she took an unsteady step back. "Nothing. I'm fine. I just need a break. Can you mind the bar?"

Without waiting for his answer, she went back to his office, hearing his heavy sigh. "Goddammit," he muttered, which Eve thought summed it up pretty well.

Chapter Twelve

The worst of Jack's anger had calmed by the time Noah got to the morgue. Ian had posted photographs of Samantha Altman's decomposed body on his board.

"Anything?" Noah asked, scanning the photos.

"Same MO," Jack said quietly. "Ket in her system, puncture wound on her neck."

"And dirt," Ian said, "in her mouth."

"What?" Noah leaned forward to get a better look at the photos. "Where?"

"You can see it in between her back molars," Ian said. "When the funeral home delivered the body, I asked them if they remembered anything different about this body."

"And?" Jack asked.

"Samantha had a viewing, and it's standard practice for them to put cotton in the deceased's cheeks to keep them from hollowing. The funeral director told me when the cosmetologist was adjusting the cotton in Samantha's cheeks, she saw dirt. She thought this was strange, but knew it was a suicide. They see all kinds of weirdness with suicides, just like we do. Some people eat dirt. We find it in their stomach contents."

"Did you find dirt in Samantha's stomach?" Noah asked.

"No, but I did find it other places. When I heard about dirt in her cheeks, I went back to all the samples Janice had taken in the first autopsy. I'd already submitted the blood samples she'd stored and they came back with the ketamine. Janice had scraped under the nails, just in case. Samantha had a lot of dirt under her nails, like she'd been digging in a garden. It's potting soil." Ian's eyes narrowed as he watched their faces. "It makes sense to you," he said grimly. "Tell me."

"He buried her alive," Noah said. "Her worst fear."

Ian stared. "Is that what the snake was all about? And the water in Martha's lungs, too? He's torturing them with their worst fears? My God, this guy is a real prince."

"And we just let him go," Jack said without emotion.

Ian's eyes grew wider. "You *let* him *go*?"

Noah shook his head. "No, we did not. Jack, we need to talk."

"Yeah, we do. But this first. Was there dirt in her lungs, Ian?"

Ian hesitated. "Yes."

Noah found himself hesitating as well. "Shouldn't that have been caught in the autopsy the first time around?"

"Yes, it should have been. Janice missed it. I don't know why, but she missed it."

"If she'd found it," Jack said, "we might have already been looking for a killer."

Ian nodded, pain in his eyes. "I know. This is going to kill her. She's a thorough ME. Maybe she was in a hurry, thinking it was a suicide. Maybe it was simple error. There wasn't that much dirt, but she shouldn't have missed it. I've informed my hierarchy and we'll have an internal investigation. In the meantime, we have to live with the fact that we could have prevented two more deaths."

"What was the official cause of death, Ian?" Noah asked. "Suffocation?"

"No, strangulation. I think she could breathe while buried. There are abrasions along her gumline." He pointed to the photos of Samantha's exposed teeth.

Noah pictured the options. "Snorkel?" he asked and Ian nodded.

"Probably. I think he took her out, cleaned her up, and hung her."

"If she could breathe, how did the dirt get in her lungs?" Jack asked.

"I don't know," Ian said wearily. "Maybe he put dirt down the snorkel on purpose, maybe it was an accident."

Noah didn't want to think about it, either way. "Anything else?"

"No." Ian began taking the photos down from the board. "I think that's enough."

Noah agreed. "We'll be in touch. Thanks." He waited until he and Jack were in the hall. "Come on. I'll buy you a cup of decent coffee. We need to clear some things up."

Jack nodded, still subdued. "All right."

Tuesday, February 23, 9:30 p.m.

"Hel*lo* there, Eve." Kurt Buckland slid onto a bar stool with a smug smile.

Eve gritted her teeth. She was getting damn sick and tired of visitors to the bar. "Mr. Buckland. Still stalking me, I see."

"Now, Eve. I'm simply sitting here at the bar, waiting for service."

"You'll be waiting a long time." She wanted to throw

him out, but Sal was their muscle, and after the "fucking pool" conversation he'd gone AWOL.

"That was an interesting show you put on at the Deli this morning," Buckland said.

She shrugged. "Believe what you want."

"It must have been hard to keep that secret from your best friend. I thought it quite interesting that Callie so adamantly insisted you weren't seeing anyone."

Eve started wiping down the bar, ignoring him as best she could. She should have warned Callie, but honestly the thought hadn't entered her mind. *I've been a bit busy.*

He slid a manila envelope across the bar. "Here are some pictures you should see."

"No, thank you. I've already seen your pictures once today."

"No, these are better. You'll see your detective isn't such a good guy after all."

Shaking her head, she turned away. "I'm not playing your game, Buckland. Leave."

He reached over the bar and grabbed her arm, his grip punishing. "I said, *look.*"

Fighting the instant panic that swelled within her, Eve calmly lifted her eyes to his and saw the crazed light of fury. "You are not a smart man, Kurt. This bar is filled with cops. I scream, and they drag you away in handcuffs. Take your hand off me. Now."

His eyes flickered, as if he'd momentarily forgotten where he was. He let her go, lowering himself back to his stool. "I apologize," he said stiffly.

Her pulse was still racing, but she kept her voice even. "I don't accept. Please go."

"Eve?" Regular Jeff Betz stepped up behind Buckland, hulking over him.

"I'm fine, Officer Betz. Mr. Buckland was just leaving." She shoved the envelope over the bar and into Buckland's hands. "Take this with you. I don't want it."

Buckland slid off the stool, the fire in his eyes now banked. "I'll be in touch."

When he was gone, she massaged her arm. It hurt worse than she wanted to let on.

"You're not fine," Jeff said. "You should get that looked at."

Eve looked up at him, her smile wan. "I've had a lot worse."

Jeff frowned, troubled. "Doesn't make it okay. You call if he bothers you again. I'm off to pick up my wife. Have Sal walk you to your car when you leave, Eve."

"I've got a ride, but tomorrow I will. Don't worry. I don't take chances." *Not anymore.*

Tuesday, February 23, 9:30 p.m.

"Why didn't you just tell me about Eve's information?" Jack asked wearily.

They'd met at the Deli, but had taken their coffee and conversation back to the privacy of Noah's car. "Because you haven't been exactly approachable today."

"I guess I deserve that. So what if it's not Girard? What do we do next?"

"Well, right now Abbott's moonlighting as a woman in Shadowland's bar, trying to attract this guy. Abbott is scarily convincing and, I think, having too much fun."

Jack's lips twitched. "Wish I'd stayed around to see that."

Some of the tension dissipated. "If Girard is our guy,

we've got surveillance tonight. Tomorrow we ask him to alibi the times Eve found the avatar files had been changed."

"But even if he was home, or at work, or anywhere people can verify his presence, he still could have gone online and made the changes. He could have just pretended to check his email. Or he could have taken a bathroom break and taken his laptop to the john. If his home or office has wireless Internet, he didn't even have to be at his desk."

"But if he doesn't alibi, we get a warrant for his computer and check online activities."

Jack nodded. "Makes sense. If he does alibi, we'll have to find something else to tie him to one of the crime scenes or the crimes in general."

Bathroom break. Jeremy Lyons. Noah closed his eyes. His tired brain was making delayed, haphazard connections. In the heat of tracking Girard, they'd lost sight of the most obvious connection. "Like Eve's list. Girard had to have had access to it. If he didn't, we have to comb through the people that did. Like Jeremy Lyons, Eve's advisor's secretary. Who knows things like her worst fear."

"Shit. Did you get any of those background checks back?"

"They weren't on my desk. I'll check tomorrow. Right now, I need to sleep."

"You want me to drive you?" Jack asked, his tone kinder than it had been all day.

"No. I'll be okay. But thanks."

"Then I'm going home." Opening the door, Jack hesitated. "Thanks for the coffee."

But Jack didn't move and Noah frowned. "Jack? Go home. Katie will be waiting."

Jack's lips twisted and when he spoke, it was with self-contempt. "If I'm lucky. She's only there because I'm on the cover of a goddamn magazine. And everybody knows it." He turned his head to look Noah in the eye. "Including you."

It was true. Katie had latched on to Jack the day after the story had hit the stands, just another woman in what had been a long line over the years. Noah remembered Eve's description of Jack. *Alone in a crowded room.* "I don't know what to say."

"I will apologize to Eve. But I didn't know how else to apologize to you."

Noah looked away, suddenly as emotionally over-whelmed as he'd been the night before when he'd called Brock. "We're a fine pair, Jack. Both of us are going home to empty beds. Yours just has a warm body in it."

Jack got out of Noah's car. "And on that bright note, I'm going home."

Noah had pulled out of the parking lot behind him when his cell vibrated. "Webster."

"It's Micki. I just got the message you left about Eve's keys. We didn't find them at the scene. We combed the entire area with a metal detector. They weren't there."

"Thanks, Mick. I appreciate you looking." He hung up, worried. Eve's keys should have been there, somewhere. Somebody had picked them up. Which meant somebody had free access to Eve's apartment. And to Eve. He shivered, suddenly much colder.

He did an abrupt U-turn. At least he could fix that.

Tuesday, February 23, 10:15 p.m.

"Here you are." He'd brought the evening cup of tea to the woman in his bed. It was a nice habit. The woman liked the tea and on the nights he went out, he added a little something more to put her right to sleep. He could come and go as he pleased and she'd never know. Then when she woke, he'd be sleeping beside her. Anything ever went wrong, instant alibi. There was beauty in simplicity.

"Thank you." She took the cup, frowning when the cat at her side jumped from the bed to wind around his legs. "Ringo likes you better. Why does he like you better? I'm the one who brought him in from the snow."

Because I put him there, knowing you'd bring him in. Ringo the cat had belonged to Martha Brisbane but had curled happily in his lap as he'd made Martha clean her hovel at gunpoint. It had given Martha great pain to watch her cat bond with the man who'd promised to kill her. Who'd followed through on that very promise.

He'd decided to keep Martha's cat. It was a memento he could enjoy in front of everyone. Visitors would pet the cat and only he would know from whence it had come. Letting the woman believe the cat rescue was her idea ensured her compliance without threat. He liked to save his threats for important things. He'd only had to strike her once and she'd learned quickly. But there were other, better ways of keeping a woman in line.

"Must be the liver on my hands," he said with a smile. *Or the blood. Metaphorically speaking, of course.* He'd have more metaphorical blood on his hands very soon.

"Must be," she said, still frowning at the cat. She sniffled a little. "Well, at least I can breathe when he's with you. I think I have an allergy."

Which was why she'd never choose a pet on her own. Not unless you counted as pets the snakes she kept in test aquariums in her research lab. And he did not. A snake was not a pet. A snake was a weapon of terror. Just ask Christy Lewis.

"I have work to do," he said. "Drink your tea. And don't wait up."

Tuesday, February 23, 11:00 p.m.

On her knees counting beer bottles in boxes, Eve did the evening inventory with a disgruntled sigh. "Sal, I wish you'd talked to me before you did that booze run. We're almost out of vodka." They went through an amazing amount of vodka. Most of the cops she'd met came to the bar to drink. A lot.

Except for Noah, a recovering alcoholic who'd ordered tonic water for a year . . . *So he could watch me.* It should have made her uncomfortable. Instead, it hurt. A lot.

Sal's shoes stopped next to her and she realized she was staring into the box, the heel of her hand pressed to her chest. "What's wrong, Eve?" he asked quietly.

Everything. "Just tired," she said, sitting back on her heels so she could see him.

Concern creased his forehead. "Go home. We're light tonight. I'll do inventory."

Only three customers lingered, but David had called to say he was running late. "My ride's not here yet, so I might as well finish. But thanks."

"Jeff told me what happened, with that reporter. You have to be more careful."

Her wrist still hurt from Buckland's grip. "Sure. Like it's *my* fault," she muttered.

"I never said that," he snapped. "Stand up. I can't get down there to argue with you."

Automatically she stood. Sal's bad leg didn't bend well. "I don't want to argue with you," she started, then stopped when he brought a bottle of wine from behind his back. She frowned at the label. "Nonalcoholic? What's this?"

"Peace offering. I'm sorry about the pool, Eve. I don't know why it hurt you, but it did, and I would never hurt you on purpose. Can't you tell me what's really wrong?"

Her eyes stung. This man had given her so much, so many chances. "Sal . . ." She looked away. "Did you ever want something so badly and know you could never have it? Something that everybody else has and you can only dream about?"

"Every damn day," he said quietly and she looked at his leg before meeting his eyes.

He was surrounded every day by men and women living his dream and he served them, always with a smile. "I guess you do." Hastily she scrubbed her wet cheeks.

"Honey, what do you want so badly that you think you can't have?"

She lifted a shoulder. "Just to be normal, I guess."

"We both know that's a total bullshit answer. But you'll tell me when you're ready." He put the bottle in her hands. "Forgiven?"

She kissed his cheek. "Of course. Thank you. I have a houseguest. We'll enjoy this."

"Uh . . . no," he said. "It's for you to take to Trina's on Sunday. Web can have this."

She looked at the nonalcoholic label, then back up at Sal. "You knew about Noah?"

"Of course. Back when he was in the academy he'd come in here, all swagger and bravado, just like all the young guys do. But after his wife's funeral he changed, fell way down the rabbit hole. He climbed out, though, and didn't come back here, for years."

Eve's breath caught in her throat. *His wife's funeral.*

Now she understood. Grief had driven him into the bottle. She wondered what had brought him out. *Poor Noah.*

"How many years?" she whispered.

"Nine or ten, at least. Then last year somebody retires, one of Web's friends. He darkens my doorstep for the first time in years, doesn't even take off his coat."

Eve remembered it well. It had been the first time she'd seen Noah come through Sal's door. He'd sat alone, the party going on around him, a tonic water in his hand.

Sal lifted her chin with his finger. "He stared at you all night. Didn't think a soul noticed him, but I did. Anybody that pays attention to you has to go through me and Josie. But I knew Web. He's a good man. And I was happy he was finally coming out of that cocoon he wrapped around himself when his wife died. Don't close your doors so quickly, Eve. You've made so much progress since you first came here, don't let it stop with the outside." He touched the tip of his finger to the scar on her cheek.

She sniffled. "I guess I'm lucky you're not a mean boss."

"So you'll take the bottle to Trina's?"

No, she thought sadly, but she made herself smile at him. "Sure."

He didn't smile back. "Trina's right. You are a lousy liar."

She was saved a reply by the jingling of the door. Automatically she turned. Stopped. And stared as Noah came through the door. Her chest went so tight she could barely breathe and she drank in the sight of him, greedily, desperately, too tired to try to hide it. It didn't matter. Everyone seemed to have known anyway.

Noah pushed the door closed and for five painful beats of her heart he looked at her.

She felt the bottle being taken from her numb hands. "Speak of the devil," Sal said quietly. "I'll just go in the back."

Noah took off his hat and she could see the flash of his eyes. He was angry. *Oh, no*, she thought, panic rising in her throat. *Not another one*. Not another dead woman. Crossing the room, he tossed his hat to the bar without a glance.

Then before she could draw a breath to speak, his hands framed her face and his mouth was on hers, hot and hungry and she couldn't breathe at all. He ended it as abruptly as he'd begun, pulling back far enough to see her eyes. "That was real," he said, his voice low and rough. "And that wasn't for my *job*. That was for *me*."

She stared up at him, stunned, her breath coming in short pants.

"And for you," he added quietly. "Especially for you." He took his hands from her face and she realized she gripped the lapels of his overcoat. Her right fist throbbed, but she didn't let go. Wasn't sure she could.

He pried her right hand from his coat, pushed her sleeve past her wrist. His face darkened. "Buckland put his hands on you. He bruised you."

Her heart beat like a rabid hummingbird and her knees were still weak as she saw the dark bruises that had formed from Kurt Buckland's fingers. "How did you know?"

"Jeff Betz called me when he left to pick up his wife. He'd heard about this morning, figured I'd want to know about tonight. Would you have told me, Eve?"

"Yes," she said, without hesitation. "He grabbed me because I wouldn't look at some pictures he had in an envelope. He said I'd see you weren't such a 'good guy.' "

"What were the pictures?"

"I don't know. I wouldn't look. He got mad and Jeff made him leave. He was scary, like he was wound too tight and the rubber band broke."

His lips twitched, surprising her. "Is that your clinical diagnosis?"

She didn't smile. "He's dangerous, Noah. You need to be careful."

His eyes narrowed and she knew he was still angry despite the little injection of humor. Deliberately he looked at the wrist he still held with gentle fingers. "Just me?"

Her knees steadier now, she tugged her wrist free and took a step back. "Okay, both of us. He didn't look quite sane for a minute." She touched the tip of her tongue to her lip. It was still tingling, distracting her from the memory of Kurt Buckland lunging over the bar. *That wasn't for my job.* "Jeff also told you that Trina was here."

"Yeah. He . . . overheard," he said and Eve rolled her eyes.

"He eavesdropped on a private conversation. You cops are so nosy."

"If we weren't nosy we wouldn't catch many bad guys. And you should know there is no such thing as a private conversation here. Did Buckland hurt your hand?"

"No, just the bruise on my wrist."

"You're going to press charges in case you need a TRO against this sonofabitch."

She knew he was right. "All right. So if you know about Trina and Buckland, you also know Dr. Pierce was here."

He winced at that. "I'm sorry. I tried to keep you out of it. I should have known Carleton wouldn't let it ride. He thought he could help you. I was going to tell you about him and let you make the decision, but I guess that's water under the bridge now."

"I guess so. He could be right. He might be able to help me."

"But?"

She moved her shoulders. "I'm not comfortable with that kind of help." She turned away from him, kneeling back down by the beer box, discomfited when he crouched beside her. He was big and warm and she wanted him to kiss her again far too much. "No other victims, right? I was worried when I saw you that you'd found another."

"No. No more victims that I know of."

"Good. I've got to do inventory before my ride comes. Go get some rest."

"Eve." She didn't look up so he gently grasped her chin and forced her to look at him. "Your ride is right here. Leave that till tomorrow. I'll take you home." His mouth bent in an awkward smile she wished she didn't find so endearing. "Hunter drove up when I did. He had a crowd in his truck. Looked like an entire college basketball team."

"He and Tom must have found a pickup game somewhere. Tom's his nephew. He's a home team star," she added, unashamed of the unabashed pride in her voice.

"Tom Hunter. I've seen him play. The kid is really good. You know him?"

Eve's brows lifted at his hopeful tone. "You want me to get you tickets, don't you?"

"I wouldn't say no." He smiled when she chuckled. "Really, how do you know him?"

She sobered. "Yesterday you asked why that man tried to kill me six years ago."

His smile disappeared. "You said he wanted to get to his wife and son. Oh." He'd made the connection, she could see. "Tom was his son."

"Yes. Tom and I both lived in the same shelter for a

while, so we kind of grew up together. After Tom's father was caught, his mother ended up marrying David's brother. The Hunters are family. Tom's the reason I picked Minneapolis."

His dark brows crunched slightly. "You picked it?"

"I'd finally decided I couldn't stay in Chicago. I had a quarter in my hand and a map on the table. Heads Carolina, tails California. Then the phone rang. Tom had just been offered a basketball scholarship here in Minneapolis. So I decided to come with him."

"Then I'm even happier he's there," he murmured, meeting her eyes directly.

Flustered, she looked back into her box. "Where is David?"

"He said he had to drive the guys back to their dorm, but he didn't want you to have to wait so he said they'd have to squeeze you in. I told him I'd take you home." He reached into his coat pocket and pulled out a plastic bag. "Peace offering."

"I seem to be getting a lot of these tonight." She peeked inside. "A deadbolt?"

He frowned slightly. "CSU didn't find your keys. Somebody could have picked them up. I'll change your lock for you."

Eve was suddenly cold. "I didn't leave my door unlocked yesterday, did I?"

His eyes flickered and she knew he agreed. "I don't know, but I'd rather be careful."

"Buckland was at the scene last night. He took pictures of my car."

Noah's eyes narrowed. "You think he has your keys?"

"It's possible, isn't it?"

His lips thinned. "Probable even." Then he stood and

pulled her to her feet, his eyes dangerous. "Let me take you home. I'll replace your lock before I leave."

Wednesday, February 24, 12:15 a.m.

Eve's cell phone vibrated on the arm of her stuffed chair. It was David, which meant he was at her front door. She'd called to tell him that Noah changed the lock, resulting in a string of harsh profanity toward Buckland. She opened the door. "Sshh," she cautioned.

She waved him to follow her to the kitchen, tiptoeing past Noah, who sat sprawled on her sofa. "He fell asleep," she whispered. "I fixed him something to eat while he replaced the deadbolt, but he was out cold. I think he's just exhausted."

"He must be, to have fallen asleep on that thing. I didn't sleep a wink last night."

"Go sleep in my bed. I'll take the sofa when he wakes up and goes home."

"Sleep in your own bed." He opened the shopping bag he held in his hand. "Blow-up mattress."

She shook her head. "It'll make too much noise when you inflate it. You'll wake him up."

"He can't have been asleep that long. Wake him up and send him home."

It would be the logical thing to do. But she shook her head again. "Let him sleep. You take my bed." David complied and Eve returned to the living room where Noah hadn't budged. He'd taken off his overcoat and suit coat to replace her lock, but still wore his shoes, his tie. And his gun.

He'll get a crick in his neck sprawled like that. She tugged on his feet, staggering under the weight of his long legs as she lifted them to the sofa. If he woke, so be it. But he didn't, not even when she took off his shoes and loosened his tie.

She should move, but stayed crouched at his side, looking into his face. Her eyes dropped to his mouth. She'd kissed that mouth. In the Deli she'd told herself it was for his job. Damage control. But she'd wanted to kiss him. She'd wanted to for months.

She relived that moment in the bar when he'd kissed her for himself. She'd wanted him to do it again, but he hadn't. He'd brought her home and kept his hands to himself. She looked at his hands, wondered how they'd feel, cruising over her skin.

After a year of *look, don't touch* this might be her only opportunity to do either. Or both. Experimentally she trailed her fingertips across the line of his jaw, hard and unyielding even in sleep. His dark stubble was rough, prickly. She skimmed his lips with one finger. Soft. They'd been hard earlier, when he'd kissed her in the bar.

When he didn't stir she became bolder, brushing the back of her fingers over his cheek, pushing his hair from his forehead, running her thumb over the ridge of his brow. He was, quite simply, beautiful. She smiled wryly, fairly certain he wouldn't like that.

She pulled her hand back before she gave in to the temptation to explore further.

"Don't stop." He opened his eyes, held hers.

She froze. "I . . . I thought you were asleep."

"I was. Now I'm not." He took her hand, held it as if it were fragile glass as he pressed his lips to her wrist where her pulse hammered. Carefully he tugged, pulling her to him, his other hand threading through her hair.

Yes. Please. "No." She lurched to her feet and he let her

go. Lying flat on his back, he looked up at her, his eyes asking the question his voice did not. Closing her eyes, she pursed the side of her mouth that obeyed. "I don't have to explain to you."

"No. No, you don't have to." He sat up. "Look at me, Eve."

"I'm sorry," she whispered, ashamed for herself and sad for them both.

He shook his head. "There's no need to be sorry. Are you all right?"

"I'm fine. I was just checking on my red-zones."

He patted the cushion next to him. "Then show me. I need to understand them."

Come on, Eve, Noah thought. *Give me this much.* He waited, exhaling silently when she picked up her computer and sat next to him, taking care not to touch him.

But she had, and it was all he'd been able to do to keep from rolling her beneath him and taking what he craved. Thankfully he'd held himself in check. Eve had always made him think of a doe, nervous and ready to flee. Tonight, she was more so than ever. But she'd ventured closer. *That has to be good enough for now.*

Beside him, she drew a breath and pushed her laptop screen back so he could see. "I'm using Greer tonight, checking out Ninth Circle for three of my red-zones."

Her scent filled his head and he tried to focus. "Three? Aren't there five?"

"Yes, but Rachel will be dancing at the casino." She said it as a professor might lecture. "Natalie is always there, playing poker. We'll go there when I'm done. There's the dancer who was with Christy."

He choked back a cough. The male avatar was dancing

with Lola, Abbott's raven-haired siren. Noah slid his arm across the back of the sofa. "What are they dancing?"

She glanced pointedly over her shoulder at his arm. He wasn't touching her, but he was in her space. But she didn't protest and he let himself relax a little. "Salsa," she said levelly. "It's not as easy it looks. You execute the dance steps with a series of keystrokes. It's fast and complex and my right hand still isn't dexterous enough."

If that made her wistful, it didn't show in her voice. Nothing showed in her voice, which had him increasingly frustrated. Over the next twenty minutes, Greer located three of Eve's five remaining red-zones. She pointed them out, and in that same professorial tone she told him everything she knew about them. She knew quite a lot actually, likes, dislikes, what they searched for in the virtual world.

"This one is Kathy," Eve said. "In Shadowland, she's a real estate tycoon. IRL, she's a retired real estate agent. She's thirty-eight years old."

IRL meant *in real life*, he recalled. "She's retired at thirty-eight? Why?"

"Kathy has a degenerative muscle disease. She's been in a wheelchair for a year now and it'll just get worse." She swallowed hard. "She told me when she came into Pandora's to buy her avatar. When she's not making deals, she plays virtual tennis. She continues the life she had in the real world, here. I didn't know she was one of my test subjects until I hacked the list, right after Martha disappeared."

"Bittersweet," he murmured. "She can do what she loves, but it's all pretend."

"Sometimes that has to be enough," she murmured, then looked up at him, her expression suddenly anxious. "Noah, she can't defend herself. If he comes after her . . ."

He frowned at the screen. "Does she live with anybody?"

"No. She lives alone with a service dog. A nurse checks in on her once a day."

"So she can't leave her house to meet him? That's been his MO."

"No, she's homebound. So she's safe, right?"

"I'll have a cruiser do drive-bys and when I leave here, I'll check on her myself." He called Abbott's cell, knowing he was still awake, and made the request. "It's done."

"Thank you," she said. Then she pulled away. "All red-zones are accounted for."

Frustrated, he kept his voice level. "So we're off to the casino?"

"Yes. Finding the last two won't take long."

Which was a shame. He wanted this time with her. Needed it. "Then let's go."

Greer was winding through the crowd when a message popped up at the base of the screen. *Can I buy you a drink tonight?*

"Him again. I swear, he hits on Greer every night." *Sorry, I'm calling it an early night,* she typed back. *Try that black-haired dancer over there. She's been doing the salsa for a while. I bet she's thirsty.*

I tried her. She was rude, too.

"I feel sorry for him," she said softly. "He's just hoping for some attention." *I'm sorry,* she typed. *I didn't mean to be rude.*

Then let me buy you a drink.

Look, I'm in a hurry tonight. How about a rain check? Next time, for sure.

The avatar's face beamed. *I'll hold you to it.*

"Will you let him buy you a drink next time?" Noah asked.

"I don't make promises I don't keep." She sent Greer to the casino and turned up the volume. He was suddenly struck by the feel of a real Vegas casino. Noise and activity . . . and anticipation. Greer stopped at a poker table. "That's Natalie."

A voluptuous redhead sat at a poker table and from the stack of chips in front of her, was doing very well. Eve paused for a moment to watch.

"Do you play?" Noah asked. "I mean as an avatar."

She smiled, faintly. "Used to, but I don't have time anymore. A few years ago, I was the one to beat. Or my Moira avatar was. She was the grand poker champion."

She picked names for a reason, he knew. "Moira. What does it mean?"

"It's a little twist on Moirae. The Three Fates in Greek mythology."

"Hm." He was quiet for a moment. Fate, not luck or skill. "So you *do* believe in fate?"

"I wish I did," she said without inflection. "Things would be so much simpler."

"Did you ever play poker IRL?" he asked wryly.

"A little five-card stud with friends, never for money. But Moira made a lot of money."

He fidgeted, her sofa poking him. "I hope she spent hers on a comfy sofa."

"No, she cashed out, and I converted Moira's Shadowbucks into real-world money."

"Which you did not spend on a comfy sofa."

She shook her head, totally serious. "I bought my freedom. A car that got me away from Chicago, first and last month's rent on this place. The rest I used to pay my first semester's tuition. After that it was touch and go, but thanks to Sal, I manage all right."

Noah thought of the last year, when she'd thought no one was watching. "You give your money away," he said, his throat suddenly tight. "I've seen you," he insisted when she looked like she would deny it. "I've seen you take dollars from your tip jar and give them away. To two women." The same two women, he realized. "Who are they?"

"They operate a women's shelter. When they need a little to tide them over . . ."

"You give it to them." He swallowed hard. "You are a very generous woman."

She looked up then, her dark eyes intense. "Fate is simply circumstance, Noah. The circumstance of birth, of ability, of events. Choice is what you do with it. I may not believe in fate," she said, "but I do believe in choice. And I believe in giving back."

People need purpose, she'd told him. *But people also need lives*, he thought, *and I've been without one too long.* And so had Eve. He was trying to think of a way to say that without seeming self-serving when a stir at the poker table broke the moment.

She turned back to her screen as a chorus of boos erupted. Crowd favorite Natalie had lost big. Raking in the chips was a male avatar, very dashing. "Who is that?"

She scowled. "Dasich. He fancies himself quite a card shark. He cheats."

"How do you know?"

"He wins too often and too well. I think he has a confederate at the table. But being in the virtual world, that's hard to prove."

"He looks like one of your designs. Very handsome."

"He is, and he proves what I've always known. Bad people rarely look bad. If bad people look sleazy, good people don't trust them. Cops like you catch them more easily. But if bad people look normal, honest . . ."

"Trustworthy?" he asked, and she nodded.

"Yeah. Then they're able to worm their way in, find the vulnerability, exploit it."

He wondered if she knew how hard her voice had become. Brittle. "And I?" he asked. "Am I one of those people looking to exploit your vulnerability?"

She glanced up, her eyes now guarded. "Yes. Not for nefarious reasons, but you have an agenda." She smiled, attempting to soften her words. "You've been alone too long, and you want someone again. For some reason, you've decided that's me."

She had a way of boiling things down to the bottom line. "But?" he asked, sharply.

"It can't be me," she said simply, then pointed at the screen. "Natalie's avatar is pissed off and filing a grievance against Dasich. Not much chance of justice, but at least she's here and not meeting a serial killer somewhere. One more red-zone to go and we're done for the night. Rachel Ward, where are you?"

Noah knew she'd tried to let him down gently, as she had the lonely avatar who kept trying to buy her a drink. He also knew he should take the hint and walk away. But he'd seen the loneliness in her eyes, too, and he wasn't giving up just yet.

She sent Greer to a stage in a dark corner where dancers writhed more erotically than animated characters should. "Rachel's Delilah should be dancing tonight."

Eve's face became troubled as she searched the area. "But she's not," he said.

"No, but the night's still young. Rachel might just be late."

"So what do we do?" Noah asked.

"I'll wait and watch. I'm sure you have other things to do."

Noah leaned back, got as comfortable as her sofa allowed. "I've got time."

She looked up at him, frowning in frustration. "You're not taking a hint, are you?"

He tried for smooth even though his heart pounded. "No. Are you throwing me out?"

Something moved in her eyes. "I made you a sandwich earlier. It's in the fridge."

He let out the breath he'd been holding. "I could eat."

She sighed. "You want some tonic water with that?"

"I hate tonic water."

"You—?" She shook her head. "Then cola or juice or milk?"

He stood when she did. "Milk. And let's be quiet so we don't disturb your guest."

Her eyes narrowed. "You sneak. You just pretended to be asleep the whole time."

He smiled, but grimly. "Like you said, I have an agenda. Let's eat."

Wednesday, February 24, 12:45 a.m.

"Your sister was arrested with a prostitute named Belle," Olivia had said when she'd picked Liza and Tom up. They found Belle pretty easily in one of the bars Liza hadn't been allowed to enter the night before.

"Detective Olivia," Belle said. "How the hell are you?"

"Wishing I weren't seeing you here," Olivia said, but

kindly. "I'm looking for the woman in this picture. Her name is Lindsay Barkley. Do you know her?"

"Yeah, I know her. We call her Little Red, on account of her hair."

"So have you seen her?" Olivia asked. "She hasn't been home lately."

Belle thought. "Not since the weekend. She was working the Hay."

The Hay Hotel, Liza thought. "I checked there last night. Nobody's seen her. Please, anything you can think of."

Belle's face was sympathetic. "You might try Jonesy. He's been watchin'."

"Why?" Olivia said, narrowing her eyes. "Why's he watching? And who?"

"I s'pose he has his reasons. That's all I know. I'd tell you if I knew. I would."

"Who is Jonesy?" Liza asked when they were back in Olivia's car.

"Minor dealer. Don't go looking. I'll ask my pals in narcotics if they know him."

"All right," Liza said. "I've got to sleep tonight. Can you call me tomorrow?"

"If I know something, I will."

Chapter Thirteen

Rachel Ward noted with bleary-eyed annoyance that her glass had become empty. "Another, please. Vodka, straight up."

The bartender shook his head. "Last call was five minutes ago. I'll call you a cab."

She glared at the man, then dropped her eyes to glare at her empty glass. She'd lost count of how many she'd had while waiting for that sonofabitch John. He'd stood her up. Got her worked up into a froth, then had stood her up.

"No, I have a ride." She pushed away from the bar, teetering in her high heels. It had been a long time since she'd worn heels. Five years. The same amount of time since she'd been to a bar. Or had sex. That hadn't ended so well, either.

She thought of Bernie, rotting in his cell, and felt a pang of regret mixed with anger. If he hadn't gone and fucked everything up . . . He'd had affairs on the road, she knew he did. She'd found countless matchbooks from truck stops and condom wrappers in his pockets. He'd never even denied it. *Patted me on the head and said men had needs.*

It still made her blood boil. And he'd expected her to be some little nun, just waiting for her man to roll out of his rig into her bed every two weeks? That hadn't been what she'd signed up for when she'd married him. He wasn't the man she'd thought he was.

That he'd been so stunned at her affairs had been a shock to her. That he'd been so angry made her furious. That he'd been capable of such brutality still horrified her, down to her bones. And that people had died in the fire Bernie set was something she still hadn't been able to forget. She could still hear their screams in her nightmares.

She'd been good for five years. Done penance. Gone to church. Tonight was supposed to be a little . . . reward. Time off for good behavior. But once again, she'd picked wrong. John seemed so nice online. So honest. And as horny as she was.

But he'd stood her up. *Maybe he came in, but didn't like what he saw and left.* She knew the years had not been good to her. In the last five years she'd aged twenty. John had seemed straight. A businessman who was in town for one night and only wanted sex. No ties, no relationship for Bernie to find out about.

Because Bernie would find out if she got a boyfriend. He had ways. She knew he kept tabs on her, even from the state pen. His letters contained sly references to her routine, to any promotions at work. To the flu she'd just gotten over. Anything to let her know he watched her, that he hadn't forgiven her.

Discovering Shadowland had been the best damn thing that ever happened to her. She could be herself, not worry about what anybody told Bernie. She could fuck twenty guys in a night online and nobody would ever know. *Sometimes you wanna go where no one knows your name. Ain't that the truth.* Looked like that was where she'd end up tonight. *I should stop for batteries on my way home*, she thought glumly.

She searched for her keys, then looked up to find the bartender giving her a pitying look. *Smug bastard.* "First sobriety test, ma'am. You gave me your keys when you sat down. That you forgot is a good sign that you shouldn't be driving. I'll call you a cab."

She knew better than to argue. She also knew she needed her car to get to work in the morning. She had a key hidden under her car. "Fine. But I'll need my house keys."

"All right." He fished her keys from a bowl, then dropped her key ring on the floor. When he bent to retrieve it, she saw opportunity and deftly grabbed one of the bottles he'd clustered on the bar as he did inventory and put it under her coat.

Second sobriety test, she thought smugly. *If the customer can steal from you, they're not that drunk.* Besides, the extra booze would help her sleep. She'd planned to have a man in her bed for the first time in five years. Sleeping alone wouldn't be fun.

The bartender wrestled with her key ring. "Here's your house keys."

She took them with a level nod. "Thanks. I'll wait outside for my cab."

"It's five degrees outside, ma'am."

"I know. I need the air. Have a good night."

Wednesday, February 24, 1:02 a.m.

Rachel hadn't wanted to meet in a coffee shop. She hadn't been out on a date in five years, she'd said when they'd made the arrangements online. She'd suggested this bar and it was fine by him. The cameras in their parking lot hadn't worked in years and it was a house of rather ill repute where patrons liked their privacy, so anybody coming here was unlikely to talk about anyone they'd seen waiting here.

He'd gotten a good bit of work done, as he'd been waiting for quite a while. Rachel Ward had outlasted all of his previous victims at nearly two hours and holding. But it was last call, so she'd be stumbling out soon.

And there she was. He frowned. She appeared to be drunk. He hoped she made it home. Having her pulled over for a DUI would be enormously inconvenient, especially as he'd gone to the trouble of readying her house for the evening.

Rachel stumbled across the parking lot in a pair of very high heels. He loved to see women in heels, the higher the better. It kept them hobbled and, he hoped, in pain. She stooped to fish a spare key from beneath her car, got in, and pulled onto the highway.

A minute later, he followed.

Wednesday, February 24, 1:40 a.m.

"Is Rachel there yet?" Noah asked and Eve looked up from the files she'd been reviewing to check her laptop screen.

"No." Rachel's avatar was still AWOL from the stage and Natalie was winning again now that Dasich had quit for the evening. "And she should be."

"I'll send a cruiser to her house," he said. "Give me her address."

Eve found it on the participant list. "And if she's not home?"

His eyes sharpened. "Then we assume he'll be following her home. I'll assemble a team and we'll be waiting to take him down." He made the call to Dispatch, then returned to the stack of graphs he'd been plodding through a page at a time. "Are you finding anything here? Because I'm not, except that grad students generate a lot of data."

After devouring a sandwich, he'd asked to see the logs Eve kept of her subjects' Shadowland play time. They'd been sitting on her sofa, poring over data for an hour. Eve stifled a yawn. "You can take this with you. You don't have to read them here. Just call me when you get word on Rachel."

He frowned, surprised. "You don't have to stay up. Go to bed if you're tired."

She narrowed her eyes at him. "You're sitting on my bed."

He looked incredulous. "You were planning to sleep on this torture device?"

"I have one bed and David's in it. Which you knew because you were awake."

"This is a two-bedroom apartment. What's in the other bedroom?"

"Boxes full of more data. I'm sorry, Noah, but you can't stay here tonight."

"Where were you going to sleep when you thought I was sleeping?"

"In my chair. Look, you were supposed to change my deadbolt, then leave. No offense intended and I appreciate everything you've done, but I'm in no danger. David put in a new security system this afternoon and he's here with me. And I have my gun. Besides, you promised you'd check on Kathy, the lady in the wheelchair, and Rachel."

"A cruiser went by Kathy's house and could see her through her front window. She was on her computer, totally alive and safe."

"How do you know? Nobody called you."

"Abbott texted me. But I did promise, so I will check on her and Rachel on my way home, even if the cruisers say everything is normal." He lifted a brow. "I also don't make promises I don't keep."

"Point taken. But you never said you would leave."

"I'll move to the chair so you can stretch out." He moved himself and the files to her chair and sat with a satisfied sigh. "Much more comfortable. Give me your gun."

"Why?"

"So I can check it out. When did you last fire it?"

"Three weeks ago when I went to target practice with Sal. If you're satisfied with my gun, will you leave?"

He just held out his hand. Rolling her eyes, she dug in her computer bag, finding the gun where it always was. Except it wasn't as she'd left it. As soon as her hand closed over it, she knew something was wrong. She drew it out, her heart pounding yet again.

Noah took it from her hand, then met her eyes. "You'd have a hell of a time hitting a target with this thing, considering it's not loaded. I'm guessing this surprises you."

Dread tightened her gut. "It had a full clip when I left the house tonight. I was so rattled by Buckland and Jeremy Lyons following me to the Deli that I double-checked."

"Someone had access to your bag. Where do you keep it when you're working?"

"In Sal's desk drawer in the back office. To answer your

next questions, the only people working tonight were me and Sal, but there is a door to the alley, for the trash."

"Give me your bag." He put on a pair of gloves and pulled out a manila envelope with her name written in block letters with a thick marker. "Feels like photos."

Her blood went colder. "That's the envelope Buckland tried to make me take."

"Then let's find out what he wants you to see so badly." He slit the envelope open with his penknife, then uttered a hoarse curse. "Sonofabitch. Sonofafuckingbitch."

Eve looked over his shoulder. And went still. In Noah's hands were photos of himself and a petite redhead, locked in an embrace as they stood on a front porch. The number on the house matched the address on the piece of paper still in Eve's pocket.

"Trina," she murmured. Trina's arms were around Noah's neck, his around her back. Her face was pressed against his neck and he looked like he was holding on for dear life. *Not good. Not good at all.*

"Sonofabitch," he repeated viciously. "She hugged me. That's all." He looked at Eve with a glare. "You can't believe this? She's my family, goddammit."

He'd misinterpreted the concern on her face. "No," she said and briefly touched her hand to his. He was shaking with fury. "I've seen her at the bar, seen her with you. I don't believe she'd do it. And I don't believe you would. So calm down."

He did, shifting back to cop. "This means Buckland was at Brock's Sunday night."

"Sunday night?"

"Well, Monday morning, actually. Must have been two, three in the morning."

"Why were you at Brock's at two in the morning?"

He shrugged sheepishly. "Why am I here with you at two in the morning?"

"That's not an answer, Noah."

"Yeah, it actually is. I went to Brock's because I needed a drink, so Brock and I boxed some, punched out my craving. Always happens when I've been to Sal's."

He said it without accusation, but she felt guilty just the same. "Because of me."

He looked her square in the eye. "Yes."

Eve set this most recent declaration aside for later consideration, focusing instead on the timing. "Monday, at two in the morning? You'd just found Martha, Christy was still alive, and nobody knew about Samantha yet."

"Except my team." He looked puzzled, then his eyes widened. "He was following me even before the serial killer story broke."

"In a very personal way. I told you he didn't look quite sane. He said I wouldn't think you were a 'good guy' after I saw these. I think he's after you and I just got in the way."

Noah massaged the back of his neck. "Why would he be after me?"

"I don't know. Do you know him?"

"Not before this. I'll report it to Abbott. Fine timing, just as we get a serial killer running around. And yes, I'm thinking what you're thinking."

"That it's no coincidence."

"Our reporter just got a whole lot less sane. He threatened you and he's hanging around my family. I need to call Brock, make sure Trina and the boys are okay."

He rose, piled the files on the floor, then paced as he dialed. He cursed and dialed another number, then a third. "Nobody's answering at home or either of their cells."

"Then go, make sure they're all right. Call me when you know."

He shrugged into his coat. "Brock and Trina are both cops. I'm sure they're fine."

"I'm sure they are, too. I'll lock the door and call you if I hear so much as a rustle."

He paused at the front door, his expression intense. "Thank you."

"For what?"

"Believing I wasn't the kind of man to cheat with my cousin's wife."

"You're welcome. Noah, call me about Rachel Ward?"

"As soon as I hear from the cruiser. I promise."

"Thank you. Be careful." She locked the door behind him, more hollow than relieved as she sat in her chair to wait for his call. She'd told him to go, but she missed him already. *I could get used to having a man in my house. In my life.*

She thought about his admission, that he craved a drink after going to Sal's to see her. He'd risked a great deal to watch her all those months. He was stubborn. *He'd probably call it determined.* Either way, he wasn't going to give up.

"I'll just tell him the truth," she said quietly. "Then he'll leave on his own. It'll be for the best." And when he was gone, she'd have her work. "If I'm not expelled." She still had Dr. Pierce's card. Perhaps it was time to start damage control on her career.

* * *

Wednesday, February 24, 1:45 a.m.

It was anticlimactic, actually. He stood staring down at Rachel Ward with a frown. She was sitting rather docilely on the counter stool he'd dragged to the middle of her basement floor. He hadn't needed to sedate her to strap her in the straitjacket and tie her to the stool. She'd had so much to drink it was a wonder she'd made it home.

She'd been a road menace, weaving lane to lane. Thankfully they had encountered no police and Rachel had managed to stagger into her house. Pushing her through her front door had been child's play. It was a disgrace. *No more bars. Insist on coffee.*

She was staring up at him, her eyes glazed. She should be coherent, conscious, ready to be scared to death. But she was nearly asleep, goddammit.

He could just strangle her, set the scene and get out, or he could wait for her to sober up. He might have something in his kit to speed her up. So to speak. Half the fun was in seeing their fear and he didn't want to give up his fun without a fight.

Wednesday, February 24, 2:10 a.m.

Eve put her cell phone on one arm of her chair and settled in, her computer on her lap and her hands wrapped around a mug of hot coffee. Buckland had unloaded her gun. *Why?* Had he planned to attack her and wanted her helpless? Or had he just wanted her to know he was there? That he could get close to her wherever she was?

"Just to fuck with my mind," she murmured. Who was this guy? And what self-respecting newspaper would hire him? Buckland was a stalker. He needed to be stopped before he hurt someone. *Too late*. She rotated her wrist. *He hurt you*.

He had. And if she hadn't worked in a cop bar and if Jeff Betz hadn't been right there, eavesdropping, he could have hurt her much worse.

Setting her mug aside she googled Kurt Buckland. And frowned. He was legit, with bylines on the *Mirror* going back years. Local stuff, neighborhood news. Of course the inside scoop on a serial killer could catapult him from Metro to the front page—and had. His "Red Dress Killer" article had been at the bottom of page one of Tuesday's paper.

With a start she realized he'd written the article on Martha's suicide she'd shown to Donner. She'd been so shocked she hadn't noticed the reporter's name. Tomorrow she'd report his assault to the police. And to his boss. He had to be stopped.

A flashing tab at the bottom of her screen caught her eye. It was the open Shadowland window. Someone was talking to Greer. *Poor Greer*. Eve had left her sitting at the bar in the cabaret, waiting for Rachel's avatar to show up. Eve toggled back and saw the bartender was scolding Greer for loitering.

Buy another drink or leave.

I'm sorry, Eve typed. *I'm waiting for someone. Maybe you know her. Delilah?*

That trash? She's not here tonight.

He said no more and Eve had Greer transfer a few Shadowbucks to the bartender's tip jar. Money talked in any world. *I need to talk to her. Who might have seen her?*

The bartender avatar hesitated, then shrugged. *That one over there, with the purple hair*. The dancer's nude body was painted with tiger stripes that clashed with her purple 'do. *They sometimes sit together at the bar while they're waiting to hook up for the night.*

You mean, like meeting guys? To take home? Does Delilah do that often?

Do you consider ten or twelve times a night often?

Ew. She'd never understood the lure of virtual sex. *Thanks*, she typed and added a few more Shadowbucks to the tip jar, then sent Greer to the stage. *Excuse me. Miss?*

The dancer was wrapped around a pole, hips gyrating in an intriguing move Eve was sure took at least as many keystrokes as salsa dancing. *I don't do girls. Go away.*

I don't want to hook up with you, Eve typed. *I'm looking for Delilah.*

She ain't here. She don't do girls neither. That one over there does.

Eve shuddered. Ew. *I don't want to hook up. I need to talk to Delilah. Where is she?*

She had a date. The gyrating hips bucked lewdly to the beat of cymbals. *IRL.*

Eve's heart beat faster. IRL? *Did she say who with? Somebody she met here?*

The dancer frowned. *I'm a businesswoman here.*

Grinding her teeth, Eve transferred Shadowbucks to the dancer's garter belt. *Well?*

Don't know his real name. Here, he goes by John. Gonna be a one-night stand.

You ever hook up with John, here in the World?

Nah, not my type. Too bookish. Get enough of that on my day job. Now go away. I can't type and dance at the same time and my set's almost over.

Thanks, Eve typed, then backed Greer out of the casino and dialed Noah's cell.

Wednesday, February 24, 2:15 a.m.

Noah parked his car in Brock's driveway, reining in his panic. They still weren't answering his calls. They'd better have a damn good explanation for this.

He knocked on their front door, scanning the road for any car that didn't belong. He was here often enough that he knew the neighborhood vehicles. But nothing seemed out of place, except that nobody was answering his knock.

He found their key on his ring and let himself in. He drew his weapon and held it to his side, creeping through the darkened house, breathing a sigh of relief when he found the boys snug in their beds and sleeping soundly. He knocked lightly on Brock and Trina's bedroom door, nudging it open when no one answered. Empty.

It was then he heard the shower. More correctly, he heard the shower stop. The master bath door opened, revealing a scowling Brock. He wore a robe that was soaked through and his wet hair stood up in spikes.

"This had better be good," Brock said deliberately, through clenched teeth.

Noah looked him up and down. "You didn't answer your phone."

Brock drew an uneven breath. "So you rushed over here in the middle of the night?"

"Brock?" Trina came through the door and Noah looked away, but not in time to miss getting a glimpse of her in a very, very small towel.

Noah winced, staring at his shoe. "I can see my concern was misplaced."

"Y'think?" Brock asked acidly. "You're not the only

one who ever has a goddamn bad day." With that he stalked out of his bedroom, grabbing clothes on his way.

"For God's sake, Noah," Trina snapped. "What's this all about?"

Noah kept his eyes averted. "We need to talk."

"Right now is not a good time."

"Yeah, I can see that." He thought of the photos in his pocket, of Buckland out there somewhere with a telephoto lens. "But it's important."

She huffed impatiently. "Fine. What*ever*. You can look now."

Noah saw with relief that she'd wrapped her body in a robe. "I'm sorry," he said. "When you didn't answer your phones, I panicked. What happened to Brock?"

"Snowmobile accident," she said briefly. "Teenager went through some pond ice. He was dead by the time Brock got to the scene. Kid was only fifteen."

Noah closed his eyes briefly. "I'm sorry, Tree. Is Brock okay?"

"He would have been better if you'd let us finish," she said dryly. "I'd say he's a little on the frustrated side right now."

"Therapeutic sex," Noah said, pursing his lips, and she nodded.

"In the shower. Kids can't hear the moans that way."

"Trina." His protest bordered on a whine and her lips twitched.

"Told you, you need to get some. At the moment, so do Brock and I."

"O-kay. I'll make this quick. A reporter got wind of this case I'm working." He lifted a brow. "The one Eve referred to tonight in the bar during your little visit."

Trina didn't flinch. "I'm not apologizing for that."

"Somehow I didn't think you would. Anyway, this reporter has been trying to get Eve to give him inside information and she refused. Tonight he got rough."

Trina's attitude disappeared. "Is she okay?"

"Other than a bruise, she's fine. He was trying to force her to look at some pictures. These." He gave the envelope to Trina and watched her face grow hot and angry.

"Son of a bitch."

"What?" Brock returned, swiping a towel over his wet head. The soaked robe was gone, changed for dry sweats. "What happened?"

Trina gave him the pictures. "Sunday. I gave Noah a hug after your boxing match."

Brock's eyes flashed. "What is this?" he snarled softly.

"Attempted extortion by a reporter who wants a story way too badly. He left those pictures in Eve's computer bag and unloaded the gun she keeps there. I saw them, knew he'd been here, and I panicked." He gestured weakly to the bathroom. "I'm sorry."

Brock sat on the edge of his bed. "I guess I can understand the urgency."

Trina put her arm around Brock's shoulders. "Those photos might have caused a major family breach, Noah. I'm glad Brock is a smart man."

"And that he trusts you," Noah said. Unlike Eve, who thought he had an agenda. *Which I guess I do.* "Keep an eye on the boys, okay?"

"You bet." Brock gave him the pictures. "You're going to report this guy, right?"

"First thing in the morning. I—" His cell vibrated in his pocket. "It's Eve. She told me to call when I made sure you were all right." He angled his body away from Brock and Trina, more to avoid the knowing smirk they shared than to hide his conversation. "They're okay," he said. "Just a . . . misunderstanding."

"That's good," she said. "Because I'm thinking Rachel's not." He listened as she explained, his jaw going taut. "You weren't supposed to approach anyone."

"Well, I did. Sue me. Noah, she's in trouble. What did the cruisers say?"

He checked his watch and frowned. "Nothing yet and I should have heard. I'll call you back." He dialed Dispatch and was displeased with what he heard. "Then tell the second cruiser to proceed at fastest possible speed. Lights, no siren. I'm on my way." He turned back to Trina and Brock, who no longer smirked. "The first cruiser came up on an accident, car slipped on the ice and hit a pole. They're with the accident victims."

"They were first responders," Trina said evenly. "You know we have to stay. It's regs."

"I know," Noah said grimly. "I just hope we're not too late. Watch the boys. I'll call you tomorrow. I have to go."

Wednesday, February 24, 2:20 a.m.

Oh God. Rachel tried to breathe, but couldn't draw a deep enough breath. He'd wrapped her arms around her. She couldn't move. Vaguely she remembered her arms being shoved into sleeves, crossed over her body. Viciously yanked as he'd rolled her to her stomach, his knee sharp in her back. He'd tied her . . . tied the sleeves.

Her chin dropped to her chest as awareness returned in jolts. White. She blinked hard. White fabric covered her to her hips. Beyond that . . . she saw her own bare legs, felt the cold air between her thighs and knew she was naked. *Help me.*

Her heart raced but her mind was still . . . slow. *Scream.* But all that came out was a muted mewling. Her mouth was taped closed. *Where am I?* Her eyes darted, frantically. *Basement. I'm in my own basement.* Sitting on a stool from her kitchen counter.

She couldn't see him, didn't know him. She flinched. He was behind her. She could hear him breathing. Then she could smell it. *Gasoline.* It burned her nose, her eyes, and she remembered that night. The gas, the smoke, the heat. The stench of burning flesh. And the screams. She heard the screams of agony of the ones that hadn't gotten out.

No. Get out. Get away. She wrenched her body, but went nowhere. *I'm tied. I can't get away.* Her heart was beating so fast. Too fast. Her head swam, dizzy. *Bernie.* It had to be Bernie. *Somehow he got out.* He'd planned this. His revenge.

He's going to kill me. She wrenched again, violently, felt the stool give, but it was brought swiftly back, all four legs on the floor with a thud that shuddered through her.

"Better," he murmured in her ear. Her head jerked to the sound, but he was still behind her. Then he walked around the stool, stopped in front of her, and grabbed her chin, forcing her to look into his eyes. *Not Bernie.* "Not fully cogent, but more aware."

Her breath hitched. A lighter. He held it in front of her eyes and flicked it to life. She reared back, unable to take her eyes from the flame. He smiled. Smugly.

"I've been waiting for you, Rachel. You thought after your public display of good behavior that you could slip into the shadows, and live the life you craved in a fantasy world. You thought Delilah was invisible, but no one is truly invisible."

Delilah. Shadowland. *John*. It had been a setup. *A trap.*

He stepped back and her eyes followed. He wore boots and . . . fireman pants over his trousers. The pants were too big, gaping at his waist. He might have looked like a clown except for the gun in his waistband. Behind him she saw a fire extinguisher. And next to that, a backpack. And on top of the backpack . . . *my shoes*. Neatly together.

"Fear is an interesting thing," he said, and her gaze ripped back to his face. He was smiling, his eyes cold and cruel. *I'm going to die.* "Many fears, like the fear of snakes, are somewhat instinctive. They represent a heightened awareness of danger. It's when those fears take control of our actions that they become phobia. You, Rachel, have an extreme phobia. Given your personal history, an understandable one."

She could feel his breath on her face. "I think your incarcerated ex-husband will get quite a chuckle out of hearing that you were incinerated. Poetic justice, wouldn't you say?"

He produced an extra-long match from his pocket, waved it like a wand. *No.* New terror shivered down her spine and she clenched her eyes shut.

"I am remiss," he said. His fingers forced her eye open and she felt wetness over her eye a split second before he pressed her eyelid back. *Glued.* She struggled when he tried to glue her other eye and he slapped her face with a snarl. "Don't move."

He stepped back, flicked the lighter, touched it to the long match. "And without further ado." A line of fire spread in a ring. *Around me.* Anywhere she looked. Coming closer. *It hurt.* Burned. *Stop. Make it stop. Make the pain stop.* The howl in her throat was muffled by the tape, her ears filled with the crackling, hissing of the flames.

And then the man was there, winding twine around her throat and all she could see was his eyes, alive and laughing. He was laughing. She could hear him laughing, far away. Then he was groaning. So far away . . .

He let out a long, ragged breath, torn between elation and fury. He hadn't held it in, hadn't been able to control it. He'd let go. And it had been . . . incredible. He shuddered, his muscles twitching in the aftermath. *Incredible.*

His eyes were inches from hers. Empty now, they'd been wide, terrified, staring up at him because he demanded it. The whores always stared up. Never down. Never again. He relaxed his grip and the twine around Rachel's throat went limp in his hands. His mind was clearing, logic returning. *Incredible, but insane.* He stepped from the carefully constructed fire zone and grabbed the extinguisher, putting out the flames, which in another few moments would have leapt free of the ring of flame suppressant he'd placed around the accelerant. The fire was out. In more ways than one.

He glanced down at his trousers, annoyed. His clothing probably had contained his ejaculate, but he had to be sure. He could leave no DNA behind. He had bleach in the back of his car. That and the fire would suffice to hide the evidence of his loss of control. Nothing of his would remain.

Wednesday, February 24, 2:30 a.m.

Harvey woke abruptly when the phone rang. He fumbled for it blindly. "What?"

"Wake up, Pop," Dell said. "Our boys are on the move."

"Where are you?"

"Following Phelps, like you told me to. Just use the GPS unit like I showed you to find Webster."

Something was wrong. There was a satisfied note in his son's tone that he just didn't trust. He swung his legs over the bed and grabbed his pants. After tonight, they'd switch. *I'll follow Phelps.* Before Dell did something foolish that they'd both regret.

Wednesday, February 24, 2:45 a.m.

"This is it? You're sure?" Noah stood on the sidewalk next to two uniformed officers.

The uniforms nodded. "Yes, Detective. The address Dispatch gave us for Rachel Ward is this mailbox store."

Noah looked around, wearily. Jack was nowhere to be seen. He'd called him three times each on his cell and his home line, getting Jack's voicemail each time. He thought of Jack's state of mind when they'd parted at the coffee shop hours ago. He could see Jack going home and getting totally drunk.

Which is his business on his own time. But this wasn't Jack's time. And Rachel's time could be running out. "Thanks." He dialed Eve. "Say the address again."

"Why? Is Rachel all right?"

"I don't know. This is a mailbox store. Check again."

She read the address again. "It's a match. She didn't give her home address when she registered for your study."

"What are we going to do?"

"What I should have done already—run her through the system. I'll call you." He got in his car and radioed in his request for addresses for Rachel Ward.

Unable to sit still, he called Jack again. Still no answer. Dispatch came back with four possible addresses for Rachel Ward, one of which was only a mile from Jack's house. *Dammit. Jack, where the fuck are you?*

Noah needed backup. His finger was a hairsbreadth away from calling Abbott, but something held him back. *Face it. You don't want to turn in your own partner. Not yet.* His mind ran through the possibilities, settling on Olivia. She was already up to speed, no onboarding required. They could split the addresses and find Rachel faster.

Olivia answered on the first ring of her cell. "Sutherland."

"It's Noah Webster. Where are you?"

"Cruising downtown, looking for a witness for a trial next week. Why?"

"I need your help."

"Where's Jack?"

"I . . . don't know."

"Oh." The single syllable said it all. "Okay, tell me where. I'll meet you."

"No, we need to split up. I've got four addresses to check for a potential victim." He gave her one of the addresses, then told her to be on the watch for an open bedroom window. If they found one, they'd be too late. If they found one, he'd need a partner.

"What about the others?" she asked.

"I'll take one and have cruisers go to the other two. Thanks, Liv."

Wednesday, February 24, 3:05 a.m.

He stepped back, surveying his handiwork. Five of six. Rachel Ward hanging by the neck had never looked better. Her feet were a little blistered, but the police would know a fire had occurred as soon as they entered her house. He wondered how quickly she'd be discovered. She'd be late to work tomorrow, obviously.

Sitting at her laptop, he went into her open Shadowland account and hung the wreath on her virtual door. He already knew he couldn't paint her avatar's face. Rachel hadn't bought her Delilah from Pandora, so he'd have to be content with hanging the dancer from a virtual rope and setting the virtual scene. He could do it in a couple of clicks, as he'd done it so many times already. Then he took her computer, let himself out of Rachel's house, locking her deadbolt behind him, and pocketed her key.

He'd driven to the edge of Rachel's neighborhood when his heart nearly stopped. Pulling into the subdevelopment was a cop. Not just any cop. A homicide detective.

Olivia Sutherland. His heart started to pound in his ears. *How had she known? Who told her to come here?* Her car slowed as she passed and he held his breath. She had no legal reason to stop him. After the police had seen the car he'd used in Christy's murder on the diner's security video, he'd changed cars and plates. All part of the plan.

Sutherland resumed driving, and letting out the breath

he'd held, he carefully pulled onto the nearly deserted two-lane highway, going east when he really needed to go west. West was toward the highway and home. But if any other cops were joining her, they'd come the same way she did and he didn't want them finding him.

Who called Sutherland? he fumed. *Who the hell had known about Rachel Ward?* Now that he was breathing again, he had a pretty good idea.

Noah Webster had the study participant list, he knew. But there were five hundred names on that list. How had they guessed that Rachel Ward was next? He'd left no pattern, left no clues that would alert them to his next victim. Webster was smarter than the average cop, he allowed, but that still didn't make him very smart. And Webster was no clairvoyant, that was for damn sure.

It had to have been Eve. He wasn't sure how she'd known, but instinct had told him the girl would be dangerous. Now he realized he'd underestimated her. He would not make that same mistake again.

He forced himself to calm and rationally think things through. Eve had known about Martha and Christy and now Rachel. *I knew they were prime targets because they were always in Shadowland. Because I'm in the game with them.* And so, he realized, was Eve. She had to be. *Clever girl.* Too clever for her own good.

He'd thought that even if she told Webster about Shadowland, there'd be nothing to fear, but he'd been wrong. He'd come too close to getting caught tonight. Eve had come too close. She needed to be eliminated. Unfortunately, she was never alone.

Lure her out, kill her. It could still work, but not as long as she was on guard, careful. He had to throw her off-balance. Scare her to death. Then he'd lure her out and kill her.

Wednesday, February 24, 3:10 a.m.

Eve was cursing herself for leading Noah to the wrong address. *But how could you have known?* She couldn't have, she knew, but what if Rachel was next? What if they didn't find her in time? Rachel Ward would be one more death on her head.

She was staring at the list, wondering how many more addresses were mailbox stores, wondering if there was a fast way to weed them out. Just in case this happened again. *It can't happen again. We have to stop this guy.*

She zoomed in on the address column on her participant list. And then cursed herself again, peering at the column next to the addresses. Social Security numbers. Dammit, she had Socials on every participant. She already knew Noah had four Rachel Wards to check out. She'd run an address check of her own as soon as they'd hung up. Socials would tell her which Rachel Ward was theirs.

She logged into the website Ethan used for background checks with the user name and password he'd set up for her when they'd talked that morning, blessing him for his foresight. She plugged in the information she knew and set the search in motion.

Rachel, where are you? Please be all right.

Feeling helpless, Eve toggled back to Shadowland and retrieved Greer. Maybe they were worried for nothing. Maybe the purple-haired dancer was wrong. Maybe Rachel's Delilah had taken a goddamn virtual football team to her virtual condo for a virtual orgy.

She thought of Sal. How right he'd been. *Aviators and orgies, indeed.*

Eve guided Greer to Delilah's condo, trepidation tightening her throat. And then she saw what she'd known deep down would be true. *Too late. We're too late.*

Slowly, she backed Greer away from the black wreath on Rachel's door, not wanting to see what was inside. Eve could still see Christy Lewis's empty eyes staring at her in real life. She didn't need to see the virtual equivalent one more time.

Four. Samantha, Martha, Christy, and now Rachel. He'd killed four women.

At the bottom of her screen the tab for the background check website was flashing. Her search was complete. *Too late.*

Blindly Eve reached for her cell and dialed Noah.

Wednesday, February 24, 3:15 a.m.

Olivia parked her car in front of the address Noah had given her and walked up to the house. It was dark. As quiet as the rest of the street. Carefully she picked her way around the back, through the snow, and looked up.

Her heart sank. "Dammit," she whispered.

The upstairs bedroom window was wide open.

Chapter Fourteen

Wednesday, February 24, 3:15 a.m.

Noah answered Eve's call on his cell. "I don't know anything yet," he said.

"I do," she said quietly.

Noah slowed his car to a stop, a block from the address he'd drawn. "Tell me."

"I found Rachel's address." It was the one Olivia was checking at this very moment.

"How?" he asked. In her voice he heard defeat and he knew. *Too late.*

"I had their Socials. We paid them a small study stipend and needed the Socials for tax purposes. I ran a background check and found the Rachel we're looking for."

"But?"

"There's a black wreath on her door in Shadowland. We're too late, Noah."

"You stay put," he ordered. "And stop feeling guilty. I'll call you when I can."

"Okay," she whispered. "I'm sorry."

"Yeah. Me, too." No sooner had he hung up than his phone vibrated again. Olivia. "You found her," he said dully.

"I'm looking at an open window, second story. How did you know?"

"Eve found her dead in the game. Call CSU. I'll be there in under fifteen."

"And Jack?"

Noah put his car into gear. "Still not answering his phone."

"Noah, we have to call Abbott. You can't keep covering for Jack."

"I know. Don't go in without me. Last time he used a poisonous snake."

"More fun and games," she said bitterly. "This guy's a vile piece of shit."

Olivia was waiting for him in front of Rachel's house. Jack was nowhere to be found.

"I think it'll be easier to get in through the back door," Olivia said.

It took only one thrust of his shoulder. "Police," Noah called, weapon drawn.

"Do you smell something burning?" Olivia murmured.

"Yeah. That's new." He lowered his weapon as he entered Ward's bedroom. There she hung, like all the others. Right down to the shoes.

"Her eyes," she whispered. This was her first time seeing it in person. There was something about the victims' eyes that didn't get captured in the crime scene photos. She touched Rachel's arm, then whirled, her own eyes wide. "Noah, she's still warm."

Noah was there in two steps. "She's been here maybe an hour," he said.

"If that." Her round blue eyes flashed fury. "A car was leaving the neighborhood, just as I was driving in. Brown Civic. I missed him. If I'd been a few minutes faster . . ."

Frustration clawed. *Dammit, if Jack had answered* . . .

He let himself finish the thought. *This woman would be alive and we'd have a killer in custody.*

"He wasn't driving a brown Civic when he followed Christy Lewis home," he said tightly. "But changing cars could be his newest up-yours."

"I remember his plate number. I'll call it in."

While she did, Noah dialed Micki, who was on her way. "We have another."

"Any snakes this time?" Micki asked and Noah crouched to check Rachel's ankles.

His stomach lurched. "No. It appears Miss Ward was afraid of fire."

Olivia finished calling in the BOLO on the brown Civic and crouched next to him, her pretty face twisted in a horrified grimace. "Aw, hell, Web," she murmured.

"What did he burn?" Micki asked.

Noah swallowed hard at the sight of Rachel Ward's blistered flesh. "Her feet."

Wednesday, February 24, 4:15 a.m.

"I thought I smelled something burning," David said, leaning over the stove where Eve had left a scorched pot. "You'll never get this clean. What were you trying to cook?"

"Cocoa." Coffee had become too much for her churning stomach. Rachel was dead. *We were too late.* "I got distracted when I was making the first batch and it scorched."

He took the mug next to her elbow and tasted it. "Not bad."

"You're not the only one who can make stuff," she muttered. "So make your own."

He took another sip instead. "Where'd you get the recipe?"

"Internet." She took her mug, sloshing hot cocoa over the sides. "Go back to bed."

"Can't. I wake up when I smell stuff burning. I'm a firefighter, remember?" He said it teasingly but she didn't smile. "Spill it." He was serious now. "Tell me what's going on."

She haltingly obeyed, starting with Buckland and the photos, ending with Rachel. David's face had darkened through her story. "Does the fact that this Buckland asshole pops up at the same time as a serial killer bother anyone but me?"

"No, it bothers Noah, too. Buckland's officially on the radar. But Buckland's been reporting for a couple years. Local color, obituaries. That he'd suddenly start killing people . . ." She shrugged. "I'm too tired to think."

"Then go to bed, honey. I'll take the couch."

"No, I can't sleep. I can't stop thinking about Rachel and the others."

"Not your fault," he said softly, tilting her chin up. "What happened with Webster?"

"Nothing."

He sat back, brows lifted. "So . . . did he kiss you yet?"

His tone was so engagingly nosy, she might have smiled. But the thought of that kiss in the bar, so . . . proprietary. So necessary. So impossible. Her eyes stung. "Stop."

"Stop what, Evie? Stop trying to keep you from making a big mistake? I have seen you through too much to let you hide again."

Misery stepped aside for blessed anger. "I am not hiding. Not anymore."

"You think just because you're not holed up in Dana's shelter anymore that you're not hiding? Give me one good reason you've written Webster off. And don't tell me it's because he's too old, because he's my age and I'll have to hurt you."

She let out a long, quiet breath. "You know why."

He stared at her in contrary confusion, and then his expression changed again to one of devastated understanding. "Oh, Evie. You can't possibly . . ."

"No, I can't," she said, twisting his meaning.

"That's not fair to Webster, or to any other man who might care about you. He might not even want kids. Especially at his age."

"I thought you were his age," she said quietly.

"I am. And I want kids. But I would be furious if a woman I cared for didn't give me a chance because she assumed she knew what I wanted. You think you know people."

His words had rattled her, but pride ran deeper than anything else. "I do."

"Because you study them? Watch them? You don't know shit, kid. You have been standing back and watching the world go by ever since Winters sliced you up."

She flinched. "You cross the line, David."

"Well, it's about time somebody did."

She stood, vibrating with ire. "Like you're the expert? You, who stood back and watched the woman you loved marry somebody else? You, who're still standing back and watching as she has baby after baby, building a family with *somebody else*?"

David jerked, his face going pale beneath his winter tan.

"Yeah," she said bitterly. "I noticed. Did you ever *think* about telling Dana how you felt all those years? Or did you *assume* you knew how she felt? What she wanted?"

The silence hung between them for what seemed like endless minutes. "I knew how she felt," he finally said. "She didn't love me. She never did. She lived her life saving other people, doing crazy dangerous things, with never a thought for herself. She didn't think about herself until she met . . ."

Eve felt a sharp stab of regret for the words she'd let fly so heedlessly. "Ethan."

He nodded unsteadily. "Then her life became precious to her, because she could see what it would do to him to have lost her. Because she loves him."

She felt lower than dirt. "David, I'm sorry."

"No. You were right. I did watch her marry somebody else, because I did love her. Still do, I guess. But if Dana had ever given me one indication she felt the same way, I promise you, nothing would have held me back. And if she couldn't have kids, I would have been sad, but it wouldn't have mattered. Maybe Webster is just a bump in the road. A practice love, if you want. But just maybe he's your chance to be happy.

"Evie, don't stand back and watch it pass by. You never know if another chance will come. It's time to trust your instincts. I'm going back to bed. Don't burn any more pots."

She watched him go, hurting. For both of them. But he was wrong. When it came to men, she had lousy instincts. And it wasn't just kids. It was everything.

For now, she'd go back to what she'd been doing. Spread across her table were the stacks of usage logs and graphs she and Noah had been reviewing. There had to be something to tell them who the next target would be before it was too late to save her.

Wednesday, February 24, 4:25 a.m.

"You should have told me Jack didn't answer his phone," Abbott said calmly, his eyes on Rachel's small house where a small army of CSU and MEs had swarmed.

Noah leaned against his car, watching the neighbors who'd gathered, wondering if their killer ever came back to the scene to watch. To gloat. "I'm sorry. I should have."

He'd called his boss with the discovery of a fourth murder, and it hadn't taken Abbott long to realize his staffing had been shaken up a little. Abbott had been most displeased.

"Next time you call out one of my detectives without my explicit permission, I'm going to kick your ass into next week," Abbott continued in the same calm tone.

"Fine. Just don't blame Olivia. She was only trying to help."

"I won't. I'm blaming you. When were you going to tell me that Jack's been late to scenes for three weeks? Or has it been longer?"

"Off and on, longer. Depends on the woman in his bed. The women go their own way, and then Jack is back." Noah shrugged uneasily. "Tonight, with him not showing up at all . . . That's abnormal."

"He's on his way. He claims you didn't call him."

Noah blinked. "What?"

"That's what he says," Abbott said.

"He's pulled that one before, too. 'Oh, my cell phone has bad reception,'" Noah mimicked. He brought up his cell outgoing call log. "I called his cell and his home line."

Abbott scanned his phone's screen. "Your fingers did a lot of walking tonight, Noah."

Noah snapped his phone shut, annoyed. "It's been an eventful day," he said tightly.

"That it has. I want you to brief me, then go home and sleep. It's going to take CSU the better part of the night to process the scene. Tell me what happened."

So Noah did, starting with Eve's discovery that her red-zone, Rachel Ward, was not where she was supposed to be, finishing with his and Olivia's grisly discovery. At this point he was reciting facts, his voice flat and expressionless from fatigue.

"We found his setup in the basement. He'd covered the windows so no one would see the flames. Smoke detectors, disabled. He let the fire lick up the stool he'd tied her to. She's got third-degree burns, feet and legs. Micki called the fire investigators."

"Okay," Abbott said. "I'm up to speed. Go home, Noah. You look like hell."

"Okay." It was testament to his exhaustion that he obeyed without argument. He started for his car, then stopped as Jack's car coasted to a stop in front of his.

Noah waited with Abbott as Jack approached, his cover-boy face haggard. And hung over. Noah recognized the look. He'd seen it in his own mirror enough times.

"Abbott said you called me," Jack said with no trace of humor. "I never got the call."

"I called you six fucking times." Ignoring the guilt in his partner's eyes, Noah went on. "The first call went out at 2:25. Rachel Ward may have still been alive then."

Jack shook his head in denial. "I swear to God I never got your call. I fell asleep."

Noah stepped closer, dropped his voice to a whisper. "After you drank how much?"

The guilt in his eyes gave way to anger. "One. Not that it's any of your business."

"No, not my business. But Rachel might think it was hers. She was busy dying while you were sleeping off your one drink."

Jack's cheeks grew dark. "You sonofabitch."

Behind them Abbott cleared his throat harshly and Noah stowed his temper. "Olivia spotted a car leaving this neighborhood at 3:15," Noah said. "The license plates were registered to Axel Girard's wife."

Jack's eyes flashed. "I told you he was the one. But *you* said it didn't make sense."

Noah had to take a step back, appalled that his hand had actually closed into a fist. He swallowed back the fury and managed to say nothing at all.

Jack flicked a glance down at Noah's clenched fist "Where is Girard now?"

"In lockup," Noah said. "I called the car we had parked in front of his house. They said the Girards appeared to have been in bed. But on the off chance that somehow Axel sneaked out to another car, killed Rachel Ward, then teleported himself home in half the time it should have taken him to drive, I had him picked up." He turned to look at Abbott. "Eight a.m. meeting?"

"Make it nine. Jack, I expect you to have a new cell phone, forthwith."

The ME techs came out of Rachel's house, pushing the gurney that held the body bag. Jack swallowed hard before turning, getting into his car, and driving away.

"I should feel bad about what I said," Noah murmured, "but I don't."

"Jack's on a bad track," Abbott said. "You can't save him from himself. Only he can."

"First step," Noah said quietly, then realized he'd said it aloud. He'd never revealed his alcoholism to anyone on the force, never even spoken of it to anyone besides Brock and Trina, until he'd blurted it to Eve. And she hadn't flinched. Now he turned to his boss, whose expression was not judgmental. Noah sighed. "You know."

"I've always known," Abbott chided. "I told you, it's my job to know my staff."

"Which is why you get paid the medium-sized bucks."

Abbott's mouth curved, but his eyes didn't smile. "Go home and sleep. That's an order. See you at oh-nine. And tell Eve I said thank you. She almost saved the day."

From under the carport in an empty For Sale house half a block away, Harvey put down his binoculars. "Webster nearly hit Phelps." He turned to Dell, who'd just arrived, his car parked down the street from Harvey's Subaru.

Still observing through his zoom lens, Dell smiled. "A crack in the blue wall."

Dell's tone had him frowning. "What do you know, son? What have you done?"

Dell shrugged. "Just gave an already shaky relationship a little push, that's all."

Harvey was quiet for a long moment. "Phelps was really late getting here tonight," he finally said. "You told me the boys were on the move an hour ago."

"It appears Phelps slept in," Dell said cheerfully.

Harvey considered the circuitous route Webster had taken, the look of weary panic on the man's face when he'd stopped at the mailbox store. He'd been racing against a clock for the past hour and here they sat, less than a mile from Phelps's home.

A shiver ran down his spine. "A woman died here. Tell me that matters to you."

"What matters to me is that V is dead," Dell said bitterly. "That *matters* to me."

"I know that," Harvey said softly. "I know that every minute of every day."

"The men who killed him walk free. Do you know *that* every minute of every day?"

Harvey leaned against the headrest and closed his eyes. "What. Did. You. Do?"

"I'm not going to tell you." Then Dell gasped when Harvey's hand shot out and grabbed him by the collar of his parka and twisted, cutting off his air.

Harvey leaned across the gearshift, furious. "You will tell me. Make no mistake. I am your father. I brought you into this world. I can—"

"Take me out," Dell sneered, his eyes flashing hate. "You know what? I'm not five years old and peeing my pants in fear of you anymore. V's not here to take my licks, so I'll take them myself. So hit me, old man. If you think you can."

Harvey hesitated, feeling a grudging respect for his younger son, who might have finally grown up. He released him with a shove of disgust. "Just tell me what you did."

"I'll get as old as you waiting for these cops to fuck up on camera. So, I decided to take control of the situation. I got us a . . . Trojan Horse."

"Make some sense, boy," Harvey snapped.

"I got someone on the inside, a woman. She's cuddled

up to Phelps, made him think she's got the hots for him. But she watches him, for us."

"And tonight? You said Phelps overslept."

Dell shrugged. "She doctored his whiskey bottle a little bit. Just to make him sleep. Obviously not too much, because he actually showed up this time."

"He hasn't shown up other times?"

"He's missed a few days. His partner's pretty pissed with him. I figure another few episodes like tonight and they'll turn on each other like the dogs they are."

What were you thinking, boy? If Phelps had been awake an hour ago, that woman might have lived. "So how have you known when they were on the move?"

"She keeps Phelps's phone on vibrate," Dell said, "and waits for a call."

"That's how you knew they were going to the Brisbane woman's on Sunday. You told me the GPS beeps when they move their cars."

"It does, but she's a little extra insurance. Sometimes I sleep through the beep."

"So instead of telling Phelps, she calls you."

"Yeah. Then she erases all of Webster's messages and calls from the incoming log. I guess somebody must have called him again after she left, woke him up."

"You dumb fuck," Harvey gritted. "If they check with the phone company, they'll prove Webster called. Then they'll be on the alert that *somebody* is *fucking* with them."

"They might. They're so mad right now, they probably won't. If they do, it won't matter, because she says Phelps does it himself half the time. Pretends like he hasn't gotten Webster's call, that he has no bars. Guy's a fuckup. I just sped it up a little."

"But this time, Phelps didn't do it himself, and this time a woman *died*. If they check his phone records, this whore of yours will be the first person they haul in. And if you don't think you'll be the first person she implicates, you're dumber than I thought."

"She won't talk and I'm far from dumb. I have it all planned out."

Harvey stared at his son, wondering how Dell had veered off course. He needed to drag his son back on task. "I'll let this go, this time. But nobody else better die because of you. That's not the way to fix this and I'm not going down with you. I'll stop the whole operation first."

"You're absolutely right," Dell said agreeably. "Gotta go." He hopped out of the Subaru and into his own vehicle and, stomach churning, Harvey watched him go.

Wednesday, February 24, 5:15 a.m.

Noah disobeyed Abbott's order to go home, stopping by the holding cell where he found Axel Girard, pacing frantically. Girard looked up, wild-eyed with panic.

"I didn't do anything. You're ruining my life."

"I'm trying to save it. I need to talk to you. Will you stop pacing and listen to me?"

Girard stopped, but his body still vibrated with pent energy. "What do you mean, save it?"

"Another woman was murdered tonight," Noah said. "A car with plates registered to your wife was seen driving away."

Girard paled. Blindly he sank to the edge of the cot in his cell. "Why?"

"Damn good question. Why do you think someone

would target you? Does anybody hate you? Have you pissed anyone off lately?"

Girard pressed his knuckles to his lips. "No. I get along well with my patients, with my neighbors. I don't have any enemies. How long will you keep me here?"

"I don't know. I need to find some connection between you and a killer."

"Oh God," Girard said, the panic returning to his eyes. "My wife and boys."

"The plainclothes detectives are still watching your house. Your family is safe." Noah left holding, finding Abbott standing in the hall outside, frowning. And waiting.

"I had to talk to him," Noah said. "Had to find out what he knows."

"And?"

"He says he doesn't know anything. I'm inclined to believe him. Well, that he doesn't know he knows, anyway. He's a squeaky clean guy who couldn't have made it from the crime scene back to his house before we had him dragged from his bed."

"Did you tell him another woman was dead?"

"Yeah. He looked shocked. I bought it."

"Okay. I was going to talk to him, too, but I'll leave him to ruminate on his nonexistent enemies for a few more hours. Now go home. Go to bed."

Wednesday, February 24, 5:15 a.m.

He was clean now, the smell of smoke gone, the clothes he'd worn tonight already decomposing in the pit. Carefully he placed Rachel Ward's shoes next to the men's Nikes he'd placed there earlier that evening. He adjusted

Rachel's left shoe, making sure it was completely straight, then tilted the round spectacles he'd placed inside one of the Nikes so that it better caught the light. *That's better.* He liked things . . . precise.

They were already at Rachel's house, the cops. They'd find nothing there that he didn't intend for them to find. He'd been precise in his execution of Rachel.

He'd thought it all through and concluded that other than speeding up his timeline, nothing terrible had really occurred tonight. The Hats knew about Shadowland. They knew about the participant list. *Neither of those things gets them even close to me.*

However, Eve's knowing about Rachel was getting too close. It didn't matter though. His sixth of the six would be a dark horse. Not on anyone's list. Not on anyone's radar.

Still, Eve's involvement had sped things up too quickly. The press hadn't caught up to what the police knew, and importantly, what the police did not know. There had not been enough time for the headlines to roil, for police failures and public frustration to mount. The Hat Squad wasn't close to being ruined. He'd have to let them spin their wheels for a few days. Give the reporters time to close the gap.

In the meantime, he needed to rest. Although he was in good shape, he wasn't as young as he once was. Pulling this off twenty years ago would have been a piece of cake. Now . . . Well, he'd need to pace himself. Cut back on the physical and ramp up the mental. Focus on Eve. She was indeed a challenge. He did enjoy a good challenge.

He opened the drawer where he kept the cell phones he took from his victims. It was quite a little walk through the past, amusing to see how far cell phone technology had progressed in the last decade. At the bottom of the drawer were the beepers, positively archaic now. But on the very top of the pile was the cell he was looking for.

He slipped it in his pocket. To make the call from here would be stupid, indeed. It was easier back in the beeper days, he thought. No pesky GPS to give the cops a technological advantage. He'd place this call from a place that would have the cops chasing their tails. A threat and a red herring. A veritable twofer.

Wednesday, February 24, 6:00 a.m.

Eve jerked awake and blearily lifted her head. She'd fallen asleep at her kitchen table, facedown on the stack of usage logs and graphs. Then she muttered a curse. She'd also knocked over the damn mug of cocoa, spilling what was left all over one of the stacks she hadn't reviewed yet.

There wasn't much cocoa to clean up, most of it having soaked through the paper. Luckily it was all stored on her hard drive. She'd print this batch again. Quickly she thumbed through the graphs until she came to a page unblemished by brown cocoa stains.

And lowered herself onto a chair. It was a graph showing steady play, upward of sixteen hours a day, and then . . . nothing. The graph was three weeks old.

Dread cold in her gut, Eve opened her laptop to the list. Subject 036 was Amy Millhouse, an ultra-user. A Google brought the results Eve expected, still her stomach turned over as she clicked the article open and read. *Amy Millhouse of West Calhoun was found dead on Sunday, February 7. She had . . .*

"Hung herself," Eve read aloud. She closed her eyes. "Of course she did."

Wearily she found her cell phone and hit dial. Noah's cell was the last call she'd made. The last five calls she'd made. "It's Eve. I need to talk to you."

"I'll be right over."

"No, you don't— *Wait*." But he'd hung up. She closed her phone, somehow unsurprised at the knock at her door, not five seconds later. He stood on her welcome mat, hat in one hand, cell in the other. Looking like . . . *everything I ever wanted*.

"I've been standing here for fifteen minutes, trying to decide if I should knock or not," he said, then one corner of his mouth lifted. "Sure you don't believe in fate?"

She opened the door wider. "No. Come in."

He did, putting his hat on her bookshelf. "No, you do, or no you don't?"

She stared up at him, her head aching. "What was the question?"

He cupped her face in his palm and she wanted to weep. "What's wrong?"

She didn't want to utter the words. Not yet. Instead she turned her face into his palm and drew a breath, then drew back, new horror registering. "Rachel was afraid of fire."

He nodded, his eyes full of pain. "Yes."

"By how much were we too late?"

"An hour. Maybe two."

She took a step back. "So while we were eating sandwiches and looking at logs and worrying about Kurt Buckland and trying to find her right address . . ."

He nodded again. Swallowed hard. "Yes."

Too late she realized he'd already put himself through this. He'd discovered Rachel, experienced the horror firsthand. She was just adding to his pain. "I'm sorry."

She wasn't sure who moved first, but she was in his

arms and he was holding her much too tightly. Except she held on just as tightly, fists pressed into his back. He was hard, he was hurting. And he was here. "Why did you come back?" she whispered.

He drew a deep breath that pressed her breasts into his chest. "I went home first," he said, so quietly she almost didn't hear. "But there wasn't anything for me there."

Oh, Noah. Eve held on for another moment, then pulled away. The words stuck in her throat. She forced them out. "There isn't anything for you here either. I'm sorry."

"I don't believe that," he said fiercely.

She shook her head, wearily. "Believe what you want. Doesn't make it any less true."

He closed his eyes. "Why did you call me then?"

Her chest hurt. "I think I found another one. Her name is Amy Millhouse."

He opened his eyes and they were blank, like all those times at Sal's. "Show me."

He followed her into the kitchen and looked at the graph, at the obituary, and his shoulders sagged. "MPD would have responded to this suicide. I must have read this report. I didn't find any scenes remotely resembling Martha and Samantha's." He went too still and she could see he'd thought of something he didn't like.

"But?" she asked.

"But Jack read half of them. I couldn't find him tonight. Rachel was a mile from his house and he didn't answer. Said he didn't get my calls. Said he'd fallen asleep."

"Sunday night, at Sal's, he checked his phone three times before you came."

"I know. Brock told me."

"Will you report him?"

His shoulders sagged further. "I already did. I had to."

"I'm sorry."

He jerked his head around to glare at her. "Stop saying that." *I hurt him.*

I never wanted to hurt him. "Sit down, Noah. I need to explain something to you."

The kitchen chair creaked under his weight. She sat, folded her hands.

"Well?" he said sharply.

"I'm trying to figure out what to say," she snapped back. "I could say, 'It's not you, it's me,' but you won't buy that. I tried 'I'm broken,' but you didn't accept that either. You read about what happened to me, with Winters."

"Yes." He bit the word. "And if a con hadn't killed him in prison, I'd be tempted to."

"You'd have to stand in line, I think. He was a very bad man. But very handsome. He had . . . charisma. Most people in his hometown liked him. He was a cop."

"I know. I read that. You said he was looking for his wife and son."

"Caroline and Tom. They'd escaped, started a new life. Tom and I became friends and he was never supposed to tell anyone what happened to him, but he had to talk to someone. He told me everything, every slap, every burn . . . Tom hated him."

"I can understand that."

"They ran away, came to Chicago. Dana, my guardian, helped women like Caroline start over." She hesitated, then shrugged. "Dana faked IDs, procured Socials."

His brows lifted. "She really put herself out there. And Hunter?"

"Knew it all. Never participated in any of the border-line illegal stuff, but he did his part, odd jobs. Kept the shelter physically functional."

"Fixed the roof?"

She smiled sadly. "Yeah. But that was long after Caroline first came. By the time I met her, Caro had her GED, a job at a university, was working on her degree. I worked for her, in the history department's office. She always made me feel like I belonged."

"Then?"

"Our old boss died and David's brother, Max, came in to replace him."

Noah was frowning. "Max Hunter. I know that name."

"Played for the Lakers, eons ago. Tall, handsome, tortured soul." *Like you*, she thought, but kept that to herself. "Max was in an accident that ended his sports career. He went back to school, became a professor, and years later, our department chair. And I did what any normal red-blooded eighteen-year-old girl would have done."

"Fell for him?"

"Like a rock. But Max only had eyes for Caroline. When I realized that, I said some things I really shouldn't have to both of them, things that with anyone else would have burned my bridges to the ground. But Caroline loved me." Eve had to clear her throat.

"What we didn't know was that Caro's ex had found her. He wanted Tom back and he wanted Caroline to pay. I'd gone to Caro's to apologize for the things I said, and Winters was there, searching for Tom. Tom was gone for the weekend. Camping trip, as I recall. Winters sized me up, saw I was young, stupid, and very vulnerable. He pretended to be a maintenance guy named Mike. He pretended to have sympathy for my *faux pas* with Max. He pretended to think I was attractive."

"You were," Noah said fiercely. "You are."

"I was. He asked me out, got me drunk. No, he bought

the beer. I willingly drank every drop he poured in my glass. I was so not legal and so didn't care. I willingly took him home and . . . willingly entertained him."

A muscle twitched in Noah's cheek, but he said nothing.

"Next morning he tried to go. I tried to keep him with me, tried to get him to want me again." She closed her eyes, this part as clear as if it were happening right now. "I put on his coat, danced a little, and a picture fell out of his pocket. A baby picture of Tom. I knew Caro had left Tom's baby pictures behind when she'd run years before."

"And then you knew," he said quietly, and she opened her eyes to see he'd paled.

"And then I knew. The rest you know. Stab, stab, slice, slice, strangle with twine, and left me for dead. I did die. Twice. I'm damn lucky to be here."

He tried to speak, pursed his lips. "Eve . . ."

"It's all right, Noah. It's past. But I need you to understand. No one can live through something like that and not be changed. Hell, I was screwed up enough before I ended up in Dana's shelter. My mother was an addict, would sell her soul for a hit."

"And her daughter, too?" Noah asked, hoarse.

"No. Because I ran. Got caught, stuck in foster. Ran again, different foster. Ran again and made it to Chicago. I would have had a hard enough time forming attachments, having a normal relationship with any man, but now . . . It's just not possible."

He met her eyes. "Why? I still don't understand."

Her cheeks heated. "Fine. After Winters, I had a hysterectomy. Everything's gone."

He exhaled. "That's it?"

She glared at him. He looked immensely relieved. "No, that's not *it*. But it's enough."

"So? You can't have kids. I don't care, Eve."

"You say that."

"I mean that."

She smiled at him, trying to lessen the sting. "You think you mean that. And if that were 'it' then I'd give you the opportunity to find out for yourself. But that's only part of it. Noah, I . . ." She shrugged, her smile gone. "I wake up at night, screaming like it's happening all over again. And I'm . . . violent. Really violent."

"You're worried you'd hurt me?" he asked incredulously.

"I know I would. Sometimes I walk in my sleep. I've woken up in the kitchen, a butcher knife in my hand. I used to lock myself in my bedroom at the shelter so that I didn't hurt anyone by accident. Most of the time I just didn't sleep. I became a creature of the night." She forced a smile. "Slept odd times during the day. Still do."

He nodded slowly. "So . . . that's it?"

She rolled her eyes. "Goddammit, what will it take to make you go away?"

"More than that. Is that it?"

"No." She stood up, poured herself a cup of coffee that had long grown cold, then set it aside. "I just don't want to be with anyone. Can't you accept that?"

"Eve, look at me." His voice was low and so warm. She turned stiffly, as if a giant hand forced her. Met his gaze because somehow he commanded it. His eyes glittered. "Tell me you don't want me and I promise I'll go away."

She wanted to. Needed to. But could not. So she closed her eyes and said nothing.

"I thought as much," he said quietly. "You need time, that's fine. I have time. You need space, I'll give you space. And if you ever tell me to go away and mean it, I will. But for now, I'm here. I came back because I needed to. Eve, I needed you."

And then he was there, his arms tight around her again. He rested his cheek against her hair and she had to try, once more. For his own good. "I'm not a good bet, Noah."

"Neither am I. Let's just see where it goes, okay?"

She remained unconvinced. "I'll hurt you," she said tonelessly.

"I'll hide the knives," he said, wry amusement in his voice, but she couldn't smile.

There was more, so much more, and she didn't have words to tell him. *He'll figure it out himself and then he'll leave on his own. And you can tell him "I told you so."*

She knew it would be a hollow victory. She pulled away. "Have you eaten?"

He frowned slightly. "Not since the last time you fed me."

"Sit." She had opened the fridge when her cell phone chirped. "Text," she said and read the screen. Then froze, her mouth open.

Noah took the phone from her hand. "'Didn't your parents teach you not to get into cars with strange men?' What the hell does that mean?"

Eve's knees went weak and she didn't fight when Noah pushed her into a chair. "That's the last thing Rob Winters said before he killed me."

Chapter Fifteen

Wednesday, February 24, 6:30 a.m.

H e closed the cell and powered it down, his text complete. That ought to shake her up, he thought with a smile. Then he got back in his car and started for home. He still had about forty-five minutes before his wife's alarm woke her up. If he wasn't at home reading his morning paper, she'd ask questions he had no intention of answering.

He was quite fortunate to have a wife who slept so soundly. Of course the occasional sedative he put in her cup of evening herbal tea went a long way toward assuring her sleep was deep when he needed it to be. He was also fortunate she was so completely absorbed in her work that she didn't notice what he did even when she was awake. She rarely read a paper, preferring science journals to television.

She moved in her own little world, after twenty years never suspecting a thing.

Nobody did. *Because I am very, very careful and very, very good.*

Wednesday, February 24, 7:05 a.m.

"Well?" David Hunter demanded. When Eve received the text, Noah had pounded on the door to wake him up. She'd been so pale, Noah had thought she'd pass out. Luckily Eve had come around on her own. Now Hunter was cooking breakfast with the intensity of a man possessed. Or a man terrified. "What are you doing to catch him?"

Noah rubbed his hands over his face. "We're running a trace on the text. So far, it's showing up as an unregistered number."

"Throwaway cell?" Hunter asked.

Noah lifted his brows. "Maybe. Anybody can buy one."

Hunter rolled his eyes. "I guess I deserve that one."

"No, you don't," Noah said. "I'm sorry. I'm just tired."

Hunter put a fluffy golden omelet in front of him. "When did you last sleep, Noah?"

"God. I don't remember. Saturday night maybe?"

"You're gonna crash if you don't rest. When do you have to report in?"

"Nine." He dug into the omelet and nearly sighed. "This is really good."

"Thanks. When you're done, go sleep in Eve's bed. I'll make sure she's all right."

She'd retreated to the shower, still pale, her eyes as haunted as if she'd seen a ghost. Noah guessed she had. "She needs to sleep, too."

"She won't," Hunter said. "Not until she feels safe. She'll catnap in that chair of hers."

"You might want to hide the knives," he said, and Hunter shot him a surprised look.

"She keeps them in a lockbox. I'll lock them up when I'm finished cooking."

"Okay, I'll take the bed." Noah blinked hard. "Who knew about the getting in a car with strangers thing? Who knew Winters said that to her?"

"We did, the family, because she told us. We never let that leak to the press."

"Somebody knew," Noah said darkly. He eyed Eve's laptop. "Can I use it?"

Hunter hesitated. "Use mine. She's a little . . . you know, about her computer."

When Hunter returned with his laptop, Noah was practically scraping the plate clean.

"You want another?" Hunter asked, and Noah nodded.

"If you don't mind." He opened the laptop. "You're a good cook."

"I get a lot of practice. I do most of the cooking for my firehouse."

"They're lucky. I eat out of a microwave except on Sundays when I go to my cousin and his wife's for dinner. If you're still here on Sunday, you're welcome."

Hunter's lips twitched. "Thanks, but you'll be happy to know I'll be gone by Friday."

Noah didn't smile. "Eve will miss you."

"I'm hoping she'll be too busy to miss any of us back home," Hunter said dryly.

"Point taken." Noah frowned at the search results on the screen. "Rob Winters gets me too many hits, most about serial killers. How many people did this guy kill?"

"At least six that we knew of. Evie would have been seven."

Noah swallowed the bile that rose in his throat. "He *was* killed in prison, right?"

"Yes. I believe it was Tom's hope that once the other cons knew Winters was a dirty cop there wouldn't be enough of him left to scrape into a baggie. There wasn't."

Hunter's voice had gone hard, making Noah remember that Winters had not only traumatized Eve, he'd traumatized an entire family. "Which prison? Was it in Chicago?"

"No, North Carolina. I can't remember which prison, but my brother, Max, will know."

"Let's not make him remember if we don't have to."

Hunter poured his omelet concoction into a skillet, a muscle twitching in his taut cheek. "When my brother found Winters, the bastard had beaten Caroline almost unrecognizable and had his hands around her throat. Max deals with the memories, with the dreams, but there's nothing about Winters he's forgotten."

Noah thought of Susan and the baby, gone twelve years now. Hardly a day went by that he didn't think or dream of them in nightmares of his own. "You're right. I'm sorry."

"No need. It was just a very bad time."

"Well, I think we can approach this from a different direction. Buckland's researched Eve's past. Let's assume he ran across Winters's threat while he was reading up in the online archives of some paper. Did Winters give any interviews before he died?"

"Probably," David gritted. "Asshole liked to hear himself talk."

Noah searched for prison interviews. Luckily there weren't that many, as Winters had not survived long behind bars. *Justice*, he thought fiercely. *I hope it hurt. A lot.*

"Here's one," Noah said. It was a transcript of a live interview in which Winters described his assaults in detail, including the "cars with strange men" comment. He read to himself, sparing Hunter the memory. Noah's head pounded as he read Winters's boasts about Eve. His jaw clenched hard, his fists harder. *I hope to God it hurt a hell of a lot.*

"It wouldn't have taken Buckland long to find it," he finally said. He remembered the look in Eve's eyes, the utter shock. The fear. And the shame. "That he'd use it to rattle Eve says quite a lot."

Hunter slid another omelet on his plate. "So what are you going to do about him?"

Noah forced his clenched fists to relax so he could pick up a fork. "I sent out a BOLO last night when I found he'd tampered with her gun. Today, Eve will file her complaint, and when I catch him, he'll wish he'd never seen a newspaper."

Hunter nodded once. "Sweet."

"What's sweet?" They turned to find Eve standing in the doorway. Her short hair stood in wet spikes. She'd been crying, hard. Hunter took a step toward her, but she held up one hand to fend him off. "Not now. Please. What's sweet?"

Noah closed the interview and lowered the lid of Hunter's laptop. "Just that you'll file your complaint and we'll put Buckland in a cage where he belongs."

"I'll drive you to the police station," Hunter said. "Sit. You need to eat. Webster needs to sleep. If you both don't start taking care of yourselves, you're going to get sick."

Unbelievably, the side of her mouth lifted in a smile. "David takes care of people when he's stressed out," she said to Noah and Hunter bristled. She sat, careful not to touch either of them as she did so. "I'm sitting and I'll eat. But I'll drive myself to the police station." Again she raised her hand as both he and Hunter opened their mouths to protest. "You can follow me if you want, but once I've filed that report, I'm going to school, where I'll be surrounded by people. I have my Abnormal seminar at ten. If I'm not expelled by the time all of this is over, I don't want to be behind."

Hunter turned his glare from Eve to Noah. "You're going to let her?"

Her face was cool and calm. But her dark eyes churned with emotion and he knew she needed at least this vestige of control. "I can't stop her," he said to Hunter, "but we'll all watch her. And I'm taking your gun as evidence," he said to Eve.

"It's okay. I have another. I have several others."

"Of course you do," Noah murmured. "It's a survivor thing. I get it. Promise you'll park out in the open and you'll stay around people."

She nodded. "I promise."

"Oh for God's sake," Hunter snarled and turned back to the counter, slicing green peppers with frustrated vengeance. "If you're going to be stupid, at least take my truck."

"Why?" Eve asked, still too calm.

"Buckland will be looking for you in your Mazda. Besides, your car needs a tune-up and it'll give me something else to do while I worry about somebody else killing you."

She rose, placed her hand on Hunter's arm and his frantic chopping stilled. "I know you worry because you love me. And I know better than anyone that I am not invincible. But if I cower here, then he wins and I lose. I promise I will be careful. I will call you every hour and if I see Buckland, I'll call 911 so fast. But I can't hide. Not even for you."

Hunter's shoulders sagged and Noah cleared his throat. "I'll follow her in and she can park in the police garage. If he follows her, we'll grab him."

"And when she leaves?"

"I'll find a way to get coverage."

Hunter nodded once. "If he doesn't get coverage, you call me, do you understand?"

She leaned up, kissed Hunter's cheek. "Completely."

Noah stood, his heart unsteady. With Hunter, Eve was unfettered and made Noah realize how much of her guard she maintained with him. But he'd promised to give her time and space. "I'm going to catch an hour sleep. Don't leave without me."

Wednesday, February 24, 9:00 a.m.

Noah gave Jack a short nod when they sat down with the rest of the team in Abbott's office. An hour of sleep had made a little difference. At least he could think again.

They were waiting for Abbott, who was still in a meeting with the brass. Noah didn't envy his boss a penny of his medium-sized salary at the moment.

There was an awkward silence as they waited. Micki and Olivia looked at him and Jack with concern. Olivia's partner, Kane, looked as if he realized he'd missed something, but wasn't going to push it because he trusted his partner to fill him in later. Olivia and Kane had one of the best working relationships of any of Abbott's staff. Noah envied them.

Ian had been at Rachel's scene and had worked the rest of the night. He looked like hell. The only one at the table fully rested was Carleton Pierce, but even he frowned as he checked each face around the table.

"What's happened?" Carleton asked. "And I'm not talking about the investigation."

"We were too late getting to the victim's house last night," Noah said. "She was already dead, by forty minutes."

Carleton's brows knit. "Who found her?"

"I did," Olivia said. "And I missed the killer by ten minutes."

"I don't understand. How did you know where to look?"

"We got another tip," Jack said tightly. "From our CI."

"He knows, Jack," Noah said. "Carleton, I know that you went by to see her last night. We were able to figure out which of the test subjects was next, but we got our signals crossed and now Rachel Ward is dead."

"I see," Carleton said, glancing at Jack's stony face. "I wish I didn't."

Abbott came in then. "Tell me we have something, people." He closed the door, his face almost as stony as Jack's. "At least balm for that ass kicking I just took. Ian?"

"I finished the autopsy. The victim had a blood alcohol of 0.15."

"Whoa," Micki said. "That made her damn near pickled. But I'm not surprised. We found a vodka bottle under the seat of her car. She'd drained it dry."

"The ket blood test isn't back yet," Ian said, "but I found no puncture wounds on her neck. I did find the same swelling around her elbows that Christy had, so I'm betting he used a straitjacket again. No defensive wounds on her hands, although there were ligature wounds at her ankles. She was tied to a chair while her feet burned."

Noah remembered. The smell in the place. Burning flesh. It still made him nauseous.

"He burned her feet?" Carleton said, hushed. "My God."

"Burns on feet and calves," Ian said. "Urine came back positive for amphetamines."

"Did she self-administer," Abbott asked, "or did he give it to her?"

"There was only one needle mark in her arm. I think he gave it to her to counteract the booze."

"He wanted her alert," Micki murmured.

"So he could scare her senseless with fire," Jack said. "I checked her background. Five years ago her ex-husband found she'd been cheating on him, so he followed her to the motel where she met her lover and torched the place. The lover and two bystanders died. Rachel was trapped. She had severe smoke inhalation and almost died herself."

"That explains the old lung scarring I found," Ian said. "I wondered."

"Where is the ex-husband now?" Olivia asked.

"State pen," Jack said, "serving twenty-five to life. And he's still there as of this morning. I had the warden himself check the man's cell."

"So this victim had a documented fear of fire," Carleton said. "The killer could have assumed this was her greatest fear."

"Or he could have these." Noah put a stack of questionnaires on the table. They'd been delivered that morning. "Filled out when subjects began the study at Marshall."

"May I?" Carleton reached for the questionnaires. " 'What is your greatest fear?' 'Why do you think you have this fear?' Samantha feared being buried alive because . . ." He flipped to the next page. "Interesting. Her cousins buried her in the sand at the beach as a child and left her there, with a snorkel in her mouth to breathe from."

"So the killer buried her alive," Abbott said.

"In commercial-grade potting soil," Micki said. "Available at any garden store. Oh, and he buried her in the bathtub. I sent a team to the apartment where Samantha lived. It hadn't been rented out yet. Or, luckily for us, cleaned very well. We found soil under the edge of the grout around the tub and a few particles in the drain trap."

"What about Martha Brisbane?" Abbott asked.

"Afraid of water," Carleton said, scanning the page, then his face bent in sympathy. "Oh. Her father drowned. Martha saw it happen. She was five at the time."

Noah clenched his jaw. "You know, I keep thinking I can't hate this guy any more, but I keep finding a way. To have read that, then to have used it . . ."

"He's a sociopath," Carleton said simply. "A sadistic sociopath. He gets pleasure from the pain of others. Christy Lewis, phobia of snakes . . . Just because." He looked up with a shrug. "That's what she wrote. 'Just because.' "

"So she didn't have any kind of traumatic event?" Jack asked.

"Or she didn't want to share it," Carleton said. "There may very well not have been one. I see a lot of patients with snake phobias and many can't tell me why. Some of it is instinctive. Snakes are dangerous and humans have developed a fear of dangerous things. Survival of the fittest and all that."

"And now Rachel Ward," Abbott said. "With her fear of fire. Does she mention why?"

"She says she's afraid of right-wing Republicans, which is a NOYB answer—none of your business. Subjects will use sarcasm when they don't want to tell you the truth."

"But," Olivia said, "he could have googled her and found that out, like Jack did."

"But it wasn't that simple," Jack said with a frown. "Somebody had to dig. I googled her first, and didn't get anything. I ran a background, saw she'd used a different name five years ago and checked the marriage licenses. I googled her ex to get the story."

Noah met Jack's eyes and gave him a "well-done" nod and was relieved at Jack's brisk nod back. "So," Noah mused, "our killer understood her right-wing Republican answer was just a ruse and dug deeper. I find that strange."

"Why?" Abbott asked.

"Exactly," Noah said. "Why? Why not just accept it at face value and pick somebody else? There are five hundred names on the list. Why Rachel Ward?"

"Maybe because she was so available," Jack said. "She was online every night."

"Possibly," Noah said. "I talked to a few neighbors last night who said she kept to herself, never went out, a real-world introvert. In Shadowland she was a cabaret dancer who'd take home a dozen 'men' a night."

"I don't get the whole virtual sex thing," Abbott said with a frown. "Is it common?"

"Not *un*common, according to Eve. Not that she gets it either," Noah added hastily.

Abbott's eyes rolled. "If Rachel had a liquor bottle under the seat of her car and a BA of oh-fifteen, he probably met her at a bar. Find out where."

"Not many bars in town," Jack muttered sarcastically. "But it's a start."

"What about the car I saw last night?" Olivia asked. "The brown Civic."

"Nothing from the BOLO," Micki said. "And Girard's wife's car was in the garage."

"I want to know what connection Girard has to this

guy," Noah said. "He's either faster than a speeding bullet, or Girard has a serious enemy."

"Who is Girard?" Ian and Carleton asked at the same time.

"Axel Girard is the owner of the car that followed Christy home," Jack said flatly.

"His wife owns the plate I saw leaving Rachel's neighborhood," Olivia added.

"He's also an optometrist," Abbott said. "And a model citizen."

"Every victim's eyes have been glued open," Ian said. "Being an optometrist can't be a coincidence. I assume he has an alibi or you would have arrested him already."

"He had a so-so alibi for Christy, but he had a hell of an alibi for Rachel," Noah said dryly. "As in two of our guys sitting in an unmarked car a few houses down, all night long."

"That is a hell of an alibi," Carleton said. "Any chance he sneaked out?"

"Possibly"—Noah shrugged—"but the timeline doesn't work unless he drove a hundred-twenty the whole way home."

"So where is Girard now?" Carleton asked.

"I had him brought in," Noah said, "more for his own protection than anything else. If anything else happened, I'd know exactly where he was. But I let him go this morning. We still have a car watching his house."

"Chat with Dr. Girard," Abbott said. "Find out why a killer has such a hard-on for him. There has to be a connection. This guy has been too damn meticulous. If nothing else, I want to know if there's any way Girard had access to that list. What else?"

"Dr. Donner and Jeremy Lyons," Jack said. "We need

their whereabouts. Right now they have the most access to study files."

"You haven't talked to them yet?" Olivia asked, surprised.

"We couldn't find Donner," Noah said. "He never showed up after morning classes. I met Lyons in the Deli with Eve, but when Jack and I went back to the university, he was gone, too. Then we caught wind of Axel Girard and spun our wheels for hours on him."

"Go back today and get their alibis for Christy, Rachel, and Martha," Abbott said. "What about your panty pervert? Taylor Kobrecki."

"We checked with his pals," Kane said, speaking for the first time. "He's in the wind."

"His LUDs show calls from Bozeman, Montana," Olivia said, "as recently as this morning. If he's with his cell, he couldn't have killed Rachel. We put Bozeman on alert."

Kane shrugged. "But it wouldn't be the first time a perp had someone else take his cell out of area to establish an alibi."

"I'd be surprised if he was that clever," Carleton said. "I checked him out. High school graduate, but barely. Special needs classes, no organization. He doesn't have the acuity to form a plan like this. I think your resources would be best used elsewhere."

"Agreed," Abbott said. "Anything else?"

"Maybe," Noah said. "Usage logs from the study show another participant who went from heavy play time to nothing, overnight. Her name was Amy Millhouse."

Jack looked perturbed. "Was?"

"Yes. She committed suicide three weeks ago."

"We checked all the suicide reports," Jack said. "Nothing looked like these scenes."

"I know, that's why I said 'maybe.' We should check it out."

Abbott gave Noah a pensive look. "Do it. Then find Donner and Lyons. Check out everyone who knew about that damn list. Olivia, Kane, find out where Rachel met him last night. Somebody has seen this guy. Meet back here at five. Web, you stay."

"I just found out about Amy," Noah said when everyone left. "I should have told you."

Abbott leaned back and studied him. "Why didn't you?"

"Eve called me this morning, after I'd talked to Girard in holding. She was showing me the graphs and Millhouse's obit when she got a text, we think from Kurt Buckland. It was a quote from the guy who assaulted her back in Chicago. She was shaken up."

"I guess so. And?"

"And this Buckland's been trying to pressure her to give him details on this case." He told him about Buckland's visit to Sal's and the photos of him and Trina.

Abbott listened, frowning. "I'll get somebody on it. You focus on this case. Got it?"

"Yeah."

"And next time, tell your partner about potential new victims before the group."

Noah bristled, but nodded. "Yes, sir."

Wednesday, February 24, 9:10 a.m.

After Winters, Eve found the shower the place to cry when people were around. The water covered the sobs and minimized eye swelling. She'd taken a lot of showers then.

Very clean, she'd been. Very clean she was now as

she sat in a chair at the police department, waiting to file a complaint against Buckland. His text had shaken her badly.

"I'm Officer Michaels," the policeman said with a kind smile. "I've seen you at Sal's."

"Bud Lite," she said, forcing a smile of her own.

"Gotta watch that waistline," he quipped, then sobered. "What happened last night?"

Eve told him, watching his brow crease as she related the details. "And this morning he texted me. Detective Webster has already started a trace." She frowned at Michaels's expression of disbelief. "You don't believe me."

"No, that's not it at all. I'm just stunned. I know Kurt and this doesn't sound like him."

Eve tugged at her sleeve, exposing the bruise that had faded a little during the night. "He did this. And another cop, Jeff Betz, saw the whole thing."

"Of course I believe you. I just never would have guessed it of Looey."

Eve sat back, her own brow creased now. "Looey?"

"Yeah. That's what some of the guys call Kurt. Don't ask me why. Before my time."

Looey. He was a semi-regular at Sal's, a Michelob man who was about fifty. The Buckland she'd met wasn't yet thirty. "What does your Kurt Buckland look like, Officer?"

Michaels put his pen down. "Why?"

"I'm wondering if we're talking about the same man. The man who grabbed me last night was about thirty, maybe five-eleven, with brown hair and brown eyes." She was studying Michaels's eyes as she spoke. "Not your Kurt Buckland."

"No." Michaels had the same bad feeling, she could see. "Let me take your statement, Miss Wilson, then I'll check on Kurt. I mean, Looey."

The man who'd threatened her was not Kurt Buckland, mild-mannered Metro reporter. That made his threat all the more bizarre and terrifying. And suddenly even more personal against Noah. "Do you have a pencil and paper?"

Michaels gave them to her and quickly she sketched the man she'd seen. It wasn't nearly the level of work she might have done before her hand was slashed six years ago, but it was a passable facsimile. "This is him," she said. "Just in case."

"Not bad. I've never seen him, but I'll take this with me when I go see Looey."

Wednesday, February 24, 9:40 a.m.

Noah got back to his desk to find Jack angrily throwing his own belongings in a box. "What the hell are you doing?"

Jack looked up, tight-lipped. "Moving."

He grabbed Jack's arm to keep him from tossing a book in the box. "Why?"

Jack faltered. "I thought . . . I assumed you'd be asking Abbott for a new partner."

Noah blew out a breath. "Dammit, Jack. He was yelling at me, not you. I should have told you about Amy Millhouse, but I just found out about her this morning." He told Jack about the latest on Kurt Buckland. "Abbott's gonna take care of it."

Jack puffed out his cheeks. "Is Eve reporting him?"

"She should be doing that right now. Did you get a new cell phone?" It was an olive branch, albeit a skinny one.

"On my list to do today. There's a store near Marshall University. I'll get one after we talk to Donner and Lyons." He met Noah's eyes. "I really only had one drink, Noah."

Noah lifted a shoulder. "Sometimes one's all it takes. Let's go."

"Wait." Jack pointed over Noah's shoulder and Noah turned.

Eve was walking toward them. For a few seconds Noah just let himself look. Her dark eyes were shuttered and there was no sign of her little sideways smile. Something was wrong. *Something new, that is.* "Can you give me a minute?" he asked Jack.

"Sure. I'll wait in the car."

Eve nodded to Jack when he passed, then fixed her eyes on Noah's, and he knew it wasn't going to be good. "I just finished filing my complaint against Kurt Buckland."

"Good." He led her to an unoccupied room and closed the door. Taking her arm, he pushed up her sleeve. "Did you show the officer this bruise?"

She tugged her hand free. "Yes. Listen. Last night I researched Buckland, found this article on your case is his first front-page article ever. Everything he's ever done has been in Metro, just like that first article about Martha's suicide."

"So he bullies and blackmails to get ahead? Extreme, but it's been done."

"I thought so until I came here today and filed my complaint. Guess what? Officer Michaels knew him. Turns out Kurt is about fifty and that everyone called him Looey."

Noah frowned. "I know Looey. He's good at darts. He's Buckland?"

"Apparently so."

"So, then . . . who is the guy who took all the pictures? And who threatened you?"

"That's what somebody needs to find out. This is personal, Noah. Against you."

"Wonderful," he muttered. "Another distraction."

"So what will you do?"

"About Buckland or whoever he is? I want to find this guy and make him pay, but right now I can't. Right now, I'm going to let the officer you talked to do his job. And right now I'm going to follow you to school. Jack and I have to talk to Donner."

"Then we need to go, because I'm late."

But neither of them moved. "I never got to kiss you last night," he murmured.

"You did, at Sal's."

"That was a little one-sided. You never kissed me back."

"I was too surprised," she said, shivering when his thumb caressed her jaw.

Jack was waiting for him and they had so much work to do, but Noah needed a minute, just one minute for himself. For Eve. *For both of us.*

"Consider this fair warning then." He covered her mouth with his, willing her to respond, and after a few pounding beats of his heart, she did. Lifting on her toes, she kissed him as she had in the coffee shop, nothing held back. Her arms wound round his neck and he pulled her closer, fitting her body to his. It was sweet and it was hot and he wanted so much more. But this wasn't the place, so he forced himself to stop.

She was breathing hard, her eyes closed. Her fingers trembled as they trailed down his arms. Pressing his palms together, she rested her brow on the tips of his fingers.

"Why?" she whispered so softly he had to lean forward to catch it.

"Why which?" he asked, gruffly.

She lifted her head, her expression devastated. "Why me? Why do you want *me*?"

"That's a longer answer than I have time for now. Have dinner with me tonight."

"I have to work."

"Then after. I'll wait."

"All right." She pushed his folded hands gently to his chest. "I need to get to class."

Wednesday, February 24, 10:25 a.m.

"Detectives, I'm so sorry I missed you yesterday. Please have a seat." Dr. Donald Donner waved at two chairs on the other side of his very disorganized desk.

"You're a hard man to find," Jack said. "We looked for you yesterday."

Donner smiled distractedly. "My wife and I went to see her mother, who's been ill."

Noah kept his expression mild—a hard thing to do when he thought about Donner's last interaction with Eve. But after getting his first look at Donner, Noah had crossed him off his list. Donner might have access to the list, but he didn't have the physical strength to hoist a woman from her ceiling. "We'd also like to talk with your assistant, Mr. Lyons, but we can't find him either."

At this Donner frowned. "He took the afternoon off yesterday and didn't come in this morning. That's not like him. He's very reliable. I don't know what I'd do without him."

You'd have to get another weasel to do your dirty work, Noah thought with contempt for the older man. But he and Jack were after alibis and for now would play nice.

"One of your studies has come up in the course of an ongoing investigation," Jack said. "The study in which participants play a game called Shadowland."

"Yes. That's the work of one of my graduate students, Eve Wilson." His lips thinned. "But I guess you already knew that. No matter. How can I help you?"

"You can start by telling us where you were last night," Noah said. "All night."

"Why?" he asked, seeming genuinely confused, and Jack frowned.

"We're investigating murder, Professor. Four women have been killed."

"What does that have to do with my study?" Donner asked.

"All four victims were participants," Noah said, wondering if the man's confusion could possibly be real. "All four were heavily into the Shadowland game."

Donner sat back heavily, disbelief etched in his face. "You're joking."

"We don't joke, Professor," Jack said, "especially not about something like this."

The color drained from Donner's face. "Four women?" he whispered. "In my study?" Then Noah's first question seemed to catch up to him as twin flags of crimson appeared on Donner's sallow cheeks. "Am I correct in understanding I am a suspect, Detective? That you want me to provide an . . . an *alibi*?"

"We're asking everyone connected with the study, Professor," Noah said. "It would make our jobs a great deal easier if we could just cross you off quickly."

"Of course," he murmured, distractedly. "I was with my wife asleep."

Noah jotted it down. "What about Monday morning between midnight and five?"

"Asleep. With my wife."

He was becoming agitated. "All right," Noah said calmly, and Donner appeared to try to regain control. "We think whoever is killing your subjects has access both to your participant list and to the questionnaires they filled out when the study began."

"Why would you think that?"

"He uses information from the questionnaires to torture them," Jack said flatly.

Donner flinched. "Torture them? He tortured them? Who are the four women?"

Noah frowned. "Don't you read the paper, Dr. Donner? Three of the victims were listed yesterday. On the front page."

Donner gestured weakly to his journals. "I don't read much news."

Okay. "The four victims are Samantha Altman, Martha Brisbane." Noah stopped when the remaining color drained from Donner's face. "Professor?"

"Martha Brisbane, did you say?" Donner asked unsteadily. "Dear God. I thought she'd committed suicide." He abruptly went silent, as if realizing he'd said too much.

"How did you know that, sir?" Jack asked quietly. "You don't read the paper."

"My graduate student, Eve . . . she told me. I didn't believe it was related to our study at the time. The others? Who were they?"

"Christy Lewis and just last night, Rachel Ward," Jack said.

"I see." He looked at Jack. "What do you need from me?"

"Anybody who would have had access to the list and those questionnaires."

"I . . . I don't know. My assistant entered the names, but the committee separated them into groups. I only saw results by subject number. Nobody was supposed to see everything. That's the purpose of a double-blind study."

"What about the questionnaires? How were they used?" Noah asked.

"They're part of a baseline measure. They form a profile, a personality index."

"Did anybody read them?" Jack asked.

"Various students," he said. "But nobody ever saw the subjects' real names. They were to input the answers in a standardized protocol."

There was nothing here they could use, Noah thought. He and Jack stood. "Thank you," Jack said. "We're trying to keep Marshall and Shadowland out of the press. We're hoping the killer doesn't know how much we know. We'd appreciate your cooperation."

Donner nodded, his face gray. "Of course," he murmured. "If you see Miss Wilson, tell her . . . Tell her I'm sorry. I should have listened to her."

"I'll tell her," Noah said. "If your assistant calls you, let us know immediately."

"Of course." They left Donner with his head in his hands, trembling.

"Well?" Jack said when they were back at their cars.

"He's too . . . frail to have done these murders."

"Mentally or physically?"

"Both."

Jack nodded. "I agree. Let's confirm Donner's alibi and find Jeremy Lyons."

Noah gritted his teeth. "Dammit, I wish I'd grabbed that little weasel yesterday."

"I think we've all been a little distracted," Jack said. "Let's pull LUDs on both Donner and Lyons and pay their wives a visit."

Chapter Sixteen

Wednesday, February 24, 11:20 a.m.

Callie, it's all right," Eve said, setting her lunch tray on the only empty table at the Deli. She sat down and slid her computer bag safely between her feet. "None of this is your fault. I should have called you, but I had no idea this guy would come to you."

An irate Callie had intercepted Eve coming out of Abnormal class, saying she had information about Noah Webster, that Eve needed to know. More "Buckland" lies.

"I can't believe I talked to him. He said you were having an affair with a married man, that Webster had a wife named Susan."

So that was her name, Eve thought. She'd died, Sal had said. More than ten years ago. With a sigh she patted Callie's hand. "Chill. I have to send a text to Webster, let him know I'm okay."

"I am chilled, knowing that guy grabbed you. You're texting? Why not just call?"

Eve hated text messaging. Even short messages made her thumb throb. "He's working. I don't want to bother him during an interview."

"Give me your phone. I'll do it for you. What do you want to say?"

"Um . . . at the Deli with Callie. Was walked over by a

large ex-wrestler named Jose. Currently surrounded by at least six cops. Am quite safe. Don't worry, Eve."

Callie shot her a curious look, then dutifully input the message. Then frowned. "What's this one from this morning?" She raised angry eyes. "Did this Buckland poser text you?"

"Yeah." And Eve was still shaken from it. "Look, I know how he found out about me. He was following Noah and I happened to be there. But how did he find out about you?"

"I don't know. A hell of a cool-headed attorney I'm going to make. He just made one false allegation and I bought it, lock, stock, and barrel."

"Don't beat yourself up, Cal. You can hardly be expected to be objective when it comes to your best friend. How did he contact you?"

"My cell at first, but I had it turned off because I was in class. He left me a voicemail asking if I knew you, but I didn't hear it till after I saw him."

"He approached you? Did he touch you?"

"No. He was waiting for me when I came out of my last class. Then he stuck Noah Webster's wedding picture under my nose, told me you were having an affair with a married man. I told him no way, you weren't seeing anyone and definitely not a married man. He gave me his card. Told me to call if I heard anything."

Eve leaned forward. "But he called you. On your cell."

Callie's brows went up. "Who would give him my number?"

"That would have been the guy you were talking to yesterday," a voice behind them said, and Eve and Callie twisted to see who spoke. It was the barista Eve had talked to the day before, when she bought the copy of *MSP* while she'd waited for Noah to come.

"What did he look like?" Eve asked.

"Short with round glasses," he said. "The one who was giving you a hard time before your boyfriend came in and kissed you."

Jeremy Lyons. Eve started to ask more, but Callie jumped in. "What kiss?"

"One of the cops from the magazine article," the barista told her. "Not the cover guy. But one of the guys inside the article."

Eve felt her cheek grow very warm when Callie started to grin. "Never mind that," Eve said briskly. "So after we left, the reporter talked to the short guy with glasses?"

"He did. The short guy was all too happy to dish. He told the reporter he didn't believe you and the cop were really a couple and he could prove it. He said he'd get your friends to tell the truth. Even said he'd get your phone number." He directed the latter statement to Callie. "The reporter gave him his card and took off."

"Took off where?" Eve asked.

"He got in his car and started driving the same way you all went."

Eve frowned at him. "You saw which way I went when I left here?"

"Sweetheart, when you two left, *everybody* watched which way you went."

Eve covered her burning face with her hands. "Oh my God. How embarrassing."

"How fascinating," Callie said with relish. "What happened next?"

"She and the Hat guy left, his arm around her, real tight," the barista said, conspiratorially. "And that yummy Detective Phelps was in the passenger seat. That made my day." He gave Eve a mock glare. "You never said you knew him."

Eve shrugged, still mortified. "Sorry, but I don't think you're Jack Phelps's type."

"I figured as much. What a waste. Look, I gotta get back behind the counter. I saw how upset you were and I wanted to let you know what I saw."

"Thank you," Eve said, sincerely. "Truly."

When the barista was gone, Callie said nothing, just sipped her coffee and waited.

Eve rolled her eyes. "I wanted to throw Jeremy Lyons off the trail. He was sure I was cooperating with the cops or the papers or both. I wanted to give him the wrong idea."

"So it was a ruse," Callie said, obviously enjoying the moment. "Just one kiss."

Eve dropped her eyes to her fidgeting hands and Callie crowed in delight.

"More than one?"

Eve's lips still tingled from it. As did every other square inch of her body. "Oh, yeah."

Callie sighed. "And you're going to find a reason it can't work. It'll be a stupid one and you'll cling to it like a drowning man clings to one of those . . . circle . . . things."

Eve had to smile. "You mean a life preserver?"

"Shut up," Callie said, but without heat. "Tell me you'll give him a chance."

"Now you sound like David."

"Who appears to be as smart as he is sexy. So what is your reason, Eve? Why have you convinced yourself this thing with Webster won't work? Don't you trust him?"

Eve shrugged uneasily. "That's the problem. I trusted him the first time I saw him."

"How is this a problem?" Callie asked, exasperated.

"Because . . . I don't just trust people. Especially men. Who look like him."

"Which is how? Impossibly handsome?"

"No. Trustworthy." Eve winced. "I know that sounds stupid."

Callie's expression softened. "Maybe you trust him because he's the one."

"I'd like to believe that." She thought about what she'd really wanted to do when he'd kissed her in that office and her face heated. "It's not wise."

"Since when have you ever been wise? Which is what you said, not two days ago."

"That was about my roof, not . . ." Not about gobbling Noah Webster in great big bites. She was still overheated, thinking about the kiss that had consumed every breath of air in the room. And she'd agreed to have dinner with him. *What was I thinking?* That she wanted more. A whole lot more. "Never mind."

"I'm getting hot just watching you get hot," Callie said. "So what was it like?"

Eve was spared a reply by the ringing of her cell phone. "Noah," she answered, ignoring Callie's delighted grin. "What's wrong?"

"Nothing," he said. "I got your text. And I needed to make sure you were all right."

"I'm fine. Noah, that Buckland person contacted Callie, too."

"How did he get her to talk to him? Did he threaten her, too?"

"No. He was trying to get information from her. He told her you were married, that your wife's name was Susan, that I was the other woman. He wanted Callie to confirm we weren't together, that I was lying yesterday when I . . . when we . . . you know."

"Yes, I know. And you were right." His voice was tight. "This is personal. He had to dig back a lot of years to find out about Susan. Sonofabitch."

"We'll figure it out," she said quietly.

He sighed. "I know. I also wanted to tell you that I don't think you need to worry about Donner. He told me to tell you he was sorry." She heard a car door slam on his side of the line. "Did you ask Sal for time off for dinner tonight?"

"Not yet." Eve glanced up at Callie, who was still watching with avid curiosity. "But I think I can find someone to cover for me for a while."

"You need me to cover for you tonight?" Callie asked when she'd hung up.

"He wants me to go to dinner with him."

"Then I'll cover for your shift. I need the money and you need the romance. Of course, if you're really not interested, I'd be more than happy to stand in."

"That's all right," Eve said dryly. "Although your sacrifice touches my heart." *Touches*. "Hey, did that guy posing as a reporter give you his card?"

"Yes, he did. I have it here." She opened her purse.

"Don't touch it. I pitched the card he gave me. Maybe they can get prints off yours."

Callie's brows rose. "Why not just give it to Noah Webster?"

"Because he's a little busy right now." Eve dug in her backpack and came up with an empty envelope. "Put on your glove, then drop the card in here."

Callie obeyed, then sat back, amused incredulity on her face. "You're enjoying this."

"A little," Eve admitted. "It's been awhile since I did anything clandestine. In the real world, anyway." She gathered her things. "It always was kind of a rush. Gotta go."

Wednesday, February 24, 12:00 p.m.

"So Jeremy Lyons is missing?" Abbott asked.

Noah slumped into one of the chairs at Abbott's table. "We stopped by his house. His wife was there. He didn't come home last night and she hadn't seen him since yesterday morning. He didn't pick their daughter up from day care and he hasn't called, texted, emailed, nothing, which she said was unusual."

"She let us search," Jack added, "but we found nothing suspicious."

"What about Donner?"

"I'd put my money on Lyons before Donner," Jack said. "Donner didn't appear to be in good enough physical shape to do these murders."

"And Lyons is AWOL," Abbott mused. "Pull Lyons's financials. See if he's gotten any big payoffs lately."

"You're thinking he sold the list?" Jack asked, then shrugged. "It's possible."

"Follow the money," Abbott said. "I requested Girard's financials yesterday. We'll look for links to Lyons, anything to explain why Axel was picked as a fall guy."

There was a light knock on Abbott's door and Faye stuck her head in. "I've got the police report on the Millhouse woman for you, Noah."

"Thanks, Faye." Noah flipped through the report and frowned. "I read this one, Jack, that first night after we found Martha. We read so many, I didn't remember Amy Millhouse by name, but I remember reading this suicide note. 'I'm sorry. God forgive me for the pain I've caused my family and my church.'"

"But we didn't see any other reports that had the shoes and the open window."

"Because this one doesn't. When the investigating officer got there, someone had already cut Amy Millhouse down and laid her on the bed. Look at the picture. Modest clothes, clean face. No makeup."

"Her eyes?" Abbott asked.

"No mention of glue," Noah said.

"Who found her?" Jack asked.

"Her mother."

"Go talk to the mother," Abbott said. "Then pay a visit to the Girards. I want to know why our guy picked Axel."

"I'll meet you at Amy's mother's," Jack said. "When we're done I'll go get a phone."

"I thought you did that this morning, before we met Donner and Lyons."

Jack jerked a careless shoulder. "I went by the store, but the line was too long then."

Noah watched him walk away, wondering how long it would take them to fall back into step. He glanced over his shoulder. Abbott watched him with keen eyes.

"Figure it out, Web," was all Abbott said.

Wednesday, February 24, 12:20 p.m.

Eve found Olivia Sutherland with her boots propped up on her desk, looking so much like her sister, Mia, that Eve had to remind herself who she was talking to. On the corner of Olivia's desk was a bust of a Greek goddess wearing her Hat Squad fedora, charmingly askew. The rest of the desk was almost painfully organized.

"Hey," Eve said.

Olivia looked up, smiling when she saw Eve. "Evie. Sorry. Eve."

"It's okay. An old friend's in town and he's been calling me Evie, so I'm getting used to it again. You remember David Hunter, don't you?"

"He's kind of hard to forget," Olivia said wryly. "We were in Mia's wedding together."

"He walked you down the aisle," Eve remembered.

Olivia grinned. "I felt my life was in danger from all the daggers shooting from the other women's eyes. So why is David here?"

"He's fixing my roof. It leaks."

"Well, tell him I said hello." She leaned back in her chair. "What brings you here?"

"I actually came to see Officer Michaels, but he wasn't there and I have a class in an hour, so I can't wait." She explained the events of the evening before.

"This guy assaulted you?" Olivia asked, blonde brows crunched.

"He did. Anyway, he gave his card to my friend." She took it out of her bag, along with a folded sheet of paper. "His prints should be there. He said he'd print it if I didn't tell him about the dead women yesterday morning."

Olivia opened the folded page and flinched. Then sighed. "Geeze. I'm sorry, Eve."

"It's okay. That's how I looked. You can still see the scar if you look hard."

"I know." Olivia shrugged uneasily. "After your last surgery, I couldn't help but look."

"I know," Eve said. "Everybody thinks I don't see them looking. Anyway, I thought you could give those two things to Latent. Maybe see if any prints pop."

Olivia's lips twitched. "You've been watching too many cop shows."

Eve smiled back. "So you'll submit them?"

"Sure. I'll take them down to Micki Ridgewell and make sure Officer Michaels knows I did it. If this guy bothers you again, call me."

Eve smiled again, ruefully this time. "After I call Noah and a list of other people."

Olivia's brows lifted. "So it's 'Noah' now? What's going on there, anyway?"

"I don't know," Eve said truthfully.

"That's fair." Olivia hesitated. "Mia asks about you every time we talk."

"I'd be surprised if she didn't. She grabbed me off the streets, you know."

"I didn't know. She never told me how she met you."

"I was a kid, living on the streets. Mia was still a patrol officer. I was running a scam with a couple of other runaways and somebody screamed 'cop.' I picked the wrong alley to duck into. Mia was there, and next I knew, I was in the back of her squad car."

Olivia grinned. "She arrested you?"

"Nah. She gave me hell and said she was taking me to somebody who could straighten me out. That was Dana and Caroline and the shelter."

"I'd say they did a pretty good job of straightening you out."

"You should tell them that. What do you say when Mia asks about me?"

"I tell her that I see you at Sal's and you look healthy

and safe. Then she always asks if you're happy and I have to tell her I don't know, that you watch us from behind the bar, but never join in. What should I tell her the next time she asks if you're happy?"

"Tell her I'm not unhappy. I've got to get to class." Eve had taken a step toward the door when a piece of paper on Olivia's desk caught her eye, a list of Twin Cities' bars. "You planning on hosting a party someplace other than Sal's? He'll be hurt."

"We think last night's victim met the killer at a bar."

Eve thought about the timeline. "It would have to be one with a late last call. We close pretty early. When I ring the last-call bell I can guarantee which customers are going to ask for another drink. It's like they'll never see alcohol again. Others toss back what's left in their glass, settle their tab, then tell me they're going to their late-night bar." She checked off several. "These are the places they tell me they're going."

"Excellent," Olivia said, scanning the list. "This will save us some time."

"Good. I have to go now. I have class at one. Don't tell Noah I was here. I'm supposed to travel with an escort but that's a pain in the ass."

"Web's worried about this guy." Olivia swung her boots to the floor in a movement that was both athletic and graceful. "I haven't had lunch yet. I'll follow behind you."

Wednesday, February 24, 1:05 p.m.

"Thanks for seeing us, Mrs. Millhouse," Noah said.

Geraldine Millhouse nodded tightly. "I always help the police," she said.

Jack had lost the toss on this one and he cleared his throat to begin. "Ma'am, we're here to talk to you about your daughter Amy's death."

"My daughter committed suicide. So what?"

"We have some follow-up questions," Jack said. "Our records show she hanged herself, but that when the police arrived, she'd been cut down. Did you do this?"

For a moment they thought she'd say no, but she nodded, stiffly. "Yes." She drew a jerky breath. "I couldn't stand . . ." Her voice broke. "I couldn't stand to see her like that."

"Ma'am, we need to know exactly how you found her," Jack said. "It's important."

"I found her hanging in her room," she said. "I cut her down and put her on her bed."

"Did you change her clothes, Mrs. Millhouse?" Jack asked and she flinched.

"No." She stood, visibly trembling. "Go away, please."

Both Noah and Jack stayed where they were.

"Mrs. Millhouse, we need to know," Jack repeated. "We think there's a chance your daughter didn't commit suicide. That perhaps she was murdered."

Mrs. Millhouse sank into her chair, the color drained from her face. "What?"

"Have you read the paper in the last few days, ma'am?" Noah asked gently.

"No. My eyes aren't so good."

Neither was her back or her hands. Noah could see the signs of arthritis. There was no way this woman had cut her daughter down, at least not by herself.

"Several women have been killed recently," Jack said, "their deaths staged to look like a suicide. Please be truthful with us. How did you find your daughter? We need to know how the room looked, how she looked, everything you can recall."

Mrs. Millhouse covered her face with her hands, a strangled sob escaping her throat as she rocked pitifully. "She was hanging, dressed like a whore. I couldn't stand it."

"Did you call someone?" Jack asked, still gently.

"My son, Larry. He came and took care of me. He took care of everything."

"We need to talk to Larry, ma'am," Jack said softly. "Where is he now?"

"At work. He works for 3M. He's a chemist."

Noah controlled the urge to snap his head up—3M made glue. A quick glance told him Jack had come to the same conclusion.

Jack's smile was both sad and encouraging. "Ma'am, it would be a huge help if you could come down to the station and tell us everything you remember about Amy's death. We'll bring you home when we're finished. Would you come with us?"

Shaken, she nodded. "I'll get my coat after I call my son."

Noah and Jack stood when she did. "Let me help you with your coat," Noah said softly. "If you give me his number, I can call your son for you."

Wednesday, February 24, 1:05 p.m.

Eve slid into one of the empty chairs at the back of the class, a few minutes late. It was Donner's once-weekly ethics seminar and she'd been dreading it all morning. Noah said Donner had apologized, but still . . .

Luckily, Donner wasn't here yet. He'd been late a lot recently, and sometimes when he showed up he was angry for no apparent reason. It was a personality change that had the older grad students worried. Even two years ago, Donner had been considered a mentor to most and a friend to some. Not anymore. *And certainly not to me.*

Her cell phone buzzed. It was Olivia. "I can't talk now," Eve whispered. "I'm in class."

"I'm out in front of your building. We need you down at the station," Olivia said tautly.

Eve's gut twisted. "Noah?"

"No, Looey. You know, Kurt Buckland. He's missing. We need to walk through the events with you. Now. I'll either drive you in or drive behind you."

Eve had already shouldered her computer bag. "On my way."

Wednesday, February 24, 2:30 p.m.

He was feeling downright lucky for the second time in twenty-four hours. Had he lingered another minute over Rachel and the crime scene last night, he would have been caught. Now, if he'd been another minute later, he would have missed Eve.

He'd gone to her apartment hoping to find her home alone, planning to force her into his SUV and bring her back to his pit. Instead, he'd pulled onto her street just as her car was pulling away. He followed, wondering if she'd seen his text, if she'd been afraid.

He so hoped she was afraid, or at the very least angry. Angry people weren't careful, weren't aware. It would be easier to force her off the road and into his SUV.

She'd be discovered missing soon enough. Her friends within the police department would make it their quest to find her killer. But they didn't have a clue. Because he'd given them none.

Wednesday, February 24, 3:00 p.m.

Jack pulled up behind Noah's car, then joined him on the sidewalk in front of the Girards' house. "You get your new phone?" Noah asked.

Jack held up a shiny new cell phone in response. "But I didn't get lunch."

"I went by the Deli," Noah said, "hoping reporter-boy would come back."

"Did he?"

"No, but I did get you an extra sandwich in case you didn't have time to eat."

Jack met his eyes for the first time all day. "Thanks. I appreciate it. I'm not looking forward to this," he said, turning his gaze to Axel Girard's front door.

"Me either, but we need to know how Girard ties, because he can't have killed Rachel Ward last night. I think Girard will be more disposed to talk to us than his wife."

"Why would you think that?" Jack asked, eyes narrowed.

"I went to see him last night. I felt I owed him some explanation after yanking him from his bed. I told him his car was seen again, pressed him to think of somebody who'd set him up. I should have told you earlier, but other things kept coming up."

Jack looked angry, but reined it in. "I guess I should thank you for telling me now."

Noah sighed. "Jack."

"Forget it. We've only got an hour before Geraldine Millhouse's son's plane gets in."

Millhouse's boss had reluctantly provided his travel itinerary. Luckily Larry Millhouse was at thirty thousand feet at the moment, unable to get cell phone calls or escape.

As predicted, Joan Girard was not happy to see them. "Go away," she said, very politely, and shut the door in their faces.

Noah knocked again. "Mrs. Girard, please tell your husband we're here."

"No!" The answer came through the closed door. "Go away."

Jack started to leave, but Noah shook his head. "Axel Girard will come to the door."

Sure enough, the door opened about a minute later. Axel Girard's face was weary and haggard. "Come in," he said quietly.

Mrs. Girard was standing to one side, arms crossed tightly over her chest. She said nothing, but her eyes were furious. "Let's sit in the living room," Axel said.

"Did you tell your wife what we talked about last night?" Noah said when they'd all sat down. "About the newest victim?"

Axel nodded. "I did."

"My husband is not guilty," Joan hissed. "But you dragged him off in the night. To jail. And our children had to see it."

"I'm sorry your kids had to see it," Noah said calmly, "but we have five dead women and so far, no one in custody. We can trace your husband's vehicles to some element of two of the crimes. Now, I don't think he's guilty, ma'am, but there is an undeniable connection. If you know anything, you have to help us, or we could have another victim."

"We can't think of anyone who hates us that much," Axel said, exhausted. "I had an argument with Mrs. Rickman about her dog pooping in our yard, but that's it."

"Do you have any contact with Marshall University?" Noah asked.

"I've taken a few classes there," Joan said, "but not in a long time. Why?"

"Mr. Girard?" Noah asked.

"I've driven past Marshall, but I've never been on the campus. Why?"

"We need to talk about tonight," Noah said, easing the subject away.

Axel's eyes narrowed. "What about tonight?"

"We'd like to maintain surveillance over you during the night. It would be," Noah rushed to add when Joan opened her mouth indignantly, "the best alibi you could hope to get. Last night we had an unmarked car watching your house. We'd like to put those detectives in the house with you tonight, watching all your doors from the inside."

"You want to put policemen in our house?" Joan asked, her teeth clenched.

"Joan," Axel said, sliding his hand across hers. "If it will put this behind us, let them. All right, Detectives. Anything else?"

"No, that's all for now," Noah said. "We'll be in touch." When he and Jack were back on the sidewalk, Noah sighed. "Somehow I knew there wouldn't be an easy connection between Girard and our guy."

"I know," Jack said, unlocking his car. "Next stop, the airport?"

"Yep. Millhouse's plane arrives in—" Noah's cell buzzed. He frowned at the 708 area code. "Webster."

"This is David Hunter."

Noah's frown deepened. Hunter's voice was slightly slurred, but there was an unmistakable undercurrent of fear. "What's wrong?"

"I called 911 first, you second," Hunter said thickly. "Someone just ran me off the road. I was headed west when a black SUV came up behind me. Lincoln Navigator, maybe two years old. It'll have a broken front right headlight. I slowed down, thinking they wanted to pass, but they pushed me off the road when we got to a curve. I fli-lipped," he stumbled over the word. "Dammit. Hurts like a bitch."

"How badly are you hurt?" Noah asked tersely.

"Hit my head. Can't get out of the car. Door's stu . . . stuck." He forced the word.

A chill raced down Noah's spine. "You're in Eve's car."

"Exactly. Find her."

"I'll make sure she's in class, then I'll meet you at the hospital."

"Fine." Hunter's voice sounded thinner. "Damn, this hurts. I think my arm is broken."

"Stay on the phone with my partner while I call her. Keep talking, Hunter." Noah handed his cell to Jack. "Somebody ran Hunter off the road," he said, fury roiling within him. "It was supposed to have been Eve." *Somebody tried to kill Eve. Buckland, or whoever he was.* "Give me your phone. I need to find her."

They switched phones and Noah dialed Eve, but her phone went to voicemail. If she was in class, she'd have turned her phone off. If she was hurt . . . "I need to get to Marshall," he said to Jack. "I need to make sure she's okay."

Jack hesitated, then grasped Noah's arm in a brief squeeze. "Try not to worry. I'll call you when I've talked to Larry Millhouse."

"Thanks." Noah took his phone back and kept Hunter talking as he headed toward Marshall where he prayed Eve was where she said she'd be.

Chapter Seventeen

Wednesday, February 24, 3:10 p.m.

"That's him," Eve said, looking at the police artist's computer screen.

"I'll get this out," Olivia said, taking a copy of the assailant's face from the printer.

"Your sketch made my job a lot easier," the artist said. "It'll give us an edge."

"If Looey's still alive." Eve's blood went cold whenever she thought about the look in the man's eyes as he'd come across the bar. *It could have been me.*

Officer Michaels had found blood in the real Kurt Buckland's apartment. He'd called it in as a possible homicide and Olivia had picked it up.

Olivia's partner Kane was taking Rachel Ward's picture to the late-closing area bars alone. While Eve knew the murder investigation should be the highest priority, she couldn't help but feel relieved that Olivia was handling Kurt Buckland's case.

"Eve." Olivia walked across the bullpen with an ashen older man. "This is Jim Rosen, Kurt Buckland's boss. Come on, let's have a seat in here where we can talk."

"I'm so sorry," Rosen said. "The paper had no knowledge of this man's actions."

"You printed his story about Martha's suicide on Monday," Eve said. "Why?"

"Kurt called me on Sunday. Said he was following up on a tip, that there was a large police presence at the home of a woman who'd hung herself and that one of her neighbors, a Sarah Dwyer, said the police indicated it had been more than a suicide."

That had been the article that had first pushed her across Noah's path. "But you only printed that it was a suicide, and back in the Metro section."

"Kurt's Metro editor and I agreed that without formal police corroboration we'd print it as a suicide. Then Monday, Captain Abbott gave a statement that Martha Brisbane had been murdered. By then Kurt had sent me emails saying he had proof on two other victims, Samantha Altman and Christy Lewis, statements from their parents saying the police had spoken with them. I've known Kurt for years and I trust him. I ran the story."

"Did he bring the story to you personally?" Olivia asked.

"No. He emailed it as an attachment. But like I said, I've known Kurt for years."

"Did you talk to him after Sunday about the Brisbane murder?" Olivia asked.

"No. I thought he was sitting at his desk in Metro. His Metro editor thought he was with me. I can't believe this." He looked genuinely devastated. "Is Kurt dead?"

"We're investigating," was all Olivia would say. "Have you seen this man?" She showed him a copy of the man Eve had described to a sketch artist.

Eve's cell vibrated in her pocket, but she ignored it, waiting for Jim Rosen's answer.

"I don't think so," he finally said. "I'm sorry."

"If he contacts you again," Olivia said, "play along. Then call me, right away."

"I will." He rose and gave Eve a pained look. "I understand this man hurt you last night. The Kurt Buckland I know never would have hurt a fly. He didn't have an aggressive nature. We certainly don't condone tactics of that kind for any reason."

"Thank you," Eve said. "I hope Mr. Buckland is found, safe."

Rosen nodded stiffly. "If you'd like, we'll put that sketch on the front page."

"Let's keep it quiet for now," Olivia said. "If he knows we're on to him, he'll bolt. If he thinks we still believe he's Buckland, he'll get bolder. If I hear anything, I'll call you."

When he was gone, Eve searched her face. "Buckland is dead, isn't he?"

"Based on the amount of blood we found in his apartment? Yeah."

Eve shuddered. "I didn't feel scared last night at Sal's. Not with so many cops around. But I feel scared now."

"Good. You should feel scared. I don't want you going anywhere alone, okay? I don't care how much of a pain in the butt it is."

"I'm not arguing with you. Did you get any usable prints from his business card?"

"Not yet. I asked Micki to send somebody from Latent to Sal's to dust the bar. If he touched it, maybe we'll get something from there."

"I polished it last night, like I do every night. I doubt you'll get anything." Eve stiffened when her cell vibrated again. She pulled it from her pocket. "It's Noah."

"Take it," Olivia ordered.

"Hey," Eve said, injecting a bright note in her voice. "I'm fine." Then everything inside her went cold once more as she listened. *David.* "Where did they take him?"

"Northwest General," he said. "I talked to the paramedics who responded. They say he's stable, he just took a hard hit to the head. Eve, he was driving your car."

Eve sucked in a breath and seemed incapable of forcing it back out. *Breathe.* "I know. I'm here with Olivia at the station. They think the real Kurt Buckland is dead. They found blood in his living room. A lot of blood." Her voice was shaking and she couldn't make it stop. "Noah, he killed Buckland. He just tried to kill me, too."

"Let me talk to Olivia," he ordered tersely.

Wordlessly Eve handed Olivia the phone. David was hurt. Stable, but hurt. *He was in my car. He's hurt because he was in my car. That was supposed to be me.*

She could hear Olivia's voice, steady and capable, but it had faded to a whisper, overwhelmed by the pulse pounding in her head. "It was supposed to be me," Eve said.

Olivia squeezed her arm. "I know. Get your coat. I'll take you to Northwest General."

Wednesday, February 24, 3:45 p.m.

He sat drumming his fingers on the steering wheel of his own car, having parked the SUV. He'd have to get that headlight repaired *forthwith*.

He'd missed. It hadn't been Eve Wilson in her car. It was Hunter. He hadn't known until he was right up against him. He'd been so surprised, he'd jerked his hands on the wheel, keeping him from delivering the ramming blow he'd planned.

The small car had veered off the road, flipping once, but it hadn't been the fiery ball it should have been. *I missed*. The only bright spot was that Hunter wouldn't be able to identify him. The tinted windows of his SUV had prevented his face from being seen.

Now getting to Eve would be impossible. He doubted the police would let her out of their sight. So now he'd have to resort to a more tried and true method.

He'd have to shoot her. Webster wouldn't like that. If the rumors were to be believed, there was a great deal more going on between Webster and Wilson than met the eye. Webster wouldn't rest until her death was avenged. No matter. He'd shoot Webster, too, eventually.

But after he'd taken the sixth of his six. This would be the victim that defied everything they'd suspected. The victim who didn't follow the rules of the game.

Wednesday, February 24, 3:45 p.m.

Olivia followed Eve and a nurse to a small room where David Hunter lay, his eyes closed. His face was bruised, one eye swollen shut, and he had a big bandage on his temple. One arm was immobilized in a splint, but other than that, he looked whole.

Olivia let herself breathe. Beside her, Eve did the same. Eve had held herself together remarkably well. *Better than I might have, under the circumstances.*

"See," Olivia murmured with more calm than she felt, "I told you he'd be okay."

"Is he conscious?" Eve whispered to the nurse.

"Yes, he is," David said. He opened one eye, squinting. "Ow. Bright light."

Eve grabbed the bed rail and held on. "Where are you hurt?"

"Cuts, bruises, and a fractured arm. They're checking my back and neck, but so far, so good." He looked past Eve and his open eye flickered with surprise. "Olivia."

Olivia moved next to Eve, keeping her smile friendly. "Long time no see."

"How are you?" he asked soberly and her heart did a slow twirl, as it had the first time she'd seen him.

"About the same. You, on the other hand, have looked better. Last time I saw you, you were wearing a tux with a carnation in your buttonhole, making every woman in the church wish you'd escort them to their seats and making them swoon when you did."

"You didn't see me the morning after Mia's wedding," he said. "I think my head felt almost as bad as it does now, although my face wasn't so ugly."

"Too much champagne will do that." She watched his eyes shadow and wondered how much he remembered of that night, of the things he'd said. And done. "But I wouldn't worry about your face," she added lightly. "You were way too pretty before."

"Thank you," he said dryly, then glanced at Eve. "She drove you down, kid?"

Eve nodded. "She kept me calm. You had me scared. No, terrified."

"I'm just glad I had the car and not you."

"Oh, yeah." Eve attempted a scoff, but it came out more like a sob. "Mr. Mario Andretti of the virtual world. More like Mario Brothers."

He looked mildly annoyed, which was encouraging. "I've raced in the real world, too."

"When you had your body shop," Olivia said quietly.

Before you gave it up for the fire department. She remembered every word he'd said that night, but she could see she'd surprised him again. "You told me you rebuilt classic cars and drove them too fast."

"The secrets champagne unlocks," he said gruffly. "I guess I'm lucky you didn't cite me for speeding." He closed his eye. "You realize he was gunning for you, Evie."

"Yes," Eve whispered. "I'm—"

"If you say you're sorry I'm going to kick your ass," David said. "After I'm able to stand up. What's Webster doing to catch this SOB?"

"Webster's not on this case," Olivia said. "I am."

David opened one eye again. "Okay. What are *you* doing to catch this SOB?"

"Right now I'm trying to understand this SOB's motives. Why Eve? Why now?"

"I think he's really gunning for Noah," Eve said again. "I'm just in the way."

Olivia wasn't so sure about that. "*If* that's true, I still don't understand why Noah."

"You don't think that's why?" David asked. "That Eve's just a by-product?"

"I might have before this. And before we found the real Buckland went missing. The guy that came after Eve isn't a reporter. We think he assaulted the real Buckland, maybe killed him."

David paled further than he already had. "Oh my God."

"We'll make sure Eve's safe," Olivia said. "But I didn't want to lie to you."

"Thank you." He glared at Eve. "You better not go to the john without protection, kid."

"I'll do what they say, David. I promise." Tentatively

Eve brushed the hair from his forehead. "I'll call your mom. Let her know what's happened."

"No," David said firmly. "That will stir up the whole family. They'll drop everything and come out here. *All* of them. It'll be like Chicago, without the Cubs."

Eve hesitated, then nodded reluctantly. "All right. If the doctor says you'll be fine, I won't call your mom. I did call Tom. Got his voicemail. I'll keep trying."

"Thanks. You're not planning to work tonight, are you?"

"No. Callie's taking my shift. I'm . . . I've got plans."

David's eye narrowed shrewdly, then his gaze lifted over their heads.

Olivia looked over her shoulder. Noah was here, making the room instantly smaller, and if she'd doubted how he'd felt about Eve before, there was absolutely no doubt now. It was written all over his face. Poor guy had it real bad. *I can sympathize.*

"I need to talk to David," she said to Noah. "Can you get Eve a cup of coffee?"

"Of course." Noah put his arm around Eve's shoulders, tenderly. "Come on."

Without argument Eve leaned against him. "I'll be back later, David."

When they were gone, Olivia pulled a chair next to David's bed and took out her notepad. "Okay, tell me what happened. Everything you can remember."

David's shoulders sagged wearily. "There's not much. I was taking Eve's car to get a few parts. I was going to tune it up. I had Hank on the radio and I was singing along."

She looked up, her lips curving. "You gotta sing to Hank. I think it's a country music law or something. What next?"

"The road was only one lane each way and I was going

the limit. This black SUV acted like it was going to pass me, then it swerved and hit me. Just once."

"Did you see the plate?"

"No. He hit his front right to my back left. I did see a broken headlight. I went into a ditch, rolled and ended up upside down. I want Eve to get protection, 24/7."

"I'll see to it. You have my word."

"Your word is good. I . . . I'm glad it's you, looking for this guy. Thank you."

His hand lay on the edge of the bed, just inches away and she wanted to touch him. Touch that face nearly every woman he'd ever met found impossible to resist. *Including me.* But because she remembered every word he'd said that night, she knew the one woman who'd somehow failed to fall at his feet was the only one he'd ever wanted.

Because she had her pride, Olivia kept her hands to herself. "We'll take care of Eve," she said briskly. "I'll leave my number with the nurse. Call if you remember anything."

She'd turned to go when he stopped her.

"Olivia, wait. There's something else you need to know."

Eve hadn't needed anyone to tell her Noah had entered David's room. She'd felt him watching her, just as he'd watched her all those months. When they were in the hall, she turned to him, her hands slipping under his coat, holding on to the warmth of his back. His arms closed around her like steel bands and he held her, saying nothing.

Her cheek pressed against his chest, she rested. He laid his cheek against her head and she felt him settle. *This is what I've missed*, she thought. *This is what they found.*

Caroline, Dana, Mia. They found a place to rest. To be safe. To not be alone.

Deep down Eve wished it could last. Deep down she let herself hope, just a little.

"I was scared to death when you didn't answer your phone," he murmured. "Please don't do that to me again."

Having someone worry over her was nothing new. But having someone like Noah worry was very new. It should feel constricting. Debilitating. But it didn't. It felt warm, welcoming, like a cozy fire on a cold day.

"I didn't mean to scare you. I was talking to the real Buckland's boss."

"I know. Olivia told me."

She pressed her face harder against him. "What could make him hate you so much, hate Looey so much? My God, Noah, Looey's probably dead."

"I know," he whispered. "We'll figure it out. Until then, you don't leave my sight."

"Okay." She held on to him until Olivia came into the hall and cleared her throat.

"He wants to talk to you, Noah," she said. "Come on, Eve, I'll get you that coffee."

Noah rested his hands on the rail at Hunter's side. "You don't look too bad."

Hunter was lying back, eyes closed. "If it had been Eve in that car, she would be dead. She doesn't have the strength in her hand to have fought with the wheel."

Noah blew out a breath. "I know. I also know Olivia's a damn good cop. She's on it."

"Last night I asked Eve if anybody's looking at this guy for the Shadowland murders. I said the timing was too co-incidental. She said it was in your mind."

"It is. And I know it's in Liv's, too. We'll be working this together."

"Well, here's another piece. I just told Olivia. Monday night when you came by, I'd put in those baby monitor cameras."

"The pink ones. I remember."

"Eve thought it was because of the Shadowland thing, that I was being overzealous. I didn't tell her this, didn't want her to worry any more than she already was. She told you she'd been having issues with her landlord?"

"She said her roof leaked."

"Yeah, well, he's pretty much let the place go to pot. When I first got there, when I was waiting for her to come back? I went up on the roof to check out the damage. The holes I found were man-made."

Noah stared down at him. "You think her landlord's behind all this?"

"God, I don't know. I almost didn't say anything because it sounds so crazy."

"No, it's good you did," Noah said. "Olivia and I will check it out."

"Olivia said Eve would get police protection."

Grimly Noah recalled the terror that had ripped him inside out until she'd answered her phone, until he'd heard her voice. Known she was all right. "Yes." *Me*.

Hunter met Noah's eyes with his open one. "Other than you?"

"Yes. If that's what she wants. Otherwise, it'll be me."

"Okay. I told her to give you a chance, but I want it to be her decision. I don't want her to feel for—" Hunter froze. "What is this ring?"

Noah looked down at his own right hand on the side rail. "My college ring. Why?"

"I never saw his face, but I saw his hands. I looked over as he was coming up on me and I saw his hand on the steering wheel. He had tinted windows on the sides and back, but not on the windshield, so I could see him. Just barely."

Noah's pulse jolted. *Something they could use.* "I take it he wore a ring like mine."

"Yeah," Hunter said grimly. "Just like that one."

"It's a common design, but a place to start. I'll tell Olivia and see where we end up."

"Excuse me, Detective." A nurse pushed in front of him. "Mr. Hunter has to go up to get his CAT scan now. You can wait in the waiting room."

"Okay," Noah said, then leaned over the rail. "Don't worry. She'll be safe with me."

Eve handed Noah a cup of coffee from the vending machine when he rejoined them. "Extra sugar. Probably not sweet enough, but the best you'll get from a machine."

"Thank you," he said. "Come on, let's find a place for the three of us to talk."

"Eve," Olivia started when they'd found a quiet corner of the waiting room, "I know you think he's got Noah in his sights and you got in the way, but we have to look at the possibility that you could be the target."

"Look at it all you want," Eve said. "It's not me."

"Still," Noah said, "we want you to make a list of everybody that might want to hurt you or has a grudge against you. Include your landlord."

Eve's eyes widened. "You've got to be kidding. Myron Daulton? If David said that, he hit his head harder than we thought."

"You're blocking Daulton from selling that building and making a bundle," Noah said.

"I know, but . . ." Eve sighed. "Okay, I'll make a list. But that guy posing as Buckland is not Myron Daulton, I can tell you that right now. Myron's about fifty and built like Homer Simpson. What about prints? Did you get any from what I gave you?"

"He's not in the system," Olivia said. "We ran the prints on that business card and the copy of that old photo you brought me, Eve. They matched prints we found in Looey's place, so we can put him there, but no match in AFIS."

Noah's brows shot up. "You were busy today," he said to Eve.

"I've had my moments," Eve said dryly. "I want to know why he impersonated Looey to start with and if this *is* personal about you, Noah—which it is—what did you do to this guy? Or what does he think you did? I've seen a killer bent on revenge up close, and this guy was all about revenge. About showing you up and making you pay."

"You and Jack should go back through your old cases," Olivia said. "For the record."

"If Jack and I arrested him, he would have shown up in AFIS."

"Not if he was a juvenile at the time," Eve said. "Or the revenge is for someone else."

Olivia and Noah shared an amused glance. "You want my job, Eve?" Olivia asked.

Eve smiled sadly. "You have no idea how much. But bum hand, so no can do."

Olivia patted Eve's knee. "It's overrated. And you can't chase your own demons. You gotta be satisfied with chasing everybody else's." She looked back at Noah. "It's almost time for Abbott's five o'clock meeting. What should we do with Eve?"

"She has to come with us," Noah said.

"Excuse me," Eve said. "I'm not going anywhere. I'm staying here, with David."

"The doctors won't let you stay with him," Noah said. "They'll watch him overnight and they'll make you leave. Plus you're having dinner with me."

Night off. *Callie.* "What about my friend, Callie? He has her cell phone number. He may know where she lives." She heard the panic in her voice and swallowed it back.

Olivia frowned. "How did he get her cell phone number?"

"Jeremy Lyons. He didn't believe me yesterday morning so he told the reporter-guy how to get in touch with my friends, who'd give him the real story."

"Where's Callie now?" Olivia asked.

"Taking my shift at Sal's."

Olivia nodded. "Then she's safe where she is. I'll make sure the word gets out that if he shows up at Sal's, they should keep him there. I'll have someone escort her home. As for you, we'll leave you here if you do not leave the waiting room. We'll give hospital security a copy of the artist's sketch, so they'll be watching for him."

"I'll stay here where it's safe," Eve promised. "I'm not stupid."

Wednesday, February 24, 4:55 p.m.

"Is Eve okay?" Jack asked when Noah sat next to him at Abbott's small round table.

He and Olivia had arrived for Abbott's five o'clock update to find everyone already gathered around the table except for Ian, who was in the middle of an autopsy.

"Yeah. She was here at the time, actually," Noah answered, "working with a sketch artist to identify the guy who's been impersonating Kurt Buckland."

Jack's eyes widened, then narrowed. "Somebody's been impersonating Kurt Buckland? When were you going to tell me this?"

Noah let out a sigh. Somewhere in his frazzled mind, he thought he had. "I'm sorry, Jack. We haven't had much time to talk today, what with us driving separately."

Abbott cleared his throat, moving over to give Olivia a seat. "Let's share all that in turn," he said frowning at both Noah and Jack. "Anything from last night's scene?"

"We got the composition of both the accelerant he used," Micki said, "and the flame suppressant. Both are common brands, available anywhere. No way to trace them. We've combed four scenes now, including Samantha Altman's after the fact. We've found no prints, no hairs, nothing to track this guy forensically."

"He's probably shaved himself all over," Carleton said. "It's common with serial killers. The really successful ones know how not to leave a trail."

"Thank goodness they're overachievers," Abbott said sarcastically. "What about Rachel Ward? Do we know where she met this guy?"

"At the Last Call Bar," Kane said. "We should thank Eve, by the way. Her narrowing the list to the later-closing bars saved me a lot of time."

Carleton turned to Kane. "Did Rachel Ward normally hang out at the Last Call?"

"No," Kane said. "The bartender said he'd only seen her last night. She was waiting for a man, and got drunker the longer she waited. He took her keys and called her a cab. I confirmed with the cab company. By the time the cab arrived, Rachel was gone."

"Security cameras?" Abbott asked.

"Broken. Probably for years," Kane replied. "No help there. I can go back tonight and see if any of the regulars spotted anyone hanging out in the parking lot."

"Do that." Abbott drew a frustrated breath. "Let me get this straight, so that I don't misrepresent us when I give the commander his evening update. We have no forensics at any of the scenes. Donner's alibied by his wife and Girard is alibied by us. Jeremy Lyons is still missing. Everyone else has a solid alibi, including the brother of the latest victim, or the first victim, Amy Millhouse."

"I thought you said you checked all the suicide reports," Carleton said.

"We did. But we missed it because her brother cut her down and changed her clothes. Cleaned her face and everything," Noah said.

"I take it you brought the brother in, then, Jack," Olivia said. "But he's alibied, too?"

Jack nodded. "He's in Interview Four with his lawyer. He was flying back from a business trip in Chicago and I confirmed that he was there this morning. I thought if Millhouse wasn't in any meetings this morning that it would have been possible for him to drive there after he killed Rachel Ward, then fly back, establishing an alibi."

"It would have been a clever thing to do," Carleton allowed. "Very much in keeping with this killer's profile. It would have been good thinking, Jack, had it worked."

Jack sighed. "Thanks. But Millhouse was in meetings from 8:00 a.m. right up until the time he left for the airport and he was in his hotel at seven. There's no way he could have made it from here to Chicago, even if he'd driven straight from Rachel Ward's house. He's not our killer, even though he works with glue. It would have been perfect."

"Did he say anything about his sister Amy playing in Shadowland?" Noah asked.

"No. He hasn't said a word. Called his lawyer right away."

Abbott scowled. "Ramsey says the most they're willing to charge him with is disturbing a corpse, and they probably won't do that. We'll talk to the brother once more when we're done here, then cut him loose."

"What about Amy's residence?" Noah asked, but Jack shook his head.

"New tenants already. I doubt we'd find anything after all this time. Building manager said they overhauled the place, painting, cleaning carpets. It's a shi-shi neighborhood."

"So do we know what the scene looked like?" Micki asked.

"Only that they changed her clothes," Jack said. "That's all Mom said earlier and brother Larry hasn't spoken. Ian will call us with Amy Millhouse's autopsy report. Amy was cremated, so we couldn't exhume her if we wanted to."

"Thanks," Noah murmured.

Jack jerked a nod. "Sure."

"We do have a little good news," Abbott said, but his expression didn't show it. "Axel Girard's financials show he was issued a credit card two months ago and it was mailed to a post office box in St. Paul."

"That seems way too obvious," Noah said, "like catching Girard's car on the surveillance video while he waited for Christy Lewis. It seems too simple."

"Because it is," Kane said. "I went to the box in St. Paul with a warrant but it was empty. There was a forwarding order—all mail was sent to a mailbox store downtown. Which was forwarded to another P.O. box right across the street."

Abbott pointed to his window. "You can see the post office branch from here."

"That box," Kane said, "was full. Mostly junk mail, but the credit card was there."

"So far no charges have been made to the card," Abbott said.

"He never intended to use it," Olivia said quietly. "He set this up, just like he's set up the scene of every crime, to divert us."

"And he was successful." Kane shook his head. "Had me running all over town, all afternoon, when I should have been talking to Rachel Ward's coworkers."

"How is this good news?" Micki asked.

"Because it adds to the profile. He's playing with us," Carleton said sourly. "He hasn't missed a step."

"Yet," Noah said grimly.

"Yet," Carleton repeated. "This man, and it's almost assuredly a man, exhibits a compulsion for order and control. Every scene, just right, exactly the same. The clues you've found are of his design—the dress, the shoes, the scene itself. No hairs, no fibers left behind. He knows what you'll look for and how you'll search."

"He could just watch a lot of television," Jack grumbled.

"Perhaps," Carleton said. "Or he could be trained."

Abbott leaned back, troubled. "He could be a cop?"

"Perhaps," Carleton repeated with a slight frown. "The need for order and control are often characteristics seen in law enforcement. No offense intended, of course," he added quickly when everyone around the table frowned. "I see a contempt for women, in the way he lures them away from their homes, and there is a cruelty as he forces them to experience their worst fears. This is also another show of control."

"Why contempt for women?" Abbott asked. "Does he hate his mother or something?"

"Not all men hate women because they hate their mothers, Bruce," Carleton said, "but it is the most common factor. We all had mothers of some kind. It's entirely possible his contempt for women stems from a poor relationship with his mother. It could also stem from abuse. I'd say that's more likely given the hands-on violence with which he kills them."

"Why glue their eyes?" Micki asked and Carleton sighed.

"He wants them to look at him, to know who it is who dominates them."

"But he doesn't sexually assault them," Jack said. "Why not?"

"He doesn't feel he needs to," Carleton said. "He's stronger than that."

"No. He's afraid of them," Olivia said and everyone turned to look at her, surprised.

Carleton's brows lifted. "Excuse me?"

Olivia moved her shoulders restlessly. "No offense, Doc, but to have them nude and tied in a straitjacket and not assault them? He dresses them up, paints their faces, gives them sexy shoes . . . Leaves them looking like whores."

Noah considered it. "He picks lonely women who haven't had physical sex with a man in some time and makes them whores in every way but the most physical way."

"And then he hangs them and waits for them to be found," Jack finished. "He never starts on the next victim until his last has been discovered."

"That's the compulsion for order," Carleton said. "Your theory is an interesting one, Olivia, but I don't see fear here. Just intelligence, power, and control."

"And arrogance," Kane added. "Setting up a post office box right across the street."

"I've met very few arrogant killers that were patient," Noah said thoughtfully. "All of his victims were discovered within a few days of their murder except for Martha. She hung there for more than a week. I wonder if he got impatient while he waited. What might he do, Carleton? If his order was disturbed?"

"I think that depends on why he's doing this," Carleton replied. "He's taunting you with clues that lead you to nothing. Maybe he just hates cops."

"Or fears them," Olivia added stubbornly and Carleton smiled.

"Or fears them," he allowed. "I've researched case studies and found nothing similar. This killer is unique."

"Three cheers for us," Abbott said sarcastically.

"Captain?" Faye peeked around the door, entering when Abbott waved her in. "We just got a call from somebody who saw the story on the TV news. She says she saw Martha Brisbane on February 13."

"The night she died," Noah said. "Who is this woman?"

"Priscilla Bolyard. She was sitting with her husband in a coffee shop and Martha sat next to the window for a long time, obviously waiting for someone, then left at 9:15."

"How did she remember the exact time?" Noah asked.

"Because her husband wanted to get home to watch a fight on pay-per-view, so they left right behind Martha. Here's their contact info—Priscilla and Stuart Bolyard." Faye made an apprehensive face. "Mrs. Bolyard specifically requested 'that handsome detective on the *MSP* cover.' They're saving all the details for you, Jack."

Jack slouched in his chair, his face darkening. "Wonderful," he muttered.

"We'll talk to them," Noah said.

"Wait," Abbott said when Noah started to stand. "Nobody leaves yet. The Buckland case. Sit down, tell us what you know, and how it connects."

Wednesday, February 24, 5:15 p.m.

Eve settled on a vinyl sofa in the waiting room and started up her laptop. David was still getting scanned, so she had time. Logging in to Shadowland, she was relieved to see Kathy Kirk wheeling and dealing from Ninth Circle. Eve made a note to ask Noah to provide Kathy protection tonight. None of her female red-zones were safe, but Kathy's condition made her particularly vulnerable.

She jumped at a sound behind her and looked over her shoulder to the door. "Sal."

"Are you all right?" Sal demanded. He came around the bank of chairs to search her face. "I just heard what happened to your friend. That could have been you."

"Was supposed to have been," Eve corrected. "I'm sorry, Sal, I should have called you to warn you about this guy again."

Sal's eyes narrowed. "Don't you worry about us. I

posted the sketch of this asshole at the bar, so if he has the balls to come back, we'll take him down."

Sal didn't often take a belligerent tone but Eve knew he was scared. And grieving. "I'm sorry about Looey."

He cleared his throat gruffly. "Looey was a good guy. Never would hurt a soul. Jeff Betz is crawling the wall, wishing he had his hands on that guy again. Eve, what's going on here? This is craziness."

"Yeah, I know," Eve said glumly. "You be careful, okay? If he comes back . . ."

"If he comes back, it'll be the last thing he does."

"Sal," Eve said, gripping his arm urgently. "Promise me you won't do anything—"

"Anything what, Eve?" he asked, too quietly. "Stupid?"

Eve felt a shiver of apprehension. "Dangerous. Sal, you're important to me."

He sighed, wearily. "Dammit, Eve. I hate that he put his hands on you in my bar."

"I know." She hesitated. "You and Josie . . . you've been so good to me. Like . . . parents. Don't flip out on me and get yourself killed. I'd never forgive myself."

He was quiet a moment. "All right. Callie's on tonight. We'll watch over her."

"Thank you. Sal, he was in your office last night. He put something in my computer bag. You should check the back door, make sure you've thrown the deadbolt."

He made a frustrated sound, a growling in his throat. But when he spoke, it was calmly. "I will. You want me to sit with you?"

She shook her head. "I'd feel better if you were watching Callie. Olivia's got all the security guys here watching for him."

He rose. "All right then. Call me if you need me, honey. I'll be here quick."

"Thank you." Eve watched him go, praying he'd stay calm. Half wishing this Buckland imposter would go back to the bar where fifty cops could bag him, and not too gently, but hoping he stayed far away from the people she loved.

Too antsy to sit still, Eve brought up a search screen and typed in Noah's name before she realized she'd planned to do so.

Nothing Olivia said had changed Eve's instinct that this "reporter's" vendetta was against Noah. *But why? And why now?* Noah's name brought back a page full of links to the *MSP* article on the Hat Squad. That was new, the article. Out in the last few weeks. *Three weeks.* Amy Millhouse had died three weeks ago. Coincidence? Unlikely.

Eve considered it. The article had brought the detectives a lot of attention, most of it unwanted. Some people, *like Sal and me*, were proud of their detectives.

But there was another element that might not take so kindly to positive press for the police. *Who?* Noah put away dangerous people. Any one of them could hate him.

"Evie? Oh my God, Evie."

Eve looked up to see Tom Hunter rushing into the waiting room. At his side was a tall young woman. She was pale, her eyes bleak and red-rimmed, and even from across the waiting room Eve could feel her desperation. Eve put her laptop aside and rose, grabbing Tom's hands. "He's all right," she said. "Take a deep breath."

Tom shuddered out a breath. "I just got your messages. I'm sorry."

"Where were you?" Eve asked, then leaned forward. "And who is she?"

"This is Liza," Tom said. "She's a friend. Where is David?"

"Getting a CAT scan. Relax," Eve said. "It'll be fine." She stretched out a hand to Liza, who stood awkwardly to the side. "I'm Eve."

Liza shook her hand, but tentatively. "Tom's told me about you."

Eve held on to Liza's hand, studying her drawn face. The girl looked as if she were about to pass out. "Liza, when did you last eat?"

She winced. "I can't remember."

Tom gave the girl a look of mild reproach. "I told you to buy food."

"I did. I forgot to eat it," she said rebelliously.

"The cafeteria is on the second floor," Eve said. "Get her some dinner."

"Okay. You want anything?"

"No, I ate lunch. And if David doesn't need me, I have a . . . dinner . . . thing."

Tom's eyes widened. "A dinner thing? Is that, like, a date?"

Eve felt her cheek heat. "Yeah, like, a date."

"Well, it's about time. Who is he? Can I meet him?"

"I think he'd like that. He's kind of a fan of yours. You two get food, then come back and let me get to know your friend."

She watched them go, speculatively. Eve had seen terror and despair in her own eyes for years and Liza's were filled with both. She also knew of Tom's penchant for helping those in need. She hoped he hadn't involved himself in anything dangerous.

Not, of course, that I can talk. David was getting a CAT scan because Eve had gotten herself involved in the Shadowland murders and then with Noah, and by association, this maniac that wanted to hurt them.

With a sigh Eve sat, continuing her search of articles about Noah. *There's something here. I just have to find it.*

Chapter Eighteen

Harvey put his microwave dinner aside when the doorbell rang. Webster was at the police station, so he'd ducked back home to grab some dinner. It had been a long week and Webster had kept some long hours, which meant Harvey had as well.

Startled to see her, he threw the door open to the woman his dead son had once loved with all his heart. "Katie, honey. What are you doing here?"

Katie came into the living room, her lovely face pale. "We need to talk."

Harvey helped her to a chair. "I thought you were at your parents'. What's wrong?"

Katie stared up at him, her eyes glazed with fear. "Where's Dell?"

Harvey sat next her, apprehension coiling in his gut. "I don't know. Why?"

"This is unbelievable." She shook her head. "Did you know what he was up to?"

"I'm not sure anymore. Talk to me."

She pressed her fingers to her mouth. "I knew he was losing it, but I never dreamed he'd . . . Dell's in trouble. We need to find him and get him out of town."

"Why? What has he done?"

"The cops say he's killed someone."

Harvey shook his head, this time in denial. "No, my son is not a killer."

"They said he killed a reporter. Kurt Buckland."

Harvey frowned. "I know that name."

"He covered V's funeral. He comes to this bar named Sal's."

Where Webster goes once a week. "I know the place. Dell killed him at Sal's?"

"No. But the cops that go to Sal's said Dell's been harassing the bartender and today he tried to kill her. They said he's been posing as this Buckland guy all week, but this morning they found Buckland's apartment covered in blood. Buckland's missing and they say Dell did it." She was becoming hysterical, hyperventilating.

"Calm down," Harvey ordered. "How do you know this?"

She blinked, as if thrown by the question. "I've been hanging at Sal's for three weeks. Kissing up to Jack Phelps so Dell could trap him. It's part of your plan."

Harvey stared. "*You're* Dell's Trojan Horse?"

She nodded. "I was supposed to snuggle up to Phelps, watch him from the inside."

"Drug him to make him sleep," Harvey said dully.

"That was self-preservation. I couldn't stand the thought of the man touching me."

"He hurt you?" Harvey snarled softly.

"No, but he's a sex addict. He blows off work for it and I'm not the first. Like Dell said, it was just a matter of time before the guy got himself fired. We just sped it up."

Harvey sat back. "So you're helping Dell fry Phelps by *sleeping* with him?"

She flinched. "The bastard deserves it for what he did to V. I'll do what I have to."

This is all insane. "Why would Dell kill Buckland? It doesn't make sense."

"Of course it does. It makes perfect sense."

Harvey and Katie swung around to look behind them. Dell stood in the kitchen doorway. He'd come in the back door. "What's this about, Dell?" Harvey demanded.

Dell's eyes made Harvey's blood run cold. "You told. You turned me in."

It took Harvey a minute, but when he understood, he lurched to his feet. "Are you saying I told the cops you killed Buckland? I didn't even know about him."

"No, but you knew about last night. I wasn't playing by your rules. Stupid rules. You would have sat, waiting and watching those two until you died. You're pathetic."

"I didn't call the cops, Dell." Harvey took a step back. "Why would I?"

"Because you lost control. I wasn't your 'boy' anymore. You couldn't stand the fact that your plan wasted a year and mine got results in three fucking weeks."

"Don't you take that tone with me," Harvey warned, but his voice trembled.

Dell laughed bitterly. "I'll take whatever tone I want. I'll do whatever I want. And you can't stop me. Nobody can."

"Dell," Katie inserted, "you've got to get away. Didn't you get my messages? I tried to warn you. The cops are passing around a sketch of you at Sal's."

"Shut up," he snarled and swung, hitting her with the back of his fist. Thrown against the sofa, she started to cry. "This is all your fault anyway, you fucking whore."

Harvey caught Dell's arm before his son could deliver another blow. "Stop it. Stop this right now. I don't know what's gotten into you, but I will not tolerate hitting a woman."

Dell made no move to wrest his arm free. They stood, nose to nose, eye to eye, and for the first time, Harvey knew true fear. "No," Dell said softly. "You just hit little kids. Well, guess what, Pop? I'm not a little kid anymore. And you shouldn't have told on me."

Harvey's heart was pounding too hard. "I didn't tell. I didn't. Tell me you didn't kill anyone and I'll hide you. Run, and I'll tell the cops I don't know where you are."

"I'm not running because I'm not finished. *You*," he barked to Katie, who was edging toward the door. "Get back here. I'm not done with you." Katie started to run, but Dell grabbed her by the hair and flung her to the sofa. "I said I'm not done with you."

Harvey took a step forward, but stumbled back when Dell's fist plowed into his jaw. Then froze when his surviving son pulled a gun with a silencer from one pocket and a pair of handcuffs from another. "I brought my own tools," Dell sneered. He snapped the cuffs on Katie, turning her facedown on the sofa. "Now you'll stay put."

"Dell. Why are you doing this? What has Katie ever done to you?"

Dell's laugh sent another chill through his blood. "You thought V was innocent, but he wasn't. He killed that guy. But do you know why he was in that store to begin with?"

"No," Harvey said, not taking his eyes from the gun in Dell's hand. "Tell me why."

"Because he needed the money. Because he wanted to buy more *stuff* for his fiancée because he was afraid she was steppin' out on him with another guy. And guess what? He was right. She was just using him, spending his money faster than he could earn it."

"It's not true," Harvey said. "Katie wouldn't have cheated on VJ. She loved him."

Dell lifted Katie by the hair again. "Tell him where you were the day VJ died."

"With you," Katie whispered, terrified.

Dell shook her. "Louder."

"With you," Katie cried. "I was with you. In VJ's bed. I was with you."

Harvey couldn't breathe. "You were sleeping with your brother's fiancée?"

"She didn't do much sleeping," Dell said bitterly and threw Katie down in disgust. "She hasn't done much sleeping any night for the past three weeks."

"You were with her?" Harvey asked, faintly. "All these nights?"

"While Phelps slept like the dead in the next room. I know. Sickening, isn't it?"

But Dell didn't look sickened. He looked . . . insane. "How could you, Dell?"

Dell shook his head, slowly. "V was always bigger than life. I can't count the times he saved me from you, taking the blame for whatever made you mad." He seemed to have run out of steam and Harvey watched, waiting for the opportunity to take the gun.

"I always wanted to be V," Dell went on, wistfully. "He got all the girls. When Katie came on to me . . . I just took what she offered. And I've lived with that for the last year."

"You seduced Dell?" Harvey whispered. "And you're still sleeping with him?"

Tears ran down Katie's face. "VJ worked all the time. I was lonely and it just happened one day. I didn't plan it."

Stunned, he stared. "But you're still sleeping with him."

"He told me he needed me," Katie sobbed. "He said we could get Phelps together. Make him pay. I wanted to make Phelps pay."

"Oh, you will," Dell said. "Don't worry. You'll have the starring role."

Harvey looked up at his son. The crazed light was gone from his eyes, replaced by an amused detachment that was more terrifying. "What are you going to do?"

"Well, I got to thinking. Wouldn't it be great if, after losing his job through gross incompetence, Phelps killed himself? Then I kicked it up. He loves women. Wouldn't it be even greater if he was discovered dead in his bed next to his newest bimbo who was shot in the head? Think about how *that* would look on a magazine cover. It would get headlines. The world would see Phelps for who he really is. It would ruin him."

"You can't do that," Harvey blurted.

Dell's eyes narrowed. "Watch me, old man."

"No, no," Harvey backpedaled, stalling for time. On the sofa, Katie was sobbing in fear. "I mean, you can't just punish Phelps. Webster was there, too. What about him?"

"Oh, I have a plan for him, too. No worries." Dell took a step forward.

"Why Buckland?" Harvey asked.

Dell smiled, enjoying his fear. "I wanted to be sure the story would get printed."

"You killed a reporter, posed as him, so that you could take over his column?"

"No. I killed him because he refused to write the story I wanted him to write. Kept whining about professional ethics and corroboration. Turns out I was right." He took another step forward, pointing his gun at Harvey's chest. "But I wasn't close to being finished.

I had days of stories left to write. You really shouldn't have told on me, Pop."

"I didn't. I swear—" There was a quiet pop and Harvey looked down at his chest in disbelief. Red was spreading across his shirt and he couldn't move. Couldn't breathe.

He fell to the floor and Dell leaned close. "You really shouldn't have hit us all those years, either, so that was for me and V." He yanked a sobbing Katie to her feet. "Time to go."

Wednesday, February 24, 5:30 p.m.

"So is this Buckland imposter connected to the Shadow-land killer?" Abbott asked when Noah and Olivia had finished the story. "Could they be the same person?"

Carleton shook his head. "Unlikely. The temperament is completely different. The imposter is reckless and the Shadowland killer is very careful and meticulous. Both dangerous, but not the same person."

"Considering we know what the imposter looks like, that would have been too good to be true," Abbott grumbled. "But the timing can be no coincidence."

"This Hunter," Micki said. "What exactly did he see?"

"A black SUV," Olivia said.

"And a ring," Noah added. He'd told Olivia and she'd already added it to the BOLO. He held up his hand. "Like my college ring, but there are a lot of people with college rings. And most schools use the same ring companies, so the designs are the same."

Kane held up his right hand. It was ringless, but he wiggled his finger. "I had one."

Olivia looked up at him, charmed. "I didn't know that, Kane. What did you study?"

Kane's smile was slightly embarrassed. "Dance. Helped me play football."

"I have one, too," Carleton said, holding up his right hand. "We're going to have a hard time tracking him down if that's the only thing we have to go on."

"I know," Noah said flatly.

"His prints aren't in the system," Olivia said, "but we've got a sketch."

"No sign of Buckland's body?" Abbott asked.

"So far, none." Olivia looked grim. "The tech guys are tracing the email he sent to the *Mirror*'s editor with the article on our dead women, we think from Buckland's laptop."

"All right." Abbott sighed. "So full circle, back to our dead women. No suspects, no forensics, and no idea who he's going to strike next. I need to decide if we're going to release the Shadowland element to the press. Pros? Cons?"

"Pro, we warn the people in the study," Noah said. "We tell participants not to leave their houses to meet strange people they meet online."

Olivia rolled her eyes. "Like they should need to be told."

"Con," Jack said, "we show him our hand."

"If you expose the connection," Carleton said quietly, "he'll change. He's stayed a step ahead of us all this time. If he thinks we know his MO, he'll find a new one."

"Which is exactly why Eve fought so hard not to be connected to this case," Noah said. "She didn't want us to lose that Shadowland advantage."

"So you're saying not to tell, Noah?" Abbott asked.

"No, I'm saying she bought us a few days, but the clock is running out for these women. We're no closer to finding this guy and he's going to kill again."

Carleton shrugged. "If women stop leaving their homes, they stop becoming victims. But you also may lose the opportunity to catch him. He's likely to go somewhere else and start all over. It's your call, Bruce."

Abbott folded his hands and pressed them to his mouth, the picture of a man with a terrible choice to make.

"If it were me," Noah said quietly, "I'd tell. He's killed five times. I don't want to find a sixth, and we can't predict what he's going to do."

Abbott raised his brows. "Jack?"

"I agree. What if we're late again? I have to live with Rachel Ward on my conscience for the rest of my life." Jack swallowed hard. "No more."

Abbott nodded. "I think so, too. I'll get the word out. I hope these women hear it."

"There are two women at high risk," Noah said. "We should call them personally."

"Get me their info," Abbott said, then sighed when the phone on his desk rang. He hit the speakerphone. "Ian, you're on speaker. We're all here. What do you have?"

"The retained blood samples from Amy Millhouse's autopsy showed ket. According to the autopsy report, the cause of death was strangulation, same as the others. There was something unusual, though. The victim's fingernails were torn and there were abrasions all over her hands. Luckily the examiner took some photos for the file."

"Defense wounds?" Jack asked.

"I don't think so. Based on what I've seen before, Amy's injuries were sustained clawing against something hard."

"Her worst fear," Carleton said. "A small space? Being closed in?"

"That makes sense," Ian said. "That's all I've got. I'll call you if I get any more."

Abbott turned off the speaker. "I'll get a statement to the press. Noah, Jack, talk to Millhouse's brother, then visit the couple that saw Martha leave the coffee shop."

"What about Jeremy Lyons?" Noah asked. "We haven't found him."

"And his financials didn't show anything irregular," Abbott said. "Kane, Lyons is yours. Find him. Olivia, find out if anyone saw our reporter-guy come in or out of Kurt Buckland's place. Have we notified his next of kin that he's missing?"

"We did a canvass, but we'll go back now that we have the sketch. Buckland's not married, no kids. Sal may know somebody to call. I think the ring won't be much help."

"Unfortunately, I think you're right. Kane, I also want you to go back to the bar Rachel Ward was at last night. Find out if anyone saw anyone loitering, waiting for her. Now I have a meeting upstairs." Abbott looked grim. "Keep me informed of everything."

Wednesday, February 24, 6:10 p.m.

Eve jumped in her waiting room chair when someone touched her shoulder. Hunched over her laptop, she jerked up her chin to see Carleton Pierce standing in front of her. She took the earbuds from her ears. "Dr. Pierce. You startled me."

"I said your name, but you didn't hear me."

Eve gestured to her laptop. "I was listening to some music. Trying to pass the time." In reality she'd been watching video from the local TV news online archive. Several of the crime beat entries were Noah's cases. But so far, she'd found nothing.

"I understand your friend was hurt. I hope he's all right."

"He will be." Rising, she studied him curiously. People from the bar often looked different when she saw them in another environment, but Pierce looked essentially the same. He wore another expensive suit, gold cufflinks winking at his wrists. "Thank you."

He took a step back and met her eyes, smiling kindly. "You've had a rough few days, Eve. I was on my way home from the police station and thought I'd stop in to see how you are."

"That's nice of you." Which made her suspicious. Which in turn made her ashamed at her paranoia. *Get a grip, Eve.* "I'm okay. I'll be more okay when they catch this guy."

"I got a call from Dean Jacoby today."

Eve's eyes narrowed. Jacoby was Donner's boss. "Why?"

"Well, because he's my friend," he said with a tolerant smile. "And because we were talking about my teaching a class next term, because Donner's retiring."

"I'm sorry," she said, then frowned when his words sank in. "Donner's retiring?"

"Yes. Apparently he gave notice a few weeks ago, but that's not for public consumption. I trust you'll be discreet."

A few weeks ago? "Of course," Eve murmured.

"At any rate, I didn't mention you to Jacoby, but he mentioned your study. The college got a request yesterday for all your project files and cooperated fully with the police. He knew I worked with the police and wanted an update. He wanted to know how the police had made the connection to Marshall's psychology department."

"And you said?" Eve said calmly.

"That I was not at liberty to disclose elements of an ongoing investigation. I wanted you to know that they're asking questions. Jacoby asked me and my wife to join him for dinner tonight. If you'd like to join us, it would be an opportunity for you to explain your actions before you're accused of anything. Once he files anything formal, you're in the system." His lips curved ruefully. "Plus, you'll get to enjoy the best prime rib in the city. If I remember grad school correctly, I ate a lot of bologna sandwiches."

She made herself smile back. "I appreciate everything you've done, sir, but I have to stay here tonight. My friend may need me. I have your card and almost called ten times. But things keep happening." She gestured to the waiting room. "I've been a bit busy."

"Are you sure, Eve?" he asked, serious now. "The police team just made the decision to take the Shadowland connection public, to warn potential victims. Soon any decisions on what, who, and when you tell will be out of your hands."

Eve's shoulders sagged. "I knew this was an eventuality. I—"

"Eve?" Tom had returned, Liza still in tow. Liza looked better but Tom was panicked. He gently pushed his friend into a chair and rushed over. "What's wrong with David?"

She realized Tom had seen Pierce and gotten the wrong idea. "Nothing. David's still getting scanned. This isn't one of his doctors." She hesitated. "Tom, this is Dr. Pierce. Dr. Pierce, my friend, Tom. Dr. Pierce's here to talk to me about . . . school."

"It's nice to meet you," Tom said, warily.

Pierce gave Tom a polite nod, then turned back to Eve. "Don't wait too long."

"What the hell was that about?" Tom demanded when Pierce was gone.

Eve sank into her chair, her head now throbbing. "Long story."

Tom sat next to Eve. "I've got time, Evie."

"Your friend looks better," Eve said.

"Yeah, and now you look like shit," Tom shot back. "Who was that guy?"

"Tom, I . . . I've done something that could get me kicked out of school."

He stared at her. "What the hell is this?"

"You know the women who've been murdered recently? The ones that looked like suicides? They were all participants in my Shadowland study."

"Shit. But how could they possibly blame you for that?"

"They can't. But I know the victims' identities because I looked at files I shouldn't have. It's cheating and I could get expelled."

Tom's face fell. "No way. You've worked so hard . . . Oh, Evie."

She patted his hand. "I know. But if it makes it any easier, I'd do it again in a heartbeat. It'll be all right, however it turns out. I'll find my feet again."

"You always find your feet," he said quietly. "I've always admired that about you."

Eve's throat tightened. "Thank you. I needed that."

He slid his arm around her in a hard, brotherly hug. "I always thought it would be Mom or Dana getting busted for breaking the rules. Never thought it would be you."

Eve's laugh was shaky. "Go bug David. He's probably done getting scanned."

"I wanna meet your date. Got to make sure he's good enough for you."

Too good for me, she thought sadly. "I'll introduce you before I leave. Now be gone."

She watched Tom go, shaken. Dean Jacoby asking questions . . . The Shadowland connection soon all over the news . . . Buckland missing and probably dead . . .

Don't think about that. She tried to draw her mind away from the fear, pulling her computer to her lap out of habit. *Think.* Buckland was missing. She'd been searching articles on Noah, but Kurt Buckland had also been a victim. She'd been so unnerved last night that she hadn't dug very deep into Buckland's articles.

Kurt Buckland, she typed into the search screen, and started reading the results.

Wednesday, February 24, 6:10 p.m.

Millhouse's lawyer stood up when Noah and Jack entered the interview room. "This is outrageous," he began. "My client—"

"Is free to go," Noah said. "But we'd appreciate answers to some questions first."

"My sister committed suicide. I don't understand why I'm here like a criminal."

Noah sat next to him. "Your sister did not commit suicide, sir."

Larry Millhouse's mouth fell open. "Are you saying my sister was murdered?"

"Yes," Jack said. "That's exactly what we're saying. We need you to tell us exactly how you found the scene, before you cut your sister down and changed her clothes."

Millhouse looked away. "She was dressed like a whore, in a low-cut red dress, and this . . . makeup. Amy never dressed like that. And her eyes . . . they were open. Glued."

"What about shoes?" Jack asked.

"High heels. Red. Amy never in a million years would wear shoes like that."

"And the window?" Noah asked.

"Wide open."

"Was there a note?" Jack finished and Millhouse shook his head.

"No," he said miserably. "So I wrote one. My mother was so upset, I just wanted to make her see that Amy really had loved her."

Jack looked at Millhouse sternly. "All of those elements are common to five murders. By altering the scene, you made it harder for us to realize what was going on before four more women lost their lives."

Millhouse glanced nervously at his attorney. "Am I in trouble?"

"The powers that be say no," Jack said. "So you're free to go."

But Millhouse didn't move from his chair. His eyes had closed, his face still pale. "Somebody killed my sister," he murmured, as if it was just sinking in. "Why?"

"We don't know why," Noah said, "but we do know that he's targeted his victims through an online computer game. Shadowland."

Larry Millhouse visibly flinched. "What do you mean?"

"You've heard of the game?" Jack asked.

Millhouse nodded, a bare movement. "I showed it to her. Then she was sucked in."

"She played a lot?" Noah asked.

"She was making money at it, amazingly. I played for fun. Amy played for keeps."

"How did she make money?" Noah asked.

"She gambled in the casino. Poker, blackjack, all the games. She won, a lot. Took her winnings, bought and sold real estate in the better neighborhoods. She converted the Shadowbucks into real-world money. She was about to quit her day job."

"So she spent time in the casino. Did she mention meeting anyone there?"

"If she did, she didn't tell me. We'd been arguing about her spending so much time in the online world. I was stunned, frankly. She'd become this wheeler-dealer, a person I didn't know. When I found her hanging there . . ." His voice broke. "Like *that* . . ."

"So you took her down and changed her clothes," Jack said quietly.

"Yes." Millhouse dropped his head to his hands, his shoulders shaking as he cried. "She was my little sister, dammit. I showed her the game. It was my fault."

His lawyer patted his shoulder. "Can he go now?"

"In a minute," Noah said, as kindly as he could. "Mr. Millhouse, this killer has taken the computers of the other victims. Did you notice anything different about the computer at your sister's apartment after her death?"

Millhouse scraped his hands down his face, struggling for control. "I don't know. We were just in . . . autopilot, you know? My mother was having chest pains and I couldn't stand the guilt. I . . . burned the dress. I told my wife to get rid of everything else."

Of course. Not that this guy would have left anything behind anyway, Noah thought bitterly, then stood. "Thank you, Mr. Millhouse."

"Do you have any leads?"

Not a one. "Yes," Noah said. "We'll call when we have news."

Noah waited for Jack in the hallway, closing the door behind them. "We know one new thing," Noah said. "Martha and Christy spent their time at Ninth Circle. Rachel divided her time between the bar and the casino. Amy Millhouse hung at the casino."

"So we know two places he hunts his victims. So how does that help?"

"I don't know yet." But Noah knew who to ask. He checked his watch. "I've got plans for dinner. Let's break and meet at the Bolyards' house at 8:30."

Jack put on his hat. "I had to cancel Katie. Maybe I can still catch up with her."

"Good luck," Noah said, and meant it.

Jack's smile was flat. "You, too."

Wednesday, February 24, 6:40 p.m.

"Eve?" Her chin jerked up when hands squeezed her knees and she met Noah's eyes over her laptop. He was crouching, looking panicked. *As well he should.*

"I tried to call you a couple of times, but you didn't answer."

She fished her cell from her bag. "I had it on vibrate and forgot to change it. I'm sorry. I didn't mean to scare you again."

The panic had left his eyes, leaving concern and an anticipation that made her own skin tingle despite her own jumble of emotion. "How is David?"

"Better. Tom's in with him now. Noah, I think I found him."

"Who?"

"The man who hates you. Sit and look." He did, sliding one arm across her back and leaning closer. Which put his face right next to hers, throwing her pulse into overdrive. Which, she suspected, was his intent. Keeping her eyes straight ahead she pointed to the picture she'd downloaded. The man had a dark beard threaded with silver, a hard mouth, and harder eyes. "Do you recognize him?" she asked, her voice a little huskier.

"No." Then he turned his head, bringing his mouth inches from hers. "Should I?"

"Yes." She cleared her throat. "Pay attention, Noah."

"I am." But instead of backing away, he came closer and there was nothing hard about his mouth when he brushed it over hers. There was instead sweetness and heat. Her eyes slid closed and she leaned into him, lifting one hand to tentatively touch his face, deepening the kiss until it was slow and unhurried, making it all the more devastating. It was sumptuous, rich and full. And right.

That rightness would make it that much harder to lose later.

She pulled away, as slowly as they'd come together, her palm still cupping his cheek. His eyes searched hers while she fought the tears that rose in her throat. It had been a hell of a day. Anyone's emotions would be on the edge.

"Sometimes," he murmured, "when you're behind the bar, you watch everyone and your eyes grow so sad. I always wondered what you saw. I'm wondering that right now."

The tears rose a little higher and she swallowed them back. "Why didn't you ask?"

Regret flickered in his eyes. "If you only knew how

many times I wanted to. But I watched you and knew you were . . . fragile. Vulnerable."

"I'm not," she protested.

"You are. So am I." He hesitated. "Eve, my mother was an alcoholic when I was a kid, out of control. I never wanted to be like her. I craved discipline and prided myself on not being weak. I joined the army, did a tour, came back determined to be a cop like my dad. He died when I was five, line of duty. That started my mother drinking."

"You got married," she said and he nodded. "But she died," she added. "How?"

"Car accident," he said briefly. "Which . . . started me drinking."

He hadn't moved, his face still hovered inches from her own. "Who saved you?"

"My cousin, Brock, at first. I spent more time at his house than mine growing up because my mom was always drunk. When I hit rock bottom, I called him, begged him to help. He took me to my first AA meeting, stood by my side while I dried out. My mom had joined AA a million times, but always fell off the wagon. I was determined not to, but it was, it is hard. Mom saw me fighting the booze, she saw me following in her footsteps and that pushed her to change. We did AA together."

"And she's still sober?"

"Ten years later we both are. She's down south now. Comes back for the summer."

"You love her," Eve said quietly, a little enviously. "I'm glad." And she was.

"Me, too. Eve, I grew up with chaos. Discipline, or the illusion of it, is important to me. I sat in the bar, watched you, and was pretty damn proud of myself for not talking to you, not saddling you with my demons. But I think I was just afraid. That if I let you in, I'd lose what control I've managed to keep. So I kept my distance."

"For a whole year?"

"You didn't help," he countered dryly. "You wouldn't even look at me. Why?"

He'd been honest. She could be no less. "Because I wanted to," she said. "I wanted you. And it scared me. It still does."

"I know it does," he said softly. "But we have time to deal with that." He returned his attention to the man on her screen. "Why should I recognize him?"

She forced her eyes away from Noah's face and her mind back to the work at hand. "This is the father of a man you and Jack *almost* arrested about a year ago. His name is Harvey Farmer. His son was Harvey Farmer, Jr., but folks called him V."

Noah nodded slowly. "Yeah, okay. I remember V Farmer. He robbed a convenience store and killed the owner, shot him in the face. We found V hiding in a friend's house. He ran, we pursued. Jack chased him and V ran across a highway to escape."

"At night, in the snow," Eve said, recalling the Buckland article she'd finally found after pages of search results. "The truck that hit him tried to stop, but couldn't."

"Right. V was dead at the scene and we closed the case. How do you know this?"

"Kurt Buckland covered V's funeral. In the Metro section." She toggled to the article. "'Harvey Farmer, Jr., known as V to his friends, was buried today. He is survived by his father, Harvey Farmer, Sr., and his brother, Dell Farmer.' Who you've met."

"The reporter? How do you know?"

"I'll show you. The father was at V's funeral and

Buckland snapped this picture of him for the piece." She clicked on a picture showing the bearded man standing at a graveside. "I think that's Dell standing next to him, but you can't see his face."

Eve brought up her favorite design software into which she'd already imported Farmer Sr.'s face, enlarged and grainy, but usable. "Take away the beard, the gray in his hair, a few wrinkles, and make his eyes a little closer together . . ." She worked steadily as she talked. "And voila. One faux reporter. Dell Farmer."

Noah blinked and stared. "Wow. That's amazing. I never would have seen the resemblance based on that little picture. It's not obvious at all. How did you see it?"

His praise warmed her. "I study faces. You know, what makes people trust one face and not another. Which features make us comfortable and which make us afraid."

"And you used that when you started up your avatar design shop in Shadowland."

She shrugged. "Might as well get some semipractical use out of it."

He was studying her again. "You trusted him," he said quietly. "Rob Winters."

She flinched. "Yes. I was young and stupid."

"And you'll never let that happen again."

"I'll never be that young again and I pray I'll never be that stupid again."

His eyes never left her face. "And you'll never trust a man again?"

"That's not it. I trust you. I never would have gotten into a car with you otherwise."

"You don't trust yourself, then. You don't trust your judgment that you trust me."

She nodded, both relieved and sad that he finally understood. "Convoluted, I know."

He rose. "I'll get Olivia this information."

"You're not going after him yourself?"

"It's Olivia's case. If she needs my help, she'll ask for it."

"Of course." Eve busied herself putting her laptop away. "If you could take me back to the station, I'll get David's truck. Callie's working tonight, so I'll just hang out at Sal's. I'm sure one of the off-duty officers will see us home, so it'll be perfectly safe."

"Eve." His eyes glittered with determination, but his voice was gentle. "Let's go to dinner. Then you can decide where you'll stay. Give me your bag. I'll carry it for you."

He understood, but he wasn't walking away. "My friend, Tom . . . wants to meet you."

Noah's eyes lit up. "The ballplayer? Sweet." He put his arm around her shoulders, possessively. "Is this like being brought home to meet the family?"

"Yes. I guess it is."

Chapter Nineteen

Wednesday, February 24, 7:20 p.m.

I do like your house."

Noah closed the oven door and turned to lean against it. Eve sat at his kitchen table, her annoyance mostly gone. "And I liked your friend Tom."

Her mouth lifted. "And the tickets to Sunday's game?"

He grinned. "Those didn't hurt." He sobered. "So . . . you're not angry anymore?"

She shrugged. "I wasn't angry. Just surprised you brought me here."

"I have to meet Jack soon, so I didn't want to spend what little time we have waiting on waiters. Next time we'll go somewhere with tablecloths and fancier food."

"Frozen pizza is fine and better than a lot of meals I've eaten."

She was nervous. *So am I.* He took the chair next to hers, took her hand. "I'm going to get to the point. You said you trusted me. Why? Is it something about me? My face?"

"I don't know why. I just do. At the risk of sounding trite, this isn't about you. It's me."

"So that you trust me for absolutely no good reason is what frightens you?"

Arousal warred with the apprehension in her dark eyes.

"I behaved impetuously six years ago," she said. "I have paid dearly for that mistake, every day since. I don't do impetuous things very often anymore."

"You play it safe. With men, anyway."

"Essentially, yes." She lifted her chin. "And I won't apologize for that."

He recognized the lifted chin as a warning and detoured, approaching from another direction. "You said you hid in the dark for two years after Rob Winters attacked you."

She didn't flinch as he'd expected. "I lived in a shelter for battered women. I rarely left the house, took most of the night shifts."

"Because you were afraid to sleep." Afraid she'd dream, that she'd hurt someone.

"Yes. I took care of the babies, ones too young to scare. My scars were bad then."

"What happened after two years?" He knew, but wanted to hear it from her.

"We unknowingly brought a murderer into our shelter, a woman who'd kidnapped a child for her own revenge. But you know this. You've read all the news archives."

He had, and had been chilled to the bone. "You saved the boy but were nearly killed."

"Alec was a brave kid. He helped save us both."

"Where is he now?"

She smiled. "Chicago. He's a senior in high school. Well-adjusted and happy."

"So what happened after you'd saved the day and the boy?"

"Dana and Ethan took the woman down, delivered her to the cops. Dana's kind of like my mom and big sister and probation officer, all rolled into one. She is best friends with David's sister-in-law, Caroline, and Olivia's sister, Mia. That's how we all connect."

"You love them, the people you left behind in Chicago. They've earned your trust."

Her eyes sharpened. "You should be the psych major."

"Just trying to understand," he said mildly. "You've been here in Minneapolis for two years, so where were you in the two middle years?"

"Hiding," she said, one brow lifted. "I'm good at that."

"I know you are. Where were you hiding?"

"Well, having a killer in our secret shelter kind of compromised our secrecy. Dana closed down, she and Ethan bought this big house, and now she's foster mom central. I could have moved in with her, but I needed my space. So I got a job at what I thought then was the perfect place—a rehab center for people who were newly blind."

Noah frowned. He hadn't known this. "Because they couldn't see you?"

"Pretty much. I liked it there. I could work on my degree at night and never needed to leave the grounds."

This made him angry. "For two years? Why did you leave there?"

"I got a kick in the ass from one of our clients. He'd lost his sight in an accident—hard enough, but he was a surgeon. His career, in his mind, was over."

"Was it?"

"Of course not. He couldn't do surgery, but he could other things. Over time, and with a lot of nagging, he began to accept that. He restarted his life, reinvented himself."

"You saved him."

She shook her head, embarrassed. "No. I was just his friend."

"I can see that." For all she'd endured, Eve was a

nurturing soul with a full heart. That was the quality that had first attracted him. "You take care of people. That's a gift."

He'd surprised her, he could see. "Thank you."

"So your friend left this rehab center?" he asked and she nodded.

"He's teaching now. But before he left, he did a little confronting of his own, with me. Told me I'd been hiding in the dark. Gave me hell. And even though Dana and all my other friends and family had told me the same thing, it meant more coming from him."

"He'd earned your trust, too."

"Yeah. He did."

"So, coming full circle, you trust me even though I've done nothing to earn it. Let me ask you something." He leaned closer. "What are you afraid I'll do to you?"

Her cheeks darkened, causing her scar to appear under the makeup she so carefully applied. He could tell her the old scar had never bothered him, even before her surgery, but he knew she'd never believe him. Not yet.

"Eve?" he prompted when she said nothing. "Are you worried you'll lose control with me?" Her eyes flashed and he knew he'd scored a hit. He didn't stop, because he knew if he had a prayer of reaching her, it would have to be now. Once she got away from him, she wasn't likely to come back soon. "Are you afraid I'll make you feel something? That after *six years* of watching from the sidelines you'll finally feel something?"

"No," she snapped. But she didn't move an inch.

"Then what are you afraid of?"

"That I'll get dependent on feeling something," she snarled. Abruptly she stood, shoving her chair. "It's better to *choose* to have no one than to get dependent on someone, only to lose him. That 'better to have loved and lost' shit? *It's shit.* I can't go through that. I won't."

He leaned back, his heart pounding as he watched her. "Do you want me, Eve?"

"Yes," she hissed. "I did the first time you walked up to the bar. You looked me in the eye and if you knew how rare that was, you'd know what it meant."

"And I didn't make a move for a year," he murmured. "You thought I didn't want you."

"It wouldn't have mattered. Knowing you were interested has been a major ego boost, but it doesn't change anything." She turned away, pretending to check the pizza in the oven, but her hands were shaking. "It doesn't make sense to go forward if we want different things. You had a wife before. I assume you want a wife again. A family."

"We covered this," he said patiently. "I told you it didn't matter that you can't have kids. I told you I'd hide the knives if you walked in your sleep. I'm a really light sleeper," he said teasingly, then sobered. "None of that matters, Eve."

"I don't believe you. You think it doesn't matter, but one day you'd start wondering what it would be like to be a dad."

"I know what it's like to be a dad," he said, more sharply than he'd intended. "I had a son. He would have been fourteen last November."

She went still. "He died in the accident, too?"

"Yes. And losing him and my wife was the hardest thing I hope I ever go through. You're right. 'Loved and lost' is shit, but I have no regrets that they were part of my life." He drew a steadying breath. "I don't need more children. If I had a baby, I'd love him, but I've done that. I don't need to do it again."

"And I still don't believe you." She touched his sleeve, her fingers trembling. "But I know you believe it." She pursed her lips, fighting for composure. "I'm not very hungry. Would you mind taking me to get David's truck now?"

He'd promised himself he'd let her go if that's what she wanted. "Okay," he said. "I'll have a cruiser watch your house tonight, wherever you stay." He got an oven mitt and pulled the pizza from the oven, then stared down at it. "You asked me this morning why I wanted you. I told you I'd tell you over dinner. Can I at least still do that?"

"Sure." It was the smallest whisper.

"It was right before Christmas, a year ago. Somebody was retiring and they had his party at Sal's. It was the first time I saw you."

"I remember."

"You were behind the bar. I remember thinking how pretty you were. My last relationship had fizzled a natural death, and I hadn't met anyone else I liked enough to move my schedule for. I thought maybe I'd say hello to you, ask you out. Then the door opened and this woman came in. Had the look of a lifetime drunk. She was dirty and she stank of sour whiskey. Do you remember her?"

"Yes, I do. A couple of the cops tried to throw her out."

"But you wouldn't let them. You sat her down, gave her some coffee, and listened while she told you her story. You even cried when she did."

"Her son had died. Christmas is a hard time for people who've lost someone."

"I know. I thought you'd let her finish her story and maybe hail her a cab. But you kept her talking, asking her questions until you had enough information to call her surviving son. He came to get her, so embarrassed, but grateful that you'd cared enough not to push her out onto the street into the snow."

"Who would have done that?"

He turned to look at her. "The dozens of bartenders over the years who did that to my mother. I'd get phone calls— 'Noah, your mom's wandering down the street without a coat.' I'd rush to get her, and find some bartender had thrown her out. Called her a bum. I guess she was, but she was still my mom. You were kind to that woman when you didn't have to be."

"I did what anybody should do."

"But few do. I came back to Sal's with Jack the next week, and the week after that. Ordered my tonic water and watched you. As time passed, I watched you be kind to more people than I can count. You asked me why I came in and ordered my water all those nights. It was because I couldn't stay away. Now I'm kicking myself for waiting so long." She said nothing and he knew he had to let it go. For now anyway. "Come on, I'll get your coat and take you wherever you want to go."

He moved toward the door, but she stayed where she stood, uncertainty playing across her face, and his heart lifted in hope. "Are we going or staying?" he asked.

"You've put me on a pedestal I couldn't possibly live up to. If I stayed, if I tried . . . you'd be disappointed."

He came back, taking her shoulders in his hands. "Maybe. But then maybe you'll be disappointed with me. But how can you know if you don't try?" He kissed her hard, relieved when she lifted on her toes, kissing him back. He broke it off, his breathing unsteady. "Aren't you tired of watching other people's lives go by? I know I am."

Her pulse was knocking at the hollow of her throat. "Promise me something."

"If I can."

"If you are disappointed, walk away. Don't stay because I'll crumble if you leave."

He let his forehead rest against hers, his hands trembling as they kneaded her shoulders. "You worry too much, Eve."

"I know," she said. "But then so do you. Can we consider that common ground?"

He cupped his hands around her face. "I think we can find better common ground than that." But he hesitated, unsure of where he could touch her. "What can I do?"

Her jaws clenched against his palms. "I don't know."

Noah felt his spine go rigid. "There hasn't been anyone since . . . ?"

She shrugged. "One. Didn't go so well."

He made his mouth curve. "So, no pressure here. I have an idea. You trust me?"

Her dark eyes had shadowed, fear crowding away all that beautiful arousal. But despite her fear, she nodded. "Yes. I trust you."

"Then get your coat and come with me."

Wednesday, February 24, 7:45 p.m.

One would think people would be more careful about locking their doors. Especially when they'd just told the police they were the last people to see a woman just before her murder. But the Bolyards hadn't been careful. And now they were dead.

By killing this couple before they could talk to the

police, he'd shown his hand. They'd wonder how the
killer had known about the Bolyards. They'd look inter-
nally, thinking they had a leak. They wouldn't suspect
each other, because that's not how cops were wired. But it
didn't matter. He'd managed any potential fallout, cut off
any search in his direction before it started with a single,
well-placed phone call. *Because I think. They just react.*

Now the only other threat to his plan, to his identity,
was Eve Wilson. She was smart, and careful. It was time
to rattle her cage harder.

Wednesday, February 24, 7:45 p.m.

Eve found herself laughing when Noah had led her into
his garage, dominated by a rather decrepit Dodge Charger. She'd picked her way through the parts and now sat
in the backseat, watching as Noah struggled to climb in
next to her.

He huffed, his breath hanging in the cold air. "See, I
told you it would be fun."

"You're going to need a chiropractor," she said.

He wedged his big body next to her. "Are you saying
I'm old?"

"No, just big."

He lifted his brows, his grin wicked. "How would you
know that?"

She shook her head, trying unsuccessfully to hide her
smile. "You're bad and it's cold. And this car definitely
has seen better days. It's not going anywhere."

"We're not going to drive it." He put his arm around
her, his gloved hand patting her shoulder through her
heavy coat. "We're going to park in it."

She looked up at him. "You're insane."

His grin softened to something so very sweet her heart turned over. "And you're smiling. That's worth a trip to the chiropractor."

Touched, she looked away. "Is this your car?"

"It is." He swatted at the vinyl roof that was sagging into the interior. "I got it a couple of years ago, but I don't have much time to work on it."

"Why this car? It looks worse than my hunk of junk."

"That's where you're wrong. This is a muscle car."

"Its muscles are atrophied," she said wryly.

He chuckled. "I drove one just like this one when I was a kid." He gave her an arched look. "I got some major action in the backseat of that car."

Her breath caught at the implicit promise. "I don't think you'll get much action tonight unless we want to explain frostbite in embarrassing places to the doctors in the ER."

"Didn't you ever park when you were a teenager, oh so many years ago?" he asked silkily and despite her winter layers and the heat from his body, she shivered.

"No. None of the boys I knew had cars unless they'd been stolen." She rested her head on his shoulder, comfortable and grateful and anticipating, all at the same time. "So how does it work, this parking thing?"

"It's pretty straightforward. I try to go as far as I can and you stop me. Of course the whole frostbite thing is an issue, so mostly we just neck. Like this." And he kissed her until her bones felt fluid and her skin became way too hot under the layers of clothing she wore. Her pulse throbbed deep, just as it had every time he'd kissed her.

She tugged off one glove so that she could touch his face, learning every texture, shuddering when he turned his face into her hand and kissed her palm. He returned to her mouth, layering pleasure on sensation without demanding anything back and suddenly she wished he would. His gloved hands were safely anchored, one on her shoulder, the other cradling the back of her head.

She pulled back, just far enough to see his eyes. They glittered in the darkness and the leashed desire she saw there stole her breath. "What do we do next?"

"Nothing you don't want to do."

It was her game then, her rules. It was terrifying even as it exhilarated. "Then try something and let me see if I want to stop you."

For a moment he remained still, then shifted to the middle of the seat, pulling her across his lap so that she straddled him. He looked up as she looked down and his hands stroked down her back, over her butt, resting on her thighs. His fingers teased, low enough not to panic, but high enough to make her heart race.

"Your sofa's a mess," he whispered, "but your chair gave me a number of fantasies."

And that fast she could see them, imagining how his bare skin would feel against hers. She covered his mouth with hers and pressed her hips into him, her body jolting with the initial shock of discovery. He'd said he wanted her. He wasn't lying.

Her eyes flew open. His face was hard. Hungry. His body was hard and full and his hips lifted in a rhythm that made her chase his movements, trying to prolong the contact. "You're teasing me," she whispered against his lips.

His laugh was soft, yet strained. "Is it working?"

"Yes."

His hands clutched at her thighs, pulling her down and grinding himself against her, dragging a muted moan from her throat. It felt good, so good, and she wanted more.

Needed more. With shaky hands she tugged at the zipper on her coat. His hands left her hips, working the zipper on the fleece she wore beneath. He yanked his gloves off, his eyes never leaving hers as his warm palms slid up under the sweater she wore to claim her breasts, the thin cotton of her bra the only thing between them.

"Yes?" he asked gruffly.

"Yes," she whispered, wishing he'd push the cotton aside, moaning when he did.

His thumbs teased her nipples and every muscle clenched harder as she lowered herself against the sharp ridge of his body. The sounds he made were harsh and full of want, and need. She took his mouth again and did some grinding of her own.

Abruptly he stopped, forcing his hands to go lax. A moment later his hips dropped back and she felt cold. They'd fogged up the car windows. His eyes were closed and his jaw tight. He was holding on to control by a thread and the knowledge thrilled.

"Why did you stop?" she asked huskily when he put her clothing to rights.

"Because I still could. In another minute I'd have tried something more."

"Maybe I would have wanted you to."

He swallowed hard. "We would have been in frostbite territory," he said quietly.

Her hand trembling, she pushed his dark hair from his damp brow. "Did you ever . . . you know . . . in the backseat?"

His unsteady grin flashed. "This time of year? No." Briefly he patted her bottom, the pat becoming a caress that made her hum with pleasure. Then his cell phone vi-

brated in his pants pocket, startling them both. "It's probably Jack."

Eve scrambled off his lap and he dug for his phone.
He listened for a minute, then flashed a quick look at Eve.
"No, she's here with me. What's the address?" He jotted
it down, his expression now grim. "I'll call Jack and meet
you there. That was Olivia," he said, hanging up and dialing again, waiting for Jack to answer. "She found Harvey
Farmer, Sr. Come on, Jack, pick up."

"That was fast," Eve said.

"Not fast enough. He's dead. Jack, dammit, call me."
He punched more numbers, climbing out of the car.
Tersely he repeated the message to call him and dialed
again as he held the garage door open for her.

"Bruce," he said, letting them into his house. "It's
Noah. Did Olivia call you? . . . Good. She called me, too,
but when I called Jack, I didn't get an answer again. At his
home or cell. I'm on my way to Farmer's, but you said to
call if I couldn't reach Jack again." He hung up, grabbed
Eve's computer bag, and kept walking. "Let's go."

"Did Olivia find the son, Dell?" she asked as she buckled her seat belt.

"No. That's why you're still with me."

"How did she find the father?"

"The LUDs from Kurt Buckland's phone showed a
phone call from that address. It's a house rented in Harvey
Sr.'s name."

He'd clicked fully into detective mode. "How did the
father die?"

"Shot in the chest. With every window in the house
open."

She felt cold herself. "He can't be the same guy, Noah.

The man killing these women is patient and meticulous. Dell Farmer was unstable."

He opened her car door. "I know. I agree and so does Carleton Pierce."

"Pierce came to see me again tonight, in the hospital. He told me you were going to go public on the Shadow-land connection, to warn potential victims."

"I should have told you. I'm sorry."

"Don't be. I just hope it saves the next woman."

Wednesday, February 24, 8:25 p.m.

"Stay here by the door and don't touch anything," Noah said to Eve.

"Okay," was all Eve said, her eyes fixed on Harvey Farmer's dead body.

"Don't look," he said, thinking he should have left her somewhere else, but knowing he wouldn't be able to think straight if he was worried about her.

"Too late," she said and waved him away. "Go. I'm fine."

No, she wasn't, but he had to do his job. "Olivia, what do we have?"

Olivia crouched beside the body. "One slug to the chest, large caliber. Body's still warm. Looks like he took a punch to the face. I've called CSU and the ME."

"The blue Subaru parked outside? I've seen it before. It was trailing me and Jack on Monday when we left the coffee shop with Eve. It's the son's."

"Wait," Eve said from where she stood, exactly where he'd asked her to stay. "Dell Farmer was there, in the cof-fee shop. How did he get to that blue Subaru so fast? The barista said Dell and Jeremy Lyons talked for a minute before he left. That's when Lyons offered to give him Callie's cell phone number. You and I and Jack were a block away by then and so was the blue Subaru."

He and Olivia shared an impressed look. "Girl thinks on her feet," Olivia murmured.

"She does," Noah said. "Dell's car is the black SUV that he used to run David off the road. The Subaru must belong to the father."

"I didn't know about the Subaru before," Olivia said. "I've got uniforms canvassing the neighborhood for anyone who saw a black SUV. Dell isn't in the Minnesota DMV database, so he's probably registered—"

"Noah." Eve stood in front of a bookshelf, her expression stricken.

He was next to her in an instant, looking over her shoulder. "What?"

"That." She pointed to a framed photo, not touching it. "That's V, the son that died. Look at the woman with him." She looked over her shoulder, eyes dark with dread. "It's Katie, from the bar. Jack's Katie. Noah, this isn't just about you. It's about Jack, too."

"Where is Jack?" Olivia asked tightly.

"Not answering his phone," Noah said, his heart starting to race. "I have to—"

"Just go," Olivia interrupted. "I'll call it in, have backup meet you there."

Wednesday, February 24, 8:30 p.m.

Eve had actually given him the idea, which was delicious in its irony. He sat in his car, watching his laptop screen as the video played. It was an interview, downloaded from the archive of a TV station in Asheville, North Carolina.

It was slightly more than six years old. It would do very nicely.

"And then what did you do?" the reporter was asking, mild revulsion on his face.

The camera switched to the handsome face of one of the more brutal serial killers he'd studied. "I killed her," Rob Winters said with a smirk. "I overpowered her, threw her on the bed, and said, 'Didn't your parents teach you not to get into cars with strange men?' Then I wound a string of twine around her neck and pulled, really hard. She fought, so I stabbed her. Six times I think."

"Eight," the reporter corrected, slightly paling. "Eight times in the abdomen."

"You must be right," Winters said with another smirk. "You reporters do your homework after all. I stabbed her, eight times. She tried to claw at me." He smiled, remembering. "Feisty little thing she was. So I slashed her hand, then her face."

"Why her face?" the reporter murmured. "I mean, you'd already all but killed her."

"Because." Winters shrugged. "Because she thought she was pretty. Because I wanted to. Because I could. She stopped fighting, so I pulled the twine again. I really thought I'd killed her. But that's okay. I'm in here, but she's out there, scarred for life." He sobered, his black eyes going cold. "So neither of us are free. I can live with that."

"I see. Well, then let's move on. What happened next?"

What happened next was Winters chronicling a chilling description of brutality, an uncontrolled killing spree that ended in his own capture. And two weeks after the interview was completed, Winters had been stabbed in the prison shower.

Because he lost control. Shame, that. Such . . . evil was intriguing on its face. Fascinating to study in depth. *I would have liked the opportunity to talk to him myself.*

But even though Winters was gone, his legacy remained. Eve Wilson was still afraid. You could see it in her eyes if you knew how to look. *And I do.*

He took from his pocket the same cell phone he'd used to text her that morning, then rewound the video to the exact frame he'd sought. He dialed Eve, then frowned. She wasn't answering. He would have loved to have heard her gasp when he played the little snippet from her past. No matter, he'd see that fear in her eyes soon enough.

When the tone beeped for her voicemail, he hit the video play button, then held the cell to his laptop speaker. When he was finished, he disconnected with a smile.

Then he started to drive, flipping his police scanner on. He wanted to know when Webster discovered the Bolyards. When Eve retrieved his little message she'd be rattled, but it was Noah Webster who'd be terrified, especially after that attempt on her life earlier today. Webster wouldn't let her out of his sight.

Which would be bad, except that he knew where Webster would be soon. *Go see the Bolyards. Find out what they know.* Like a good soldier, Webster would follow those orders. Where Webster would be, so would Eve.

I'll be ready.

*   *   *

Wednesday, February 24, 8:45 p.m.

"Oh my God." Noah ran from the curb to Jack's house, pulling Eve by the hand, then he stopped, his stomach dropping to his feet. ME techs were going into Jack's house, a folded body bag on their gurney.

Abbott met them at the door, looking grim. "Jack's not dead," he said.

Noah's breath shuddered out as he pointed to the ME gurney. "Then who?"

"Katie. She was shot in the head with a gun from Jack's collection."

"He didn't do this," Noah started intensely, but Abbott held up his hand.

"Jack's on his way to the hospital. He's in bad shape."

Noah felt his legs tremble and resolutely locked his knees. "What happened?"

"We found an empty liquor bottle next to his bed, but the paramedics thought he'd taken some pills, too. We couldn't find any pill bottles."

Noah wanted to say Jack wouldn't have done that, but he wasn't sure that was true.

"Jack was the one who chased V Farmer into the highway," Eve said quietly. "This is part of Dell's payback."

"You know Jack didn't kill Katie," Noah added and Abbott nodded.

"But we're following procedure. No accusations of cover-up. Noah, you can't go in."

Noah closed his eyes, knowing Abbott was right. "Tell me what you saw."

"Katie was lying in the bed, shot in the head." Abbott hesitated. "She'd been beaten up. Jack was lying next to her, passed out, his gun on the nightstand, with the bottle.

If we'd discovered this tomorrow morning, Jack would have been dead. It was a good thing you called me when he didn't answer. And, Eve, nice work. Olivia told me that you made the connection from the news archives. And seeing Katie in that picture with V Farmer will be important to clearing Jack."

Eve's nod was calm, as was the hand she rested on Noah's back. "Are you assuming Dell killed his father?" she asked.

"Yes," Abbott said. "Why?"

"Because I'm wondering why he did it. And who else is on his list."

"It's fair to say you are," Noah told her, trying to stow his worry.

"And you," she replied. "Where did they take Jack?"

"County," Abbott replied, "but they won't let anyone see him. I've called his father and I'm about to meet him at the hospital."

"I need to talk to him," Noah said. "He thought I was asking for a new partner today. He took Rachel Ward's death hard. I want him to know he's got my support."

"And you'll be able to tell him that, after he's stabilized," Abbott said. "For now, the best thing you can do is your job."

"You're right. We were going to check on that couple who phoned in the Martha tip. The Bolyards. I still have time to do that. Eve can stay with me while I talk to them."

"No problem," she said. "I have my laptop. I can keep busy wherever."

Abbott walked with them, waiting until Eve was in Noah's car and her door shut before motioning Noah a few feet away. "If Jack survives, he won't be on his feet for a while. You're going to need a new partner to see you through this investigation."

Noah didn't want to consider either option, but knew Abbott was right. "Who?"

"I don't know yet. If this had been next year, I'd say Olivia, because Kane's up for retirement soon. I'll make some calls and let you know as soon as I do." He looked over Noah's shoulder to where Eve waited in the car. "She needs to go to a safe house."

Noah thought of all the years she'd hidden in that shelter. "I don't think she'll go."

"Convince her," Abbott said tersely. "I can't have you carting her around with you. If you can't find a safe place outside, we'll find a safe house and keep her inside."

Noah nodded, once more knowing Abbott was right. "Anything else?"

"Just focus on your own case. Five women dead."

"I haven't forgotten them, Bruce," Noah said levelly, then was saved anything further when a sleek Mercedes drove up.

Carleton Pierce got out, his face tight with concern. "What's going on?"

Abbott's brows bunched. "What are you doing here, Carleton?"

"I have business with Jack."

"What kind of business? Why did he call you?" Abbott pressed, but Carleton's eyes were fixed on the gurney being pushed out Jack's front door, the body bag zipped.

"Oh my God. Did Jack . . . ?"

"Why did he call you, Carleton?" Abbott asked again.

Carleton's eyes never left the body bag on the gurney. "I can't tell you that."

"That's not Jack," Noah said and Carleton's startled gaze swung to meet his.

"Then who is it?"

"Jack's girlfriend," Abbott said. "Why did Jack call you? I need to know."

Carleton's shoulders had sagged in relief, but now they were straight again. "Bruce, don't ask me. I can't tell you. Where is Jack?"

"Probably in the emergency room by now," Abbott said darkly.

Carleton's eyes grew wide again. "Why?"

Abbott's jaw was tight. "He may have mixed alcohol and downers."

Carleton let out a quiet breath. "Dammit. What's Jack's prognosis?"

"Not good." Abbott watched as the MEs loaded Katie's body into the rig. "But better than hers at the moment. I don't mean to be rude, Carleton, but we have work to do."

"Fine. If Jack survives, tell him I stopped by, won't you? I'll see you both tomorrow at morning meeting." He drove away without another word.

"Unhappy shrink," Noah noted.

"Not my job to keep him happy," Abbott snapped.

"He's not allowed to divulge patient information, Bruce. You know that. That he was here means Jack was more affected than either of us thought."

"I know," Abbott said grimly. "And that's not good for Jack."

"When Jack wakes up, tell him I don't believe he did this, okay?"

Abbott's angry expression sagged. "Sure. Now go and do your job. Keep me posted. And follow my orders on the safe house for Eve."

* * *

Wednesday, February 24, 8:45 p.m.

"Your uncle seemed nice," Liza offered quietly. They'd left the hospital when visiting hours were over and were in Tom's car, headed downtown. "I'm glad he'll be okay."

Tom's jaw was hard. "I can't believe somebody tried to kill him. Or Eve."

"You're lucky to have a family," she said and watched his shoulders sag.

"Don't give up hope. Lindsay may still be out there. How's your mom?"

"She's okay. I still haven't told her. She's pretty fragile right now." Liza felt terrible lying to him, but if he knew her mom was dead, he'd force her to live somewhere else. For now, she needed the freedom to move and search. "If you need to be with your family, it's okay. I can look for this Jonesy guy myself." Olivia had never called with information on the one person that prostitute said might have seen Lindsay.

"I'll go with. I'm worried about Eve. I don't want to be worrying about you, too."

Wednesday, February 24, 9:25 p.m.

"You were remarkably calm," Noah commented as they drove away from Jack's.

"Not really," she said honestly. "But I didn't think I was helping you by falling apart. Why was Pierce here and what did Abbott say to make you so upset?"

"Carleton said he had a meeting with Jack tonight."

"*Meeting* meaning *appointment*. Not good for refuting Jack's attempt at suicide."

"Exactly. Neither of us is terribly thrilled at the moment."

"And? Noah, I want to know what Abbott said. I know he was talking about me."

He glanced over at her. "What makes you say that?"

"Because he looked me square in the eye while he was talking to you."

Noah sighed. "He wants you to go to a safe house."

Eve smiled mildly even though her insides churned at the thought. "No," she said, then moved on before he could argue. "How about you? Are *you* all right?"

He said nothing for a moment. "No. I haven't had the best relationship with Jack."

"I could tell. Sal told me that Jack went through partners pretty quickly."

"The last few years, that's been true," he said, guilt in his voice.

"Noah, even if Katie was a plant, Jack allowed her into his home. His bed. He let down his guard with a woman he barely knew."

Noah aimed a long look at her, before turning back to the road. "I meant to tell you. Amy Millhouse was the first victim. Her brother altered the scene, which was why we missed it. He said she sold real estate, but mostly hung out in the casino. High roller."

"The dancer friend of Rachel's said he picked her up in the casino, so we know he's been hunting there. It makes sense that he'd go there for Amy. He went to where the heavy users were. I have one other red-zone case that never leaves the casino. She was there last night, all night, just like normal. But she could be at risk."

"Natalie," he remembered. "She plays at the table with the avatar who cheats."

"Dasich," she said darkly. "I need to check on Natalie. She should be there now."

"You can access the game from here? Right now?"

She drew her laptop from her bag. "I've got a wireless card, so I'm good anywhere."

"After you check on Natalie, see if Amy Millhouse has a black wreath on her door."

"Will do." Eve navigated Greer first to the casino, where Natalie's avatar sat in her usual place. Unfortunately for Natalie, Dasich was there, too, and had the lion's share of chips. "Natalie's losing, but she's safe. I'll go to Amy's now."

She sent Greer on to Amy's house and frowned. "Yes, there's a black wreath on Amy's door. There wasn't one this morning." She turned to Noah, troubled. "He put the wreaths on Christy's and Rachel's doors as soon as he killed them, but waited on Martha and Samantha until you realized they were there. Amy didn't have a wreath this morning. How did he know you knew? None of the press picked up on that yet."

"How did he find out about any of them?" he asked irritably.

"He found out that you knew about Martha, Christy, and Samantha through Dell's article. I heard a report on the radio this morning about Rachel's murder when I was driving in to work. But how did he know about Amy?"

"Jack and I went to see Amy Millhouse's mother today and Jack escorted her brother from the airport to the police station. I suppose he could have been watching us."

"Like Dell Farmer did," she said, "except he's all wrong for this." The car pulled to the curb and slowed to a stop. "Why are you stopping here?"

"This is the Bolyards' home. They may have been the last people to see Martha Brisbane alive, other than her killer. Come on, you can't stay out here alone."

"I have my headphones," she said. "I can always put them on if you need privacy."

"I may ask you to." He put on his hat and for a minute she let herself stare. "What?"

"I like the hat," she said, her voice husky. "I always have."

He looked at her for a long moment, most of his face cast into shadow by his hat brim, but she could feel the heat of his gaze. "Let's get this done. I'd like to spend some time with you tonight." With that he came around to her side, opened her car door, and pulled her to her feet. Barely feeling the cold, she followed him up the Bolyards' driveway, staying back a few steps when he rang the bell.

There was no answer, so he knocked on the door, hard.

"Maybe they went out?" Eve asked tentatively and he frowned.

"Maybe. But they were expecting us. The wife wanted to meet Jack," he added bitterly. Eve ran her hand down his back, wishing she could comfort him. He straightened his shoulders. "I'm okay. I need to do this."

"This" was his job, she knew. Finding, stopping a killer so that he could somehow balance the scales for his partner. He walked back to the driveway and peered into the windows cut high in the garage door.

"Come on," he said, his voice now hard, and her stomach clenched.

"What?" she said, following him around the back of the house, through the snow.

"Both of their cars are parked inside the garage. They're home." They got to the back of the house and he held up his hand, palm out. "Stay here."

She nodded, forcing herself to breathe as, gun drawn, he approached the kitchen door and exhaled a weary curse. She took a few steps forward and could see through the window. "Oh God," she murmured.

Two people lay slumped over the kitchen table. There was a lot of blood. Noah pulled on the door and it opened. Eve didn't move another step as he went into the house, checked for a pulse. Then he backed out, touching nothing else.

"They're dead," he said flatly. "Come on."

Once again she followed him, this time back to the car where he grabbed the radio and called for backup. And CSU. And the ME.

Wearily he propped his elbows on the wheel and pressed his thumbs to his temples.

Eve ran her hand down his arm. "Who knew they'd seen Martha Brisbane?"

"My team, the person who took their call, and anyone else the couple might have told. They were so set on meeting Jack because of that damn article." His mouth twisted. "Who knows who else they bragged to?"

"But that would only matter if the person they bragged to had something to hide."

He looked at her, intense. "So either they knew the killer and didn't know it . . ."

The dread in her gut matched that in his eyes. "Or you do," she said.

Chapter Twenty

Webster was here, as was Eve, just as he'd known they'd be. This was the prime moment, when Webster was shocked by finding the bodies of the Bolyards and before everyone else showed up. If he could get Webster, Eve would be ripe for the picking.

But Webster had pulled his car ten feet too far. He lowered his gun, frustrated. He couldn't get a straight shot and didn't dare move closer. Ever the cop, Webster still had his own gun drawn and though it pained him to admit it, Webster was a better shot. *If I miss, I'm dead.* He didn't plan to die. Not tonight anyway.

Phelps just might. It was the spark he'd been waiting for. The press would be all over the story and it would come out that Phelps felt guilt over the death of Rachel Ward. Rather than letting the press catch up, this was the perfect time to throw his final punch.

The Hat Squad would be defensive. They'd say they'd warned the Shadowland study participants of impending danger. That the women of the Twin Cities were safe.

Then by end of the day tomorrow another victim would be found, with no tie to the study, and the Hat Squad would be left with no clues, no defense. No plan.

The press would crucify them. It was perfect. They'd

be publicly fumbling, humiliated. Justifying their incompetent investigation while juggling avoidance of any appearance of cover-up in the case of Jack Phelps.

They'd be thrashing about, trying to regain face, looking for suspects. He'd hoped Axel Girard would be good for more than a few days of confusion, but that was all right. The squeaky clean optometrist had never been his planned fall guy.

He'd sown the seeds for two new suspects, providing hours of enjoyment as the Hat Squad's wheels continued to spin. He'd had the suspects in his plan from the start.

The first backup cruiser was stopping in front of the Bolyard house. Soon the place would be crawling with cops. He'd retreat for now, disappointed but undamaged.

Eve could no longer hurt him with her forays into Shadowland, but that no longer mattered. It no longer mattered how much aid she gave Webster, because the role of her study, and of Eve herself, were finished. He no longer needed to silence her.

Now he just wanted her. Partly for revenge, it was true. But it was more than that.

He'd been stunningly aroused watching Winters recall the moment he'd "killed" Eve Wilson, and how she'd fought for her life. *I want that fight. That fear. I want the power of my hands around her throat.* There was also the aspect of ego, he had to admit. Succeeding where a celebrated killer had failed would be so very satisfying.

He started his car, slipping quietly away into the night.

Well, that was interesting, Dell thought, watching through his camera zoom as the dark car drove away. *Somebody hates Noah Webster as much as I do.*

He was certain the man driving away didn't know he'd

been watched. If he had, he wouldn't have aimed a gun at Webster's car. Apparently, he hadn't had a good angle or he'd gotten cold feet, because he'd left without firing a shot.

Dell noted the man's plate and returned his attention to Webster, who sat in his vehicle, looking very sad. He should look sad. His partner had just been found in bed with his dead girlfriend. It would make beautiful headlines. *More beautiful had Phelps's "suicide" been successful*, he thought bitterly. That Phelps had been discovered before he was fully dead was frustrating, to say the least.

That Dell hadn't been the one to write the headline was frustrating as well. He could still be submitting stories as Buckland had his old man kept his damn mouth shut.

I didn't do it. What bullshit. Harvey had threatened to tell, and he had. But when time came to pay the piper, Harvey had whined like a little girl.

V always said he would. V always said they could make him cry if the two of them had joined forces as kids. *But I was always too scared.* Tonight he had not been afraid at all. He'd been angry and justified.

But now Webster knows who I am. Webster had gone to Harvey's house. They'd found the old man's body. He'd heard the chatter on the scanner, the BOLO issued . . . *for me.* But they'd missed on his vehicle. They had him in a black Lincoln Navigator.

Just like that gun-pointing guy was driving. Dell grinned as things fell into place. Unless Webster had three guys on his ass, the guy in the Navigator was the Red Dress Killer himself. Dell put down the camera and pulled out his BlackBerry, doing a reverse search on the Navigator's plate. Then frowned at the name that popped up.

Donald Donner. Where had he seen that name before? *Oh, yeah.* That was the name he'd seen on the door behind that douche Jeremy Lyons's desk at Marshall.

"I don't think so, Dr. Donner," he murmured. "I saw him first. He belongs to me."

But first, headlines. He couldn't write them, but he'd make damn sure someone else did. He dialed a number he'd found in Buckland's contact list. "Hi. I have a tip for you . . ."

Wednesday, February 24, 9:55 p.m.

Eve was cold despite the car heater Noah had left running at full blast.

She'd seen four dead bodies tonight. She included Katie in that number, the sight of the body bag fresh in her mind. *I saw her Sunday, called her a bimbo du jour.* Eve wondered what Katie had done to warrant Dell's wrath. Or if the man had simply lost it.

He killed his father. *And tried to kill me.* And David. She groaned. She needed to call David. He'd be worried sick. She dug her cell from her computer bag, wincing at all the calls she'd missed.

"I'm sorry," she said before David could snarl. "I've been busy. This guy who hurt you—"

"I know. Olivia called me. She's stepped up security here at the hospital."

Eve's blood ran colder. "She thinks he'll come after you? He was trying for me."

"She said she's not taking any chances. Are you okay?"

"Physically, I'm fine. Emotionally . . . I've seen four bodies tonight."

"Webster let you?" He sounded outraged.

"He won't let me out of his sight. What he sees, I see."

He grunted at that. "Tom told me you had a dinner thing. How did it go?"

Eve found the one side of her mouth lifting despite everything. "Not bad."

"A glowing endorsement coming from you. I'm glad. You deserved it."

"Get some sleep. I'm safe." Hanging up, she reached into her bag for her laptop and her hand brushed the hard bulge in the zippered pocket. The image of Harvey Farmer flashed into her mind, dead on the floor of his living room, a hole in his chest. Dell was out there, somewhere. The gun she carried would do her little good in her computer bag unless she intended to hit him with it.

Lifting her head, she looked both ways out the window before slipping her gun from the bag to her coat pocket and suddenly felt much safer. She opened her laptop to make sure Natalie and Kathy were safe as well. They were, Kathy's avatar on her Ninth Circle bar stool and Natalie's still at the poker table.

Natalie was losing big. Dasich, conversely, had a mountain of chips. *So not fair. Guy's a damn cheat.* Eve watched the next hand go to Cicely, the avatar who always sat next to Natalie's. Once she'd had Greer bump into her to get her screen name, to determine if Cicely was one of her subjects. She wasn't.

At least not that you know of. A new chill chased down her spine.

"Shit." *I have a dozen avatars. Any one of them could, too.* She could have red-zones she'd never identified. And at the moment she had no idea what to do about it.

A roar from the casino had her looking down. The Cicely avatar had won a hand she shouldn't have. It was extraordinarily lucky, totally skillful, or totally cheating.

Natalie agreed, filing a formal complaint. A brawl was building. More fun and ga—

Eve was yanked from the action by a knock on the car window that had her stifling a yelp. She rolled down the glass, drawing a breath. "Captain Abbott, you startled me."

He didn't smile. "Did Web tell you that we've arranged a safe house for you?"

Eve smiled, brightly. "He did. Thank you for your concern."

Abbott opened her car door. "I'll take you there now. Come with me."

Eve leaned back, shaking her head. "I've made alternate arrangements."

"You can't stay here. This is a crime scene."

Eve looked up at him, keeping her expression bland although in her mind, her eyes were narrowing suspiciously. "I'll leave as soon as my ride gets here."

Abbott's jaw clenched. "What are your alternate plans?"

The hairs on the back of her neck lifted. "I'm staying with Sal and his wife," she lied.

"I cannot have Webster distracted. This mess with Jack is bad enough."

"How is Jack?" she asked, changing the subject before he decided to call Sal.

"They've pumped his stomach, but he's not out of the woods. Don't change the subject, Eve. I don't want Noah to miss a threat because he's looking after you. It could mean his life. Or yours."

Put that way, Abbott made sense. "I understand."

"Then you'll back away from him until this case is resolved."

Eve studied his face, harshly illuminated by a street-lamp. "I will not be a distraction."

He glared at her, knowing she had not agreed. "See that you don't."

He closed her car door and had started to walk away when Noah emerged from the Bolyards' house with Micki Ridgewell, both looking grim. Eve muted Shadowland, so she could listen to what was being said outside the still-open car window.

"Time of death?" Abbott asked Noah.

"Between seven and eight," he replied and Eve's heart sank. That would have been when they'd been kissing in the backseat of his old car.

"Any indication of what they'd planned to tell you?" Abbott asked.

"No." Noah rubbed the back of his neck. "But they did make a phone call at 7:47."

Micki pointed to a local TV news van that was just slowing to a stop. "To them."

A woman approached wearing a stylish coat and high heels. "I'm Regina Forest," she said. "Can you tell me what's going on here?"

"This is a crime scene," Noah said. "You'll have to leave."

Forest's expression became a deliberate mix of horror and interest. "Mr. Bolyard?"

"No comment," Noah said, but before he could step away Regina came closer.

"Stuart Bolyard called our office. Talked to one of our staff members." Her eyes narrowed, catlike. "I'll tell you everything I know if I get an exclusive."

"Depends on what you know," Noah said. "So what do you know?"

"Mr. Bolyard said he'd seen the Red Dress story on the news and recognized one of the women. That he'd seen her at a coffee shop and that he'd called the police for a meeting. I asked why he just didn't tell the police everything when he called and he said his wife was 'into celebrities.' She wanted to meet Jack Phelps. Where is Phelps?"

"Not on duty right now," Abbott said. "What else?"

"So you already knew all that?" she asked. "He also said he saw a man leave just after them." Her smile bloomed, cagily. "And that he didn't tell you."

Noah's smile was unpleasant. "Ma'am, we have an ongoing homicide investigation, as you're well aware. Please don't play games with us."

"Wouldn't dream of it. The staffer called me to the phone and when I introduced myself, Mr. Bolyard said his wife wanted to meet me, too, and be on TV. I told him I'd need to hear more. He told me he'd seen the man again, in the same coffee shop. Said he was a professor at one of the local colleges. Fifties, horn-rimmed glasses and a bow tie, and that his hands shook when he drank his coffee."

Donner, Eve thought. To his credit, Noah didn't blink.

"Do you know him, Detective?" Forest asked shrewdly.

"Did Mr. Bolyard approach this man?" Noah asked instead of answering.

"Yes. When he saw him today he asked if he was the one who'd left with the woman who got killed. He said the professor got angry and denied it. So, *do* you know this man with the bow tie?" She wagged her finger. "And no fair answering with a question."

"We may," Noah said. "As soon as we confirm, we'll

give you your exclusive. And you'll hold back on broad-casting the tape your assistant is shooting right now?"

Forest scrutinized him. "Sure. Just don't double-cross me, okay?"

"Wouldn't dream of it," Noah murmured as another car raced up the street, stopping behind the news van with a screech of brakes. Two men emerged, one with a camera.

"Detective Webster?" The one without the camera jogged across the street. "Can you comment on Detective Phelps's attempt at murder-suicide?"

Forest's brows shot up and Noah's eyes flashed dangerously.

"No comment," Noah said softly.

"I'd say that qualifies as a double-cross," Regina Forest said, equally softly, and motioned at her assistant in the van to keep rolling tape.

The reporter looked annoyed that he'd been scooped. "Nelson Weaver, the *Mirror.* Is it true that Jack Phelps murdered his girlfriend and OD'd on booze and pills?"

"No. Comment," Abbott repeated forcefully.

Forest's lips curved, this time in disdain. "Nelson, I think we should grab a coffee. Chat." She walked away, the confused newspaperman at her side.

"God*damn* it," Abbott muttered. "So much for Jack's privacy."

"But now we know who killed five women," Noah said, sounding oddly disconnected. "I'll go pick up Donner."

Abbott turned slowly toward Noah's car, as if remembering Eve still sat there. "I'll send a squad car to Donner's house to hold him there, then *I'll* pick him up. Drop her off at Sal's before you meet me at Donner's."

*   *   *

Well, that was interesting, too, Dell thought, watching through his zoom. The guy from the *Mirror* he'd fully expected since he'd called him, but the chick from the TV news was a bit of a surprise. Looked like Phelps would be covered coming and going.

Phelps could still die, he thought optimistically, *but even if he doesn't, his face will be plastered all over the Twin Cities*. A murder-attempted-suicide by a cop was big enough to be picked up by CNN. Hell, maybe even big enough for Yahoo.

Everyone had read that *MSP* article and thought Phelps was a god. Now they knew he was a murderer and a coward. In other words, everyone would know the truth.

"Now, on to Webster," he said with a big grin. He knew how to hit Webster where it would really hurt. The man cared for his family.

Wednesday, February 24, 10:15 p.m.

Noah clenched his steering wheel as he drove away from the Bolyards' house. "What happened between you and Abbott?"

"He wants me out of the way so you won't be distracted. I told him I'd comply."

Noah tamped down his temper. No easy feat. "By going to Sal's?"

"I figured Sal would cover for me. Abbott tried to take me to the safe house himself and that wasn't going to happen." She drew a breath. "Noah, I don't know what to say."

He gave her a hard glance. "About what?"

"Those people, the Bolyards . . . They were killed while we were . . ." She shrugged.

"I know. But you told me that Jack made a bad choice, letting a woman he didn't really know into his bed. You were right. The Bolyards made a bad choice, too. They could have told us what they knew and we could have picked Donner up before he shot their heads off. They didn't. They wanted their fifteen minutes of fame."

"Looks like they got it," she said sadly. "But back to you. Abbott's right. I'm a distraction to you right now. Drop me off at Sal's. I'll go home with Callie and ask one of the cops to follow us. I'll even call you when I get there so you know I'm safe."

"I've got an idea that I like better. Brock and Trina's house," he said, then blinked when she forcefully shook her head.

"*No.* They've got kids. No way will I lead Dell to them. I'll go to a safe house first."

His heart squeezed hard. He hadn't expected her to say that, but now that she had, he was totally unsurprised. "They sent the kids to Brock's dad for the night. He's a retired cop and understands what's going on. The boys will be perfectly safe there. I called Brock while I was in the Bolyards' house and he says it's fine with them." He lifted his brows, engagingly, he hoped. "Trina is a really good cook."

"I don't want to put them out. And what about Callie?"

"I can have her taken to Brock's, too. You girls can do each other's nails and stuff."

She laughed, shaking her head. "Would it keep you non-distracted?"

"Yes."

"Then I'll go. Thank you for finding a different way."

She studied his face, hers troubled in the darkness. "Do you believe Donald Donner killed five women?"

He looked over at her. "Do you?"

She wagged her finger. "No fair answering with a question," she said, mocking the Forest woman, then shrugged. "No, I don't. He's angry, but forgetful. Sometimes he'll be teaching and just trail off, staring into space. He forgets what he's assigned. His obsession is getting published. I don't think he has the mental organization to do these murders, or frankly the physical strength. He's pretty old."

Noah nodded thoughtfully. "What you said."

"But you're picking him up anyway."

"Oh, yeah," he said grimly.

"I'm assuming this couple saw Martha at the Deli," Eve said, "because that's where Donner goes for lunch. Whether or not he'd go there on a Saturday night? Don't know."

"Hopefully the Deli's security video will shed some light." He glanced at the computer on her lap. "Did Donner know about Shadowland? I mean, did he play?"

"I don't know what he did at home. He needed me to explain the game to him, every time we talked. If he was faking his forgetfulness, he's a damn good actor."

"I agree. Did you check on your red-zone cases? Are they where they should be?"

"Yes." She squeezed his hand lightly. "I'm sorry about the Bolyards. About Jack, about all of this."

"Not your fault."

"I don't mean that. I'm not apologizing that it happened. I'm . . . sorrowful. Sorrowful that you have to see all this pain and death and that it hurts you."

Emotion, exhaustion, exhilaration . . . all welled up in

a wave that closed his throat. This is what he'd missed. What he wanted. What he needed. Unwilling to trust his voice, he pressed her hand to his cheek and held it there.

Wednesday, February 24, 10:30 p.m.

The Bolyards hadn't locked their back door. Donner appeared to be more careful with his locks.

He broke a pane of glass in the basement door, reached in, and twisted the doorknob from the inside. A quick survey of the house revealed Donner and his wife were not home. *Dammit.* Donner was supposed to have been here tonight. They'd had an appointment. *Bastard stood me up.*

I should have grabbed him before I killed the Bolyards. This could be tricky. He could only hope that, wherever Donner had gone, his alibi would be as shaky as before.

This did save him from having to kill Mrs. Donner, though. Killing people not in his original plan chafed at him, and he was still plenty chafed over the Bolyards.

I should have stayed outside that coffee house and waited, like I did with the others. But the night he'd met Martha had been so damn cold. He would have drawn more attention to himself sitting outside in his car than going inside. But now he had two unplanned murders and a lot of extra effort to explain it away.

He had to hurry. The TV news reporter had probably already shown up at the Bolyards' house to get the interview he'd promised from Stuart's home phone, only to find Webster's crime scene instead. Pretty soon this place would be crawling with cops. They were supposed to find the house empty, because he'd taken Donner.

He went straight to Donner's bathroom and frowned. Both toothbrushes were gone, as were several toiletries, leaving gaps in the row of bottles and cans on the bathroom shelf. The Donners had gone away for more than the evening.

In Donner's kitchen, however, he had to smile. There was a lone highball glass on the table. He sniffed at it. Donner had been drinking bourbon. He'd make sure the sixth of his six victims had a bottle in her house. He dropped the glass in a plastic bag.

Donald Donner had never been a real suspect in Webster's eyes, but even Webster wouldn't be able to explain away hard evidence.

As for Donner's whereabouts . . . On a hunch he hit redial on the kitchen's cordless phone and hung up before the number could connect. Committing the number to memory, he took out his BlackBerry, connected to the Net and did a reverse call lookup.

Ah. The number belonged to Adele Donner, Donald's mother. He'd confirm it, of course, but instinct told him this was where Donald had retreated.

He dialed 411, let it connect, then hung up when the operator answered. He'd knocked Adele's number from the last-called spot so the cops couldn't do what he'd just done. They could get the number from Donner's LUDs, but that would take them time.

Time was something he didn't have a great deal of. He left the way he'd come, and none too soon. As he rounded the block, a squad car entered the neighborhood, lights blazing but siren silent. *Sorry, boys. Dr. Donner has left the building.*

* * *

Wednesday, February 24, 11:00 p.m.

"Nice place," Eve murmured. Brock and Trina lived in a brick house with a chimney from which a cozy stream of smoke billowed. Just looking at it made her queasy.

"Nice people," Noah said quietly. "Why are you nervous?"

"It's serious when you meet family."

"You know them from the bar."

"This is different. This is . . . personal."

"Damn straight it is. You introduced me to Tom tonight," he noted.

"I know." Her face still heated in embarrassment at the stern way Tom had studied Noah, as if Tom were the father and she were an errant teen. "Kid's a pain in the ass."

"He loves you. You're his family. And I passed muster," Noah added with an arched brow, then he smiled. "Trina already likes you. Why are you nervous?"

"I don't know. Maybe my spider senses have been on tingle mode so long today, my nerves are shorted out. I don't know how you cops cope with all the excitement."

He came around to open her door. "Normally it's not this exciting. Normally it's all paperwork. Don't forget your phone."

Her computer bag had fallen on its side and the phone had slid out of the front pocket. Out of habit she flipped it open. "I've got a million missed calls."

"You'll have time to catch up inside," he said, a little impatience in his voice.

She made her feet move. He had work to do and she was distracting him again. "Sorry. I procrastinate when I'm nervous."

"Well, stop it. You don't need to be." He put his arm

around her shoulders and she leaned against him, hip to hip, her head on his shoulder as he walked her to Trina's front door. "Feels nice, doesn't it?" he murmured in her ear and she shivered.

Because it did. And that made her nervous, too.

He sighed. "Just enjoy it, okay?"

She realized she was holding her breath. "God. This shouldn't be so hard."

"Try to relax. I'm the least of your worries right now."

"That's what you think," she muttered, then jumped when the cell phone in his pocket vibrated against her leg.

"Eve, relax. Trina doesn't bite. Not anymore, anyway." He was smiling until he looked at his caller ID. "It's Abbott." He stopped on the front porch and took a step back, turning his face away as he listened to his boss.

Eve didn't want to know what was happening. The day was catching up to her and she was suddenly overwhelmed. *No more. Not tonight.* But Noah's call wasn't quick and too much energy had her flipping her phone open to look at the incoming calls.

Oh God. It was the same number that had sent the text. She lifted her eyes to Noah, who was now pacing the width of the driveway as he talked with Abbott in low tones she couldn't hear. Her hand trembling, she hit the speed dial for her voicemail and put the phone to her ear.

"Didn't your parents teach you not to get into cars with strange men?"

She was breathing hard, the cold air hurting her lungs. Her knees gave way and she sank to the edge of the porch, numb. It was him. *Him.* It couldn't be. He was dead.

But it was. The voice that taunted her nightmares until she woke screaming. Her phone slid from her fingers, hitting the porch with a clatter that brought Noah around.

He ran to her, dropping to one knee in the snow. "What?"

"Him." She shook her head hard, trying to clear it.

"Dell Farmer?"

"Yes. No. *God*." She was hyperventilating and she pursed her lips, made herself breathe through her nose. "It was a voice message. Winters's voice."

Stunned, Noah did a fast take. "Are you sure?"

She ground her teeth. "Fucking sure. I hear that voice in my dreams. Dammit."

"Sshh," Noah soothed. He took her phone, punched in the numbers to replay the message. And his face grew grim. He pocketed her phone and helped her to her feet. "I'll tell Olivia. We'll find him."

"How did he get it? How did he get his voice?" She heard the hysteria in her voice, tried to battle it back. "How did he know?"

"I don't know. Maybe from an old interview. I found a few on the Net this morning. Try to breathe, honey. It's just words. Winters can't hurt you now." His arms were around her, holding her up. "He can't ever hurt you again."

She thought of Harvey Farmer and Katie. And Kurt Buckland and David. "But Dell can. He wants to. He won't give up."

"Breathe." He pounded on Brock and Trina's door, loud enough to wake the dead. But nobody answered and he pounded again, harder. "Open the damn door."

It opened only a few inches, Trina's face peeking around the edge. "Noah," she said brightly. "Eve, what a surprise." Then she frowned. "*Go*," she mouthed. "*Now*."

"Goddammit, Tree, I don't care if you're both naked and having sex from the damn chandeliers. *Move*." Noah knocked the door open with his shoulder.

Trina's words hadn't matched the look in her eyes, Eve thought numbly. Slowly, the look in Trina's eyes sank in. *Run*. Pulse shooting like a rocket, Eve backed up, but it was too late. Trina was yanked from sight and Eve heard a loud thud a split second before a hand grabbed her arm, dragging her inside.

"*No*," Noah thundered, trying to yank her back. Eve thrashed like a wild cat. But it was too late. She went still when a gun was shoved against her temple.

Noah had gone still as well. "Dell Farmer," he said quietly.

What a shock, Eve thought, her mind racing now, even as her body was motionless.

An arm locked over her throat, squeezing. "The great and powerful Noah Webster," Dell scoffed. "You couldn't have found your own ass in the dark."

"I seem to have found you," Noah said calmly, his focus on Dell's face.

Dell scoffed again. "Yeah, right. Only because my old man gave me up."

Noah looked surprised, though none of his focus dulled. "No, he didn't."

Eve could see Trina, hands and feet bound, lying dazed against a wall. *Where's Brock?* Then Eve was lifted on her toes, Dell's gun digging harder into her head.

"Don't lie to me, Webster," he snarled.

Eve found her voice. "He's not," she said. "*I* found you. It wasn't that hard."

Dell stiffened and for a split second the pressure from the gun slacked away. But he recovered and Eve winced in pain when he ground the barrel harder. "You're lying."

"I'm not. I found an article by Kurt Buckland, with a nice photo of your father standing at V's graveside. You resemble your dad." She paused for effect. "Or you did, until you killed him. You don't look much like him anymore, what with that hole in his chest."

"Shut up." But she could feel a slight tremble in Dell's hand.

She could see Noah watching, waiting, alert. She felt the weight of her own weapon in her pocket and hoped to keep Dell distracted enough that he wouldn't feel it, too.

"You killed your father for no reason, Dell," Eve said softly. "He didn't tell on you."

Dell was shaking now. "Shut up. Damn you."

"Did he tell you he was innocent? Beg for mercy? Did you shoot him anyway?"

His arm tightened around her throat. She lifted higher on her toes, trying to breathe.

"Let her go, Farmer," Noah said, his voice as calm as hers had been.

"No. *No.* You killed, too, Webster. You started this."

"I didn't kill your brother, Dell," Noah said. "He was running from a crime. We were pursuing. That's what we do."

"He didn't *do* anything."

Eve could smell his desperation, a rancid odor.

"He killed a store owner," Noah said reasonably. "In cold blood."

"Only because she drove him to it."

"She? You mean Katie?" Noah asked.

"Yes. He wasn't bad. V wasn't bad." But he didn't sound so sure now. Eve sensed his confusion and remembered the night before, that brief moment when she'd reminded him he was in a bar surrounded by cops. Rage had become confusion, then he'd swung back to cold control. Dell was there, right now, in that moment between rage and control, and Eve prayed Noah was paying attention. Turning herself into dead weight, Eve lifted her feet and wrenched from his grip.

"Drop the gun, Farmer," Noah demanded, even as she hit the floor, rolling away.

Curled into a ball, she turned her head enough to peek out. Noah held his gun steady on Dell, but Dell held his gun on Eve. The two men stared at each other.

"I'll kill her," Dell said, his voice coldly mocking, just like the night before, "while you watch. You're going to kill me anyway, just like you did V. I'll take her with me."

Eve slid her hand into her coat pocket and pulled out her gun. She lurched to her knees, holding her aim steady at the hand that held the gun.

"No, you won't," she said, and Dell's head whipped around, eyes wide and startled.

It was all Noah needed. Quickly he closed the gap, twisting Dell's wrist painfully as he shoved him to the floor, his own weapon shoved against Dell's spine as Dell fought wildly. Noah grunted as he struggled for control of Dell's gun, one knee jammed into his back, the other pressing his arm into the floor.

"Get back," Noah snarled to Eve. "Get out of here. Now."

"I'll kill you," Dell was screeching at the same time. "I don't care which of you."

Eve crawled a few feet toward Dell and pointed her gun at his head. "Stop it," she snapped. "Or I'll shoot your damn head off. You don't want to die, Dell. I've been there, and trust me, it ain't fun. I'm not lying. And I'm not afraid of you."

Dell stared up at her, eyes full of hate. In seconds Noah knocked Dell's gun from his hand, then cuffed his hands behind his back. Kneeling on Dell's bucking legs, Noah looked up, his eyes dark with fury. "What part of 'Get back' did you not understand?"

"I couldn't hear you," Eve said blandly. "He was screaming 'I'll kill you' too loudly."

Noah rolled his eyes, tersely called for backup, then looked at Trina, who'd struggled to a sitting position, her hands and feet bound. "Where's Brock?" he demanded.

"Bedroom," Trina said. "He was going to kill us when you got here, make you watch."

Eve was on her feet. "I'll go." Her heart surprisingly steady, she ran to the back, stopping to grab a kitchen knife. Brock was on the bedroom floor, tied and gagged. But his eyes were open and furious. She pulled the gag from his mouth.

"Is everyone okay?" were the first words from his mouth.

"Yeah. Are you?" She winced. "Ooh. That's a nasty bump on your head."

He rolled his eyes. "How much will it take to wipe this picture from your mind?"

Eve chuckled as she sawed at his ropes. "We'll negotiate."

Chapter Twenty-one

Wednesday, February 24, 11:20 p.m.

Noah blew out a relieved breath when Eve emerged with Brock, walking unaided. "You better be happy they're not hurt, you little shit," Noah muttered.

"I would've," Farmer snarled. "I would've killed all of them while you watched."

Noah held on to his temper. Barely. He'd recited Miranda, but Farmer had screamed through it. Farmer starting screaming again as Brock ran to his side, holding Farmer down while Noah dug plasti-cuffs from his pocket and secured Farmer's kicking feet.

Eve cut Trina's bonds and helped her to the sofa amid Dell's promised retribution, delivered at a pitch that could shatter glass.

"You guys need a medic?" Noah asked.

Brock and Trina checked each other for injuries. "Nah," Brock said, "I think we're good with just some ice. Eve has informed me I have a nasty bump." He lifted his brows in an attempt at levity. "I never would have known otherwise."

Now that it was over, Noah chanced a look at Eve and his heart tumbled. She stood, still calm, holding one of Trina's butcher knives in her hand. Noah stood, wincing a little. He lifted Eve's chin where a bruise was forming, his jaw going hard. "He hit you."

"I'm okay. Really."

"You were a hell of a lot better than okay." Needing to hold her, but aware of Brock's and Trina's curious eyes avidly watching every move, Noah stepped back. "I'll call Abbott. The three of you should go ice yourselves."

Brock helped Trina to her feet. "I'll have bourbon with my ice."

"I'm not on duty," Eve shot back, laughing as she walked with them to the kitchen.

She was a fascinating woman, Noah thought. So often, she stood back and watched the world go by. But when she found herself thrust into it, she . . . sparkled.

Distraction? Perhaps. But a welcome one. He glanced down at Farmer. And now that this SOB was in custody, she was no longer in danger. She needed no safe house.

He could take her home. *Or to mine.* He swallowed hard as he thought about taking up where they'd left off earlier that evening. But other priorities came first.

Noah took his cell from his pocket, his adrenaline already receding. Abbott had told him Donner was gone and commanded him to meet him and CSU at Donner's house.

"Bruce, it's Noah," he said when Abbott picked up.

"Where are you?" Abbott asked acidly. "And what's all that racket?"

"At my cousin's house and the racket is Farmer. I brought Eve to stay with Brock, but Farmer was already here, waiting. Long story short, he's cuffed and lying on the floor."

"My God," Abbott said, the acid drained from his tone. "Is everyone okay?"

"Brock's got a bumped head. Trina, Eve, and I have some bruises. Farmer's alive." Two uniformed officers came through the front door. "Backup just arrived."

"Good. It'll be a pleasure to see him rot in prison. I'll let Olivia know."

"What about Donner?"

"Still no sign of him," Abbott said, but Noah's attention was suddenly fixed on Farmer who had stopped screaming and was now laughing like a crazed hyena.

"Wait," Noah said to Abbott, then crouched next to Farmer. "What's so funny?"

"You," Farmer said. "Looking for Donner. He almost got you good tonight."

"What are you talking about?"

Farmer shrugged, a smirk on his face. "You'll see. Or maybe you won't, then *pow*. It'll be night-night-Noah and your pretty Eve, too."

Noah leaned in close. "Tell me what you know," he said quietly.

Farmer's smirk grew more mocking. "Or you'll do what? Other than kill me, there's nothing more you can do to me." His smirk became a sneer. "So go fuck yourself."

Noah rose and nodded to the uniforms. "Take him in. Mirandize him again. He screamed while I did it and I don't want any sleazy lawyer saying he never was advised of his rights. Keep him restrained, and watch his damn feet," he called after them.

"What did he mean?" Abbott asked. "Night-night-Noah."

"I don't know. But he'd heard Donner's name before." Then Noah remembered. "Of course. He was at Marshall yesterday. He met Jeremy Lyons, who works for Donner.

He might have met Donner then. What did you find at Donner's house?"

"Broken glass in a back door, nobody home. Looks like he and his wife went away."

"Damn. Do we know where?" Noah demanded.

"I've got a request for his LUDs in process, Noah," Abbott said. "And a BOLO. None of the neighbors know where they might have gone."

Noah sighed. "I really believed Donner wasn't our man. Now, he's bolted and Crazy Boy Farmer says he's out to get me. I should have had surveillance on him all along."

"I put surveillance in front of the two women's houses you sent me, Natalie Clooney and Kathy Kirk. For now, we have Eve's frequent users covered, so his victim pool has been warned. You go home, get some rest. You've had a pretty busy day."

Noah found himself too relieved to argue. "Haven't we all. How's Jack?"

"Still critical. They said they'd know by morning. I'll call you with any news."

Thursday, February 25, 12:25 a.m.

Noah turned off his engine and everything went silent as the two of them sat in his driveway. They had been inordinately lucky.

Or fate had smiled. Eve wasn't sure which she believed anymore.

She only knew the silence had grown louder with every mile. When he hadn't taken the turnoff to her apartment, she'd known this moment was coming. Her mind kept going back to the backseat of his old car and inside her whirled arousal . . . and fear. A lot of fear. In her mind she knew it was unfounded. Noah wouldn't hurt her.

After staring straight ahead at his garage door for a full minute, she chanced a glance at Noah from the corner of her eye. He looked grim. "I don't know what to do next," he confessed and she saw compassion as an easy way out for them both.

"Noah, you're tired. Take me home and get some rest, just like Abbott ordered."

"Do you want that?" he asked, and her pounding heart pounded harder.

"If we go inside, what happens next?"

He didn't blink. "We can sleep. Or not. Your call."

Everything inside her clenched. "Can we just dip our toe in and see where it goes?"

"We can do anything you want, Eve," he said, volleying the ball into her court again.

"It's just . . ." She shrugged. "The last time I had sex with a guy he tried to kill me."

Now he blinked. "You said there'd been another between then and now."

"One other that didn't go very well. Actually, it didn't go at all."

His dark brows went up, hidden beneath the brim of his hat. "Why not?"

"He couldn't. He really tried, but he . . . couldn't."

"Did you love him?"

"No. It was more like a mutual favor between friends." She pursed her lips. "Yeah."

Noah pushed his hat back on his head and stared at her. "I don't understand."

"Well, remember that doctor? The one who'd had the accident?"

"You had *sex* with *him*?"

"Well . . . no. Which is the point. He and I got to talking one day and I wondered if I still could. You know, if everything still . . . worked. He said he'd be willing to try."

"What a guy," Noah said dryly.

"Yeah, well." Eve chuckled awkwardly. "It's kind of funny now, but it sure wasn't funny then, for either of us. I think I was more upset for him than about myself."

"Not surprising," he murmured.

"About a year ago he called me. He's met someone and he's happy. And functional." Her smile was half fond and half embarrassed. "He made sure I knew that."

"What a guy," Noah said again. He hooked his finger under her chin, tugging until she looked up at him again. Then his head dipped, his mouth covered hers, and he kissed her so thoroughly her toes curled in her boots. He pulled back just far enough to see her face. "You want to dip your toe in, Eve, or do you want to dive into a cold pool?"

In his eyes was heated challenge she couldn't ignore if she wanted to. And, to her relief, she found she didn't want to. "Cold pool," she said and his eyes flashed, with triumph probably. But that was okay because she was feeling triumphant herself.

Noah paused long enough to throw the deadbolt on his front door and take her computer bag and coat. Then he took her hand and led her back to his bed.

He'd had a flash of insight at Brock and Trina's. For all Eve's outer calm, she was timid. Terrified even. The last six years of her life had been all about dipping her toe in.

But he'd watched her when she was put face to face with people. She interacted. She came alive. She just needed that nudge. *So did I.* He'd needed whatever had put them together. Call it fate or luck or whatever, he didn't intend to spend another day watching her over his tonic water.

He stopped next to his bed, set his gun on his nightstand. Then he slid his hands into her short hair and took her mouth the way he'd wanted to from the first moment he'd laid eyes on her, letting her feel what he'd kept pent up for one very long year. With a low, satisfied hum she leaned up into him, grabbing his wrists for balance, then her hands slid down his arms, under his suit coat, flattening against his back. With kissing she was comfortable. He prayed she'd be comfortable with what came next.

"These are the rules of this game," he said against her lips. "You say 'stop' or 'wait' at any time and I will. But if you say nothing, I keep going. Okay?"

"Okay," she said breathlessly, her fingers digging into his back. "Just hurry."

But he wouldn't hurry. He'd given them the nudge they needed, but had no intention of flying so fast that they missed the trip. He spent time on her mouth, kissing her long and deep and lush until the hands that gripped his back slid up his chest and around his neck. He ran his mouth over the cheek she could feel and down the scar she couldn't.

He ran his lips down her neck, over and past the leather choker he'd never seen her without, until he got to the collar of her sweater. She'd pushed his suit coat off his shoulders and to the floor and was tugging his shirt from his trousers and it was all he could do not to throw her on the bed and plunge deep.

But he didn't hurry, didn't rush. Didn't push her. Didn't need to. She was struggling with the buttons of his shirt and he pulled back to give her room.

She looked up, her eyes dark, intense. "My hands are clumsy."

"I don't mind." When she'd finished, he shrugged out of the shirt.

For a moment she simply looked at him and he felt oddly . . . humbled. "I always wondered what went on under your suits," she said softly. "I never thought I'd find out."

"I'm glad you were wrong."

She smiled at that, shyly, but her hands were clenched together. She was nervous again, but she hadn't told him to stop, so he started anew. He kissed her until she kissed him back and her hands unclenched, flattening on his chest, and he shuddered.

He'd missed this. Needed this. He dropped his head to her shoulder. "Don't stop."

"I won't." And she didn't, fanning her palms back and forth, exploring.

He lifted his head and watched her face as she touched him. She'd needed this, too. "I like the summer," he said abruptly and she looked up, surprise in her eyes.

"Why?"

"Because you have this shirt that you wear to the bar." He trailed his fingers up under her sweater, along her stomach, and felt her muscles clench and quiver. "It's cut high. When you twist a certain way, I could see part of your tattoo. What is it?"

She swallowed hard. "Why don't you find out for yourself?"

"I could do that." He pulled her sweater over her head, revealing a plain, serviceable bra that shouldn't have made his mouth water, but it did. Gently he pushed her to the bed and followed her down, running his fingers over the skin he'd bared.

He pressed his lips between her breasts then forced himself to lift his head. "This drove me crazy all summer." Vines crept up from the waist of her jeans, curling this way and that. Some bore tiny flowers. In some places the vines were thicker than others.

She was holding her breath. He ran his fingertip over one of the thicker vines, felt the hardened, raised skin beneath. And understood. They were the scars from the eight times she'd been stabbed. She'd turned something horrific into something beautiful.

He waited to meet her eyes, waited until he'd shoved all the sorrow and rage back deep, where she couldn't see. Waited until the only thing left was pride. And desire. "This is one hell of a tattoo," he said, his voice between husky and hoarse.

She breathed then, her tension ebbing. "It keeps going. You know. Down."

Noah's mouth curved even as his fingers itched to rip the jeans from her body and see just how far down the vines dipped. "I can see that."

She exhaled through her teeth. "Hurry, Noah."

But he wouldn't let himself be hurried. He kissed the skin above her bra, then below it until her shoulders lifted from the bed, seeking more. Finally she threaded her fingers through his hair and pulled his mouth to her breast and he gave in, sucking hard through the cotton, groaning when she pushed the fabric away.

She twisted higher, humming her pleasure when he

took her other breast in his mouth. "More," she whispered. "Do more. Please. Don't make me wait anymore."

His hands shaking, he yanked the jeans and lace panties down her long legs, leaving her naked and wide-eyed, waiting for his reaction.

He had to wait, to make sure his voice didn't crack like a teenager's. "I always wondered what went on under your clothes. I never thought I'd find out."

She said nothing, still waiting, and his heart squeezed even as his body throbbed.

"Eve, I imagined a lot, but never like this. You're beautiful."

Her eyes closed and her throat worked. "Hurry," was all she whispered and he knew she was terrified. Noah wanted to curse, no, to kill the man who'd left her scarred and scared. But that wouldn't help either of them now.

No pressure, he thought and let his own trousers drop to the floor in a jingle of keys. She flinched, just a little, but he saw. So he lay down beside her and started again, kissing, caressing, until her hands relaxed and her hips lifted, her body seeking his.

"Please," she whispered. "I'm ready." But her eyes were still closed.

"No, you're not." He kept his voice soft. "Look at me, Eve."

She opened her eyes. There was arousal there, but still too much fear. He brought her hand to his lips, then down his body, wrapping her fingers around him.

"That feels so good," he said huskily. "I want you to feel good, not afraid." He covered her mouth with his once more and teased her, working one finger up into her, then two until her hips moved restlessly and little cries burst from her throat.

Now, he thought. It had to be now. Slowly, carefully, he pushed inside her, watching her face. When her eyes met his, relief hit him like a brick. Arousal had won.

And so had Eve. He started to move, never taking his eyes from hers, and when they clouded with pleasure he felt like he'd conquered the whole damn world. When she came, convulsing around him, he dropped his head to her shoulder and followed.

In the minutes afterward, he felt dizzying relief. He might have had more powerful orgasms, but never one more satisfying. There would be time for powerful later. Now he rolled them to their sides, and savored what they'd done.

Eve blew out a breath. "I'm glad that's over," she murmured.

Startled, he blinked down at her. "Excuse me?"

She winced. "I didn't mean it that way. I meant . . . hell. We dove into a cold pool and I was so scared, but you . . . you were so patient with me. You couldn't have enjoyed that very much." Her brows lifted. "Although you were exceptionally functional."

He snorted a surprised laugh. "I'll have you know I enjoyed it very much. As did you."

She smiled shyly, charmingly. "I did."

"Now that we're finally in the pool, we'll both enjoy it more the next time."

"Next time?" She looked intrigued. "When might that be?"

He laughed again. "Give me a few minutes."

"Thank you," she murmured. "For understanding that I needed the shove."

"Thank you for trusting me." He raised one brow. "And for . . . you know."

"I do know," she said sagely. "I'd be interested in knowing again. If you don't mind."

"I think I can sacrifice."

Thursday, February 25, 12:30 a.m.

He drove by Adele Donner's house, pleased to see Donald's car in the driveway. The house was dark, its occupants tucked into bed. For now, the fact that Donner was staying with his wife and very elderly mother made for a wonderfully thin alibi.

He'd let the Hat Squad have Donner for a little while. They'd question. Interrogate. Use their tough, scary voices. Donner would deny and tremble. Maybe they'd arrest him right away, but Donner had sufficient assets to pay the bail the judge would set. Then later, he'd take him and hold him where no one would find him.

The cops would search high and low, while the press seethed and the public's respect for Hat Squad seeped away. And when they'd been sufficiently humiliated, Donner would be found, having hanged himself, his suicide note a full confession.

Webster would close the case, defeated and maligned. *And then I go back to the way things were.* Quietly eliminating the dregs of society nobody would miss.

He drove away from Adele Donner's house. It was time for the sixth of his six to die.

*   *   *

Thursday, February 25, 12:30 a.m.

Virginia Fox looked in the mirror, sighed angrily. She was not a beautiful woman, and that always mattered to men. She had hoped that this man would be different, but she knew he wouldn't be. His screen name was Dasich. His real name was John.

He was a newbie to Shadowland, eager to learn, and like all the men, he knew how to sniff out the women who could actually accomplish something. She'd helped him along, shown him the ropes, knowing he'd find some excuse to skip away when he'd learned his fill. So she'd been shocked when he wanted to meet.

More shocked to learn that he lived nearby. In Wisconsin. He wanted a late-night meet. Said he worked strange shifts, but Virginia knew the code. He was married and cheating on his wife. It didn't matter. It would never go as far as sex. It never did.

Men took one look and went running.

She wasn't a troll. "I may not be beautiful like Natalie, but I'm okay," she snarled to the mirror, angrily slashing lipstick over her mouth. *Pretty Natalie, smart Natalie. The "I-just-got-a-promotion-and-a-big-raise" Natalie. The "I'm-your-new-boss" Natalie.*

"Fuck Natalie." She threw the lipstick in her purse.

She'd brought Natalie into Shadowland to take her down a few pegs. *Make her compete in my world.* But some evil genie demon had touched her and Natalie was good at poker, too. *Fucking pact with Satan.* "She used me. Took what I knew and got me thrown out of my own place."

Turned on me, reported me for cheating. It wasn't fair.

Wasn't right. *I spent months building my skill points. Months.* And now, it was all gone. Taken away by . . .

Natalie. "God, I hate that bitch."

John had been right about her all along. *Using me, just to make her look better.*

Virginia would have the last laugh. At least tonight she'd be meeting a man, unlike Natalie who'd be home playing poker, all alone. Sucked into the game.

Virginia hoped Natalie got addicted. Maybe she'd lose her job. Virginia brightened. *Hey, that was possible.* Then Natalie would lose her swanky house, her nice car. *And where do you think she'll come crawling?* "Here," Virginia snapped aloud, pulling her front door closed behind her. *And then it'll be payback time.*

She threw her purse into her car so hard it bounced. "I'll kick your ass to the curb so hard it'll leave skid marks. Tell *me* not to meet my man tonight. Tell *me* it's not safe." Greedy bitch. She just wanted all the men, the money, and the power all for herself.

Well, John was one guy Natalie wasn't going to get. Virginia would see to that.

Thursday, February 25, 12:30 a.m.

He pulled into the parking lot, gratified to see Virginia's car parked outside. She'd been so easy to lure, so jealous of her friend Natalie. He was sure Natalie had no idea how much her "friend" despised her. Everything had come so easily for Natalie, her career, her family, even the men that had come in and out of Natalie's life. Men she took for granted while Virginia had been forced to listen to Natalie's exploits.

Virginia had invited Natalie to the Shadowland poker table to get some payback, instead finding this an area where Natalie also excelled. He had to admit, in all his years he'd met few opponents so formidable. He'd actually never planned to kill Natalie Clooney. She was the closest to real competition he'd ever met. When he went back to the quiet killing, he'd reregister in Shadowland and buy another avatar. The poker table was a place he'd really grown to enjoy, so he'd go back.

And when he did, there'd be no Virginia to spoil his game. When he'd come along, Virginia had been ripe for the picking. It wasn't hard to get her help in beating Natalie at poker. It wasn't hard to lure her into side conversations where she bared her soul on topics from the boss that was against her, to her fear of the dark, to her incompetent therapist. He pitied anyone who had to listen to that woman for any length of time.

He despised a whining woman. His mother had whined. All the time. Finally, he'd grown tired of her. He imagined the world was weary of listening to Virginia Fox, too.

Soon, the world would be a little bit quieter.

Thursday, February 25, 1:45 a.m.

Eve lay with her head pillowed on Noah's shoulder. Her fingers toyed with the coarse hair on his chest that rose and fell as he slept.

But she was wide awake, mind and body. Noah hadn't lied. They'd both enjoyed it a lot more the second time. She shivered, remembering, mind and body.

A whole lot more. The first time hadn't been a dive into

a cold pool, as much as a protracted glide. The second time? Most definitely a dive, fast, furious, and satisfying.

She stretched sinuously, aware of every well-earned twinge. It was as if he'd used up all of his slow and gentle the first time. He'd finally lost control, plunging hard and deep, ruthlessly dragging her along for one hell of a ride.

When she'd come, she'd felt alive. *Invincible*. And when he'd come, she'd watched his face and finally felt beautiful again. *Whole*. For the first time in a very long time.

And now, in the quiet, she wondered if she'd ever have gotten to this place with anyone else. She thought about Callie's theory that she'd trusted him because he was "the one." Perhaps. Perhaps not. Whether that was true or not long term, he was definitely the one for now and Eve felt a gratitude that she suspected he would reject.

Her eye caught a small picture on the nightstand and gingerly she reached across him to grab it, taking care not to wake him. They'd turned out the bedroom lights, so she rolled away from him to hold the picture up to a shaft of moonlight coming through the curtains. It was a woman with a small child and she felt the slickness of the wood, worn smooth by a caressing thumb, and she pictured him sitting in his bed staring at the family he'd lost. Her throat closed and the hope and beauty she'd felt fizzled a little.

He'd never get a family like this again. *Not with me*.

"That's Susan," he said quietly and she jumped. "And Noah," he added. "My son."

She pulled the blankets up to cover herself. He eyed the movement, his eyes taking on that blank expression she now knew hid his heart.

"I didn't mean to wake you," she said as he sat up, pushing a pillow behind his head.

"I wasn't asleep. I was just enjoying holding you. It was a long time coming."

"Yes, it was." She held out the picture and he took it, his eyes still blank.

"Susan was a clerk in ballistics," he said. "I'd just finished the academy, and didn't have a hundred dollars to my name. Somehow, she was still interested in me."

Eve's throat tightened. She had no problem visualizing any woman falling for Noah Webster. *I did, the first time I saw him.* "She was beautiful. So was Noah, Jr."

He smiled then, wryly. "Noah the fifth. Poor kid."

His smile loosened the vise around her throat, just a little. "So your mother wasn't being professorial when she named you Noah Webster. I wondered."

"My mom can't spell 'professorial' without Webster's dictionary," he said, genuine affection in his voice. "She's a smart woman, but can't spell to save her life. There's no actual family connection to the dictionary Noah, other than some great-great way back who thought it was a name with stature."

"It is," she said. "And it suits you."

"It's my name, like it or not. Mom had to name me Noah, and I had to name him Noah." He studied the picture with a sigh. "I thought my life was over when I lost them."

He seemed to want to talk, so she obliged. "You said there was an accident."

"Yeah. Stupid teenager driving a car packed with his friends, coming home from a football game. The radio was too loud and they were having too much fun. Ran a red light. I swerved to avoid them, skidded on some ice, ran off the road, rolled down a hill."

He'd recited the story as if it were a police report. "And the stupid kids?" she asked.

"They fled the scene, but one of my friends from the force caught up with them later."

Beneath the blankets she felt cold and pulled her knees to her chest. "And then?"

"We'd landed upside down and I'd been knocked out cold. When I came to, Susan was bleeding out, begging me to wake up, to help the baby. But it was too late." He swallowed hard and deliberately put the picture back on his nightstand. "I heard her voice in my mind for a very, very long time."

Eve's cheeks were wet. "It wasn't your fault."

"No. Didn't change the end though."

She rested her chin on her knees. "Winters is like a bad song that won't get out of my mind. He died in prison. Some con stabbed him in the showers."

"I know. I'm glad, because I would have been tempted to do it myself."

He was totally serious and bizarrely that made her feel safe. "The day I found out he was dead, everyone had gathered at Caroline's, you know, Tom's mother. They were having a picnic. I wouldn't go, so Dana stayed home with me. I couldn't face anyone."

"Understandable."

"Perhaps. I wonder what would have happened if someone had shoved me out of the house that day. If I'd have hidden in the dark for so long."

"You can't second-guess, honey. Trust me, I did it for a long time. And every time I'd just find myself staring at the bottom of an empty bottle."

"You're right. I know that and I'm not blaming anyone. Except maybe myself."

"Well, that needs to stop, here and now." He swiped at her wet cheeks with his thumb. "You beat him, Eve. You survived."

"So did you."

"Barely, and with a lot of help from my family, but I did. And here we are."

So where will we go? Eve looked across him to the picture of the beautiful family he'd lost. "I can't give you a family like you had."

His jaw tightened. "And I told you that didn't matter."

"And I still don't believe you. You're such a good man. You should be a dad. I just wanted you to know that if you change your mind . . . that it's okay. I'd understand."

Even in the darkness she could see his eyes flash. "Eve, you are really pissing me off." Abruptly he slid down, lying flat on his back, glaring up at the ceiling. Then he sighed. "Are you going to sit over there all by yourself all night?"

"Probably not," she said cautiously.

"Come here." He waited until she complied, settling her head against his shoulder. "You might decide you don't want me," he said pragmatically, although she heard the vulnerability in his voice. "Some young guy comes along . . . you may decide that's what you want. We can't know what will happen, Eve. For now, this is what we have."

She tilted her head back to look at him. "For now, this is what I want."

Too many emotions shifted in his eyes for her to read any of them. "Good," he said. "Now go to sleep. I have it on good authority that you can only live one day at a time."

She cuddled closer, her palm resting atop the coarse dark hair that covered his chest. She was absurdly happy he had a hairy chest. It wasn't something she'd ever thought she'd experience, this tickling against her palm, the feel of his heart beating steadily beneath her fingertips. The smell of a man as she nuzzled, satisfied. And she realized she was simply, absurdly happy.

"Eve?"

"Hmm?"

"What was it like to die?"

She lifted her head to look into his face, unsurprised to find his green eyes blank, waiting. "I'm sure it's different for everyone."

"What was it like for you?"

Her eyes flickered to the photo. How excruciating to know those he loved most were in pain, be forced to hear his wife's desperate cries, and be helpless to save them.

"It . . ." She searched for the right word. "It lured. Come. Rest. I wasn't afraid, but I was angry. I was only eighteen and I didn't want to go. I flatlined twice. The time in between I could hear the medics yelling to stay with them and I wanted to scream, *'I'm trying.'* It was then I became afraid. It was like . . . quicksand and I couldn't get footing and it all slipped away again. The second time was harder. I wanted to just rest. But I fought. And I made it back. I hope that's what you wanted to hear."

"I always hoped she wasn't afraid," he said hoarsely. "But I wanted her to fight."

Eve brushed her fingertips over his cheek. "Did she love you?"

"Yes."

He said it with an assurance that made her eyes sting. "Then I'm sure she fought. But when she was too tired to fight anymore, I'm sure she felt safe. As did your son."

He swallowed hard. "Thank you."

She kissed him, softly. "You're welcome." She'd started to slide back to his shoulder when his hands gripped her face, pulling her back to his mouth for more, and she gave it to him, in seconds the kiss exploding. He grabbed her hips and, as in the backseat of his old car, swung her over to straddle him.

"Please." The word ground from his throat as he ate at her mouth. It was he who begged this time and Eve felt powerful. The first time he'd been patient, the second he'd lost control, but this time he needed her.

He was suddenly, fully aroused and Eve lowered herself onto him, taking him inside her. Her breath caught when his fingers dug into her hips, bringing her down hard, making her feel every inch of him. She sat back, and he went deeper still.

"You feel so good," she whispered, hissing out a breath when his hands covered her breasts and she began to move. He matched the frantic rhythm of her hips, her name a chant on his lips as he begged her not to stop.

She couldn't stop. It was a wave, an incredible towering wave, and she rode its crest until he groaned, rearing up to close his mouth over her breast, hungrily suckling, his hands hard on her back pressing her down, his body twisting up.

Then the wave broke and she cried out. She wrapped her arms around his head and held him close as she rode it in, barely hearing his cry as his body went rigid, jerking against her. His shoulders sagged and he buried his face between her breasts, his muscles twitching as he came back to earth with her.

Without a word he sank back against his pillow, bringing her with him, his chest heaving as he struggled to catch his breath. A laugh bubbled up and out of her, a purely happy sound of delight. "Are you always so . . . functional, Detective Webster?"

"No." He pressed a weary kiss to the top of her head. "You're good for me, Eve."

And somehow it was that simple. That easy. "You're good for me, too." Her arms slid around his neck and his hands moved down her back to close over her butt possessively, kneading so very gently. And finally, sleep came.

Thursday, February 25, 3:15 a.m.

He let out a shuddering breath mixed with a groan. *God.* After killing Virginia Fox, he'd needed that. His heart pounding in his chest, he released the throat he clutched and sat back, staring at the woman on the narrow, filthy bed in his basement. He didn't know her name and he didn't care.

He climbed off her, his body still twitching in climax. He'd nearly lost it at Virginia's house, holding on by a mere thread as he'd silenced her for eternity. Because it hadn't been Virginia's face he saw, but Eve's. He'd imagined it to be Eve's throat, Eve's terror.

As he'd dressed Virginia, staged the scene, then hoisted her body onto the hook in her ceiling, his hands had been shaking like a schoolboy's. But he'd maintained control, even as he'd completed the final detail on his final victim. The pièce de résistance.

He had finished with Virginia, finished with his six, but a fire had raged within him, his mind churning too violently to think. So he'd driven blindly into the city, chosen another that no one would miss. Now, he could think again. He looked at the dead stranger in his bed. Soon, he wouldn't have to pretend to see Eve's face. Soon it would be Eve in that bed, her terror that propelled him upward.

Tomorrow, he'd have the look on Webster's face when he gazed up into Virginia's face. The sight of her remains would remain in the cops' minds for a very long time. They would feel responsible. They'd been so certain that they understood him, that they could predict him. That they'd warned the potential victims.

They knew nothing. It would eat at them, taking apart their confidence brick by brick.

It had been a good night. Once he cleaned up, he could go home and sleep. He was tired, but it was a good tired. The sixth of his six was finished. The Hat Squad would be exposed for their hubris and incompetence. And he would relax and enjoy the show.

He pulled back the concrete slab and frowned. He'd have to lay off for a while after this. Apparently too many bodies at the same time slowed the process. He grimaced at the sight of Jeremy Lyons's hand poking up out of the layer of dirt and lime.

He cut the ropes binding his latest prey, then stopped, staring at her face. But it wasn't tonight's dead hooker he saw. It was . . . Sunday's. Wild dogs. He'd told her she'd be torn apart by wild dogs. Her eyes had been blue, the roots of her hair auburn.

His mind clear, the association clicked. He'd seen that face. Tonight. *Where?*

In the hospital. She'd looked tired and . . . terrified. Leaving the dead hooker where she lay, he went to the drawer next to where he kept all the old cell phones. It held dozens of wallets and driver's licenses. He found the license from Sunday's whore. Lindsay Barkley. He found her cell phone in the next drawer and turned it on, clicking through the photos she'd stored there. There she was. The girl he'd seen tonight.

Why was she at the hospital? He thought hard, remembered the tall young man who'd been with her, and drew a breath. The young man knew Eve Wilson.

Perhaps the girl knew nothing. But he would not take that chance. He looked at Lindsay's license. He knew where she'd lived. He'd swing by on his way into morning meeting. Have a little chat with the girl. He'd take care of her easily.

He grabbed tonight's hooker by the ankles and dragged her to the pit. It was pretty full, but he thought it could accommodate two more. Lindsay's sister and Eve were both tall, it was true, but both were slender. They wouldn't take up too much space.

And then no more for a while, he told himself. Which was not a problem. Once this endeavor was complete, his stress would recede to a manageable level and in a few months when he hunted his next prey, so would have the pit.

Thursday, February 25, 3:30 a.m.

Olivia's cell phone rang, rousing her from what had been a very pleasant dream on the cot in the break room at the station. Dell Farmer was a tough nut to crack. Kane and Abbott had taken a turn questioning him while she caught a few winks. Blinking hard, she flipped her phone open. "Sutherland," she said, swallowing a yawn.

"It's Tom. Tom Hunter."

Olivia sat up and turned on the light next to the cot. "Is David all right?" Of course he was. He had to be. The hospital would have called her if there'd been any issues.

"Yeah. I talked to him around ten and he was going

to sleep." On the other end, she heard Tom sigh. "This is going to sound so paranoid and you're going to be mad."

"I've got security on your uncle," Olivia said as kindly as she could. "He'll be fine."

"Olivia, I was out tonight. With Liza."

Olivia's eyes narrowed. "Define 'out.' As in 'on a date'? Or as in 'hunting bad guys'?"

"The second one. Wait," he inserted before she could explode. "We found what we were looking for. That guy the prostitute mentioned last night, Jonesy, we found him."

"And you didn't think to mention this to me?"

"You would have yelled because we were out looking."

"Damn straight I would have yelled," she yelled. "Your mother asked me to watch out for you, Tom. You're making trouble for me."

"I'm twenty," he said quietly. It wasn't bravado or posturing. Tom Hunter had been forced to be a man, to defend his battered mother, before his seventh birthday.

"All right," she said, just as quietly. "You found Jonesy. Had he seen Liza's sister?"

"Yeah. He said he'd been watching the cars picking up hookers, writing down license plates. If they were rich . . ."

"He'd blackmail them. Wonderful. So he saw Lindsay getting in a car?"

"Yeah, but he said he didn't have the list anymore, that he'd sold it, and he didn't remember what kind of car, but he remembered the date and time. I didn't believe him, but I got him to tell me who he'd sold the list to."

Olivia sighed. She knew Jonesy. "How much did you pay him?"

"A hundred."

"*Tom.*"

"I *know*," Tom spat, frustrated. "He said he sold it to some guy named Damon. Another hundred got me Damon's 'business address.'"

A shiver tickled down her spine. "You're on thin ice, kid. Damon is a major dealer."

"I figured that out. I found him, told him what I wanted. He looked at his list. And this is the paranoid part. He said he saw her get into a black SUV. Lincoln Navigator."

Olivia blinked, wondering how many Navigators could be on Twin City roads.

"You know," Tom said when she said nothing. "Like the one that hit David."

"Yeah, I got it. That's weird, but not impossible." Besides, they'd gotten Dell Farmer. *But not his SUV.* He'd been driving a beat-up old Corolla and had just laughed uproariously when she'd demanded to know where he'd parked his Navigator.

"I know and I almost didn't bother you with it. But I figured better safe than sorry."

"Damon didn't happen to share the license plate, did he?"

"No, and frankly I didn't want to push it. He scared the bejesus out of me."

"That's the first smart thing I've heard you say all night. Dammit, Tom, he would have stabbed you as easy as breathing. I'm shocked he told you anything at all."

"He's a basketball fan," Tom said wryly. "I had tickets in my pocket. If you don't pick him up sooner, I know where he'll be sitting come game time on Sunday."

Olivia massaged her temples. "Your mother is going to kill me."

"My mother and Dana *taught* me. All those years in the shelter, the new identities, transporting women and kids in the dead of night . . . No way Mom can yell at you."

"Good point. Okay. Here's the deal. I don't tell your mom what you've been doing and you don't go out with Liza alone anymore."

"She's not going to give up until she finds her sister. Or her body."

Sisterly bonds. That Olivia understood. "Tomorrow I'll go with you. Where's Liza?"

"I dropped her off at her apartment. I walked her to the door," he added defensively.

"You're a good man. Maybe too much so. No more sleuthing by yourselves. Deal?"

"Deal. Thanks, Olivia."

"Tom, wait. Where are Liza's parents in all this?"

"Her mom's sick, and Liza doesn't want to worry her yet. No dad in the picture."

"Okay. Let me see what I can find. Get some sleep." Troubled, Olivia hung up, then placed a call to an old friend in narcotics. Hopefully they'd have enough to bring Damon in and she could find out what he really knew.

Chapter Twenty-two

Thursday, February 25, 4:00 a.m.

He was so tired. He parked his car next to his wife's BMW and was tempted to go to sleep right there in the garage, but his wife would wonder where he was when she awoke to an empty bed. He didn't hate his wife. They had a mutually beneficial relationship. She received a generous allowance for her support, showed up on his arm at all the right functions, never expected sex, and conscientiously kept his secret.

Or what she believed to be his secret. Through twenty years of marriage, she'd believed him to be gay. It wasn't the optimal solution, but it did explain to her satisfaction why he never touched her. He closed the door into the kitchen, frowning when he switched on the light. Something was different. It took him only a second.

She'd moved the cat's bowl. He didn't like it when she changed things. She knew this. It had been the only occasion he'd needed to strike her during their marriage. She'd learned quickly and kept things the way he liked ever since. Until tonight.

He opened cupboards, careful not to wake her. He didn't care a whit if she got her beauty sleep, but she was his cover. That's all she'd ever been. The cat's bowl was nowhere to be seen. Maybe she'd broken it and hoped he wouldn't know.

He always knew, could always instantly see any item out of its place. He climbed the stairs, his temper seething. It was exhaustion and he reined his temper in. He'd deal with her in the morning, after she'd woken to see him soundly asleep beside her.

He'd brought her a cup of tea tonight, as he always did. Laced it with enough narcotic to have her sleeping through the night, as he always did when he was going out. As he'd done every night this week. He closed the bedroom door behind him.

And stopped. She wasn't in the bed. Carefully he turned. And stopped again.

She was sitting in one of the chintz chairs by the window and in her hand she held a gun. His heart began to beat harder. He recognized the gun. It was one of the many he kept at his place. She'd been to his place. "What's this?" he asked quietly.

"I didn't drink the tea tonight," she said. "Or last night. Or the night before." She paused meaningfully, tilting her head. "Or the night before that."

Sunday. "Why didn't you drink your tea?" he asked, injecting a note of hurt into his voice. She was small, manageable. Taking the gun would be no issue.

"Because of your cat. I was sneezing all the time, so I took an allergy pill."

"What does this have to do with the tea?" He took a step forward and she brought the gun up, smoothly. Interesting. They'd been married twenty years and he never knew she could handle a weapon. Looking back, he probably should have asked.

"Don't come any closer," she said and he could hear

the underlying fright. Panic. Disgust. "And keep your hands where I can see them. The allergy pill interacted with whatever it is you put in that tea. It made me sick. I threw up the tea. And I was awake when you came in on Sunday night. Monday morning, actually. You were out all night."

"I was with a patient," he lied.

"You had sex. I can always tell. I thought you'd gone discreetly about your business with your newest boy of the month. Which was fine, but then you were gone Monday night, too. You slipped into bed, thinking I was asleep. I smelled perfume. *Ladies' perfume*. I could accept your alternate lifestyle. I was willing to be your cover. But you were cheating. With *women*."

He tilted his head, feigning puzzlement. He needed to get to the gun in his pocket. "Let me get this straight. You're angry because I'm not gay?"

"Don't," she said, disgusted. "Don't even try to charm me. I followed you."

He narrowed his eyes. "And?"

"I *know* what you did. I *saw* you last night. I followed you to your other house, saw you change cars, then I watched you wait for that woman outside that bar and follow her home." She sat back and leveled him an even stare. "I thought, 'He has another home. Another life. Maybe even another wife. That's why he doesn't want me.' I couldn't stand wondering, so I went back to that house today."

His fists clenched. "You had no right."

She laughed, hollowly, dully. "My God. You can stand there and speak to me of *rights*? I saw your basement. Your . . . shoes. My God. You're a monster. How long? How long have you been killing?"

"Thirty years," he said, oddly pleased that he could finally tell someone.

She shook her head, helplessly. "I . . . opened the pit. I can't stop thinking about it. I see that hand, sticking up, every time I close my eyes. Why did you do it?"

"Because I wanted to," he said simply and she shook her head in disbelief.

"You're a monster. And no one will believe that you're capable. You have everyone fooled. Everyone but me. I know what you are and you aren't going to get away with this." She started to pull the trigger, but he was faster. He leapt forward and wrested the gun from her hand, her cry of pain barely registering. He tossed the gun to the bed and dragged her up against him, his arm over her throat. Her gun had no silencer and the shot would wake the whole neighborhood.

Pulling his own silenced gun from his pocket, he pulled her to the bathroom and shoved her into the tub, holding her as she fought. "Just one question. Where is my cat?"

She twisted to stare up at him, defiant in her fear. "Dead," she spat.

He clenched his jaw. "You bitch." Then he shot her in the head, stepping back as she slumped. "I should have stayed single," he murmured, panting. "Dammit."

Now he'd have to explain to their friends where she'd gone.

Thursday, February 25, 7:00 a.m.

Coffee. Noah drew a deep breath, the aroma teasing him awake. Sex and coffee. He wasn't sure a man needed a whole lot more than that. He rolled out of bed, a little creaky after tackling Dell, but his mind was alert. He hadn't gotten any calls during the night, so Natalie Clooney and Kathy Kirk, Eve's last two red-zone cases, were all right.

He still didn't believe Donner had killed five women, but he had the very bad feeling that Farmer's mocking "pow" and "night-night-Noah and his pretty Eve, too" were more than petty taunts. Donner was involved, or he wouldn't have run.

Pulling on pants, he found Eve sitting in his kitchen wearing only his shirt, frowning at the morning's newspaper headline. He pressed a kiss to the back of her neck and stole a look down the shirt at her breasts. "I like you in my shirt," he murmured.

She looked up over her shoulder, her dark eyes troubled. "Sit down."

She gave him the front page and he hissed an oath. "I guess we expected this," he said grimly. HAT SQUAD MURDER-SUICIDE, the headline read. He scanned the article, keeping his temper in check. "They make it sound like we know Jack did it."

She got up to pour his coffee, then set a mug next to his elbow and leaned over his shoulder, her cheek pressed against his. It was the support and affection he'd craved, and greedily he took it in.

"They mention Farmer's capture," she murmured, "and his father's murder a few pages in, but nobody's tied their motive to Jack and Katie."

"We should have tied it together for them last night."

"Why didn't you?"

"It's an internal investigation now. They'll have to clear Jack."

"I called the hospital this morning. They're not giving out any information."

"Abbott said he'd call when he heard something. I guess no news at this point is still good news. I wish *MSP* never published that damn article. When you were untying Brock last night, Dell was screaming that the magazine made us look like gods."

"I thought 'white knights,' when I first read it." She kissed his temple. "You want some eggs? I can't do omelets because I couldn't find the knives."

"You started talking in your sleep, so I got up and locked them in my gun safe. I'll make you a key so you can get to them when you're awake."

She sighed wearily. "I'm sorry."

"Don't be. We both bring baggage, Eve. We both have nightmares." He hesitated. "Mine are especially bad whenever I go to the bar."

Now she looked away. "So if we . . ." She picked at the shirt of his she wore. "If this continues, I'd have to quit."

"I wouldn't expect that, Eve. I know what Sal and Josie mean to you, and you to them. But I can't visit you there." He tugged on the tail of his shirt, pulling her to his lap. "If this continues, we'll both give and take. In the grand scheme, your job, my knives, not a big deal."

She leaned her head against his shoulder. "I dreamed of him last night."

"I know. It gave me chills." Bone deep chills that had kept him awake for a while.

"I wish I could make them stop."

"They'll pass, Eve, the dreams and the voices. Mine took years, yours may take longer." He took her hand, threaded their fingers together. "It'll be all right."

She pressed their joined hands to her lips. "I believe you." Then she abruptly turned his hand over, her expression suddenly taut. "Dell Farmer wasn't wearing a ring."

Noah stared at his hand, his chest growing tight with dread. "No, he wasn't."

"David said the man who ran him off the road was wearing a ring, like yours. So either David was wrong, Farmer lost his ring, or . . ."

"Or somebody else ran David off the road." He closed his eyes, trying to remember the scene at Harvey Sr.'s house. "The father wasn't wearing one either." He dug his cell phone from his pocket. "I'll call Olivia."

As he dialed, there was a knock at his front door. He opened his door to Olivia, holding her ringing phone. "We gotta talk, Web." She pushed her way in before he could say another word, then stopped, her eyes gone wide. "Well, hello, darlin'."

Eve halted her attempted flight and leaned against the wall, arms crossed, long legs bare. Her face was red, her scar visibly white. "Olivia," she said, warningly.

"I was going to ask if you had a good night, Web, but I can see that you did." She looked at Eve. "And next time my sister asks if you're happy, I'll know to say yes."

Noah dragged one hand down his face. "Give us a minute to get dressed. There's coffee in the pot. We need to talk to you about Dell Farmer."

"That's why I'm here. He was tracking your car, and Jack's. I found the device under your engine block. Jack's car had one, too."

"Well, that explains a lot," Noah said. "I wondered how he seemed to know when to follow us. He was at every victim's scene and there when we interviewed the families."

"I checked Katie's cell LUDs," Olivia said. "Lots of calls to Dell's cell matching up to calls made between you and Jack, going back about three weeks."

"Since *MSP* hit the stands," Eve said, "and Katie hit on Jack."

"She was tipping off Dell every time Jack got a call. Have you heard anything?"

"They won't tell me anything," Olivia said, "except that he's not conscious."

"Farmer wasn't wearing a ring," Noah said abruptly.

"Somebody else ran David off the road," Eve said. "Somebody else was after me."

Olivia didn't look surprised. "Farmer wasn't driving a black SUV last night. And he seemed to think it was really funny when we questioned him about it."

"He said Donner 'almost got you good tonight,' " Noah said slowly, a piece falling into place in his mind. "Did you trace any of his calls to that reporter from the *Mirror*?"

Olivia's lips thinned. "The one who wrote that trash story on Jack? Yeah, his number's in Dell's call log, not fifteen minutes before the reporter showed up."

"At the Bolyards' house," Noah said. "He knew that's where we were. And that reporter's first question wasn't about the Bolyards' homicide, it was about Jack."

"Dell was there," Eve said. "He saw something. He saw someone try to get you."

"Get us," Noah corrected. "That somebody tried to get you first, yesterday."

"He was there, outside the Bolyards'," Olivia said. "They both were. Dell and the killer. The other killer." She scrunched her eyes. "Sorry, it's been a long night."

"Why? Why me?" Eve asked, but by the look in her eyes Noah knew she knew.

"It's all about Shadowland," he said. "Your test. Your subjects."

"We almost got him coming out of Rachel's," Olivia said. "Because you alerted us."

Eve leaned against the wall, stunned. "And now he wants me gone. Damn, why do I always get involved with these people? I'm a goddamn trouble magnet."

"Dell started with the 'pow' shit when he heard me say Donner's name, and the Bolyards told that TV reporter that it was Donner that followed Martha out that night."

Eve shook her head. "I still can't see Dr. Donner killing five women, Noah. I can't."

"I'm having trouble with it myself. But we won't know until we find him, and he's run."

"Could Dell know where he is?" Eve asked uncertainly and Olivia shook her head.

"He wouldn't talk. And I don't want to start out offering him any deals."

"Let's talk it with the team," Noah said. "We'll get dressed and follow you in."

Thursday, February 25, 7:30 a.m.

"Hurry," Liza muttered, rushing down the stairs of her apartment. "Be late, be late." The words were for her school bus. If she missed the bus, she'd have to walk three miles and miss the test she had first period. She burst out of the apartment building, relieved to see kids at the bus stop at the end of the block.

"What's your rush?" Liza heard the silky voice a moment before she felt something sharp at her back. "Scream and you die," a man's voice promised softly.

She sucked in a breath to scream her lungs out anyway, but his hand covered her mouth, yanking her head backward. He was strong, dragging her into the alley between her building and the next. Fear gave her strength and she flailed, biting his hand. The gun abruptly disappeared from her back, but she was stunned by a blow to the side of her head. Dazed, she tried to fight, until a needle pricked her neck.

Seconds later he had her under his arm, dragging her through the snow. She could see an outline of a dark vehicle ahead. She tried to scream, but she couldn't move her mouth. Couldn't move anything. *Tom.* He wouldn't know she was gone for hours.

He pushed her eyelids closed and she couldn't open them. "Your sister is dead," he whispered in her ear. "And soon you will be, too." Then she landed hard on the floorboard of his backseat and the car drove away.

Thursday, February 25, 8:00 a.m.

The mood around Abbott's table was silently grim as the team waited for Abbott to return from his meeting with the commander. Noah had put Eve at his own desk with orders not to move for anyone. Right now she wore the biggest target of them all.

Olivia and Kane were tired after their fruitless hours in Interview with Dell. Micki also looked exhausted, having coordinated multiple crime scenes. Ian had actually fallen asleep sitting up. Four new bodies in the morgue kept the MEs busy through the night.

Carleton's shoulders sagged, his eyes on Jack's empty chair. No news was no longer good news.

Abbott returned, and one look at his face said his meeting had not gone well. The commander had a right to be perturbed. Five dead women and they didn't have shit.

Abbott threw a stack of local newspapers on the table. The headline on every one was Jack's alleged murder-suicide, but each had an equally damaging variation on the *Mirror*'s NEW RED DRESS VICTIM FOUND, with the details of Rachel Ward's death. Below the headline was the smaller "Two Witnesses Slain" and "Cops Have No Leads."

Ian jerked awake as the papers slid across the table, Micki patting his hand silently.

"Jack is unchanged," Abbott began tersely, saying nothing about the newspapers. The headlines spoke for themselves. "The doctors aren't hopeful. His dad's with him."

Noah closed his eyes until the fury passed. "Do we know what he took?"

Abbott pursed his lips. "This is delicate. Internal Affairs has the case, but we all know Jack was set up. I've been given clearance to give you certain information as it may connect to Dell Farmer, which may connect to Donner ⋯."

"Which may connect to five dead women," Noah said bitterly. "So IA's helping us?"

"More like reluctantly cooperating. There was Oxycodone and Valium in Jack's whiskey bottle. The empty prescription bottles were in Dell's car."

"At Rachel's he swore he'd only had one drink," Noah said hollowly. "Katie must have been slipping stuff in his booze all along. I blamed him for getting there too late."

Olivia gave his arm a brief squeeze. "You didn't know, Noah."

"Jack was late a lot before Katie came into the picture," Micki added softly. "It was a perfect storm, I guess."

Carleton nodded wearily. "Apt description," he murmured. "Such a waste."

"Were Dell's prints in Jack's house?" Noah asked.

"Yes," Abbott said. "Dell was there. So far, however, we have not found Dell's prints in Donner's house, so it seems their only connection is Dell's rant last night."

"What about Donner?" Noah asked. "We get his LUDs yet?"

"Still waiting for them," Abbott said. "When we're done here, we'll go search his office at Marshall, and check his next of kin. I got the warrants signed overnight."

"We?" Noah asked.

"We," Abbott confirmed. "Until I get you a new partner, we're riding together."

It was going to be a very long day. "Okay."

"Glad you heartily approve," Abbott said dryly. "Kane, anything on Jeremy Lyons?"

"Security at Marshall found his car in one of the lots last night," Kane said. "He hasn't called home, hasn't used his credit cards, didn't pick his kid up from day care."

"So Lyons is either gone under or dead," Abbott said. "Putting us no closer to determining who's doing this. The one bright spot is that the two potential victims Eve identified weren't contacted and are still safe."

"He could be done," Olivia said. "We almost caught him coming from Rachel Ward's. Maybe that was enough to convince him to stop."

Carleton looked unconvinced. "I don't think he'll stop until you stop him or until he accomplishes whatever it is he's trying to do."

"What *is* he trying to do?" Abbott snapped. "Goddammit."

Carleton appeared unoffended. "Do *that* to you. Make you ruffled. Throw you off."

"Well, he's doing a damn good job," Abbott grunted. "But I take your point. Once we find Donner, we'll start getting some answers."

"God, I hope it is him," Noah murmured.

"But you still don't think it is," Abbott said, then shrugged. "He framed Axel Girard, Donner could be a setup, too. We need to know what Dell knows and how he knows it."

"We should be careful with Farmer. His reality isn't cogent. He ain't right," Carleton added dryly when everyone gave him a puzzled look. "We need to consider what he says accordingly."

"Right now he's all we have," Abbott said, "cogent or no. Ian, anything?"

"The Bolyards were shot with the same gun, a nine-mil. Harvey Farmer and Katie Dobbs were killed with a same, but different gun, higher caliber. Katie's face had lacerations and bruises, probably from a fist." He hesitated. "Katie had had intercourse an hour before her death. Unlikely that it was consensual."

Noah gritted his teeth. "Jack did not rape her. Dell did," he said even as a new wave of nausea rolled through him at the thought of what Dell might have done to Eve.

"I told IA that," Ian said quietly. "Based on the blood spatter, Katie's body temp, and the chemical levels in Jack's blood, he was already unconscious when she was shot. It might have been harder to definitively say that, however, if we hadn't gotten there when we did. That open window would have muddied things considerably."

"So," Abbott said, "we need to at least ask the question. Open windows at Harvey's house and Jack's. Any chance Dell could have killed five women?"

Carleton shook his head. "It's far more likely Dell just picked up this element of the Shadowland killer's MO. He seems like a quick study, writing news articles that Buckland's editor accepted as genuine. He's not a stupid man."

"Just not cogent in his reality," Abbott said sarcastically. "Olivia, Katie was his brother's fiancée, but he used her to hurt Jack. There's something there. Use it to froth him up. Get him agitated, then get him talking. I want to know what Dell saw last night. Micki, anything from the Bolyard house?"

"No forced entry. So far no forensics. Looks like he caught them by surprise at dinner. The wife was probably shot from the doorway. She fell face-first into her dinner. The husband was collapsed over her, probably protecting her."

"Would have better protected her by not confronting Donner in a coffee house," Abbott grunted. "What else?"

Micki produced a small plastic bag. "Cat hair, found in Rachel's living room. It matches cat hair we took from Martha's carpet. It doesn't give us any more on the killer's identity, but it's a connection to give the DA when we finally catch him, just like this one." She put a photo on the table. "Christy, leaving the diner. Look at her shoes."

They did, everyone frowning. "And?" Noah asked.

"They're Manolos, four hundred bucks a pair," Micki said.

"Spendy," Olivia said. "I still don't get it. Why are the shoes important?"

"Because they weren't in her closet, they weren't anywhere in her house," Micki said.

"His souvenirs," Carleton said. "It's very common for serial killers to take souvenirs, and shoes are among the most common things to keep. Again, nice connection once you find him, but not terribly helpful to me in forming a profile."

Micki looked unhappy. "I'm done now."

"It's good work, Mick," Abbott said, trying to smooth over Carleton's tone.

Carleton winced. "I'm sorry. I didn't mean to be dismissive. Knowing he collects things is just more of the same. It doesn't help me, help you." He glanced at his watch. "I have a patient at nine. Call me if there's any change in Jack's condition."

"Will do," Abbott said, then turned back to the team. "Today, we focus on finding Donner and cracking Dell Farmer. Noah, you and I will go to Donner's office at Marshall and execute the warrant. Olivia and Kane, you've got Farmer."

"What about the coffee shop?" Noah asked. "The TV reporter said that Bolyard saw Donner there. They'll have tapes. Eve says Donner eats at the Deli. Let's start there."

Abbott shook his head. "I went by the Deli as soon as they opened this morning. Security video is only of the register and the barista didn't remember Martha, Bolyard, or Donner. Let's meet back here at two. I have a press conference at three, so get me something." He met their eyes, grim. "A killer would be nice. Web, you're with me."

Noah stopped at his desk to get his hat and coat and found Eve staring at her laptop screen, her expression intent. "What are you doing?" he asked.

"Trying to keep busy. Natalie won big at the casino last night because Dasich and one other player got thrown out for cheating and—" She pursed her lips. "I'm babbling. Dr. Pierce stopped by on his way out. He said he had dinner with Dean Jacoby last night. They know it was me. He said Jacoby wants to see me this morning, but I told him you'd made me promise to stay here."

He wasn't sure what to say. "Eve, you did the right thing. Whatever happens."

"I know," she said, then smiled, ruefully. "Luckily I'm a damn good bartender so I'll still have one career. You take your desk. I know you've got work to do."

"It's okay. You stay here. I'm on my way out."

"Noah?" She stood as he buttoned his coat. "They're releasing David from the hospital this morning and I have to take him home. I can't stay here forever."

Yes, you can. The thought rose above the worry and he tucked it away. There would be time for that later. He looked at Abbott, who was waiting impatiently. "Bruce?"

Abbott looked irritated. "I'll have someone drive her over later. Now let's go."

"Captain, wait." Faye hurried up to them, a paper in one hand. "Donner's LUDs. His last call went to 411 at 10:40, but the one before that went to his mother, around 6:00 p.m. Here's her address. You want me to have the locals meet you there?"

Abbott grabbed the papers greedily. "Yeah, call 'em, but tell them to stay back until we get there. Thanks, Faye. Noah, let's roll."

Thursday, February 25, 8:30 a.m.

Olivia and Kane were preparing for another go at Dell Farmer when Olivia got a call from narcotics that left her smiling, albeit grimly.

"What?" Kane asked when she hung up.

She told him about the call from Tom Hunter in the middle of the night and the dealer Damon who might have license plate info. "Two SUVs could be a coincidence, but

we can't afford to assume. That was my old pal in narc.
They have Damon in custody."

"How much did he have on him?"

"Recreational. But that violates his parole, so we're in
business. I want to know if he saw the license plate on that
Navigator."

"He's gonna want a deal," Kane said glumly, in his way
that reminded her of Eeyore.

"I know. Let's go to the DA, see if he'll give us wig-
gle room."

Kane paused at the bullpen door. "What about her?"

Olivia turned back to look at Eve, who sat at Noah's
desk, hunched over her computer. "She's digging in that
game, hoping to find something we can use."

"Wish I'd never heard of that damn game," Kane said
as they walked to the elevator.

Olivia punched the button so hard her finger buckled.
"Don't we all?"

Thursday, February 25, 8:45 a.m.

Liza screamed. She was running, couldn't get away. Lindsay chased her, her face gray, gaunt. *Dead. She's dead,
she's dead*. But the scream never made it out of Liza's
mouth, coming out as a muffled grunt. Her body wasn't
moving. She was tied, she realized. Her hands and feet
were tied. She breathed through her nose.

Her mouth. It was taped shut. It came back in a rush.
The man, his hand over her mouth, the sting of a needle
on her neck. *What did he give me? Where am I?*

She opened her eyes a slit, relieved when her lids

obeyed. It was dark, and they were moving. *A car.* She remembered his car. *I'm in the trunk.*

Do not lose it now, she commanded herself. She focused on the breaths she took. And as her pulse steadied, she knew she was not alone. She could smell . . . blood.

Oh my God. Lindsay. She clenched her eyes shut, refusing to look. *Maybe he lied, to scare you, to make you obey. Maybe she's alive, maybe she needs you. Open your eyes and look. Dammit, girl, look.* Her heart pounding in her ears, she made her eyes open, blinking to see in the darkness. Then saw what she'd smelled.

She froze, the scream trapped in her throat. *Eyes. Open eyes. Staring at me.*

Lindsay was dead. *I will be, too.*

Thursday, February 25, 9:15 a.m.

Noah checked out the car in Adele Donner's driveway, his gun drawn. "Covered in snow. Been here all night." He and Abbott went up the front walk while two uniformed officers went to the back. They had the exits covered.

Abbott rapped on the door, hard. "Police," he called. "Come out, Donner."

The door opened, revealing two women, one about ninety and the other perhaps fifty. "We're both Mrs. Donner," the older woman said, her chin up. "What do you want?"

Donner's mother and his wife. The wife's eyes were red and swollen and she cried quietly. The old woman's eyes, though, were clear and cold as ice.

Abbott looked over their heads. "Step aside, ladies. Please."

"Do you have a warrant?" the ninety-year-old demanded.

"Yes," Abbott started, but Noah held up his hand.

"Mrs. Donner, you know why we're here. Please don't make this any harder."

Donner's mother's chin wobbled, her only sign of weakness. "He's not here."

Abbott's jaw hardened. "What do you mean, he's not here? His car is here. His wife is here. Where is your son, Mrs. Donner?"

Donner's wife wiped her eyes. "He's out back. At the pond."

Noah started to run. A single set of footprints marred the snow and by the look of them, they weren't fresh. From the snow that had filled them, they were hours old. No footprints came back to the house. Donner had left during the night and not returned.

Noah strode through the snow, motioning to the uniforms to spread out. But when he got to the pond he abruptly stopped. His breath hung in the air as he stared at the bench at the pond's frozen edge. He lowered his pistol. No need for it now.

"Goddammit," one of the uniforms cursed, barely managing to stop before stepping in what had been Donald Donner's brains. "What the fuck is this?"

Noah pursed his lips, swallowing back the bile. Animals had done what animals do, but there was enough of Donner left to see the pistol in his ringless right hand.

He turned to find Abbott staring as well. Together they walked back to the house and knocked on the front door again. This time Donner's mother let them in.

"We want this to be over," she said with dignity, then placed their hats on a sideboard before leading them to the living room where Donner's wife sat in a chair, sobbing.

Adele Donner lowered herself to a sofa, looking every one of her ninety years.

"He had a brain tumor," Adele said. "The doctors gave him less than a thirty percent chance. All my son wanted was to see his work published one more time." She took a sealed envelope from the table beside her and gave it to Noah. "He wrote you a letter, Detective. He told me to give it to you."

"He never would have hurt anyone," Donner's wife said. "He couldn't live with knowing that his study . . . That all those women died."

"When did he shoot himself?" Noah asked softly.

"About eight o'clock last night," Adele answered. "That bench was his favorite spot."

Eight o'clock, Noah thought. *Before the last call from his home phone went to 411.*

"You heard the shot?" Abbott asked.

Both women nodded. "And we knew it was over," Adele said. "It was what Donald wanted. He'd suffered so much, I couldn't tell him no."

"Why didn't you call 911?" Abbott asked, more gently.

Adele Donner cast a quick look at her daughter-in-law. "I don't drive at night, and last night she . . . well, she just couldn't drive. We decided that we'd drive into town this morning, to see the sheriff."

Donner's wife closed her eyes. "My mother-in-law wanted to call 911. But I didn't want to be here when they took him away."

Noah stood, his shoulders heavy. "We'll get someone out here to take care of him."

In the car Abbott was grim. "He still could have done all five murders, you know."

"I know. But do you think he did?"

"No. What does the letter say?"

Noah scanned its contents. "What you'd expect. He does give his regards to Eve."

Abbott started the car. "I'm sure you won't mind passing that on."

Noah's jaw tightened. "Why are you being like this? We wouldn't have a case if she hadn't come forward."

"She didn't come forward, Noah. We had to drag her in here."

"Not true. You've always been reasonable before. What's the problem now?"

"The problem is that she continues to be a distraction."

"She's a target."

"Then put her in a safe house. You know I'm right."

Abbott was right. Then again, so was Eve. But Abbott's order would keep her safe.

"If you don't, then I will," Abbott said quietly. "I mean it, Noah."

Noah nodded. "Okay. I'll take her back to Brock. Will that work?"

"I'll take her," Abbott said, irritated. "I want you focused. And I swear, if I have to tell you that one more time . . . Well, I won't tell you. I'll just yank you from this case."

"Okay," Noah said, teeth clenched. "I hear you."

Thursday, February 25, 10:45 a.m.

"I'm not going to Brock's," Eve said, putting her laptop in her bag. "His kids can't stay away forever and I will not put this target I'm wearing on their heads." She looked at Abbott, resigned. "I'll take the safe house."

"Eve," Noah started, but she lifted her hand to stop him.

"Do safe houses have cable?" she asked Abbott, and to Noah's surprise, he smiled.

"All the channels you can surf," Abbott said, "and free wi-fi to boot."

Her lips curved. "Can I order any takeout I want?"

"Don't push it, Eve," Abbott said dryly. "Let's go."

"Wait," she said. "Noah, what about David? Who's going to take care of him?"

"His brother Max," Noah said. "He'll stay with David until he can go back to Chicago."

Her eyes widened in surprise. "You called Max?"

Noah shook his head. "No, I called David. Apparently Tom called his stepfather last night and told him the whole story. Max left Chicago a few hours ago."

She looked up with a forced smile and he knew how much this pseudo-incarceration was costing her. "Will you come to see me?"

He kissed her brow, not caring who saw. "You bet. Now go." He helped her with her coat and watched her walk away, chin lifted in the gesture he'd come to expect.

The phone on his desk rang and he picked up, his eyes still on her. "Webster."

"My name is Natalie Clooney. T-the officers l-last night . . . Th-they said to call you."

Noah cupped the phone, dread pooling at her hysterical stutter. "Eve. Tell Abbott to come back." Dropping his hand, he answered the call. "What happened, Miss Clooney?"

"My f-friend. Virginia. She's d-dead."

Noah sank into his chair as Abbott approached grimly, Eve following behind. "How?"

"Sh-she's hanging." Natalie was sobbing. "Her eyes . . . They're gone."

Thursday, February 25, 11:10 a.m.

Noah had tried to mentally prepare himself for what he'd find in Virginia Fox's house, but there was no way he could have. He looked up into her hollow eye sockets and it was all he could do to keep his stomach in check.

"Donner didn't do this," he said hoarsely.

"No, he couldn't have," Abbott said, his voice dull.

"Why not?" The question came from Carleton Pierce, who had just arrived behind Ian Gilles and the ME techs. Carleton stopped dead in his tracks as he entered the room. "Holy God."

Noah stepped back as Micki snapped pictures of the scene. "Donald Donner committed suicide last night. Sometime around eight o'clock."

Carleton did a double take. "He did what?"

"He killed himself, okay?" Noah snarled, then forced himself to calm. "I'm sorry. It's been a bad day. Donner was dying. He shot himself last night."

"I don't even know why I'm bothering to photograph this scene," Micki muttered. "It looks like all the others."

"Except the victim," Noah said. She was dressed like the others. Same dress, same shoes, same makeup. Everything except the eyes. "Virginia was not on Eve's list."

"What? How do you know?" Carleton asked.

"Because Eve just called me. She's sitting at my desk, checking the damn list, and this woman is not on it. And if we don't find him, she could be next."

"She won't be next," Abbott said. "Kane's taking her to a safe house as we speak."

Noah turned to Carleton. "Virginia wasn't on the list, but she was a close friend of Natalie, who's been one of Eve's red-zone cases for weeks. Why did he change now?

Every victim had been on that list. Why choose one who was not?"

"I don't know," Carleton said tersely. "Maybe just to throw us off."

"Well it did." Noah went to the living room where Natalie sat on the sofa, rocking herself, her face dangerously pale. "Miss Clooney, I need to ask you a few questions."

"Of course," Natalie said through bloodless lips.

"You said Miss Fox was a programmer."

"Office assistant, actually, She and I started out at the company together."

"In the same office?"

"No. I got my certifications and was promoted a few years ago. I'm the director of our department. Virginia reports . . . reported to one of my people."

"Did she mention any boyfriends, any new relationships?"

"No. Well, yes, but not in the real world."

"In Shadowland, then."

"Yes. She met this guy at the poker table. Oh God." She started to cry again. "I told her about the warning I got from Captain Abbott. She said that I was just trying to keep her from having a life. Now she's dead." She covered her face and rocked.

"I know this is hard, but stay with me. You two played in Shadowland together?"

Natalie lowered her hands and drew a breath. "She loved to gamble in Vegas, but she lost a lot when the market crashed so she started virtual gambling. It was cheaper."

"You're doing great. Now, how did you come to be part of the Shadowland study?"

"She saw the ad in the paper and said I'd enjoy the game. I asked her if she was going to do the study, but she said she got enough of shrinks in therapy. But it seemed important to her that I play, so I joined."

"I understand you're a pretty good poker player."

"I'd never played before. But I pick things up pretty easily. We played poker together, every night. Last night we had a fight. A terrible fight."

"Tell me what happened."

"I was winning and she seemed happy for me. But a few weeks ago she met this other gamer and she changed."

Eve had mentioned this. "Dasich. He and your friend were thrown out for cheating."

Her eyes widened. "How did you know that?"

"We've been keeping an eye on you, in the virtual world and the real one. But we didn't know about Virginia. What was she afraid of, Miss Clooney?"

"The dark," she said thinly. "Virginia was terrified of the dark."

"Do you know why?"

"Yes. Her family lived in Japan in '95 when they had that big earthquake in Kobe. She was trapped in the dark for three days, dead people all around. Ever since, she couldn't stand the dark. Always kept a light on in every room."

So the sonofabitch takes her eyes. "Thank you. I'll have an officer take you home."

Chapter Twenty-three

Thursday, February 25, 11:10 a.m.

It's that damn list," Eve said, sitting at Noah's desk. Olivia and Kane stood ready to haul her off to the safe house at Abbott's command. *Not yet. I need to think.*

"But the Fox woman isn't on the list," Kane said.

"Exactly. It's to throw us off," Eve said. "He knew we had the list."

"There is no 'we.' " Olivia frowned. "There is us, and there is you. You are not part of this anymore, Eve. You're in too much danger already."

"And I'll continue to be until we catch him. Where is Jeremy Lyons?"

"Still missing," Kane said. "No credit card activity or contact with family and friends."

He could be dead. Or he could be a killer. "You've checked the grad students' alibis. Donner didn't do it, because you've got one more and he was dead when it happened."

Olivia and Kane shared a look. "Eve, you're leaving," Olivia said calmly. She pulled Eve to her feet but Eve yanked her arm away and sat back down.

"Let me think. Virginia wasn't on my list, but she and Natalie were friends. Sit down, Olivia. Please. I need to do this. There is something here." Eve stared at the list on her laptop screen. But the answer wasn't here. She logged back in to Shadowland as Olivia gave in, pulling a chair behind her with a frustrated sigh.

"Abbott's gonna have my ass in a sling," Olivia grumbled.

Eve didn't respond. She was pulling up user accounts.

"What are you doing?" Kane asked standing behind her.

Eve rubbed her forehead. "Don't ask, don't tell. I hacked in, okay?"

"Cool," Kane said, impressed.

"Don't encourage her," Olivia hissed, then sighed. "What are we looking for?"

"I'm not sure. This here is Virginia Fox's account. And this is her poker avatar, Cicely." She pointed to the screen. "Cicely used to sit next to Natalie's avatar at the poker table. But Virginia's got other avatars. This one she bought from Pandora. From me, I mean." Eve's eyes narrowed and her heart started to beat harder. "No way."

"No way what?" Kane demanded, hulking over her shoulder.

Eve clicked on the Pandora avatar. "She changed the face. She changed my code."

"Like the killer did to his victims' avatars," Olivia said.

"Is it like a fingerprint?" Kane asked. "The code change?"

"No. I mean, I use software packages for design like everybody else does, so my code's not unique. But the pattern and placement of the change is the same as what we saw with Martha and Christy's avatars. Either Virginia showed him how to change Pandora's faces or he showed her."

"How can you figure out which?" Kane asked.

Eve went to the messaging area. "You can talk in the World, or you can send private messages, avatar to avatar. So nobody knows your real name or account name."

"Virginia sent messages to somebody?" Olivia asked, leaning forward. "Please?"

"Yeah, she did." Eve clicked through them. "We're lucky she kept them. Here's the message where she sends him the text to cut and paste to make the changes." She looked over her shoulder, met Olivia's eyes. "Three weeks ago."

"When all this started," Olivia said. "Who did she send the message to?"

Eve clicked the message header open and was unsurprised. "What a shock. It went to Dasich. Damn it, I knew something was wrong with that guy. Virginia's Cicely and this Dasich were thrown out of the casino last night for cheating."

"So how do we find a live body for this Dasich avatar?" Olivia asked.

"I access his account," Eve said, already typing.

"How, if you don't know who he is?" Kane asked.

Eve hesitated. "Accessing an account starting with the avatar takes the highest authority. After all, sometimes you want to go where no one knows your name."

"Do you have this authority, Eve?" Olivia asked quietly.

"Yes. I kept upping my privileges until I'm executive level, but I haven't used it yet. I didn't need it before, because I knew the victims' real names from the study, and Virginia actually registered with her real name. When I go backward, from the avatar to the account, I may raise flags at ShadowCo." She turned to look at Olivia again. "I don't want this coming back to hurt Noah or any of you."

"What about you?" Olivia asked.

Eve shrugged. "They could prosecute. Then again, if we save the day, who knows? At a minimum, I'll be a goddess to hairy-palmed hackers everywhere. But it's too late. I already did the search, and . . . we have a winner. The Dasich avatar is owned by the account of Irene Black."

"So Irene Black is a man?" Kane asked.

"Irene Black could be anyone. I told Abbott that nobody uses their real name when they register. That Virginia did is a surprise. I didn't." She opened Irene Black's file. "These are all the avatars this gamer owns, five of them. Looks like he bought all but one from Pandora's shop. See, here is Dasich, the poker player." Eve clicked on each one, then abruptly sagged back in her chair. "Oh my God."

"What?" Olivia leaned closer. "What?"

"That avatar. It's Drink Guy. He trolls Ninth Circle, asking females if he can buy them a drink. He hit on my Greer avatar every time I went through the bar. That's how he hunted."

"All right," Olivia said urgently. "If nobody uses their real name, how do we find him?"

"Follow the money," Kane murmured. "That's what Web was doing, when I went all over town tracing Axel Girard's credit card. Can you access Irene's financial info?"

Eve clicked, then frowned when a scolding message popped up. " 'You do not have access to this information. Account blocked.' " She looked up at Kane, frustrated. "Apparently, there's a super-executive access for credit card info. And I probably just shot a big ole flare to ShadowCo that I'm here." Rapidly she logged out. "If they're any good, they already know where I'm sitting. Dammit."

"We'll deal with the fallout," Olivia said. "We have one

name. Irene Black." She pushed her chair away and pulled Eve to her feet. "Put on your coat. Kane, get her out of here and into that safe house before Abbott gets back and kicks our asses."

Eve buttoned up her coat. "You're not coming?"

"No, I'm going to call Abbott with this, then I'm going to have another go at Dell. I'll visit you, bring you a cake with a file in it," she joked soberly. "This will be over soon."

"I hope. Tell Noah . . ." Eve's cheeks warmed. "Tell him to be careful."

"You bet. Now get out of here. You're safe with Kane. I trust him with my life."

Blinking away her fatigue, Olivia watched them go. Six dead women, two Lincoln Navigators, a lunatic Farmer, and a drug dealer named Damon. And now they'd added one Irene Black to the mix. She'd pulled out her cell to call Abbott when it rang in her hand. It was the DA's office. "Sutherland."

"It's Brian Ramsey. I've got a little good news. I'm authorized to deal with your dealer, Damon. Meet me in Interview in twenty. I hope you find what you're looking for."

"Yeah. Me, too." Olivia set out to meet Ramsey, calling Abbott on her way.

Thursday, February 25, 11:30 a.m.

Eve's mind was still racing as she and Kane went down in the elevator to his car. "All right, so we have Irene Black, but it still comes back to the list. Whoever did these murders had access to that damn list."

"Jeremy Lyons did and he's missing," Kane said.

Eve sighed. "Donner did and he's dead. I guess knowing he was sick puts some of his responses into a different light. He was running out of time."

"He wanted to leave a legacy," Kane said quietly. "Most people do."

"True. I wonder if he really believed we were testing often enough or just convinced himself we were. I tried to tell him that we were affecting people's lives, but without the personality testing scores, he wouldn't believe me."

"I doubt it would have mattered."

She looked up at him as the elevator doors slid open. "What do you mean?"

Kane shrugged. "He was dying. Desperate. Desperate people do unexpected things. It's possible he would have ignored the results even if you'd done the tests."

"No, he couldn't have ignored them. He wouldn't even have seen them. The results went straight from the independent third-party therapist to the committee. It was part of the checks and balances. If personality tests started showing huge swings, as they would have done with the red-zones, the committee would have stopped the study."

"My car's on the right," Kane said as they walked through the parking garage. "So who was this third-party therapist?"

Eve stopped. "I don't know. I wasn't supposed to know, just as I wasn't supposed to know the subjects' real names."

Kane had stopped, too. "Would Donner have known who it was?"

"Yes." She let out a breath. "And what Donner knew, Jeremy knew. He told me so."

"And would that person have had access to the list?"

Eve opened her mouth to reply, then watched in shock as Kane dropped to the cement floor of the garage like a rock. She looked up, stunned.

Between two parked vehicles a man wearing a fedora was sliding a club into his coat pocket. In his other hand he held a gun with a silencer. "I'd say he almost certainly would have access to that list."

She stood, staring into a face she knew. But that she had never quite trusted. Then instinct surged. *Run.* Eve swung her computer bag at his arm, knocking the gun from his hand. His grunt echoed as the gun skittered a few feet away.

She turned and ran as fast as she could. Then stumbled to her knees on a cry of pain when fire bored through her thigh. *Goddammit. He shot me.* She pushed herself to her feet and had gotten a little farther when he came from between two parked cars and dragged her backward. His arm was over her throat, bending her backward, cutting off her air.

Eve grabbed at his arm over her throat, trying to breathe, trying to drag in air to scream. Then she felt a prick on the side of her throat. In seconds her body went limp, her vision blurred. From far away she heard his voice in her ear, distorted and slow.

"Eve. Didn't your parents teach you not to get into cars with strange men?"

Thursday, February 25, 12:10 p.m.

Noah burst into the bullpen, followed by Abbott and Micki. His heart was pounding out of his chest. Eve was gone. "What the fuck happened?"

Kane sat at his desk, an ice bag on his head. Olivia stood at his side, pale, but her eyes were clear and focused.

"Status?" Abbott demanded. He'd barked orders into both his cell and the radio the whole way back from Virginia Fox's house while Noah drove like a bat out of hell.

"Garage is locked down," Olivia said steadily. "BOLO is out, cars all over the city are on alert. I put a watch on the interstates and roadblocks at the major arteries out of town. State patrol is en route with air support."

Abbott's nod was tense. "Good work." He gave Kane a visual once-over. "You didn't see him?"

Kane shook his head miserably. "No."

"What happened?" Noah bit out.

Kane looked up, pain in his eyes. "One minute we were talking, the next I was waking up."

Olivia sat next to him. "Kane came to about seven minutes later and called it in. I looked at the security video right away. Somebody came up behind him and hit him with a club. Eve slung that computer bag of hers at him and ran. She knocked the gun away, but he got it back." She hesitated and Noah's heart stopped.

"What? What happened?"

"He shot her in the thigh, then dragged her away." Her hands were shaking. "A different camera showed him put her in a black BMW, plate registered to Donner."

Noah wouldn't think about what he'd just seen, the grotesque butchering of Virginia Fox's eyes. He wouldn't think about what a killer was doing to Eve, right this minute.

Except it was all he could think about. *Don't hurt her. Just don't hurt her.* But he would hurt her. He would kill her. *Stop it. Be a cop, for God's sake.* Noah clamped his fingers into his head and made himself look up. "How badly was she bleeding?"

"Not gushing," Olivia said, "so it's unlikely he hit anything vital."

He hit something vital. He hit Eve.

"I'm sorry, Web," Kane said hoarsely.

"Not your fault." Numb, Noah sank into a chair. "What did he look like? He was on the camera, for God's sake."

Olivia shook her head. "Not when he was hitting Kane. He came up between a minivan and an SUV. All you can see is Kane dropping. Once he'd shot Eve, he kept between the cars and when he dragged her he was bending over. He's on the short side. I'm guessing he's five-eight. He was wearing a beige overcoat with the collar up and a black fedora so you couldn't see his face. I already asked for the video to be sent up, so we can look at it again. I put everything we have in the BOLO. Everyone is searching."

"How did he get out of the garage? How did he pay?" Noah asked desperately.

"He was there less than thirty minutes," Olivia said wearily. "He put his ticket in the slot and the arm went up. No charge. God, Noah, I'm sorry."

"Then he'd parked here before. He knew if he was there less than thirty minutes that he'd be able to exit without needing a credit card or going through the attendant booth."

"I thought of that. Right now security is checking the tapes for that BMW on other days that it might have parked here."

"And I put a team in the garage," Micki added, "in case he left something behind when he struggled with Eve."

He nodded numbly. "Dell. He knows something. We need to make him talk."

"We tried all night," Olivia said harshly. "He won't talk."

Let me talk to him, Noah thought viciously. *He'll talk to me.*

"Don't even ask," Abbott warned.

Noah looked away. *Think.* "What did we find on Dell? In his vehicle?"

"The GPS tracking screen," Olivia said. "Kurt Buckland's cell phone and a couple of untraceable cell phones. A copy of *MSP*. Newspaper articles about you and Jack going way back. All your cases. Transcripts of times you'd testified in court."

"Lots of pictures," Micki added. "Going back months. We found cameras in both Dell's and Harvey's cars, so they were both surveilling."

"Let me see the pictures," Noah said, his voice flat.

"Noah, just go home," Abbott said. "We've got eyes all over the city searching for his car. Everyone understands the urgency. We will find him."

"Let me see the fucking pictures," Noah repeated, hostilely, and Abbott shrugged.

"Fine, let's see them. Faye," he called, "get the head of security up here with a copy of the tapes. I want to review them myself."

As a group they moved to Abbott's office and Micki dumped a stack of photographs on Abbott's round table. "I don't know what you're looking for, Web," she said.

"Neither do I. Where are the cameras?"

"In the evidence room," Micki said. "I'll get them." She left as Olivia's cell rang.

Olivia grimaced at the ID. "Ramsey's waiting for me in Interview with Damon."

"Go," Abbott said. "Good luck."

Noah didn't look up when she left. He was sorting photos with single-minded focus. There was something here. *There has to be.*

Thursday, February 25, 12:10 p.m.

Didn't your parents . . . Eve couldn't breathe. She could only stare up into Winters's face as he grabbed the twine and pulled. *Can't breathe. Going to die. Again. Didn't your parents— No. I won't go there again.*

She opened her eyes with a hard jerk and found herself looking into the amused face of Dr. Carleton Pierce. He smiled at her, patting her face mildly. She tried to bite him but when her head turned it moved slowly, as if through molasses.

"What did you give me?" she asked him, her words slurred.

"Ketamine. Don't worry, it'll wear off. And it's not addictive, although that doesn't really matter. You wouldn't be living long enough to care if it were."

"Noah . . . will find you."

Pierce laughed out loud. "No, he won't, my dear, but you go on thinking that if it makes you feel better. How's your leg?"

"Shot," she said, her teeth clenched. She was lying on the backseat of his car and her thigh burned where his bullet had pierced her flesh.

"Well, I've bandaged you up," he said, mockingly benign. "Don't want you to bleed out. I'm not done with you. In fact, I haven't even started." He smiled and Eve tasted true fear. She'd seen that smile before, on Winters's face . . . *before he killed me.*

"Very good," he said. "I can see the fear in your eyes. Did you like my message?"

Pain mixed with fear to back the breath up in her lungs. "I thought it was Dell."

"And it suited me for you to think so. But now, I find I want the credit." He reached in his pocket and pulled out another syringe and she twisted hard to roll, move, anything to get away. But his knee clamped over her thighs. "It'll hurt less if you don't fight me." He plunged the needle into her neck. "That will hold you until I get you where we're going. Listen, Eve." He put a microrecorder near her ear and clicked a button.

And once again Eve heard Winters's voice. "I stabbed her, eight times. She tried to claw at me. Feisty little thing she was. So I slashed her hand, then her face."

"Why her face?" another man asked. "I mean, you'd already all but killed her."

"Because she thought she was pretty. Because I wanted to. Because I could."

She was fading fast, faster than before. She blinked hard, and clicking off the recorder, Pierce leaned close. "I'll kill you," he whispered, "because I can. Because I wish it. Because it will give me pleasure. But it won't be quick. You'll wish you were dead, but I won't make it as easy as Winters did. Don't worry, Eve. You'll see."

He stepped back, drawing sweet cold air through his nostrils. This was going to be so good. He'd been in a constant state of arousal since he'd forced Eve to the back of his wife's car. The knowledge he'd been carrying his wife and Liza in the trunk all this time . . . This was going to be so good.

He wouldn't limit himself to killing her only once. Eve

had died twice before. *I'll let her relive that, moment by moment, again and again.* He had visions of his hands around her throat, taking her almost to death. Then letting her come back. And letting himself go. Again and again. It was going to be an amazing experience.

He slid from the backseat and looked both ways. No one was coming. He'd pulled to a side road, well outside the city limits, a smart move given the chatter on his police scanner. They were searching the city and the highways, but they'd never look for him way out here. Still, he needed to hurry. He was only another twenty minutes from his place.

He prepared another syringe to administer to Eve just before he took her into the house. She was tall, and stronger than she looked. She'd nearly gotten away, back in the garage. *Bitch.* He rolled his shoulder gingerly. That computer bag of hers had been as hard as a brick. That's why he always went for the petite types. They took far less effort to subdue, leaving him more energy for the main event. He didn't want to fight with Eve again until he had her tied to the narrow bed in his basement. But when he was ready . . . He liked it when they fought on his terms. It made it so much better. Eve was going to be the kill of his life.

He went around to the trunk to check on his other passengers. His wife was still quiet. Being dead did help that. And Liza was still in a stupor. She wouldn't give him much trouble. She'd been bordering on catatonic since she'd realized she was riding with a dead woman. She probably still thought it was her sister. That made him smile.

"You shouldn't have come looking for your sister," he murmured. "And she shouldn't have been a hooker. But she was, and you did, and now you're mine."

He closed the trunk and headed for his place. Arranging the details to explain his wife's upcoming extended absence had taken most of the morning. It was only sheer luck that he'd been back to his car in time to hear police scanner chatter about the discovery of another homicide. He couldn't let the opportunity to watch Webster's horror at his final "Red Dress Kill" pass by unenjoyed. And it was good that he had not. Good to know Donner was dead before he set him up any further.

Of course the best thing to come out of his visit to Virginia's this morning was the news that Eve was going to a safe house. Once she'd been so ensconced, it would have been nearly impossible to get to her without arousing suspicion.

Taking her in the police garage had been a necessary risk. And, he had to admit, an awesome thrill. But even better thrills were to come.

Thursday, February 25, 12:45 p.m.

Noah put his head in his hands. Eyes all over the city and no one had seen anything. She'd been gone an hour. Time enough for whoever took her to be miles away. "Where's Pierce? We need a better profile."

"I'll call him," Abbott said and Noah began searching each pile of photos again as Micki returned with two cameras, both with a long-range zoom.

"Here it is," she said. "And I think I found out what he meant by 'he almost got you.'"

She showed Noah the view screen, pointing at the shadowy interior of, surprise, a black SUV. "Whoever that is had a gun trained on you and Eve."

"Thanks," he murmured.

"Farmer's got pictures here of you in front of Jack's house last night," she went on, "but most of the rest of what's on this memory card he's already printed out."

"So we keep looking," he said, and started searching again. Everyone at the table picked up a stack, even though none of them knew what they were looking for.

Abbott rejoined them. "I left Carleton a message. Give me those pictures, Noah. You've looked through them twice already. Look at something different."

Noah handed him the photos from Martha Brisbane's and picked up a new stack. They were from Christy Lewis's house. Monday night. He put the pictures in sequential order, trying to remember what had happened that night three days before.

They'd arrived first, he and Jack. There was a picture of him taking Eve out the back of the patrol car and the officers uncuffing her. He'd put her in his own car and then the rest of the team had arrived in waves—Ian, Micki, and Carleton.

That was the night Jack was afraid of the snake. Noah saw the picture of Jack leaving the house, getting in the car with Eve. Then Ian left, he remembered, followed by Carleton. Noah frowned, not knowing how to order some of the pictures. He squinted at one, unsure of even what or who it was.

"This is Eve's car parked in front of Christy's," he said. "But who is this?" He angled the picture toward the light. It was a man, hunched over near the hubcap.

"That's Carleton," Micki said. "I'd recognize those Bruno Maglis anywhere."

"Is it always the shoes, Micki?" Abbott asked, exasperated.

"Christy's shoes might be important," she insisted stubbornly, "no matter what *Dr. Pierce* said. Noah, are you okay?"

Noah had brought the picture to an inch from his eyes, still squinting. "Is this still on the memory card of Farmer's camera?"

"Yes." She began scrolling back through the pictures Farmer had taken. "Why?"

Noah could feel each beat of his heart. "Just enlarge it. I want to see his hand."

Noah took the camera, willing his hands not to shake. "He has a ring like mine."

"So?" Abbott said. "He showed us his ring yesterday."

"Those are Eve's keys in his hand. Somebody stole Eve's keys that night."

Abbott frowned. "You can't be serious, Noah."

"Eve dropped her keys. Micki, you said CSU combed the area and didn't find them."

Abbott still shook his head. "Assuming those are her keys, just because he took them doesn't mean anything."

"They're hers," Noah said stubbornly. "When we were searching for her keys, she said she had a police whistle on her key ring, and there it is. Somebody broke into her apartment that night while she was here, with us, but there was no sign of forced entry, because he used her keys. Later that night I changed her lock, and a few hours later that person came back. We assumed it was Buckland."

"You mean Dell," Abbott corrected.

"*Whatever.* Listen to me. When I got to the Bolyards' last night, my first thought was how did someone know to kill them? Could it have been one of us?"

"That's absurd. Bolyard confronted Don . . ." Abbott's voice trailed. "He never talked to Donner. Donner was being set up. Whoever made that call to the TV news, lied."

"Exactly. Bolyard might have told someone else, but the only person that would benefit from their murder was the one he'd seen in the coffee house. It wasn't Donner. Also, Pierce was at Christy's scene Monday night because he was here when I got Eve's call. He was at Virginia Fox's this morning, but he wasn't here when Natalie called. How did he know to come to Virginia's house? Did you call him, Bruce?"

Abbott slowly shook his head. "I thought you did."

Micki and Kane were shaking their heads as well. "Liv didn't," Kane said. "We were together until I . . ." He swallowed. "Until I took Eve to the garage."

Noah nodded grimly. "So none of us called him and Virginia's name wasn't on the list. But he knew we'd go there. Sonofabitch wanted to watch us."

"I can't believe this," Abbott said. "It is too incredible. I've known Carleton Pierce for years. Years."

Noah leaned in close. "Think about it, Bruce. He was there at Virginia's when you said Kane was taking Eve to the safe house. Then he was gone. Twenty minutes later, Eve is gone."

Abbott pursed his lips. "He was more upset about Donner's suicide than Virginia Fox's murder. He set Donner up, but didn't know he'd killed himself."

Kane went still. "Right before he hit me, Eve and I were talking about her study. She said Donner had appointed an independent third-party counselor in case anyone in the study became unstable or suicidal. She didn't know who that was. I'd just asked her if that person would have access to the subject list."

Abbott's jaw twitched. "Donner knew. Who else would know?"

"Jeremy Lyons," Noah said. "But he's missing. Where is he? Did we get his LUDs?"

Abbott riffled through the papers on his desk. "Yeah. Faye gave them to me before my meeting with the brass, but we rushed to Donner's." He handed the papers to Noah.

"These are home LUDs," Noah said. "We asked for Jeremy's cell, too."

"Cover letter says no cells in his or his wife's name," Abbott said.

"They had pay-as-you-go phones," Kane said. "Mrs. Lyons said they were counting pennies."

Noah scanned their home LUDs and a number jumped out. "This is the same number that called Eve's cell—twice. One was a text, the other a voicemail."

"That number called the Lyonses' home phone at least once a day up until Monday, right at 5:00 p.m.," Abbott said, looking over Noah's shoulder.

"When Lyons picked up his kid from day care," Kane said. "That's Jeremy's cell."

"What text and voicemail did he leave for Eve?" Micki asked.

"Rob Winters's last words," Noah murmured. "Eve's worst fear. We thought it was Dell Farmer, but it was Jeremy Lyons."

"It was Jeremy Lyons's *phone*," Kane corrected.

Noah looked at Kane. "You think Jeremy's dead."

Kane looked miserable, but he nodded. "He was a weasel to Eve, but everyone swore he loved his kid. He never picked her up on Tuesday and never called home."

Noah stood up. "I'm going to his house. Pierce's house."

"And then what?" Abbott said. "A shoe next to Eve's keys isn't enough for a warrant."

"I don't care." Noah grabbed his hat, but Abbott grabbed his arm.

"Sit down, Noah." His voice was like a whip. "We're not going to run off half-cocked. We're going to call Ramsey, see what we need to get a warrant. In the meantime, Kane and Micki, go to Marshall, serve the warrant on Donner's office, see if he mentions Pierce anywhere. A known association would get us a warrant for Pierce's house and office. See if anybody saw Pierce with Donner. Take his picture in a six-pack of mugs."

"I'm not going to just sit here," Noah said. His voice trembled and he didn't care.

"Yeah, you are. But we'll call Donner's wife. See if he had a calendar or diary. We'll ask if she's seen Pierce with him. We'll follow the law. Mick, you drive. Kane still looks a little dazed. Call me when you find anything, even if it's nothing. Go."

Thursday, February 25, 1:05 p.m.

"That was good work," Brian Ramsey said as the officer led a grumbling Damon to a cell. "I didn't have to deal as low as he wanted and you got what you needed."

Olivia looked at the license plate number Damon had provided. "I hope it's legit."

"Well-heeled gentlemen venturing to the wrong side of the tracks for tricks make good blackmail victims. Nobody wants their wives to know they've been trolling."

"Thanks, Brian. I'm going to call this in, see who it belongs to."

He put his briefcase back down. "Have to say I'm

curious." Then he rolled his eyes when his own cell rang. "I miss the days of bad reception."

Olivia moved to one side of the room to give him privacy. "Hey, Faye, I've got a Wisconsin plate for you to run."

"You need to get back here, girl," Faye said. "It's a zoo."

Olivia straightened, her already queasy gut churning. "Why? Is it Jack? Eve?"

"No. No news there. They looked through those pictures and think it's Dr. Pierce."

Olivia sank back against the corner of the steel table. "What?"

"You heard me. Carleton Pierce. So give me the plate. I'll run it."

Stunned, Olivia did and felt the table shudder when Ramsey sat on his corner. She turned to find him looking at her, looking as poleaxed as she felt.

"It's Abbott," Ramsey said. "He wants us both in his office."

Keeping her phone to her ear, Olivia made her feet move and was in the hall when Faye came back. "Got a name for you. Black, Irene, age sixty-two. The address is a PO box, Eau Claire, Wisconsin. Mean anything to you?"

"Yeah. It does." *Irene Black got around.* "Give the info to Abbott. We're coming."

Ramsey glanced at her as they jogged to the exit. "Who does the SUV belong to?"

"Our Shadowland hunter."

"So now we have an address?" he said, but she shook her head.

"A PO box. He's done this before. It's a shell game. I'll meet you at Abbott's."

She was three steps from her car when her cell rang again. "Sutherland."

"It's Tom Hunter."

He didn't know about Eve. Neither did David. Dammit. "Not a good time, Tom."

"Wait. I tried to call Liza, but she's not answering her phone. I got worried and called the school, but she never showed up today."

Olivia rested her pounding forehead against her car. "I'll send a car to her address."

"I'm here now. Olivia, she's gone and her neighbor says her mom died last year. She was living all alone with her sister." She heard him suck in a panicked breath. "I knocked on every door in her building, showed a picture I took from her apartment. One old lady said she saw her getting into a car with a man. She said Liza looked sick."

Olivia felt sick. "What kind of car?"

"Black BMW."

Bile burned and Olivia swallowed it back. "Meet me at my office. Don't ask questions. Just get in your car and meet me as fast as you can."

"You know something. What? What do you know?"

"Tom, you need to stay calm. I need you calm. Eve's gone."

He sucked in another breath. "Does David know?"

"Not yet. Meet me at my office. Now."

Thursday, February 25, 1:20 p.m.

Eve shuddered out a breath. It had been harder the second time, waking up. The images had been more intense, Winters's voice more real. *Because I wanted to. Because I could.* She'd been helpless, unable to move, unable to scream.

Just like that night five years, eleven months, and

eleven days ago, she thought and with sudden clarity realized she'd never screamed. Not once when Winters was killing her.

I never screamed for help. I lay there and let him do that to me. Today, in the parking garage, she'd run, but she hadn't screamed for help. *If I'd screamed . . .*

Awareness was returning slowly, the fog clearing from her mind.

Back then, it wouldn't have mattered. Back then, Dana's Chicago apartment had been in such a bad part of town that nobody would have helped her. But today . . . *Dammit. I was in a police parking garage and I never made a sound.*

And none of that mattered right now. Her breathing had quieted from harsh pants to slow drags of air. The air was cold and dry. It stung her nose, burned her throat. Her mouth was like cotton. She smelled sweat. Vomit.

I'm cold. She let out a breath, struggling for calm when panic speared. *I'm naked.* Her wrists were tied behind her head. Her ankles were tied, together and to the bed.

She kept her eyes closed, afraid of what she'd see.

Next to her she heard the sound of metal clashing. Scraping. Swishing. She'd heard that sound before. Panic became a live thing when she realized from where.

He was there. Sharpening a knife.

"I really like your tattoos," he said companionably. "It's like a paint-by-numbers set."

She kept her eyes closed. *Why?* she wanted to scream, but he'd already told her that. *Because he wished it. Because it gave him pleasure.* He knew her worst fear and was using it. He knew how. He studied the mind, behavior, phobia.

"You used their worst fears against them," she said, her

voice cracking from the dry air. "Martha and Christy and the others. Why? Did it make it more *fun*?"

"It did. And knowing yours will be even better."

She flinched when he came close. She felt his heat, then smelled the metal of his knife beneath her nose. "Open your eyes, Eve, or I'll open them for you."

She remembered Christy Lewis's eyes, glued open. Eve forced her eyes to open, holding her cringe inside. His face was inches from hers, his eyes bright with anticipation. He brandished the knife in front of her eyes, then trailed the tip down her face, over her old scar. She couldn't feel it, but she wouldn't tell him that.

"It's like a road map," he said, amused. "I just have to stay on the lines. Or maybe I'll make a few new ones."

She fought for something to say. Something to throw him off-balance. Anything to buy her time. Noah and Olivia were searching. She just had to give them time.

"I know who you are."

"I should hope so. I did give you my card." He smiled at this.

"No, I know who you are in the World. How many times did you beg women to buy them a drink? How many times were you rejected?"

He looked bored. "Avatars, Eve. It's all in the appearance."

"Not entirely. There is substance and there is style. You had no style. *Dasich*."

His eyes flickered and she could see she'd surprised him, but he recovered quickly. "So I played a little poker. *Greer*."

He took a step back and she had to control another cringe. She was naked. So was he. But he never sexually assaulted his victims. Noah had said so. But Pierce was erect. Aroused. Why had he not raped them?

"You never assaulted your victims," she said levelly and he paused, studying her.

"No, not sexually," he agreed. "Not *those* victims." He smiled again. "But they were special. A project, if you will."

Eve swallowed, forcing herself not to stare at his groin or his knife. She would not give him power over her fear. Instead she focused on his eyes. "You left those women hanging in their homes. Why did you bring me here? Wherever here is."

"Like I said. The six were special. The rest were not. Dregs of society nobody cared about. I brought them here and here they died." He grabbed her hair, forced her head off the bed, forced her to look at the wall. "Look," he mocked, "and *try* not to be afraid."

The strangled sound she heard came from her own throat as she stared.

Shoes. The wall was lined with shelves and the shelves were lined with shoes. Her breath was coming hard again and all she could hear was the pounding of her pulse in her ears. He leaned close and tilted her head higher. "See anything familiar?"

My boots. He had them arranged side by side, the calf folded over at the end of the top row. She sucked in a breath that made her cough. He grabbed a water bottle, held her nose until her mouth opened, and forced her to drink. "Normally I don't give my guests refreshment. But I think you'll be here for a while."

He set the bottle and the knife aside and hoisted himself on the bed, straddling her. He leaned in close and put his hands around her throat. She realized then that he'd taken off her choker and her throat was totally exposed.

"I've always wondered," he crooned. "What was it like to die?"

His hands had not tightened. *He's playing with me.* Like he played with Noah and the Hat Squad. *Hat Squad.* The *MSP* article had filled Dell Farmer with rage. Pierce's first victim had gone missing at the same time. It made sense.

"What was it like when the cops got all that attention in *MSP*?" she asked. Contempt. He needed to hear contempt. "They collect men's hats." She lifted one brow. "You collect women's shoes. Tough guy you are. Where did you get the hat you wore today? eBay? Because you didn't earn it."

She grunted when he hit her with his fist. She tasted blood and felt satisfaction.

Astride her, his chest rose and fell with his angry breaths, but he calmed himself quickly. A quick glance showed much of his sexual prowess had also calmed.

"You think you're smart," he said, sliding his hands around her throat again.

"I'm just a grad student. You're the professional. You're the shrink." She made herself smile, with pity. "And you just did."

Her head swung hard to one side as he hit her again, then his hands took her throat and tightened. She couldn't breathe. White lights danced in front of her eyes. *Can't breathe.*

His face loomed close, his eyes dark with fury. "You are nothing. I say if you live or die. I hold the power here. You are nothing."

She held still until the panic overruled and she bucked,

trying to throw him off. The pressure on her windpipe increased and the fringes of her vision went dark. It all went dark, and then abruptly he let go.

She gasped, dragging in air.

He sat back, his jaw cocked, his eyes hard. "You are tied to a bed in a place where no one can find you," he said flatly. "You are mine. I will have your respect." He leaned close, his thumbs on her windpipe. "Even if I have to kill you to get it."

Glad he'd made her drink, Eve found moisture in her mouth and spat in his face. His eyes flashed rage and he raised his fist. Then he lowered it and lifted his brows.

"Unwise, Miss Wilson. I hold the power here and I know how to wear you down. I will enjoy wearing you down." He climbed off her and went to the wooden staircase where he'd hung his trousers. From one of the pockets he drew a syringe and she stiffened. He smiled. "What shall I whisper in your ear this time?"

She didn't care, because every time he sedated her was time he wasn't strangling her and time Noah could spend finding her. Still, she didn't want to look too grateful.

"Please, don't." She shrank back. "Don't drug me again." *Do it. Do it.*

He leaned in, jabbed the needle in her neck. "When you wake, I'll be carving your face like a Halloween jack-o'-lantern. No one will ever look at you again."

She thought of Martha and Christy as the room began to blur. And Virginia. He'd do it, she knew. And he'd enjoy it. *Hurry, Noah. Please.*

Disgusted, he grabbed the knife from the table and turned to the stairs, stopping when he saw a slight movement from the huddled form in the corner. He crossed the room and backhanded her, taking pleasure in the whimper she emitted.

"You're next." Then he grabbed his pants from the newel post and went upstairs, slamming the door behind him. Broodingly, he sat in his kitchen and looked out the window at the woods surrounding his place. *I underestimated her. I let her unnerve me.*

She would pay. He pulled his laptop closer, searched, and found a photo a Chicago tabloid had printed after Winters had carved her up. He printed it out and slapped it on the table. He was a man of his word. When he was finished, she'd look like that again.

Immensely cheered, he made himself a sandwich and sat down to watch the news. It was all about Virginia Fox and the Red Dress Killer. There would be a press conference later. He'd have to make sure he tuned in.

For now, he needed to regroup, clear his mind. Out of habit, he started to log in to Shadowland, then stopped. She knew he was Dasich. That meant Webster probably knew, too. They might be watching.

No matter. He'd create a new account, a new profile. It was, after all, the place you went when you wanted no one to know your name. He'd buy a new avatar, go back to the casino, and start anew. He liked the poker table, always had. He'd made a lot of money in back-room poker games over the years, enough to retire young. With his wife gone, he didn't have to share. Now, what to call his new Shadowland persona?

He thought of the woman in his basement. *Iblis*, he typed, and smiled. He was certain a woman who named her guardian avatar "Greer" would recognize an ancient form of Lucifer. *And just as Lucifer crushed his Eve, I'll crush mine.* As he'd crushed every woman he'd thrown into his pit or hung from a rope.

He thought of Irene, hanging from the tree branch, so long ago. He would have preferred she'd gone undiscovered for days, weeks, however long it took for the vultures to pick her bones clean. Unfortunately John had come home unexpectedly and found her hanging. Like the good son, John had called the sheriff. John had known he'd killed her. But his brother had said nothing. *Because he hated her as much as I did.*

But that was done. If nothing else, Irene had done him a service. She'd shown him how mind-clearing a good killing could be. And she'd taught him to play poker. So now he'd return to Shadowland and play, just for a few minutes. Just to clear his mind. And then he'd go back down there and . . . *take what's mine.*

Chapter Twenty-four

Thursday, February 25, 1:20 p.m.

So what do you have?" Brian Ramsey asked, setting his briefcase on Abbott's table.

Abbott had been waiting for them at the table. A very pale Noah sat off to the side, watching the security video from the parking garage on a small TV. He was hunched over, his face inches from the screen, a remote clutched in one hand.

Olivia flinched at the image of Kane dropping to the concrete and Eve's stunned face. She'd watched that clip ten times, her gut roiling each time Eve was shot, injected, then dragged away. She couldn't imagine what Noah was going through, but on some level he appeared to be holding up.

"Not much," Abbott said grimly. "We're hoping you can be creative. One photo of a shoe next to Eve's keys. It's Pierce's shoe." He slid the picture across the table to Ramsey. "Someone broke into her house with her keys that night, then returned later."

Ramsey shook his head. "It could be anybody's shoe. What else?"

"Two," Abbott said, "we have a photo from the parking garage security camera."

"Can't see his face," Ramsey remarked blandly. "Or his shoes. Or his height. Next?"

Abbott looked frustrated. Noah hadn't said a word, his gaze fixed to the small TV. Olivia wanted to gently pull him away, to take the remote from his hand, but she understood the value of *doing* something.

"Three," Abbott said, "we have pages from Donner's datebook. His wife found it with his things. She scanned it into her computer and sent it as an email attachment. Shows six meetings with a C.P. One was for last night, but Donner was already dead by then. Mrs. Donner said her husband was seeing a counselor as part of his cancer treatment. She said she knew he knew Pierce, but thought it was only socially."

"Now we're getting somewhere," Ramsey said. "Where is this datebook now?"

"Locals got it from Mrs. Donner," Abbott replied. "She's grieving, but cooperative."

"So we're good on chain of evidence. What else?"

"The black BMW," Abbott continued. "One's registered to Mrs. Pierce. The plates the garage camera caught were Donner's, but Donner's plates are on his car, in his mother's driveway."

"The BMW plates are duplicates," Ramsey said. "Okay, keep going."

"I don't have any more," Abbott gritted out. "Isn't that enough?"

"I have more," Olivia said. "A black BMW was used to abduct Liza Barkley this morning." She explained her phone call with Tom. "Liza's sister, Lindsay, was last seen getting into a black SUV, registered to Irene Black."

Ramsey lifted his brows. "So you said before. Who is Irene Black?"

Olivia looked at Abbott, who shrugged. "Tell him," he said.

Glancing at Noah from the corner of her eye, Olivia did. "Eve found the account the killer used in the game, by following messages sent by Virginia. The name on the account is Irene Black. She couldn't get an address or financials because she didn't have the access and the program booted her out."

Ramsey closed his eyes. "Eve hacked in, didn't she?"

Noah's shoulders stiffened, the only indication he was still listening. He'd rewound the video to the beginning and was watching it again. *Torturing himself*, Olivia thought.

"Yes," Olivia said to Ramsey, flatly. "When we find her alive you can arrest her."

"But you got an address," Abbott said.

"A PO box in Wisconsin, from the license plate of an SUV that abducted a missing hooker," Olivia said tautly. "That should expand the good doctor's psych profile."

Ramsey looked pained. "It's not enough. Basically you have Donner's datebook and Pierce's wife's black Beemer. Everything else is fruit of a poisoned search."

"The plate from Damon isn't," Olivia insisted.

"But it only connects to Pierce because of what Eve found in the game," Ramsey said, frustrated himself. "I wish I could help you, but I can't. Even if I wrote a warrant based on that information, no judge would sign it." He rose, sliding the photos back across the table. "Call me when you have more."

Olivia watched him go, her heart in her throat. "Dammit."

"Get him back." The growl came from Noah, whose face was an inch from the TV screen, his body vibrating like a plucked string. "Now. Get Ramsey back *now*."

Ramsey waited for the elevator, looking miserable. "Brian," Olivia called. "Come quick."

They ran back to find Abbott squinting at the TV screen. Noah had frozen the video to a single frame. Eve was being dragged by a bent-over figure in a tan overcoat. The coat's lapels were turned up and his fedora was pulled low, hiding his face. The frame was frozen with the man's gloved hand on the handle of the back door of a black BMW.

"Look at the window," Noah said urgently, enlarging the picture.

"Stop. Freeze it," Ramsey commanded. Because there, reflected in the window glass for one frame only, was the face of Carleton Pierce.

Noah looked over his shoulders, his eyes blank. "Is this enough?"

"More than enough," Ramsey said. "Get moving. I'll call you when the warrant is signed."

Abbott was already putting on his coat. "Liv, you're with me. Noah, you stay here."

Noah rose. "No. I'm coming. I'll follow orders once there, but I'm not staying here."

Abbott took a second to assess, then nodded. "All right. One false move and I'll have you removed. Clear? Olivia, have Kane track the Wisconsin PO box for Irene Black, then you and Micki meet us at Pierce's. Thanks, Brian."

"I'll follow you in a few," Olivia said. "I'm expecting Tom Hunter any minute. I need to get Liza Barkley's description out on the wire."

*   *   *

Thursday, February 25, 1:50 p.m.

"We have a warrant," Abbott said as he and Noah got out of the car in front of Pierce's very expensive home. Micki was already waiting with the CSU team.

"He's not here," Micki said, and although Noah had expected it, his heart sank. "A neighbor saw Pierce leave this morning driving his wife's car, a black BMW. It's not here, either, just Pierce's Mercedes."

"Noah, you take the upstairs," Abbott said, "I'll take the main floor and Micki, you have the basement. Let's go in."

Pierce's house was as quiet as a tomb. Abbott announced them loudly, while Noah ran upstairs, heart in his throat, despite the certainty that Eve wasn't here. *She was still alive.* He had to believe that, or he'd lose his mind.

He searched two empty bedrooms before he found the master. The bed was tidily made and nothing seemed out of place. But he could smell bleach. He moved to the master bath and gasped a breath. The odor was so strong here, his eyes watered.

Not Eve. He would not let it be Eve. He stepped back, touching nothing, and went downstairs to find Micki. She was in the kitchen, opening cabinets.

"Basement was clear. Nothing but spider webs. These cabinets are arranged by type, each box and can alphabetized. Textbook obsessive personality our good doctor has," she said, then held up a can of cat food. "I haven't seen a cat. Have you?"

To *hell* with the *cat.* His heart clambered up into his throat. "No, but somebody used extra-concentrated bleach in the master bathroom."

She grimaced. "Oh, hell. I'll get up there in a second."

She opened the trash can and dug a minute, coming up with an opened cat food can in one hand and something shiny in another. "Look."

Noah was losing patience. "I don't care about the damn cat," he ground out.

"Look," she repeated, more forcefully. "This collar has Martha's cat's name on it."

He took the collar and held it up to the light. "Ringo."

"I saw some old vet records in the trash Olivia and Kane cleared out of the empty apartment next to Martha's. Pierce took her cat."

"So he's an animal lover," he snarled. "Damn it, Micki, it doesn't help us find Eve."

"You're thinking like a man, Noah. Think like a cop or get out. It's all important. Like the cat hair Pierce tried to dismiss this morning. Think."

"You're right." He tried to think. "He dismissed Christy's missing shoes, too."

"Called them souvenirs," she said. "Said shoes weren't special enough. I'd say a cat would make one hell of a special souvenir. Sonofabitch was mocking us. We'll treat the master bath with Luminol, see what he was trying to hide with the bleach. We'll also see if we can link it to the bleach he used at Rachel's."

"Because it's all important," Noah murmured. "You're right. I'm sorry."

"It's okay. Go find Abbott. He'll keep you focused."

Abbott sat in Pierce's study, behind his desk. Noah steeled himself to say the words that were choking him. "I think he killed someone in the master bath. It reeks of bleach."

Abbott considered. "I don't think he brought Eve here,

Web. Neighbors said he left with the Beemer, and it's not here. I don't think he's been back."

Noah let the breath he held slide out. "Thank you. I needed to hear that."

"It's okay. I don't think I'd be holding up so well in your shoes. I'm not finding anything incriminating here in his desk, just a lot of old tax files."

Noah pushed at the stack of papers. "He's got copies of his wife's W-2s, so we know where she works. She's not here and he took her car this morning."

"And the bathroom reeks of bleach," Abbott said grimly. "I'll call her employer. You keep looking for something we can use."

Noah took a walk around the office, looking for anything out of place, finding it in a door wallpapered so skillfully that its outline nearly disappeared into the wall. For a moment hope soared. *A secret room. Eve.* But the door opened easily and the disappointment tasted bitter on his tongue.

Behind the door there was a walk-in closet. *Think like a cop.* He dropped his eyes to the carpet. There was a deep groove in the carpet a fraction of an inch from the edge of a filing cabinet, as if it had recently been moved.

Noah hefted it to one side, surprised when it moved easily. Behind it in the wall was a small safe. "Now we're in business," he murmured. He re-entered the office just as Abbott was hanging up.

"Pierce's wife didn't show up for work this morning," Abbott said.

"If he did kill her," Noah said, "why now? According to those tax returns they've been married for twenty years."

"I don't know, but this is interesting. She's a biologist at an animal research lab. And guess what species they keep there? Timber rattlers."

Christy Lewis. "Pierce's wife helped him get the snake, or he got in with her key."

"Her boss doesn't think she'd remove an animal from the lab. He says she's very dedicated. He's checking key card access. The lab is checking their snake 'inventory' now." Abbott shuddered involuntarily. "God."

Noah thought of Jack and how terrified he'd been. "Pierce must have laughed at Jack for being so afraid," he said bitterly. "I found a safe back here. Let's get it blown."

Thursday, February 25, 1:50 p.m.

"Where is she? Goddammit, Olivia, where is Eve?"

Olivia looked up to see three men rushing toward her desk. Two were tall, dark, one with a cane and one with his arm in a sling. The other was lanky, blond, and old beyond his twenty years. The Hunter men had arrived. David, his older brother Max, and Tom, who looked as if he'd been crying. David had let the question fly across the bullpen and two detectives had already grabbed him and were trying to hold him back.

"It's okay," she called to the detectives. "Let him go." Olivia hung her head for a minute, digging deep for the energy to do her job and be the friend they'd need. She rose and met each man's eyes in turn. "We don't know where she is, but we know who took her. Come on, I'll tell you what I can."

She led them to the same small room she and Eve had used when talking to the real Kurt Buckland's boss at the

Mirror only the day before. "Sit, please. I don't have the energy to keep looking up at the three of you." It wasn't a quip, wasn't a joke. It was the weary truth, and the men sat, Max between them.

"We want to know what's going on," Max said with quiet authority. The older brother and Tom's stepfather, he'd clearly taken charge. "Now."

"Of course. How's your arm and head?" she asked David, taking charge back.

"Fractured and pounding," he said between his teeth. "You know my brother Max."

She met Max's steel-gray eyes, identical to David's. "I met you at Mia's wedding. All right, here's what I know. First, we took Dell Farmer into custody last night after he tried to kill Eve and one of our detectives."

"Farmer ran David off the road," Max said, but Olivia shook her head.

"No, he did lots of other really bad stuff, but that wasn't Farmer."

David had gone white beneath his winter tan. "If Farmer's in jail, then it's this . . . Shadowland guy."

Olivia nodded. "Yes. We had Eve en route to a safe house when she was taken."

David surged to his feet. "How did this happen? Webster promised he'd watch her."

"Sit down, David," Olivia commanded, and vibrating with fear and rage, he obeyed. "Noah was at the scene of another homicide."

David looked ill. "Six. That was number six."

Olivia hesitated. "Yes."

"He's killed more," Max said thinly.

Olivia nodded. "Yes."

"He's got Liza, too?" Tom asked, more calmly than his elders.

Olivia nodded. "Yes. And I don't know why or how it connects, so don't ask, but it does. Your black SUV tip may be really important, Tom."

David and Max turned to look at Tom. "What black SUV?" David asked.

"Who is Liza?" Max asked at the same time. "What is this?"

She met Tom's gaze. "You play the white knight, you gotta come clean. Tell them the details, but later. I have to go and so do all of you. I have a house to search."

Max had returned his sharp gaze to her face. "You said you knew who had Eve."

"Yeah, and I'm not going to say who, so don't ask." There was a commotion outside and one of the detectives who'd stopped David stuck his head in the door.

"You've got someone here demanding to see you, Detective Sutherland."

Sal burst through the door. "I heard. Down at the bar, I heard." His eyes were red-rimmed. "Dammit, Olivia, what happened?"

"Sal." She gave him the two-minute version, then rose. "You guys can't stay here." She held up her hand to quell the four dissenting voices. "Sal, take them back to your place. I'll call you when I have any news. I promise. Now go. I have work to do."

Thursday, February 25, 2:20 p.m.

"Luminol was positive," Micki said, joining Noah and Abbott in Pierce's study. "Blood in the tub. I've got a tech checking the drains." She stuck her head into the walk-in closet. "How's that safe coming, Sugar?"

"It'd come faster if you all would be quiet," Sugar Taub said testily from the closet.

Noah was pacing a groove into the carpet, but abruptly stopped at a section of books when a title caught his eye. "It's in German," he said, and Abbott came to look.

"I found books in French over there. Carleton is, unfortunately, a very smart man."

But Noah wasn't listening, instead staring at the book spines. "This one's by Freud. *Das Ich und Das Es.*" He heard a piece of the puzzle fall into place. "*Das Ich.* Dasich. He was the avatar that played poker with Natalie Clooney and Virginia Fox."

"What does *Das Ich* mean?"

Noah googled it on his cell. "The book is *The Ego and The Id.* This says that the ego's job is to find balance between the primitive drives of the id and reality."

"The drive to kill is pretty damn primitive," Abbott said. "Smug sonofabitch."

"That's what Eve called Dasich," Noah said. *She's been gone three hours.*

"Don't think about her right now," Abbott said. "We're getting closer."

His words were punctuated by a satisfied "Ah," from the closet and Sugar and Micki emerged with a stack of thick file folders.

"Give me the folders," Noah said and crowding around Pierce's desk, they searched the contents. "Bank statements. This one looks like his family account."

"His wife has her own," Micki said, looking at another stack of statements. "Regular transfers from the main account, barely enough for groceries and gas. He had her on an allowance. Based on the order of the kitchen, he likes control."

"Order," Noah murmured. "He said the killer liked order. He was right."

"Control often masks fear," Micki said. "Remember that Olivia said he was afraid of his female victims? She was right."

Beside him, Abbott let out a low whistle. "Look at these. He's got three-quarter mil stashed away. Let's freeze all his accounts. Make it hard for him to run."

After he finishes what he set out to do. Noah pushed Carleton's own words away as ruthlessly as the images of his victims and opened another folder. "PI reports. PI's name is Hugh Robard. Subject of surveillance is John Black of Fargo, North Dakota."

"We need to find John and Irene Black," Abbott said, darkly.

"And the PI," Noah said.

"I don't know, Web," Micki said doubtfully. "The last report's dated ten years ago. But it's worth a try," she added, more upbeat, and he knew his devastation was showing.

"Let's go back to the office and make our calls there," Abbott said. "I've got a press conference at three. I'll tell them we've issued an arrest warrant for Carleton Pierce."

Thursday, February 25, 2:20 p.m.

The pain . . . the pain was unbearable. She lifted her hands to her face and touched bone. Her hands were covered in blood. He cut me. My face. My face is gone.

No. She threw her head back and gasped in a breath.

And bucked. She couldn't breathe. Something covered her mouth. She twisted, trying to get away.

"Stop. Don't scream."

It was a snarled whisper and Eve dropped back, shuddering. What covered her mouth was skin. An arm. Eve breathed through her nose, nodding hard. The arm moved and a body collapsed across her legs, sending fire through the hole in her thigh.

"If you scream, he'll come back."

Eve struggled to lift her head, then sucked in a stunned breath. "Liza."

Liza was tied, hands and feet behind her back. Her lips were pursed and she took short, staccato breaths through her nose. "Who is he?"

"Police psychologist. Why did he take you?"

"I've been looking for my sister." Liza lifted her head and her eyes were haunted, horrified. "She's dead. Her shoes are up there. He showed them to me."

It took a moment to trickle through the fog in her mind, but when it did, she was sick. For Eve, the shoes were vile, horrific reminders of past victims of Carleton Pierce. For Liza . . . it was the sister she loved. *Dear God.* "We have to get out of here."

Liza gave her a hard look. "How? He took the knife."

"I don't know yet."

"He put me in his trunk." Her eyes were haunted again. "There was a body in there. He said it was his wife. He put her in the pit."

Eve's blood chilled as this newest horror registered. "What pit?"

"It's a door in the floor. He pulled a handle and it slid back. He dumped her in. He said that's where my sister was. He said there was room for two more."

Don't panic, don't panic. "We're not going to die. How did you get over here?"

"I rolled. I didn't want you to scream."

"That was smart." Eve craned her head up, but from where she lay she couldn't see much. "Can you see anything we can use for a weapon? Anything sharp?"

"There are some drawers behind you, but they're above my head unless I can stand up. Which I can't." There was a sound above their heads and they both looked up.

"He's coming. Go back to where you were," Eve hissed. "Play dead if you have to."

"I've been playing dead. He thinks I'm catatonic, he said. What will you do?"

"I don't know yet, but whatever happens, don't let him know you're awake. Do not let him see your fear. He feeds on our worst fears. Now go." Liza obeyed, rolling back to her corner awkwardly while Eve tried to think of what to do. How to escape.

Understand him. She'd scored a direct hit on the *MSP* link to his manhood, but she couldn't count on that working again. She lifted her head to look at the shoes. Most were women's shoes, but three pairs from hers were a pair of men's Nikes. Sticking up out of the Nikes, she could see a pair of wire-framed glasses.

Like Jeremy Lyons had worn. *Kane was right*, she thought. *Jeremy's dead.*

She closed her eyes, fighting despair. *Noah, where are you?* He was looking, she knew. *Look harder.* She lifted her head again, made herself truly see what was before her eyes. With the exception of Jeremy's Nikes and a pair of men's work boots on the bottom shelf, most of the shoes were . . . fuck-me heels, for lack of a better term.

Dregs of society, he'd called them. *Prostitutes.* He'd

killed prostitutes. She ran her gaze over every pair, until she came to the very first pair on the far left of the first shelf.

They were old, worn. Matronly, even. The shoes of his first victim?

Irene Black. The name rushed into her mind and she wondered if the woman had been more than a fake name for a Shadowland account.

The door opened and Pierce sauntered down the stairs, naked again. She put her head back on the pillow and closed her eyes. She had to be mentally ready.

"Too late, Dr. Pierce," she taunted. "I'm awake and you missed the show."

"No." He took the rest of the stairs in a giant step, throwing his trousers on the post and grabbing her hair. "You didn't scream. They always scream."

Thank you, Liza. "Maybe I've developed a tolerance. Maybe you mixed it wrong."

"Maybe I should just carve you up anyway," he sneered. "That scares you. I can tell. Your eyes flicker when you're afraid."

He had recharged. He was once again aroused. He straddled her again, hands on her throat. She bucked to try to throw him and he only laughed.

"More, Eve. The more you fight, the more I enjoy it."

"Do you enjoy it?" she flung back. "You never had sex with any of your victims. Can you even do it?" *MSP.* He'd fizzled before her eyes. *Make him do it again.* "Or does that tiny dick of yours disappear before the main event?"

"Are you begging me to rape you, Miss Wilson?" he asked, but she'd seen the flicker in his eyes. She'd rattled him.

"I'm saying you couldn't if you wanted to."

His face darkened. "Soon, all you'll be saying is 'stop.'" He tightened his hands around her neck, cutting off her air. She fought to get him off, but he pressed his knees into her ribs, like a rider controlling a horse. His hands got tighter and his face got closer and his hips began to thrust. She could feel him, hard against her breastbone.

She fought harder, twisting, and heard the faraway sound of his laugh. She could smell him, the musk, the smell of sex. *This is what he does. He's almost there.* In a surge of strength she forced a single hoarse syllable from her mouth. "Who?" But all that emerged was a mangled *Huh.*

He paused, his breath hard and hot and fast against her face. Revulsion roiled through her. The blackness was claiming the edges of her vision once again.

His lips curved in a triumphant smile, even as his muscles quivered, straining toward release. "Help?" he asked, smug now. "Was that a plea I heard?"

He loosened his grip a fraction and began thrusting again, harder, faster. "Beg, Eve, yell for help and I'll let you breathe."

She pulled in as much air as she could. "Who . . . is Irene Black?"

He stopped like a rock, shock flattening his face. "What?" he asked ominously, but against her his erection had abruptly shriveled and his hands had gone slack.

Yes. "Irene Black." She took a deep breath. "I said *Irene Black.* Who is she?"

His face retreated a few inches. She watched him battle for a blank face. "Nobody."

Eve's laugh was hoarse and brief. "You're a lousy liar. Who is she?"

"How did you find that name?"

"Don't you want to know?"

He struck her, hard. "Tell me."

"Untie me and I'll tell you."

He hit her again, harder. "Tell me or I'll kill you."

Eve's head was spinning. "You're going to kill me anyway, so go to hell."

He grabbed her throat and shook her. "Tell me. Who else knows? Did Webster tell you that name?"

The white lights were back, dancing before her eyes. He let go, clutching her hair in one hand and hitting her with the other. She dragged the air in, the room now spinning. There was a greasy roiling in her stomach and she threw up.

All over him.

"Dammit," he hissed. He leapt off her and delivered one more blow to her head. And the spinning room went dark.

Thursday, February 25, 2:45 p.m.

"Captain, two things," Faye said when Noah and Abbott were back in his office. "We got a hit on Mrs. Ann Pierce's plane reservation. She was supposed to leave for Los Angeles this morning and never showed up for her flight."

"Find out how and when she paid for the ticket," Abbott said.

"Cash and yesterday evening," Faye replied. "She bought it at the airport counter. I already asked. Second, Lieutenant Tyndale from Fargo PD is on line one."

Abbott contacted the Fargo PD to locate John Black as soon as they'd left Pierce's house. Kane had traced Irene Black's Wisconsin PO box to a mailbox store in New Germany, a rural town nearly an hour from the Cities.

Because Pierce had forwarded Girard's mail a third time and he was obsessive about order, Kane was trying to determine where the mail was being forwarded from there.

Noah had discovered that PI Hugh Robard disappeared without a trace ten years ago, about the same time the reports ended. *And somewhere, Pierce still has Eve.*

Every muscle clenched, Noah sat on the edge of Abbott's desk. Abbott's eyes were sharp. "You will not engage this witness," Abbott said. "You aren't here, understood?"

Abbott had sent him home, but Noah had thrown any pride he had left to the wind and begged to stay. There would be nothing at home to do but pace, and worry. And drink. "I understand," Noah said. "Please, just hurry."

Abbott hit the speaker button. "This is Captain Abbott. Who is this?"

"Lieutenant John Tyndale, Fargo PD. I have John Black here with me. I need to tell you up front, John's a good man. I've known him for more than twenty years."

"We appreciate his help. What can you tell us about the man in the photo we sent?"

"His name is not Carleton Pierce." It was John Black who spoke. "It's Edward Black. He's my younger brother. We haven't spoken in twenty-seven years, since our mother died."

"Your mother was Irene Black?" Abbott asked.

"Yes. Ed made it look like she killed herself, but I always knew he did it. He hated her." Black sighed. "He had good cause. We both did."

"What was his good cause? And why did you think it was no accident?"

"My mother was a drunk," Black said baldly, "and a gambler. The only time she was ever sober was when she had cards in her hand. Sometimes she'd take him to games with her. He was small and cute and nobody knew she was using him to cheat."

"Was there abuse?"

"She never sold us, if that's what you're asking, but we were dirt poor. Lived in a filthy, rusted-out trailer. Rats ate at our toes in the night. She traded food stamps for booze, so yeah, I guess you could say she abused us."

"Did your brother hate all women, or just your mom?"

"I'd say all women. Eddie had a hard time getting dates. He always blamed it on being short, but most of the girls in town were afraid of him. Eddie took a knife to school, threatened a kid with it. Kid was a bully, but Eddie ended up in juvie for a year."

"You said he made it look like your mother committed suicide? How?"

"I found her hanging from a tree outside, but she never could have managed it."

"Let me guess," Abbott said quietly, "whatever she stood on was too short to reach."

"How did you know?" Black asked suspiciously.

"He's done the same thing here. Six times. So was there no investigation?"

Black said nothing for a long moment. "I cut her down. Nobody knew it was fishy."

Abbott waited as Noah's impatience grew. None of this was helping.

"Why?" Abbott finally asked.

"Because she deserved it," he said harshly. "She never sold us, but she brought home any man who'd buy her next bottle. Sometimes they'd sneak from her bed in the night. I was big and could fight them, but Eddie was little. As I got older, I'd stay with friends to get away, but Eddie didn't have many friends. He was stuck. I know some of those guys hurt him. One boyfriend in particular.

"I'd come home sometimes and see Eddie, cowering in the corner like an animal. Once I saw his eyes, and I knew. I should have told. I should have told," he said again. "But that boyfriend was big and mean and I was barely fourteen myself. So I cleared out, moved in with a friend whose mom didn't drink. There was food on the table and clean sheets on the bed. In other words, I saved my own hide. When I found her hanging, I cut her down and told the cops what they wanted to hear to make it all go away. I thought I was doing the right thing. I had no idea what he'd become."

"Why that day?" Abbott asked. "Why do you think he picked that day to hang her?"

There was another silence. "Eddie was almost eighteen, he'd just gotten out of juvie. That day he'd taken a girl from town on a date, played up the bad-boy image. I guess she wanted a thrill. But I guess Eddie couldn't . . . perform. I heard she was laughing at him, that she was telling everyone she'd laughed at him while he tried and couldn't.

"When I heard that, I knew he'd killed our mother. He blamed her. I would have, too. If I'd told the truth, he would have gone to jail as an adult and I knew what would happen to him there. I figured he'd already done his time and maybe I felt guilty for never helping him. I wish I'd told the truth. I wish I'd known."

Me, too, Noah thought woodenly. *I wish you'd told the truth, too.*

"What happened to your brother after that?" Abbott asked.

"I picked up, landed here in Fargo, made a life. I never heard from Eddie again."

"He made a life here, as a psychologist," Abbott said.

Again, Black went quiet. "So he pulled it off after all. He was supposed to be in juvie till he was eighteen, but he got out early. The school and the local cops fought hard to keep him in, but there was a shrink working with him, said he'd rehabilitated. I guess Eddie had him pretty fooled. I remember going to family court for the hearing. The shrink wore fancy clothes, used big words, and dazzled the judge. He made the cops look like rubes. Eddie told me *that's* where the power was. That if you took a cop's gun, that he was just a bully. I think Eddie'd had his share of bullies in juvie. He said he'd go to college, be one of those smart guys. I told him it would never happen."

"Why?"

"Because colleges didn't let in people like him. Poor, with a record. I guess he listened to me more than I thought. I guess he became somebody else."

None of this was finding Eve. "Hurry up," Noah mouthed and Abbott glared at him.

"We need to find him," Abbott said. "He's abducted at least two more women."

"I know. Lieutenant Tyndale told me. I want to help you, but I can't. I don't know where he'd hide. Like I said, I haven't spoken to him in nearly thirty years."

"Well, thanks for talking to me," Abbott said wearily. "And you should watch your back, Mr. Black. He's got reports on you and your wife and kids. I guess he worried you were the one person who could identify him."

Noah stared blindly at Abbott's phone after he'd hung up. "That was useless."

"Faye's doing a property search on Irene and we've got roadblocks set up on every artery in and out of the Cities." Abbott's eyes were kind. "Go get us some coffee, Noah."

What he really needed was a drink. *Just one. Just to even my nerves.* He knew it was a lie. Knew one would never be enough. And if they didn't find her in time . . .

Noah gave Abbott a shaky nod and walked to the coffee pot in the bullpen, stood there for long minutes as he stared, fighting the urge to smash the glass pot. Smash everything in the damn place, then go hunt for something stronger to wet his lips. To give him courage. Or maybe just to forget how damn scared he was.

In his mind he saw the victims hanging . . . Pierce had been hanging his mother, each time. *And now he has Eve. My Eve.* He couldn't think like a cop anymore. *I can't.*

"Noah." Noah looked up. Brock was coming down the hall, still in uniform. "I came as soon as I heard. Any news?"

"No," Noah said. "Nothing."

Brock put his arm around Noah's shoulders. "I'll buy you a coffee in the cafeteria."

"I'm sorry I didn't call you."

"Noah." Brock's voice was gently chiding. "Eve's smart and brave. She'll hold on."

He looked straight ahead, seeing nothing. "If I don't find her? How will I hold on?"

Brock sighed. "Sometimes you have to take one minute at a time."

As the elevator doors slid open, Noah's cell phone buzzed in his pocket. His pulse shot up when he saw the caller ID. "Olivia, what is it?"

"I just got off the phone with Abbott." She hesitated. "He ordered me not to tell you. I hope I'm doing the right thing."

Noah pursed his lips in desperation. "Goddammit, Olivia, tell me."

"Faye just took a call from Martha Brisbane's vet, about her cat."

Noah hissed out a breath. "Who gives a fuck about that damn cat?"

"Listen," Olivia snapped. "The vet called to say Martha's cat had been dropped off outside the gate of the Green Gables Kennel in New Germany yesterday. The security camera outside picked up a woman and a black BMW, registered to Pierce's wife."

Noah went still. "New Germany? That's where Irene's PO box is being forwarded."

"I know, Kane told me."

"Why would Pierce's wife drop off the cat? And how do they know it's Martha's?"

"Don't know why the wife did it, but Martha had the cat chipped. Vet scanned it and Martha's name came up. He'd read about her murder, called it in. I'm going out there."

"Thank you," he said fervently, then hung up and stepped into the elevator Brock had been holding open. "I'm going to New Germany."

"I figured that out myself," Brock said wryly. "Gonna tell me why?"

"Depends. You gonna turn me in?"

Brock studied him as the elevator descended. "I call shotgun."

Noah nodded hard. "Thanks."

* * *

Thursday, February 25, 3:00 p.m.

He sat in his kitchen, looking out the window at the woods, clean again after showering off Eve's filth. The swaying trees always calmed him, but today, they did not.

Irene Black. How had Eve known? Who had she told? *How can this hurt me?*

Irene Black was a common enough name and the PO box he'd set up in her name was out of state. Highly unlikely they'd find it. This was the Hat Squad after all. Not the world's greatest intellects.

They would never have gotten this far without Eve. He tightened his fist against his kitchen table. She needed to pay. Next time he went down he'd tape her mouth and glue her eyes open. He wanted to hear her beg for her life, and she would, once he'd worn her down. Once he'd worn her down, he'd take off the tape and her pleas for mercy would be music to his ears.

For now, he couldn't let her get in his head. She knew too much. For now, he'd make her show him the fear. He'd glue her eyes open and make her show him her fear.

He hadn't glued her eyes, he realized. It was always the first thing he did, so that he could see their terror as soon as the ketamine wore off. When the ket wore off, they thrashed like wild animals, making it impossible to get the glue on their eyes.

Why had he not with Eve? *Because I want her unfettered fear.* He wanted her to look up at him with glassy-eyed terror because she could do nothing else.

She was a worthy opponent, but *he* held all the power. She'd tell him how she found Irene Black. Eventually. Until then, he was safe. There was nothing to link him to Irene. Nothing linking Irene to this place.

His only loose end was his wife's disappearance, and he'd handled that, too, sending a text to Ann's boss from her cell saying she'd had a family emergency. He'd sent the text while sitting at a rest stop off the interstate, an hour away. In a few days, he'd send a registered letter to her boss, giving her notice, that she was needed back home. He'd met her boss, a cold, efficient man. Another lab tech would be hired and Ann would soon be forgotten. Meanwhile, her body would be decomposed in his pit.

Movement on the television caught his eye. *Ah. The press conference.* He grabbed the remote and turned up the volume. This was what he'd been waiting for. The press was about to crucify the police. *Six dead women, no suspects. Red Dress Killer on the loose. Cops have no clue.* He couldn't wait for the accusations to fly.

Abbott climbed to the podium, looking positively grim. *This* was entertainment.

"Thank you," Abbott said. "As you know, a sadistic killer has been preying on the women of the Twin Cities for the last three weeks."

Sadistic killer. It was good for a start. In tomorrow morning's meeting he'd give Abbott a few more psychological terms to use for his next press conference.

"This morning, we discovered a sixth victim," Abbott went on. "Her name was Virginia Fox. Last night we asked you to post warnings to women participating in a Marshall University study involving the Shadowland computer game. Today we know this killer's victims are not constrained to the game."

"Gotcha," he crowed. "All bets are off and nobody feels safe."

One of the reporters rose. "Can you comment on the arrest warrant you issued?"

He leaned forward with a frown. Donner was dead. Lyons was missing and Girard had been cleared. Who was Abbott planning to arrest?

"Yes," Abbott said. The screen split, showing Abbott on one side and on the other . . .

- *Me.*

"At 2:30 today we issued a warrant for the arrest of Dr. Carleton Pierce."

He could only blink in stunned disbelief as flashes went off in Abbott's face. Then he lurched to his feet, pushing his chair back. "No. *No.*"

"We do not do this lightly," Abbott was saying. "Dr. Pierce was considered a colleague and a friend. We don't know why he has done this, but we have definitive proof linking him to these crimes. We have three missing women and would like your help." Abbott's face disappeared completely, three pictures taking his place. "Dr. Ann Pierce, the wife of the alleged killer, Miss Eve Wilson of Marshall University, and Miss Liza Barkley." Abbott continued to talk as the photos remained on screen.

"Take it down," he ground out. *"Take my picture goddamn down."*

But it stayed, for everyone to see. It wasn't possible. It wasn't happening. *But it was.*

"The suspect was last seen in a black BMW, last year's model. He's also been seen in a black Lincoln Navigator. We've listed the license plates he's used on our website and in the press release you've been given." The pictures cleared and Abbott was looking sternly into the camera. "This man is armed and dangerous. If you see him call 911 immediately. If you have information as to his whereabouts, here is our hotline.

"We know you join us in condolences for the families

of his victims and prayers for the women still missing. I'll take your questions now."

He sat back in his chair and pulled trembling hands over his face. *They knew. How did they know? They're coming. They're coming for me.*

"Stop it," he snapped, slamming his fists into the table. "Think."

They didn't know about his place, this place. His sanctuary. The deed to this house was not in Irene's or anyone else's name. *They can't find me here.* There's still time to get away. But his hands still shook as he pulled his laptop closer.

"Consolidate your finances," he muttered. "Put your money where you can get to it." Then he'd get in that old brown Civic he'd bought to frame Axel Girard. They weren't looking for that car anymore. He'd take Eve and the girl as hostages and he'd drive.

Where? Where can I go? Everyone knows my name. My face. Damn you, Abbott.

But he knew it wasn't Abbott he should damn, or even Webster. It was that woman downstairs. His eyes narrowed. Eve.

Stop it. Stay calm, focused. Get your money. He logged into his bank account and his heart stopped. *Frozen. Funds unavailable.*

"No. Goddammit, no." His fingers few over the keys as he checked his offshore accounts. *Frozen. Funds unavailable.*

They'd frozen his accounts. They'd been in his house. *In my things.* The account information had been in his safe . . . along with all of his information on John.

Even Webster was smart enough to connect John and Irene Black.

He put his head in his hands. He needed to get away. *Now.* He grabbed his knife and headed down the stairs.

Eve heard his voice upstairs. He'd sounded angry. There'd been cursing. That was a good sign. Noah was close. She needed to buy just a little more time.

Opening her eyes a slit, she could see Pierce marching down the stairs, fully clothed, his hair still wet, his knife clenched in his hand. Under his arm he had folded blankets. She closed her eyes, hoping he'd think she was still unconscious. She hadn't been long, but Liza hadn't responded to her whispers and she feared what had happened while she'd been out. *Don't be dead.*

Pierce walked behind her, then reappeared with a very still Liza wrapped in one of the blankets and heaved her over his shoulder. He took Liza up the stairs, ignoring Eve. If he was in a hurry to leave, it meant Noah and the cops were on their way. She had to do whatever it took to keep him down here, where Noah could trap him.

Pierce would have to untie her to get her out. She could only pray he didn't sedate her again. Sedated, she couldn't fight him. And fighting him was exactly what she'd do. If he didn't sedate her, she'd have a split second to act when he cut her loose.

Upstairs, she heard a door slam and he came down the stairs, moving more slowly this time. He was tired, she realized. He'd probably never had to carry a body *up* those stairs. Eve kept her eyes closed, body lax. *Don't use the needle. Don't use the needle.*

She heard him approach, felt him stop next to her. "Wake up," he said and smacked her face. He leaned over, placed the blade against her throat. "You're either good or you're out cold. Let's see how good you are."

Chapter Twenty-five

Thursday, February 25, 3:15 p.m.

Do you have any idea where you're going?" Brock asked.

They were speeding toward New Germany and all Noah had been able to think was that Eve could be there. Hurt or . . . *Don't go there. You can't go there.*

He looked over at Brock. "The kennel was called Green Gables."

"I know it. They train hunting dogs. It's a damn big kennel, Noah. Acres of land."

"Olivia said a woman dropped off the cat driving Ann Pierce's BMW. Assuming it was Ann Pierce, how would she pick that kennel, just out of the air? She must have passed it at some point."

"Or she's a hunter," Brock said. "But let's go with your line of thought. This road continues for miles. The houses are usually at the end of long driveways. Did you find any property out here owned by this Pierce guy?"

"No. The only house in his name is the one he lives in."

"There's the kennel up on the right," Brock said.

Noah checked the driveway, then passed the kennel without slowing down when he saw Olivia's car parked in front.

Brock turned to look behind them. "Looks like your friend beat you here."

"I know. I don't want to get Olivia in trouble."

"You can't do this on your own, Noah. This area is too remote. You need an aerial view to know where all the houses are. You'll need search crews and dogs."

"I know," Noah said, then focused on the vehicle stopping ahead. "Or . . . a postman."

The postman had pulled his truck to the side and was stuffing letters into a mailbox. He looked up in surprise when Noah got out, showing his badge. "I'm trying to locate one of your residents. We think he may be able to help us with an investigation."

"I've seen your face before. I delivered a lot of *MSP*s out here."

"I'm Detective Webster," Noah said. "I'm looking for a man named Pierce."

The old postman shook his head. "I don't know that name. Sorry, can't help you." He started to move, but Noah put out his hand, desperation rising to close his throat.

"Wait, please. If you know who I am, you know what's been happening this week."

The postman nodded. "I read the paper, but I don't know that Pierce name."

"Okay." Noah's mind was racing. If Pierce had mail in Irene Black's name sent out here, it meant he came out here. His wife knew about the kennel, so she'd been out here, too. It was a long shot, but he had to try. "What about deliveries? You say you delivered *MSP* magazine out here. What about other magazines?"

The postman frowned severely. "I can't tell you that."

Noah closed his eyes briefly, fighting for control. "This man has killed six women, maybe more. He's abducted two more women that might still be alive. If you can help me, I won't tell a soul how I got the information. I promise. *Please*. Please, help me."

The postman looked away for a long moment, then back. "What kind of magazines?"

"Psychology, computer magazines, game magazines." Noah concentrated. The wife was a biologist. "Animal magazines. Dogs, cats. Snakes."

The postman shook his head. "I haven't seen anything like that. A lot of our folks have their magazines sent to post office boxes, too."

Which Pierce would have done. Dammit. Noah started to turn away, then stopped. He'd come too far. There had to be something . . . "What kinds of deliveries would have to be delivered to an actual address, not a post office box?"

"Packages. Those PO boxes don't hold that much."

Packages. Noah blew out a breath, watched it hang in the air . . . just as it had as he'd stood looking up at Martha Brisbane Sunday night. He pictured her as she'd hung there in her low-cut red dress, her stiletto-heeled shoes on the floor beneath her feet.

Her dress, her shoes . . . they'd been identical to all the others. Same style, just different sizes. Ordered from an online shopping club, Micki had said days ago.

"What about packages from The Fashion Club? It would have been a few weeks ago. It had dresses and shoes."

The postman went still. "High-heeled shoes? Red?"

Noah nodded, trying to keep calm. "Yes."

"I left the box on the front porch. A few days later I delivered another box. The first one was still there, its bottom frozen to the porch. The box was wet from the snow and it fell apart. It was filled with shoe boxes. The same red, pencil-heeled shoes. I assumed it was for some play or dance troupe, you know, where they all had to dress alike."

Noah's heart was pounding in his ears. "Where did you deliver the boxes?"

"About two miles up the road. I'll draw you a map."

Two minutes later Noah was in his car, slamming the door as he punched the gas.

"You found it then?" Brock asked.

"I hope so." He hit redial on his cell phone, getting Olivia on the first ring.

"You . . ." she fumed. "You lied to me. You said you'd stay back at the station."

"I found him," Noah said, ignoring her very justified tirade. He gave her the address as the road the postman had indicated came into view. "I'm going in. Back me up."

"Noa—"

Noah closed his phone and handed it to Brock. "If she calls back, you answer it."

Brock was giving him a wary look. "You're gonna get your ass fired for this."

"Not if I win." He thought of Eve and Liza and every woman Pierce had left hanging from her bedroom ceiling. Of Virginia's hollow eye sockets. "If I lose, I won't care."

Thursday, February 25, 3:15 p.m.

Don't be afraid. Don't flinch. Even if it hurts. She smelled the metal of the blade, heard it scrape her skin. Down the scar on her cheek, she realized. The cheek that had had no feeling for almost six years. She smelled her own blood. Knew he'd cut her.

Panic welled up and she fought it back. How deep had he cut? *It doesn't matter.* Noah had noticed her before the scar was gone. And if it did matter to him . . . *If I'm still alive to worry about it, that'll be good.*

Pierce grunted, evidently convinced. "All right. You're unconscious."

She focused on even breathing as he cut the twine that had tied her bound wrists to the bed. But her wrists were still bound. *He didn't cut my hands free. Dammit.*

He took her wrists and brought them over her head, resting them on her stomach. He paused. *He's looking at me. Waiting.* She kept breathing and kept her eyes closed.

Noah rolled his car to a silent stop, diagonally behind the open garage. Inside was a Lincoln Navigator, a black BMW, and a brown Honda Civic with the trunk lid up.

Heart pounding, he got out of his car moving noiselessly, weapon drawn. Brock followed, watching his back. Inside the truck was a huddled figure wrapped in a blanket. *Be Eve. Be alive.* He pulled the blanket aside and blew out a breath. It was the girl he'd seen with Tom Hunter the night before. She was nude, bound, her mouth taped, her eyes staring up at him desperately. Her skin was already blue.

He peeled the tape back from her mouth. "Hurry," she whispered, teeth chattering. "He's got Eve in the basement. He's got a knife."

Noah pulled the blanket back up over her, shrugging out of his own coat to wrap her in it. She'd be dead from exposure in minutes. "How many doors to the basement?"

"One. From the kitchen."

"Stay with her," he said to Brock and took off at a run, ignoring Brock's hissed command to wait for backup. The house was eerily empty, the television set to the news. Abbott had just finished his press conference.

It was safe to assume Pierce knew he was a wanted man. It was safe to assume he'd do anything, as he had nothing to lose. Noah was at the door to the basement when he heard a crash that sounded like a wall coming down. He started to run.

Eve sat up, breathing hard, blinking to clear her vision. Her leg burned, but what she saw was far better than she hoped and ironic as hell. The shelves of shoes had come down. She'd waited until he'd bent to cut the twine at her feet, then she'd shoved her body down the cot, knees bent, and kicked him backward. Caught unawares, he'd gone sprawling against the wall, knocking all the shelves down.

One wood shelf had smacked his head and he lay unmoving. Shelves and shoes covered him in a heap, so that only his feet showed. Eve was bizarrely reminded of the red-and-white-striped stockings of the Wicked Witch and half expected his toes to curl.

"Eve!"

Slowly Eve looked to the stairs, sending the room into a spin. Noah was leaping, taking four stairs at a time. He rushed to her side, pale, holstering his gun. *White knight*, she thought as he grabbed Pierce's knife from the floor and cut the twine that bound her feet. Then she saw movement behind him and screamed, hoarsely. *"Noah."*

Pierce had risen from the shoes and was running to the stairs. In two steps Noah was on him, gun drawn. Then Eve heard a sickening crunch, metal to bone. Noah dropped to his knees and Pierce remained standing, holding a shovel like a bat.

Pierce swung again, but Noah rolled, the shovel head hitting his shoulder instead. A moment later, Noah tackled him and Pierce went down.

On his hands and knees, Noah blinked hard, trying to see. Pierce was on the floor, scrabbling backward. He plowed a fist into Pierce's face, feeling satisfaction when the cartilage in Pierce's nose yielded like butter. But Pierce rolled to his feet, standing behind him. Noah twisted, found himself looking into the barrel of a .22 with a silencer.

"Hands out, Noah," Pierce said. "I want to see them."

Noah held his hands out. His own gun was three feet away, dropped when he'd been hit by the shovel. Too far to grab. He watched Pierce, waiting for the time to move.

"This is the way I always wanted you to die," Pierce said with a smile, even though blood gushed from his nose. He stood over him, staring down. "On your knees, looking up at me."

Noah was breathing hard, his ears still ringing from the blow. "There are police surrounding this place. If you kill me, you'll still go down."

"But I will have killed you," Pierce said, reasonably. "And I have a hostage."

Noah didn't think he'd ever adequately describe the expression that crossed Pierce's face next, a combination of surprise and . . . annoyance. Noah leapt, wresting the gun from Pierce's hand, but he didn't have to exert much force. Pierce slumped to his knees, then fell flat on his face, Eve falling with him. Her hands were still bound and she wore nothing except the satisfaction on her face. Her left hand still clutched Pierce's knife as it stuck from his back, blood soaking his tan overcoat.

"No, you do not have a hostage." She lifted her eyes. "Are you all right?"

Noah crawled to her, checking her for injuries. "I'm fine. What did he do to you?"

"I don't know," she said, dully. "What did he do to me?"

"He hit you. Oh, Eve." She looked like Brock had on Sunday night.

She grabbed his arm, clumsily. "My face. Did he cut my face?"

Noah wiped the blood away from her cheek. "Not much. Nobody will be able to tell." It was then the shoes sank in. "Oh my God. Micki was right. The shoes."

Eve blinked slowly. "He killed all these women. They're under us, right now."

He'd deal with that later. She looked like she was going into shock. He tried to stand up, but came back hard on his knees. The room was spinning so he crawled to get a blanket on the floor next to the bed. He wrapped Eve in it, then pulled her to his lap, holding her close, giving her his warmth. "You're like ice."

She stared at the knife protruding from Pierce's back. "Did I kill him?"

"I hope so," he said fiercely.

Olivia came down the stairs, her gun at her side, then stopped short. "Holy shit," she muttered. She knelt at Pierce's side, put her fingers to his throat. "Alive, but barely." She took her radio from her belt, called the all-clear and requested three more gurneys, then knelt beside Noah, reaching for Eve. "Let her go, Web."

Noah shook his head, sending the room spinning again. "No."

"Noah," she said gently, "you've got a huge gash in the back of your head and you are bleeding a river. In about three minutes you'll be flat on this floor yourself. Let her go so I can cut this twine."

Reluctantly, Noah let go. Olivia efficiently cut the twine from Eve's hands as the medics thundered down the stairs. Eve met his eyes as the medics lifted her to a gurney. "He killed his wife. She's under the floor. They all are. Jeremy Lyons, too."

A second medic was pushing Noah to a gurney. "Wait." He blinked at the floor, saw a handle. "Open it."

Olivia yanked, then gagged when a concrete slab rolled back. "Oh my God." She covered her mouth as she stared into the pit. "That's his wife, Ann Pierce."

A man's hand stuck up out of the dirt. "Jeremy Lyons," Noah whispered. "Kane was right. So was Micki."

Olivia pulled the slab shut. "You can tell them yourself, once you've had stitches. Take him," she said to the medics. "Don't let him argue."

Noah let the medic roll him to his side to tend to his head. "Do me a favor."

"The ER docs'll give you a local when they give you the stitches," the medic said.

"No." Noah pointed to Pierce's barely breathing body. "His bus? Drive it real slow."

Thursday, February 25, 6:15 p.m.

"Oh, Eve."

From her hospital bed, Eve turned to see Callie standing in the doorway, distress on her face. "You should see the other guy," she said, trying for light, but her voice still too hoarse.

"We tried," Callie said, utterly serious. "But they wouldn't let us in the morgue. Sal wanted to be sure he was really dead, but the ME said we'd have to take his word for it. Good for you, girl."

Carleton Pierce had bled out as the helicopter transporting him had touched down on the hospital's roof. "I don't feel bad," Eve murmured. "I suppose I should, but I don't. I feel pretty damn good."

Callie carefully sat on the edge of her bed. "As you should. Where's Noah?"

"On the phone." She smiled, gingerly. Her face still hurt from Pierce's fists. And his knife. She fought back the shudder and thought of good things. "Jack woke up. The first person he asked for was Noah. They're talking now."

Callie squeezed her hand gently. "That's good. Maybe Jack will pull it together. Listen, you've got a crowd waiting to see you. Are you up for visitors?"

Eve raised her hand to her throat, knowing what it looked like. Pierce had cut away her choker, exposing what was still a nasty scar. Then she shrugged. "It is what it is," she said. "Let the visitation begin."

"I went by your place, grabbed you some clean clothes, a robe, and this." Callie reached into her pocket and pulled out another choker.

Eve's eyes stung. "Thank you. For knowing it would be important."

"Don't start crying or you'll have me crying again." She busied herself helping Eve into the robe and fastening the leather choker around her neck. "Sal will be chomping at the bit. He closed the bar so he could be the first one here. He only let me in first to get you presentable. He was the pillar of strength, keeping everyone's spirits up, taking care of your Chicago friends." She dropped her voice. "Then when he got the word that you were okay, alive, he broke down. Cried like a baby. So did Jeff Betz."

Eve sniffled. "That's so sweet."

"And your friends from Chicago? They wanted to be here when you woke up, so Jeff gave them a ride in his cruiser, lights flashing."

"David's was the first face I saw when I woke up from the surgery to sew up my leg." Eve made a face. "It was like a bad rerun. His face is always the first one I see when I wake up from an attack by a homicidal lunatic." But it had been such a relief. Max and Tom had been on the other side of the bed. Her family had rallied.

"You could certainly wake up to a lot worse," Callie said. "As wake-up-to faces go, David's would be the one I'd choose, every time. So, you ready?"

Eve drew a breath. "Let 'em in." No sooner had she uttered the words than Sal was there, his arms around her, hard and safe. He was trembling, she realized. No, he was crying. The tears she'd blinked back burst free. "I'm okay," she said, patting his back. "Totally okay."

He nodded, his face pressed against the curve of her neck. "Don't ever do that to me again," he grunted. He pulled back and wiped at his eyes, unashamed.

Callie handed her a tissue. "Or he'll fire you. He said that on the way over, about six times."

Sal shot her a dirty look. "I was emotional."

Eve patted his cheek. "I think you're sweet," she said. "But fiscally irresponsible. I can't believe you closed the bar. There's a game tonight."

"Nobody was there anyway," Noah said from the

door, and as always, he took her breath away. It didn't seem to matter what kind of doorway he stood in, the result was the same. "It appears they're all downstairs, waiting to see you."

Sal twisted around to stare at Noah, then looked back at Eve with a satisfied smirk. "So I suppose you'll be taking that bottle to Trina's on Sunday after all?"

She met Noah's eyes and in them saw everything she'd ever wanted. "I suppose I will." She struggled to sit up. "Now, how about those visitors? I hope they brought flowers. I haven't had flowers since the last time I got kidnapped."

Thursday, February 25, 8:30 p.m.

Olivia gratefully wrapped her hands around the cup of coffee Kane had coaxed from the vending machine in the hospital's waiting room. "Thanks, I needed this."

"You need to go home, Liv," he said gently.

"I will. I just want to check on Liza and Eve first."

"Is Micki still at the scene?"

Pierce's basement had been a hellacious discovery, branded into her memory. "Yeah. Probably will be for days. If you don't mind, I don't want to talk about that now."

"Okay." In true Kane fashion, he was quiet until she was ready to talk again.

"I called Social Services," she finally said. "Got a nice place for Liza."

"That's good."

She looked away, too close to tears. "Kane. The bodies in that pit . . . it was horrible."

He brushed his big hand down her hair. "See the ladies, and I'll take you home."

"You're a fine chauffeur. You got your lights smacked out today, too. I'll be okay. But thank you." She drew a breath. "Let's go."

They went into Liza Barkley's hospital room where the girl lay, grimly coherent. She remembered everything, Olivia knew. Liza had her arms crossed and stared straight ahead. She was alive, but her sister was not, and that put the girl on a long, lonely road.

Tom sat at her side, quietly, not touching her. He stood when Olivia and Kane entered. "I was with Eve, but she had a crowd."

And Liza was all alone. Olivia stood by her bed, touched her shoulder. "I found a really nice place for you to go when they let you out tomorrow. The woman that runs the home is a personal friend of mine. She'll take good care of you."

Liza looked up, her eyes dead. "Thank you," she murmured. "For everything."

Olivia met Tom's eyes, saw the helplessness there and knew how he felt. "You both have my number. Call me day or night if you need me. I'll let you rest now. I'll be back tomorrow when they release you."

Olivia was at the door when Liza spoke again. "Detective. Did he live?"

It was, perhaps, the one bright spot. "No."

Liza's eyes flickered wildly, but her voice was calm. "My sister. Did you find her?"

"Yes." And she could see it in her mind. Probably always would.

Liza nodded. "I understand."

"You two did good. We might not have found him in

time without that license plate. Try to sleep now. Tom, I'll see you later."

Outside, she slumped against the wall and shuddered.

"There wasn't anything left of her sister, was there?" Kane asked.

"No," Olivia said hoarsely. "Just bones."

"Jennie's downstairs, waiting for me." Jennie was Kane's wife. "You're coming home with us. You're not going to be alone tonight, Liv," he added sharply, when she tried to argue, then he smiled to soften his words. "I'll carry you out of here if I have to."

Olivia nodded wearily. "Okay. Just for tonight." She didn't think she could be alone tonight. "Let's go by Eve's room. I'll make it quick."

Thursday, February 25, 8:45 p.m.

They'd all come, Eve thought, still a little stunned. Fifteen minutes before she and Noah had been sitting in her hospital room, Noah sporting a thick bandage on his head and she with her leg elevated, the bullet hole wrapped and treated.

And then, the horde had descended. *My family. They came.* Dana and Ethan, Caroline and Max, Mia and her husband, Reed. David had called them and without a second thought, they'd come. They were noisy and laughing and joyful.

And mine. The tears came again in a torrent, but that was okay, because they'd all been crying, too. Dana had plopped her pregnant self down on the bed beside her and hugged her like she'd never let go while everyone eyed Noah as if he were an alien from outer space.

A new roar of welcome rose when Olivia came into the room. "I just came to check on the patient," she said, her voice falsely bright, then stopped short when she saw Mia standing by the window next to her husband. "I didn't know you were here." Then Olivia burst into unexpected tears and tried to escape, but hit the wall of Kane.

Mia put her arms around her. "I didn't want to distract you," she said. A homicide detective herself, Mia understood the pressure. *Olivia, trying to find me and Liza before it was too late. And dealing with what Pierce left behind.*

"Come," Mia told her sister. "Reed will take us back to our hotel and we'll have chocolate. It'll be all right." Mia and Kane shared a knowing glance. "Thanks, Kane. We've got her now." Then she looked at Eve. "*Try* to stay out of trouble, kid, okay?"

Eve watched them go with a sigh. She knew Mia had come as much for Olivia as she had for her and that was as it should be.

"Mia will know what to do. I can't imagine . . ." *I won't think about the pit. Not tonight.*

Beside her, Dana hugged her hard. "You're here," she said firmly. "And okay."

"And you hacked into ShadowCo." Ethan pretended to wipe a tear from his eye. "I am so proud. I'll contact them on Monday, tell them they have a network security issue."

"Then I want half the commission when they hire you to fix it," Eve said.

"A third," Ethan said. "Okay, half," he amended when Dana elbowed him.

"You led her into this life of hacker crime," Caroline said, amused.

Max scoffed at that. "You all did, with the clandestine

activities and taking care of people whether they wanted it or not. Speaking of clandestine activities, where is Tom?"

"He went to sit with Liza," Eve said and they all sobered again. "Poor kid. I wish . . ."

Dana leaned her head against Eve's shoulder. "We'll just be there for her."

Like Dana always was for me. "I know."

Caroline stood. "We're out of here now, but we'll come back tomorrow. We're staying at a hotel about three blocks from your place. When you get out, we'll have Dana's baby shower in our room, then we have to be getting back." She looked up over her shoulder at Max. "Your mother will be tearing her hair out with all the kids."

Between Caroline's and Dana's toddlers, Dana's fosters, and Mia's adopted son, Max and David's mom had ten kids under her care. The horde, squared. It made Eve smile.

"Mom loves it," Max said. "Don't let her fool you." He leaned over and kissed Eve on the forehead. "Three times is your charm, kid. No more getting kidnapped, okay?"

Eve laughed softly. "I'll do my very best."

Friday, February 26, 3:00 p.m.

"The real Carleton Pierce was a poor kid from a small Colorado town," Abbott said when they'd all rejoined around Abbott's table the next day. Olivia and Kane were there, Ian and Micki. And Eve. She sat at Noah's side, listening as everyone brought a little bit of the story together.

The only one not here was Jack. Nobody was sure when he'd be back at work. But he was alive and that's all that mattered for now.

Dell Farmer had been charged with the attempted murder of Jack, along with the murders of Katie Dobbs, Harvey Farmer, and Kurt Buckland. *MSP* planned to do a follow-up article to be sure everyone knew what had really happened.

Noah didn't plan to buy a copy.

In the last month, Pierce had taken the lives of six women as the Red Dress Killer and four others to cover his tracks—Ann Pierce, Jeremy Lyons, and the Bolyards. Then there were all the women in his pit. Noah pushed them to the edge of his mind for the moment, concentrating on Abbott's summary of what they'd discovered in the last twenty-four.

"The real Carleton Pierce graduated from high school the spring after Eddie Black hung his mother," Abbott went on. "His home address was on a copy of the acceptance letter the university had sent. The real Carleton's parents had died in an accident. He was taken in by a local family and the town came together to care for him. He graduated valedictorian, earned a full scholarship to the U. His town pitched in, bought him a used car, had a nice pot-luck to see him off, and never saw him again."

"He sent a thank-you card," Kane said, "and a few Christmas cards. But he never came home. They had old high school yearbooks in the town library and they faxed us his picture. Their Carleton Pierce looked nothing like ours."

"So what happened to the real Carleton Pierce?" Ian asked.

"We may never know," Noah said. "Based on what we know of the real Eddie Black, the real Carleton Pierce is dead."

"We found a .22 slug in his wife's head," Ian said.

"Same as the gun he used on Jeremy Lyons and the Bol-yards." He looked at Eve. "And to shoot you."

Noah pushed that image away, too. Eve was fine, but she almost hadn't been.

"We've pieced the story on Ann Pierce," Noah said. He'd talked with her employer that morning. "She'd bor-rowed cash from a friend at work to book that flight to LA, the one she never showed up for. Apparently Ann Pierce had friends that Carleton didn't know about. We think she dropped off the cat because she didn't want to leave it alone, because she may have planned to kill Pierce herself."

"We found another gun in their bedroom closet," Micki said, "with Ann's fingerprints on it. We're guessing she figured out what he was doing and Pierce killed her first."

"What I don't understand," Ian said, "is why he kept the cat?"

"Pierce kept souvenirs," Micki said. She was pale, her eyes drawn. They weren't close to being finished process-ing Pierce's basement. "Shoes, driver's licenses, wallets, cell phones. I think he kept the cat as a souvenir of his Red Dress murders."

Abbott sighed. "We found three dozen pairs of shoes in his basement. From the driver's licenses, he hunted these women from as far east as Chicago and south as Omaha. He consulted on a few of his own murders of local prosti-tutes, as part of the homicide investigation. Brian Ramsey is pulling his hair out. Innocent men in prison, every case Pierce testified in up for appeal. This isn't going away for a long time."

"We'll be able to close some of our own cold cases," Noah murmured. "Including the disappearance of Roger Eames, twenty years ago. He was a laborer, did odd jobs. We found his driver's license at the bottom of Pierce's drawer."

"And his work boots in the pile of shoes that fell off his shelves," Olivia added flatly. "Still had cement in the treads. Apparently, Roger Eames dug the pit."

"The deed to the house was in his name," Abbott said. "We never would have found the house that way."

"How did he find out about your study, Eve?" Ian asked.

"When Donner was diagnosed with cancer, his doctor recommended a list of therapists," Eve said. She'd talked with Donner's wife and mother that morning, trying to understand how her study had gone so wrong. "One of them was Pierce. Over the course of his therapy, Donner mentioned the study, said he needed an independent third-party consultant. Pierce was intrigued and he volunteered."

"When Pierce knew we had the participant list," Noah said, "he knew Jeremy Lyons had to go. As Donner got sicker, he'd passed more authority and access to Lyons."

"We found Jeremy's laptop in Pierce's New Germany house," Micki said. "He'd sent an email to Pierce with the list as an attachment. We found all the Red Dress victims' computers in the New Germany house, in fact."

"Martha used her stool at Ninth Circle to solicit business for Siren Song," Abbott said. "We're not sure if she became obsessed with the World to support her phone sex business or turned to phone sex because it allowed her to never leave her PC. Her heaviest call volume was in the hours the other victims were killed, so that's probably why she met Pierce so much earlier than the others."

"Which turned out to be important," Micki said, her brows raised.

"As did the cat and the shoes," Noah said. "You were right. And Kane, you were right about Jeremy. Pierce used his phone to leave the text and voicemail for Eve. Sitting right outside Abbott's window as he did so. One more of his up-yours."

"Like *Das Ich*," Eve said. "Dasich. I can't believe I didn't see that. All my avatars' names had meaning. I never looked at his."

"Hindsight is twenty-twenty, Eve," Abbott said kindly. "For all of us. We've checked out Pierce's computers, too. He had two, and accessed Shadowland from both so he could have two avatars active at once, never considering anyone was watching him."

"Why Axel Girard?" Ian asked. "How did he pick him?"

Noah sighed. "Axel was his optometrist. Eve realized Pierce resented us for the *MSP* attention, that he never got credit, but he used that anonymity, believing Axel would never have cause to link him to this case."

"The trigger was *MSP*," Eve said. "For both Pierce and Dell Farmer."

"We'll think twice before granting any more interviews," Abbott said.

"And then we'll just say 'no way in hell,'" Noah added.

"When will you release the bodies of Pierce's victims?" Eve asked Ian.

"Today," he said. "Why?"

"I plan to go to their funerals," she said.

"Eve," Abbott said, "you don't believe any of their deaths are on your head, do you?"

"No." She gave Abbott a sad smile. "But they were vulnerable to Pierce because all they had was a virtual life. They looked for happiness in an imaginary world because they couldn't find it in the real one. There but for the grace of God . . ."

Abbott's gaze was respectful. "If you'd like someone to go with you, I will."

Eve looked surprised and touched. "I'd like that. Thank you, Captain."

"What about you, Eve?" Olivia asked. "Have you heard from the university?"

"Yes. Pierce was lying to get me to leave with him. The dean never contacted him. Dean Jacoby called me this morning. Under the circumstances, there will be no sanctions. We'll regroup, retool the study with appropriate checks, and begin again."

Abbott blew out a breath. "I think we've covered everything. Everybody go home."

Eve rose, leaning on the cane the hospital had given her until her leg healed. "Actually, we're on our way to Sal's. We're having a baby shower there for my friend. You're all invited and Sal says the drinks are on him today."

Except for me, Noah thought. He'd decided not to go and after he'd explained, Eve's family had offered to change the venue. But it meant a great deal to Sal and therefore to Eve, so they'd kept the shower there. They'd have an early dinner with her family before they all went back to Chicago and they'd planned an alcohol-free meal.

Noah was looking forward to it. Now, he'd drop Eve off at Sal's for the shower and go see Jack. They had much to discuss.

* * *

Friday, February 26, 8:30 p.m.

"That was nice," Noah said, helping Eve into his car after every member of her family had hugged them both. "I especially liked all the stories about your misspent youth."

"I wasn't that bad. I imagine Brock's got stories on you that are as good or better."

"Good point." He dropped a kiss on her lips and she kissed him back. "Although I wonder if Caroline and Dana know they've been immortalized as avatars."

Eve winced. "Caught that, did you?"

"What, that Pandora's face is Caroline's and Greer the Guardian looks just like Dana? I saw it the minute they walked into your hospital room. But I won't tell. Just tell me I'm not in your avatar collection." He'd meant it as a joke, but she hesitated. "Eve?"

"Well, remember when you asked me if you needed a virtual warrant to enter one of the condos and I said I had connections and could get one? Well . . ."

He gave her a mock glare. "Just tell me I'm wearing appropriate attire."

She snickered. "You do have a hat. The rest is . . . let's just say I imagined well what went on under your suits. Really well. I'll have to show you later."

He laughed out loud and it felt good. "Where to?"

"My place."

"My place doesn't have a leaky roof."

"But I need to pack a bag." She aimed Noah an arched look. "Plus, I think we still have some unfinished business having to do with a certain stuffed chair."

He looked at her leg, his blood already heating. "Can you?"

"I'm young. I heal fast. Very, very fast." She lifted her brows. "Can *you*?"

He snorted a laugh. "I'm functional. Very, very functional."

"So shut up and drive, Web."

He obeyed, making the trip to her place in record time, then carrying her up the three flights of stairs to her apartment. He'd started by romantically cradling her close, but after the first flight flung her over his shoulder while she laughed out loud.

"That was a one-time deal," he said, breathing hard, but the sound of her happy laughter had been worth it. "Open the door so I can collapse."

She obeyed, then they both stared at David Hunter, who sat in her stuffed chair, arm in a cast, looking as if he owned the place. "I thought you went home," she said.

David's dark brows lifted. "I did."

Noah's eyes narrowed. "You're going to live here? With Eve?"

David chuckled. "Not exactly. I'll live downstairs."

"You are renting from that scum-sucking bastard, Myron Daulton?" she demanded.

"No, *you* are renting from *me*. And in six months, your lease is up. If you choose to renew, I'm going to have to raise your rent." David grinned. "I bought the place."

Eve's mouth fell open. "You bought . . . this place? This place should be condemned."

"Nah, it's not in such bad shape. See, on Wednesday morning I was up on the roof, patching your leaks, all of which were man-made, by the way."

Eve narrowed her eyes. "I knew it. And Callie said I was being paranoid."

"Well, you weren't. Anyway, this guy pulls up in a

fancy car and calls up to me to come down, that he owns this place and I'm trespassing."

"Eve's landlord wouldn't allow you to fix her roof?" Noah asked.

"Because he's a scum-sucking bastard," David said affably. "You'd said he just wanted to sell the place, so I decided to buy it."

"Just like that?" Eve said. "You'd buy an old house like this?"

His smile softened. "Yeah. It's an investment."

Her smile softened as well. "That's sweet. Except for the part about raising my rent."

David grinned. "Yeah, well, not by much. A few bucks. If you're still here."

Eve sat down on the sofa. "Wait a minute. So what are you using for money?"

"I got a good deal. Myron didn't want me telling anyone he'd sabotaged the roof, so he heavily discounted the asking price."

"But what are you using for money?" she repeated. "You're not rich."

David sat back and studied her face. "I sold my garage."

Eve's mouth fell open again. "Your body shop in Chicago? You've had it for years."

"Yeah, I know. I've had somebody running it for me, ever since I joined the fire department, and that guy's been asking to buy it. So I sold it."

Eve's mind was reeling. "Just like that? My God."

"And I gave my notice to my captain at the fire department," David added.

Noah sat down beside her, heavily. "Why? You weren't hurt that badly . . ."

"No, it's nothing like that. I applied with the fire department here and in St. Paul."

Eve sat back, stunned. "David. I can't keep up."

He smiled at her. "Actually you led the way. Gave me the push I needed anyway. You were right. I was hiding in Chicago, just like you were. I decided it was time to start fresh, just like you did." He gave her a wink. "Maybe I'll be like you when I grow up."

"So what if you don't get the job here?" Eve asked, bewildered.

"Then I'll fix this place up, flip it, buy the place next door and do the same. You reinvented yourself, Eve. It's about time I did the same."

"I don't understand," Noah murmured. "Do I need to?"

She smiled serenely. "No. It's all good. I'm going to pack a bag and go to Noah's. This chair is the only furniture I want. The rest can stay with the house."

"The rest can go in a bonfire," David said, shaking his head.

"If I decide not to stay with the new management," she said archly, "I'll move my chair to Noah's." She glanced up at Noah. "If you can't bring the mountain to Mohammed."

Noah's lips twitched. "I see."

She smiled at him. "I thought you might."

"I don't want to see," David said with a scowl.

"Exactly my point," Eve said, rising. "There are some things family shouldn't see."

David watched her go back to her room, contemplatively. "Make her happy, Noah."

"That's my plan." Noah gave David a measuring look. "You do body work?"

The measuring stare was returned. "Some. Why?"

"I've got this '69 Dodge Charger that's been sitting in my garage in pieces."

Hunter nodded. "I can help with that. And if I don't get a firehouse right away, I might start up another shop. You know this starting all over might not be so bad."

"We all need a nudge sometimes." Noah stood as Eve re-emerged, a bag over one shoulder. "Life's too short to stand back and watch from the sidelines."

She tilted her head, hearing the last part of the conversation, her lips curving in that half smile that had first attracted him. "No more dipping our toes in. From here on out, it's just one big cold pool. Cannonballs, big splashes. *Babe*."

Noah laughed as David grimaced. "Sounds painful," David said.

Eve pressed a hard kiss to Noah's mouth. "Actually, the water's warm. Ready?"

And Noah found that indeed, he was.

About the Author

KAREN ROSE is an award-winning author who fell in love with books from the time she learned to read. She started writing stories of her own when the characters in her head started talking and just wouldn't be silenced. A former chemical engineer and high school chemistry and physics teacher, Karen lives in Florida with her husband of twenty years, their two children, and the family cat, Bella. When she's not writing, Karen is practicing for her next karate belt test! Karen would be thrilled to receive your e-mail at karen@karenrosebooks.com.

He watches their every move . . .
And he's closer than they think.

Don't miss Karen Rose's
next pulse-pounding thriller!

❧

Please turn this page
for a preview of

Silent Scream

Available now in mass market.

Prologue

They'd shown up. He had to admit he was surprised. He didn't think they'd had the cojones, especially the girl. Of all of them, he hadn't thought she'd follow through.

Four college kids, all dressed in black. Four college kids with way too much time. Two of them with way too much of their daddies' money. If all went according to plan, a great deal of their daddies' money would soon belong to him.

It was rule number one of his world—if people didn't want to be blackmailed, they shouldn't do bad things. Rule number two—if they did bad things, they should be smart enough not to get caught. The four college kids weren't very smart.

From the cover of the trees the condo developer had taken such pains to preserve, he watched the four approach, while he filmed every step they took. Their faces were plainly visible in the moonlight, and although he'd bet their daddies' money they believed they were being stealthy, they moved with enough noise to wake the dead.

"Wait." One of the four stopped. His name was Joel, and of the three young men, he had been the most enthusiastic proponent of their plan. "Let's think this through."

Interesting. Conflict always added a little excitement. Unseen, he kept filming.

"No waiting," the girl said. Her name was Mary, and she was a bitch. "We agreed. All of us, Joel. This condo has got to go. We have to send a message."

"She's right." This from Eric, the so-called brains of the group. As if. "This is our one chance to make a difference to these wetlands. If we do nothing, this whole lake will be nothing but condos." He turned to the large brute standing behind him. "The guard will be doing his outside sweep in two minutes. He'll exit the building from the service door in the back. You know what to do. Come on, people. Let's roll."

The brute was Albert, pronounced without the *t*. French Canadian, he was at the university on a hockey scholarship. Right wing. Hell of a checker. Albert set off around the building, obediently. His research had revealed that Albert was quite the juvenile delinquent, back in the day. He was quite certain Albert would know exactly what to do.

The show was about to begin. *Hurry,* he told himself, taking his second camera from his pack. This was his stationary camera and was attached to a small tripod which he stuck into the soft ground, positioning the lens just in time to capture Mary, Eric, and Joel entering a stairwell door on the east side of the condo.

The door had been propped open with a rock, probably by a construction worker who'd wanted to save a little time and effort. The best security system in the world could be neutralized by lazy workers. Apparently the College Four had done their homework and knew exactly which door would be open. Kudos to them.

Leaving his stationary camera running, he moved the

way Albert had gone, arriving just as the guard exited, right on schedule. Five seconds later the guard lay unconscious on the ground. A satisfied Albert slid a small club back into his pocket.

All caught on my tape. Albert's family was dirt poor, so there was no money now, but there was a good chance that Albert would someday have an NHL salary ending in lots of zeros. *I can wait.* Eric and Joel both had daddies rich enough to fill his bank accounts for now. As for Mary's daddy . . . some paybacks didn't require a dollar sign.

Some paybacks are personal.

Within another minute, Mary emerged from the side entrance and joined Albert. Both stared up at the windows, waiting.

He waited with them, from a safe distance away. He saw the first wisps of smoke rise in the upper floors. Mary threw her fist in the air with a whispered "*Yes.*"

Minutes later there was lots of smoke, on every floor. But the side door had not opened again. Mary took a step forward, the triumph on her face turning to concern, but Albert stopped her, his beefy hand closing around her arm.

"They're still inside," she said, yanking at her arm. "Let me go."

Albert shook his head. "Give them another minute."

And then the door burst open, both Eric and Joel gasping for breath. Mary and Albert ran to the wheezing boys, pulling them away from the building.

"Goddamn idiot," Eric snarled, jerking in huge breaths. "You nearly got us killed."

Joel fell to his knees, spasms of coughing shaking his body. He looked up, his eyes terrified, desperate. "She'll die."

Mary and Albert shared shocked looks. "Who will die?" Albert asked carefully.

Joel scrambled to his feet. "A girl. She's trapped. We have to get her out." He started to run. "Dammit," he cried when Eric and Albert dragged him back. "Let me *go*!"

Mary grabbed Joel's face. "There's somebody in there?" She flashed a panicked glare at Eric. "You said nobody would be in there. You said it was safe."

"Nobody's supposed to be in there," Eric gritted through clenched teeth. "Joel didn't see anything. Let's go before somebody sees the smoke and calls 911."

"She's in there," Joel insisted, hysterical now. "I saw her. Look!"

As a group they looked up and he followed suit, pointing his lens upward as a collective gasp rose from the group. In that moment, he saw her, too. A girl, her fists banging on the window that had been designed to provide a view of the lake, not an escape. She was young, a teenager maybe, her mouth opened on a terrified cry they could not hear. Her fists pounded weakly now, her face pressed to the glass. Then her hands flattened against the window as she slid from their sight.

Joel gave a final, desperate yank. "She's going to die. Don't you care? Nobody was supposed to get hurt. Let me go. I've got to get her out."

Mary grabbed his hair. "Stop it. You go back in there and you'll both be dead."

Joel was sobbing now. "Then call 911. Please. Dammit, please."

"Listen to me," Mary said, her voice low and urgent. "If we call 911, we all go to prison. Prison, Joel. That's not going to happen. Stop this, right now."

But Joel wasn't listening. He thrashed, trying to escape their grip like a man possessed. Behind his head, Eric gave Albert a grim nod. Albert pulled the club from his pocket and a second later Joel collapsed, just as the guard had done.

"Let's go," Eric said tersely and he and Albert picked Joel up and carried him through the woods to where their car was parked.

Mary gave a final look back up at the now-empty window. "Shit," she hissed, then turned and ran, passing the struggling boys to pull at the chain-link fence they'd cut on their way in. "Hurry. Shove him through."

Well. He lowered his camera, watching as the taillights from their car disappeared. That had been a lot more exciting than he'd thought it would be. A simple arson would have been good for years of blackmailing fun. But murder trumped arson and just about anything else. He had several clients who would agree to that.

He quickly packed his two cameras and the tripod. Smoke was billowing into the sky and he heard the pop of glass as windows began to burst. The authorities would soon be here. *And I will be long gone.* Hefting his backpack, he jogged around the building to the lake side where he'd left his boat tied to the dock.

"You there. Stop." It was a thin, ragged cry, but he heard it. Spinning around, he found himself face-to-face with the security guard, who staggered forward, dazed. Blood oozed from the open wound on his head. Albert hadn't hit him hard enough. The man held his radio in one bloody hand, a gun in the other. "Stop or I'll shoot. I will."

Not today, Pops. Calmly he drew his own gun and fired. The guard's mouth fell open in shock. He dropped to his knees, then collapsed for the second time that night.

"Shoulda stayed down, Pops," he muttered. He ran to his boat and dropped his pack inside. With a quiet roar, the motor engaged. Quickly he pulled off the ski mask he wore. If anyone saw him now he could claim he'd seen the smoke and was coming to help, versus trying to flee. But nobody saw him. Nobody ever did.

Which made listening to their whispered secrets so much easier. He patted the cameras in his pack. Which made taking their money so much easier still. *I love my job.*

Oh my God oh my God oh my God. From behind the tree where he'd hidden, Austin Dent watched the small boat speed away, his hands pressed to his mouth. The guard was dead. That man had shot him. *Dead.*

They'll say I did it. Run. I have to run. He took a few unsteady steps backward, lifting his eyes to the burning building once again.

Tracey. She'd been behind him as they'd run from the building. But when he got out, she wasn't behind him anymore. And when he'd turned back . . . All he could see was smoke. A sob of anguish rose up in his chest. *Tracey.*

In the distance he could see the lights flashing. They were coming. The cops were coming. *They'll take me away. Put me in a cage. No. Not again. I can't do that again.* He stumbled back a few more steps, then turned and started to run.

Chapter One

Minneapolis, Minnesota, Monday, September 20, 12:40 a.m.

"Higher, Zell," David Hunter said into his radio, his voice muffled by the mask covering his face. He turned his shoulder into the wind that blew the acrid smoke into the night sky. Suspended four stories up, the bucket in which he stood held firm. The belt anchored him to the apparatus, but his legs still clenched as he held his position.

"Going up." Jeff Zoellner, his partner, operated the lift from the base of the ladder.

David adjusted the angle of the nozzle mounted on the bucket as he rose, aiming at the flames that had consumed the lower two floors of the structure before they'd arrived. None of them had gone in. Too dangerous. Their only hope was to control this fire so that it didn't spread to the trees surrounding what had been a six-story luxury condo.

Thank God this place isn't finished. In a few weeks there would have been people inside. *There may be one.* The guard was missing. If he'd been on one of the lower floors, he was dead. If he'd made it a little higher, there was still a chance of saving him.

Arson. David's jaw clenched as the platform rose.

Had to be. He'd seen it before, up close and way too personally. The wind shifted again and he flinched when the flames lurched his way. For a split second he lost his footing. *Focus, boy. Stay alive.*

"David?" Jeff's voice was urgent amid the crackling. "You okay?"

"Yeah." The platform rose a few more feet, lifting him alongside a large picture window. Every condo on the upper floors had them. He saw no flames, but smoke billowed from the smaller windows which had already burst from the heat.

But all the picture windows were intact. Made of impact-resistant glass, they didn't burst. They also didn't open. They were for the view of the lake. Not for escape.

And then he saw them. His heart began to race faster.

"Stop." He leaned over the edge of the bucket in which he stood, so he could get closer to the window. It couldn't be. *Nobody's supposed to be inside.* But it was.

"What is it?" The platform lurched as Jeff hit the brakes.

Handprints. The faint outline of small handprints that somehow . . . shimmered in the light from his spotlight. *What the hell?* "Handprints." And streaks, made from fingers clawing at the window, trying to escape. "Somebody's in there. We have to go in."

VISIT US ONLINE

@ WWW.HACHETTEBOOKGROUP.COM

AT THE HACHETTE BOOK GROUP WEB SITE YOU'LL FIND:

CHAPTER EXCERPTS FROM SELECTED NEW RELEASES
•
ORIGINAL AUTHOR AND EDITOR ARTICLES
•
AUDIO EXCERPTS
•
BESTSELLER NEWS
•
ELECTRONIC NEWSLETTERS
•
AUTHOR TOUR INFORMATION
•
CONTESTS, QUIZZES, AND POLLS
•
FUN, QUIRKY RECOMMENDATION CENTER
•
PLUS MUCH MORE!

BOOKMARK HACHETTE BOOK GROUP
@ WWW.HACHETTEBOOKGROUP.COM.

If you or someone you know
wants to improve their reading skills,
call the Literacy Help Line.

WORDS ARE YOUR WHEELS
1-800-228-8813